The Midnight Clear:
Stories of Love, Hope & Inspiration

The Midnight Clear:
Stories of Love, Hope & Inspiration

KNB Publications, LLC
http://www.knb-publications.com

KNB titles are published by:

KNB Publications, LLC
P.O. Box 831648
Stone Mountain, GA 30083
Email: info@knb-publications.com

ISBN: 0-9742207-0-1

ISBN 13: 978-0-9742-2070-3

First Printing: November 2006

Printed in the United States of America

Table of Content

Foreword from the Publisher, Kendra Norman-Bellamy

I feel quite blessed to have been chosen to publish this wonderful collection of stories. I remember the moment the thought to create *The Midnight Clear* was placed in my heart. The idea for this project came through two male vessels that I have not yet had the pleasure of meeting. Therefore, I, in part, dedicate this book to them for their inspiration.

Several months ago, I was contacted via email by Bobby Minor, a dynamic rising keynote speaker. In his note, the opportunity was extended to me for participation in a nonfiction anthology that was being spearheaded by Johnny Wimbrey, a colleague of the legendary Les Brown and an extraordinary world-class lecturer in his own right. As I accepted the challenge of being a part of my first nonfiction venture, the concept of the book that these two gentlemen presented to me took root in my heart and blossomed into the concept for *The Midnight Clear*. So, to both Bobby and Johnny, I extend my gratitude.

The purpose of this particular collection is two-fold. Through KNB Publications, LLC, I wanted to produce a project wherein nationally acclaimed authors and novice/aspiring writers could collaborate, and the end result be a creative literary masterpiece that readers would enjoy. Perhaps most importantly, I wanted to provide a window of opportunity for gifted, but undiscovered writers to realize their dreams of becoming published authors. Through *The Midnight Clear*, God allowed me to achieve both the goals that were set forth at the start of this vision. So, of course, I thank Him for His infinite wisdom. He is faithful!

To all of the new and rising authors who came together to make up this compilation, thank you. This is only the beginning. Your creative gifts will continue to make room for you.

A special note of appreciation goes out to my sisters of the pen and nationally acclaimed authors, Patricia Haley, Tia McCollors and Stacy Hawkins Adams. Thank you for agreeing to join me in this project. Without doubt, your combined talents helped to make this book a success.

To the readers...sit back and enjoy! And may these stories remind us all of the One who makes our midnights clear.

Chapter One

Stacy Hawkins Adams discovered a love of writing in first grade. Family, teachers and even young friends (who dubbed her an author-to-be before she reached adolescence) nurtured her gift.

She is the author of two widely acclaimed Christian fiction novels, *Speak To My Heart* and *Nothing But the Right Thing*, through which she uses the lens of faith to explore the true-to-life struggles faced by twenty- and thirty-something-year-old men and women. Her novels have been feature selections of the Black Expressions Book Club and Sybil's Book Club on the Tom Joyner Morning Show, among others.

Before becoming a full-time author, professional speaker and freelance writer, Stacy served as a social issues reporter and newspaper columnist for thirteen years. Her freelance articles have appeared in *Heart & Soul* and *The Crisis* magazines, *USA Today, The Richmond Times-Dispatch* and Crosswalk.com. She also pens an online column for an early childhood initiative created by Virginia's current Governor.

Stacy is a graduate of Jackson State University and has participated in several creative writing workshops. She aims, through her writing, to help people live their faith authentically and experience God's unconditional love. She lives in Richmond, Virginia with her family and is working on her third novel. To learn more about Stacy's work, visit her at www.stacyhawkinsadams.com.

Her contribution to *The Midnight Clear* is entitled, **The Inheritance**.

The Inheritance

The legal-sized white envelope stood out among the stack of green, red, cinnamon and gold ones Gabi Spencer gathered from her mailbox. Her name was neatly typed on the correspondence and bore a familiar return address.

"Interesting," Gabi said softly as she climbed the stairs to her second-floor apartment. Once inside, she plucked the envelope from the pile of Christmas cards and rested her purse on the table in the foyer. She turned on the floor lamp in the living room, sank into the black leather sofa and carefully opened the letter with a fingernail.

Dear Ms. Spencer:
On behalf of Cora Lynn Smith, I am contacting you on the six-month anniversary of her death, as she requested in her will. Ms. Smith indicated in that document that the final disbursement from her estate would be distributed to Bruce Spencer, Monique Spencer-Davis and you on Christmas morning at her Mesa, Alabama residence. Ms. Smith specified that none of you be allowed to receive your inheritance unless you gather at her home on Christmas Eve and Christmas Day. I will visit the residence on Dec. 25 to document your presence and deliver her final gift. If you have questions or need more information, I can be contacted via the telephone number provided below.

Sincerely,
Slater Hill, Esq.

Gabrielle laughed out loud. Slater Hill, *Esquire* couldn't be serious. She rose from the sofa and ran her fingers through her silky deep brown curls.

She paced for a few minutes and toyed with the idea of calling her sister, who obviously had received a similar letter. What would they say to each other after all this time? Gabi paused and read the letter again.

Even from the grave, Aunt Cora was trying to keep her family together. The more she thought about it, the less surprised she was.

Letter still in hand, Gabi entered her cozy kitchen and turned on the fluorescent overhead light. She carefully replaced the letter in its envelope before laying it on a counter and opening the fridge to forage for dinner.

A container of shrimp fried rice, left over from the night before, stared at her. She scooped the contents onto a plate and began reading the letter again as the food warmed in the microwave.

The shrill ring of the telephone interrupted her, mid-sentence. Gabi glanced at the Caller I.D. before removing the cordless from its wall cradle.

"Hey Dee," she said to her best friend. "Looks like my plans to spend the holiday with your family have changed."

- - -

Snow in Alabama. Just in time for Christmas. Aunt Cora couldn't have planned it better if she had been alive to fast and pray for a picture perfect family gathering. The precipitation fell in light, fluffy mounds, some melting as soon as it touched the still-warm ground.

Gabi knew it was enough to send local residents on a bread and milk run to the town's two grocery stores. After their pantries were stocked, few people would venture outside until the sun melted enough of the snow for them to see the roads.

Aunt Cora would have been among that number.

Gabi turned the rental car onto Alcorn Lane and crept toward the end of the road. A year earlier, she had sped down this wide, tree-lined street, past the houses occupied by long-time family friends and former classmates, eager to reach the four-bedroom white clapboard house so she could wrap in a hug the regal, elderly woman watching for her from the front porch.

Today, though, she purposely prolonged the journey, lingering in memories of the past year that unfolded in her mind like a movie: Aunt Cora's cancer diagnosis nine months ago that had left her unable to work her part-time seamstress job. Monique and Steve's decision to sell their small rancher in the town five miles away and move into Auntie's home with their infant son, Steve Jr. Bruce's attempts to also move in after he left his wife. The ugly words she had exchanged with her sister and brother that left her vowing to never return to Mesa again.

3

Gravel crunched beneath the tires, despite the padding of snow, as Gabi turned into Aunt Cora's long driveway. She basked in the final strains of Donny Hathaway's "This Christmas" softly playing on the radio, and stared at the place that had once been as familiar to her as her shadow.

For Gabi, 102 Alcorn Lane had stopped feeling like home when Aunt Cora kissed her goodbye and shooed her from the bedroom so she could take her final breath. Since that day, she, Monique and Bruce had let old grudges and new differences cement the wall already forming between them. Without Aunt Cora around to douse their flaring tempers or guilt them into getting along, it had been easy to retreat to their own corners of the world.

For Monique, that meant remaining in Aunt Cora's house with her husband and son and honoring Aunt Cora's memory by living for God in a fashion that Monique was certain would have pleased her auntie.

For Bruce, it had meant snatching out of life, whatever happiness he could, because Aunt Cora had been the third person to show him that tomorrow wasn't promised.

And for Gabi, the baby of the family, moving on had meant leaving Mesa to find herself. It had meant crafting a new family, made up of friends who cared about her – flaws, quirks and all – and accepting that while Mesa, Alabama was stamped on her birth certificate, it was okay if the place wasn't stamped on her heart.

Those decisions had worked for each of the Spencer siblings, until now. Aunt Cora had known that after her death, she would have to force them to bond.

Gabi stepped out of the car and pulled her hat down over her ears. Even with snow, the temperature in Mesa was nowhere near as cold as it could get on a sunny, dry winter day in Philadelphia. Maybe, she thought, she was protecting herself from the chill within.

She pulled her suitcase from the trunk of the two-door Subaru and climbed the steps to the house. Before Gabi could ring the bell, Monique opened the door and stood there, expressionless, holding Steve Jr.

"You got the letter."

Gabi nodded.

Monique opened the door wider and stepped aside.

4

Welcome home to me, Gabi thought.

She walked inside, rested her suitcase on the worn linoleum and canvassed her surroundings. Little had changed since she had been there for Aunt Cora's death and burial in early June. The mauve walls were still lined with pictures of Gabi, Monique and Bruce from pre-adolescence through adulthood. Monique had added a few of Steve Jr.'s preschool shots to one area.

The cushioned mahogany pieces of furniture were still covered by a plastic film, in case of childhood spills. The out-of-tune piano remained in the corner, partially hidden by the heavy deep golden drapery. The house still smelled of lavender, but now it mingled with the scent of cigars and fresh bread. Monique had always loved to bake.

The sisters awkwardly faced each other. Instead of opening her arms for a hug, Monique brushed past Gabi and lowered her head.

"You can stay where you usually do," she said. "I haven't changed anything. Steve Jr. needs to potty. We'll be back in a minute."

Gabi entered the room she and Monique had shared as children and touched the ruffled lime green curtains that covered the room's single window. She sat on the double bed and sighed.

How did we get from there to here?

By dinner, an easy silence had settled between the sisters. Steve Jr. shyly played near Gabi, inching closer every few minutes until he mustered the courage to crawl into her lap for a game of patty cake.

It didn't take long for Gabi to fall in love. Her nephew had a smooth coffee complexion similar to hers and the long eyelashes to match. When he smiled, the two-year old's dimples were deep like his Uncle Bruce's. Otherwise, he was all Monique – long limbs, thin frame and high forehead.

Gabi shook her head. "Has Steve made this boy undergo a DNA test?"

Monique laughed genuinely. "Nope, but he's threatened to do that with the next baby, if it doesn't come out looking more like his side of the family."

Gabi looked up at Monique, one eyebrow raised.

Monique shrugged. "I'm due in June, right around Steve's birthday."

5

And the anniversary of Aunt Cora's death. Neither of them said what they were thinking.

"Congratulations," Gabi said. "What do you want?"

"A healthy baby, that's all. But you wouldn't understand."

There it was. Gabi rose and sat Steve Jr. on the chair. She walked toward the oven and stirred the pot of Gumbo her sister was cooking for dinner.

I will not allow her to make me feel bad about a mistake. I will not sink to her level.

"Thank God for second chances," Gabi finally said, in as lighthearted a tone as she could muster.

"Humph," Monique said. "If God has given you a second chance, where's your man? Where's your baby?"

Gabi spun away from the stove, clutching the wooden spoon she had been stirring with. "Don't start with me, Monique. I don't need to hear your condemnation – again – about a split-second decision I made during an emergency. You might be a preacher's wife and you might have a pretty decent relationship with God yourself, but don't you go judging mine."

Monique smirked. Before she could respond the kitchen door creaked open, ushering in a burst of frigid air. Covered with a light dusting of snow, a taller, broader, muscular version of the sisters tumbled into the kitchen.

Without acknowledging their presence, Bruce closed the door behind him and plopped a covered dish on the kitchen counter. He turned away from them and stepped out of his boots.

When he faced Gabi and Monique again, he looked from one to the other and shook his head. "If I didn't know better, I'd think you two were twins." He laughed at the irony of his comment. "Now that would be interesting. Merry Christmas, ladies. I fried the turkey."

Gabi's feet wouldn't move. Part of her wanted to run to her brother and forget all that had happened between them. The other part was wary, afraid that just like Monique had done minutes ago, he was preparing to aim a missile straight at her heart.

What to do? Fight fire with fire.

"This is going to be a long few days, huh?" Gabi said. "How can the two of you stand to be in my presence, with my sinful self?"

Monique took the question seriously.

6

"I'm just honoring Aunt Cora's last wish. I loved her enough to do that. She left me this house. What more could I want? This holiday gathering isn't about collecting some sort of inheritance for me – it's about respecting what Auntie wanted."

Bruce snorted. "Who you trying to impress?"

Monique rolled her eyes. "You're the one hard up for something more than what Aunt Cora's already given you, Bruce. She left you her three rental properties and a nice lump sum of cash. What'd you do with it, lose it all at one of the riverboat casinos in Hattiesburg?"

The anger that flashed in his eyes let Gabi know Monique was closer to the truth than Bruce would ever admit. She sighed and turned back to stirring the pot of gumbo, feeling as if she'd suffocate. Nothing had changed. Monique was still playing the holier-than-thou saint and Bruce was still the black sheep of the family. And she…she was still the one who could never do enough, be enough or apologize enough to make up for the lives she had taken. Suddenly, she was tired of it all.

She turned off the fire under the gumbo and turned toward her siblings, who continued to glare at one another across the kitchen. Gabi walked toward the center of the room, until she stood between the two of them. She placed her palms flat on the table in front of her and closed her eyes.

"You know what?" she began softly. "I promised myself after our holiday fiasco two years ago that I wouldn't spend another Christmas with the two of you, because somehow you manage to always dampen the joy this season is supposed to bring. And every year it's the same tired argument."

Gabi opened her eyes and looked from her brother to her sister. "When are we going to grow up and stop playing the same sick roles we've played in this family since Mama and Daddy died? When are we really going to forgive – and realize that some things don't need to be forgiven, they need the power of grace? Are we going to spend the next twenty-four hours teaching Steve Jr. the value in hating your brother or sister? Can't you see that's what Aunt Cora was trying to stop?"

Monique grabbed her son off the chair, where he had silently been watching the exchange between the adults. He rested his head on her shoulder and sucked his thumb as Monique scowled and walked over to Gabi.

7

"You've moved your little self up to Philadelphia, gotten some education and think you know it all now. You think that psychology degree gives you permission to diagnose us? Well, baby girl, I know the Lord, and He is my counselor."

Gabi threw her hands in the air and left the kitchen. She walked toward the bedroom, where she planned to spend the rest of the evening reading, watching TV or doing anything but arguing.

"You know what, Monique?" she called as she rounded the hallway corner and turned the doorknob to the bedroom. "God is my counselor, too. You'd think He would give us the same advice."

- - -

Tears poured from Gabi's eyes as she clutched her silver cell phone. Mama Ruth waited silently for her to pull herself together.

"You know, Gabi," she finally said, "this really isn't about you. You can go ahead and pack your bags and catch the next flight out of Alabama. You know you're always welcome at my home, and we'd love to have you for Christmas again this year.

"But your Aunt Cora knew what she was doing when she stipulated in her will that exactly six months after her death, the three of you make time to spend time together."

The tears began to abate as Gabi listened to her former college professor, the woman who had become a surrogate mother, of sorts, to her. Ruth knew about the mistakes Gabi had made. She knew about Gabi's worst fears and about her dangerous temper. She knew about Gabi's tendency to run from uncomfortable situations and turn cold to keep people from seeing her pain simmering beneath the surface.

She viewed today and the next as turning points in Gabi's efforts to heal and move forward. If Gabi ran away again, she'd have to keep returning to Mesa until she got it right.

Mama Ruth wanted to tell Gabi that, but then again, she wanted Gabi to realize it for herself. Only then could the deep losses Gabi had suffered throughout her life fail to keep her locked in a prison of guilt. Only then, could she accept that she was human, just like her siblings, with no more power to control the course of life than they possessed.

- - -

Just as the sun was setting and Steve Jr. sat in his play pen, marveling at the Christmas tree lights, a red-eyed, but solemn Gabi

8

emerged from the bedroom. Steve and Bruce sat in front of the flat screen television, engrossed in the fourth quarter of a football game. She walked past them and entered the kitchen, where she found Monique kneading dough for the yeast rolls she made every year.

Monique looked up at her and returned to her work.

Gabi pulled out a chair and sat at the table to watch. She was fascinated by Monique's back and forth arm and wrist motions and the strength required to make the dough as pliable as possible. Gabi had never been patient enough to learn how to make rolls, but Monique had become Aunt Cora's pet student soon after they had come to live with her.

Even so, Gabi had continued to feel Monique's resentment for the attention Aunt Cora showered on her. She'd felt it from her brother, too. Tonight, though, on the eve of Aunt Cora's favorite holiday, she wanted to confront the curses that had kept her from connecting with her siblings. She had apologized more times than she could count, but this time, she wasn't going to play the martyr. Instead, she started with the bread.

"Let me help you shape the rolls."

Monique gave her a startled look. "What? Miss Prima Donna wants to help make rolls?"

Gabi held her attitude in check. "You know, Monique, the reason I never cooked was because you were so good at it. If I couldn't be as good at it as you, I figured I should focus on something else. Since I excelled in school, I turned my attention to the books."

Gabi could tell that her revelation had, for once, left her sister speechless. They spent the rest of the evening working together to prepare the Christmas meal. Other than the three of them and Monique's family, Bruce's ten- and twelve-year-old daughters would be coming for dinner.

Monique patiently showed Gabi how to make dressing without having to add Stouffer's or use a recipe. She walked Gabi through the process of making sweet potato casserole, and macaroni and cheese that didn't come from a box.

At a little after midnight, the sisters were exhausted. For the first time since they were very young, they felt a closeness they each had believed was no longer possible.

"This is what Aunt Cora wanted, you know," Gabi said.

9

Monique smiled halfheartedly and rubbed her growing tummy. She flicked off the lights in the kitchen. "I know, Gabi, I know."

The Spencers slept late on Christmas morning. The ringing telephone introduced them to the holiday – the first major one they would celebrate in Aunt Cora's home without her.

Gabi's eyes fluttered open and filled with tears when reality hit her. She heard Monique stirring in the hallway, answering the cordless phone that was charging in its base on the cherry wall-length table.

"Yes, Mr. Hill, we're all here. You can come by now or later, whatever you'd prefer."

Gabi sat up and put her feet in her slippers. She entered the hallway at the same time as Bruce, who had slept in the guest room and had also been awakened by the attorney's phone call.

"When's he coming?" he groggily asked Monique.

She shrugged. "He was pretty vague. I think he wants to get this task out of the way, but he doesn't want us to pretend to be together for Christmas and then go our separate ways once he leaves."

Minutes later, the energy of a child-occupied house bubbled over when Steve Jr. woke up and scampered to the Christmas tree with his father at his side. The little boy's squeals over Elmo, a super-sized fire truck and a toddler sized basketball goal were rivaled only by his father's glee. By the time Steve Jr. waded through the gifts that mostly bore his name, he was beaming like a child overdosed on sugar.

It took half an hour for Monique to lure him to breakfast. With him as the center of attention, any lingering issues from the day before were forgotten.

Slater Hill rang the doorbell at ten-thirty, just as Gabi emerged from the shower. He waited until the three siblings were dressed and assembled in the living room. Respectfully, Steve Sr. took his son outside to play with a brand new football.

Bruce sat on the sofa between Gabi and Monique. He took each of their hands in one of his. Monique seemed surprised, but complied.

Grateful for the progress she and her sister had made the night before, Gabi silently uttered thanks for her brother's peace offering. She squeezed his hand and looked expectantly at Slater Hill.

"You know, none of us really needs anything else from Aunt Cora," Bruce said softly. "Maybe we don't even want to hear what Mr. Hill has to say."

Gabi tossed around that idea and decided he had a point. Aunt Cora had taken out life insurance policies on herself and had left one to each of them. The sizable payouts, coupled with insurance money from their parents' deaths, had left the siblings very comfortable.

Monique nodded. "He's right, Mr. Hill. We don't have any material wants, thanks to Aunt Cora and our parents. We got together this Christmas because we loved her and we wanted to do as she wished and try to work out our differences." She looked at Gabi. "I don't know if we'll succeed, but we're trying."

Slater Hill cleared his throat and glanced at his watch.

Gabi remembered that this was a holiday for him too; he obviously had someone waiting.

"Really, you all," he began, "this won't take very long. I think you'll appreciate this gift, because it's one from Ms. Smith's heart rather than her bank account."

The siblings exchanged curious glances.

"What gives?" Bruce asked.

Slater Hill handed over three envelopes bearing each of their names in Aunt Cora's loopy, cursive handwriting. On each envelope she advised in parentheses, "Please read aloud." The envelopes were also numbered, indicating that as the oldest, Bruce, should read his first.

Before he could begin, Slater Hill asked to be excused. "My work here is done. Ms. Smith wanted me to deliver these letters and make sure each of you was present to hear them read aloud. It was her hope that if nothing else, her gift to you this Christmas would be the gift of a connection to each other that you pass on to your children and grandchildren, and any other children you take into your hearts. Have a Merry Christmas."

Slater Hill closed the front door behind him as Bruce opened the envelope and cleared his throat:

"My handsome Bruce, when you moved into my home seventeen years ago, you were deeply lost and filled with anger. Who wouldn't be, tragically losing your parents as you did during your senior

11

year of high school? You stood on the verge of manhood, yet your father still had so much to teach you; your mother, my sister, still had many more hugs to give.

"I'm writing this letter as I near my homegoing to heaven to ask you to understand that no one and nothing could have prevented their plane from crashing. It is not Gabi's fault. Instead of traveling to her national cheerleading competition, they could have been on their way to see you play football or Monique participate in an orchestra concert when the accident occurred. Only God knows why they died the way they did and when they did.

"But they loved you enough to make sure you'd be taken care of. They knew that I would love you and your sisters like the children I never was able to have. The Bible says that love covers a multitude of sins, Bruce. You have surely committed them as I have. So have Gabi and Monique. Even so, God, through His never-ending grace, has given us chance after chance. All these years later, it's okay to be angry and hurt by your parents' death, but it's not okay to keep blaming your sister. It is not okay.

"I'm not there anymore to referee, but you have to learn to love each other, no matter what. You three are all you have. The way you decide to move forward today will determine whether this family dies on the vine or flourishes to God's glory and honor. It is the only gift I desire. Although I wasn't your birth mother, I was with my sister as she prepared to give birth to you. I am your mother in my heart and soul. As that, I say to you, please give the gift of love to yourself and to others, especially your sisters."

Bruce leaned forward and hung his head in his hands as Monique, in a trembling voice, read her letter:

"I can hear you now, my sweet Monique, grumbling about the fact that I've left you something else in my will. But don't worry – I know you don't need material goods to be happy.

"What I offer you instead is the gift of truth. I tried to share it time and time again while I lived, but I'm faithfully believing that God will open your ears and your heart in a powerful new way through my written words.

"Monique, I know you love God and He surely loves you. I want you to consider, however, that God doesn't live in the building

at Elm and Hunter streets that opens every Sunday and Wednesday to usher in His spirit. I used to think that, too, until I really got to know Him. He dwells in your heart and in your soul right now. I urge you to seek Him, Monique, and to develop a relationship with Him that will allow you to see past the rules and restrictions imposed by the church to the grace and mercy emanating from Christ's heart.

"For too long, you too, have blamed Gabi for your parents' untimely death. Can you even imagine what kind of burden that is to place on fourteen-year-old shoulders?

"You've doubled the guilt and grudges by blaming Gabi for the miscarriage you suffered five years ago, when she was driving you to Montgomery. Had the deer hit your car that night, who knows how you might have been injured? She swerved to save your life, Monique. She didn't know it would cost you your baby. Forgive her. Allow her to heal from the guilt she feels every time she's with you and you remind her what she took from you – twice. Remember that God holds no grudges – He didn't against Moses or against King David when he purposely murdered a man and took that man's wife. Gabi lost a lot too."

Monique could hold the dam no longer. She shook with sobs and uttered, "I'm sorry" over and over, hugging herself and rocking back and forth. "I'm sorry Auntie. I'm sorry Gabi. Forgive me God."

Now it was Gabi's turn. Her face was already streaked with tears and she wasn't sure if she could speak.

Finally, the pain that had burnt her soul all these years was being acknowledged. Finally, she was experiencing some of the earthly redemption she knew God had long ago granted her. It rivaled any gift she could have found under the Christmas tree or in her stocking this morning. Aunt Cora had delivered it from the grave.

She didn't think she could read her letter. Could any of them stand any more?

Bruce looked up at her, his face broken with pain. She knew he understood her hesitance.

"You have to."

Gabi slowly opened the envelope and took a deep breath. She tried to compose herself enough to keep her eyes clear. If they

13

blurred with tears, she knew she'd never make it through the first page.

Monique leaned back on the sofa and mopped her face with one hand. "Go on, Gabi. Read it."

It began the same as the others, with a greeting filled with love.

"The others always thought I doted on you too much, that you were my favorite. I simply tried to put myself in your shoes: How would I feel if I had begged and pleaded with my parents to fly to Florida to see me compete in my first-ever cheerleading competition, one in which I didn't even have a starring position? How would I have felt if that plane had crashed, killing everyone on board and ending my family as I knew it?

"For a teenager and the youngest in your family, I knew you were carrying a huge burden, Gabi. It wasn't that I loved you more than your siblings; I just knew that in order for you to survive this ordeal, you needed to be shown more love and grace - until you got to know God for yourself. I knew it would happen eventually. I knew you'd find Him in your darkest hours. That was always my prayer, that you would turn to God and not to drugs, alcohol or something worse to numb your pain. And when you did seek God, I saw you blossom. Your heart for God shone through your spirit and in your eyes. And yet, pain and guilt still lingered there, too.

"So then, my gift to you today is the gift of freedom. I declare that you are free from the "what ifs," "How could I's?" and "I'm sorrys" you've been uttering to members of your family since you were fourteen. You are a beautiful creation of God. You did nothing to kill your parents. You did not intentionally wreck a car so you could kill your just-pregnant sister's unborn baby. The God we love doesn't orchestrate such evil and neither did you.

"Please free yourself. Please love yourself. Do whatever it takes to achieve those two goals, but in the process, don't give up on loving your brother and sister. You three are connected by blood, by faith and by love. A long time ago, you forgot that. This Christmas is the perfect time to remember."

Gabi, Monique and Bruce rose from the sofa and held one another in tender embraces.

14

Before long, Steve Jr. raced into the living room to announce in his two-year-old grammar, that more snow was falling. Steve Sr. followed him into the room and paused at the scene before him.

Monique took a swipe at her damp cheeks and smiled at her husband. Gabi grabbed her hand and Bruce's. She led them toward the kitchen and motioned with her head for Steve and Steve Jr. to join them.

"Come on. We've got some new Christmas traditions to establish. Starting with those rolls I helped bake."

Chapter Two

Sherri Lewis authored her first book at the age of six. Her family considered her pencil and crayon on brightly colored construction paper creation a masterpiece. She continued to enjoy writing short stories and poems throughout her young adult life.

Her writing was put on hold while she attended Howard University as an undergraduate, then Medical School at the University of Pennsylvania. The writing bug bit again a few years ago and pencil, crayon, and construction paper were replaced by laptop and printer. She has completed two inspirational novels, one of which, *My Soul Cries Out*, is set for release in 2007.

Sherri is co-founder of the Atlanta Black Christian Fiction Writers' Critique Group. She is also a member of the American Christian Fiction Writers and president of the organization's Southeast Atlanta chapter. She lives in Atlanta, Georgia.

Her contribution to *The Midnight Clear* is entitled, **Christmas Fruit**. It is her first published work of fiction.

Christmas Fruit

I *hated* Christmas.

I was born on Christmas day. You'd think that would be a good thing. But while other kids got parties, presents and specialized birthday cakes, my birthday got absorbed into the holiday. My gifts said "Happy Birthday/Merry Christmas" and Mom stuck a candle in a sweet potato pie. Like that was the same as a birthday cake with my name on it.

Then my father died of a massive heart attack on Christmas day six years ago and my mother of a broken heart a week before Christmas a year later.

If that wasn't enough, my husband was killed three years ago by a drunk driver who'd enjoyed too much of the Christmas spirits. I guess it was grief – a few days later I had my third miscarriage. The day after Christmas. After that, I lost my hope of ever having the family I'd always dreamed of.

Truth be told, Christmas hated me. I'd been through years of psychotherapy and spiritual counseling. My heart was healed in the name of Jesus and I had overcome by the blood of the Lamb…and all those other wonderful scriptures I quoted daily, Praise the Lord.

Honestly, I kept God and His promises at arms length. I knew I'd go to heaven when I died and just needed to go through the motions until that blessed day came. I was still saved and loved God. Just didn't have any hope of being happy in this life *ever* again.

My best friend didn't help matters. She was a Christmas fanatic, determined she could pull me out of my funk with her overabundance of Christmas joy. I avoided her as much as possible from mid-November until January. On Christmas Eve morning, she called, frantic that she had promised to bake someone 500 Christmas cookies and there was no way she could finish on time. She begged me to help.

As much as I wanted to say no, that was something I could rarely do to Charlene. She saved my life on many occasions after my husband died. The Holy Spirit brought her to my house at all the right times – those times when I slit my wrists, swallowed a bottle

18

of sleeping pills and drank myself into a near coma, she showed up just in time to get me to the ER. She finally convinced me that if any of my plots worked, I wouldn't end up in heaven with my family. Last thing I needed after all this hell on earth was to end up in hell for eternity.

So I mentally prepared myself for an afternoon of torture – sipping eggnog, eating fruitcake and listening to Charlene singing off-key Christmas carols at the top of her voice.

When I walked into Charlene's house, I inhaled the scent of pine, cinnamon, apples and spices. Nat King Cole's voice floated through the air to greet me. Everywhere I turned, there were wreaths, bows, ornaments, and lights – the house was a blur of red, green and gold.

"You really outdid yourself this year, Charlene."

"Isn't it wonderful?"

"Bah humbug."

Charlene laughed. "You're hopeless."

Within three hours, we finished the rest of the cookies. Then Charlene ushered me into her family room loaded with kids' toys and clothes. She volunteered at several children's homes throughout the year and played Santa Claus at Christmas. She handed me tape and wrapping paper, indicating that I was to help – ignoring my aggravated glare.

When we finished wrapping the gifts, Charlene placed the cookies in several large tins. "Wanna take a ride with me?" she offered.

"Where are you going?"

"After I drop off the cookies, I'm gonna take these presents to Momma Bey's house." She said it innocently, like it was no big deal.

Momma Bey was one of the mothers of our church who ran a foster home. She adored children and couldn't stand to see one without a good home. No telling how many of them she had running around that huge house of hers.

Charlene knew I avoided children like the plague. They brought up sad memories and lost dreams of not being able to have my own family.

"No." I said it firmly enough to let her know one of her begging sessions wouldn't work.

19

"Pleeeeeeeeease, Faith."

"No." I stood and picked up my purse and coat to show her the consequences of continued pleading.

Her eyes pierced my conscience. "You really should go see Momma Bey. It's the least you could do."

I refused to let guilt force me into doing something I knew would leave me depressed for days. I shook my head.

"Fine, Miss Grinch. Help me load the presents in the car before you retreat back to Hermitville."

Hermitville was Charlene's name for my house. My life, really. My husband's huge life insurance policy kept me from having to work, so I only ventured out of the house to shop for food. My days were spent sitting home in the dark, or watching television, surfing the internet, or losing myself in a book.

If I went to church, I sat on the back pew, interacted with no one and was at the door before the pastor could breathe the benediction. Charlene was my only friend and only meaningful human contact. I figured if I didn't get close to anyone, I didn't have to worry about them dying on me. My friendship with her kept me from slipping too far into the abyss.

I silently loaded packages into Charlene's SUV.

"Here, let me back out so we can get the rest of the presents in."

Charlene's garage was small and full of junk so it was a tight squeeze to get the back door fully open. She got in and turned the key. She frowned. She turned the key again and looked up at me.

"It's just cold. Pump the gas a few times and try again." I rubbed my hands together.

After ten more minutes of trying, it still wouldn't start.

"You're gonna have to take me."

I stiffened. "Charlene. I...can't."

"You'll be fine. They're mostly older kids anyway. Most of the children have been placed elsewhere since Momma Bey got sick." She gave me a "I never ask you for much" and then a "you really owe Momma Bey big time" look.

"Just take my car. I'll wait here 'til you get back," I said.

"Stop playing. You know I can't drive a stick."

- - -

We pulled up in Momma Bey's driveway. I didn't budge.

Charlene stared at me. "Are you crazy? You'll freeze out here

20

in the car."

"I'll be okay."

"At least come in and say hello. She misses you."

I bit my lip and shook my head.

"Fine. I'll get the kids to help me bring the stuff in." She slammed the door when she got out. Sometimes I wondered how long Charlene's patience with me was going to last.

Moments later, two older boys came out to the car and unloaded presents. Each time they came back and opened the doors for more packages, the fierce Detroit cold overpowered my car's heater pumping full blast. Soon I was shivering and couldn't feel my feet.

On the last trip, one of the boys asked, "It's cold out here, Miss. Ain't you comin' in?"

I shook my head. "Can you send Miss Charlene out, please?"

"She praying for Momma Bey. She real sick."

Ten minutes later, I couldn't feel my hands. I got out and slammed the door. Pain shot through my wrist as if the bones cracked from the cold. I silently cursed Charlene under my breath. Only for a second. It wasn't her fault Momma Bey was sick.

I stepped inside the door and was instantly enveloped by warmth. Not only the physical heat, but the overwhelming feeling of...home. There was a huge fire roaring in the fireplace. A teenage boy stood over it proudly, like it was his special project.

I smelled turkey and dressing, sweet potato pies, greens and macaroni and cheese. I had been to enough of Momma Bey's Christmas dinners to know the menu by heart. Momma Bey became my mom after my parents died. Just being in her house again made me realize how much I missed her. Missed...people.

I surveyed the room just to see how bad my day was about to get. The kids were gathered around the ceiling high tree checking out the boxes. There were only four of them and they were older. Young children were the one thing that could break down the carefully placed barriers around my heart. Their smiles, hugs and kisses and pure innocence *almost* made me want to feel again. Just hearing a child laugh was enough to send me into a depression for days.

But these kids were older. I was safe. I rubbed my hands together and stomped my feet. I might stay around for a while.

21

Charlene was right. I was long overdue for a visit with Momma Bey.

I felt a tug at my coat. At the *bottom* of my coat. From a height that could only be...

I looked down into beautiful, hazel eyes on a caramel brown face with the cutest pudgy cheeks that begged to be pinched. Thick, sandy brown curls surrounded a little girl's face.

"Are you Miss Charlene's friend?" Her small, squeaky voice was serious.

I nodded.

"Can you pray for Momma Bey, too?"

"Miss Charlene is praying for her." I tried to tear myself away from those eyes.

Huge tears pooled at the rims of them. Her bottom lip trembled. "But she needs you, too. Please lady, if you don't help pray..." she looked around at the other kids and lowered her voice as if she knew a secret they didn't – "Momma Bey might die." The tears spilled over onto those sweet cheeks.

My iceberg of a heart threatened to thaw. She put her small hand into mine and pulled me toward Momma Bey's bedroom. I resisted slightly and she leaned forward, determined to put all her strength into dragging me to that room.

As we approached the door, I recognized the fervor in Charlene's voice. It had brought me back from the brink of death on many occasions.

To tell the truth, I had a lot of nerve not wanting to pray for Momma Bey. She had warred for me in prayer against the spirits of suicide and depression in the hospital after my repeated attempts. She came to sit with me at the house to make sure I didn't try to hurt myself again. I could hear her pacing the floors all night, praying. I owed her and Charlene my life.

The little girl led me to the side of the bed opposite where Charlene was praying. She climbed up onto the bed and laid her hands on Momma Bey's chest, bowing her head and moving her lips ever so slightly. She couldn't be older than five but seemed to know just what an intercessor should do. She must have been with Momma Bey for a while.

Charlene stopped for a second and glanced up at me, then down at the little girl, then back up at me. She closed her eyes and

22

continued to pray.

When we finished praying, the little girl stood on the bed and turned around to me. "Thank you, lady." She threw her arms around my neck.

I froze. Slowly, I lifted my arms to return her embrace. *Crack.* The ice around my heart was melting by the second.

"Hey, baby." Momma Bey's eyes lit up with surprise when she saw me. I had never seen her look so bad. Her usually glowing, brown skin was ashen gray. Her eyes were glassy and cold, lacking the life they usually sparkled with. Her pleasing plumpness had wasted away to thin gauntness.

I glared a silent message at Charlene. *Why didn't you tell me how sick she was?*

Charlene's eyes flashed back. *Would it have made any difference if I had?*

Momma Bey said, "I see you met Hope." Upon hearing her name, the little girl went to lie at Momma Bey's side. Momma Bey lifted an arm and rubbed her back.

I inched closer to the bed. "Hey Momma. It's good to see you. Sorry I haven't been by to see you before –"

"Shhhh, baby. It's all right. You know I know." She reached out a hand.

I took it. Her grip was still strong and full of love. Hope scooted out of the way as I sat on the bed and embraced Momma Bey. She felt so thin and frail I started to cry. When I pulled back, she wiped my tears.

"Stop all that, baby. I'm so glad I got to see you before..." She looked down at Hope and stopped talking.

I shook my head. "Don't talk like that. You're gonna be fine."

She looked at me like she was preparing herself and didn't need me to play games. "Hope, go in there with the big kids."

Hope kissed Momma Bey's cheek, slid off the bed and scampered out of the room.

Momma Bey motioned for Charlene to sit down. "I want to thank you for helping with the kids this last year. Your being here kept the state from taking my children away. I know that kept me alive longer."

Momma Bey's quiet strength faded for a minute as a tear slid down her cheek. "I'm glad the state is letting you take Hope for

23

now. I pray a good family adopts her before she gets too much older. I need to know my baby girl is going to be okay."

I looked from Momma Bey to Charlene. Why hadn't she told me she was taking in a foster child? Guess she was afraid it would send me to Hermitville forever.

"You know I'll take good care of Hope, Momma Bey."

Momma Bey squeezed my hand. "And you." She smoothed a weathered hand across my cheek. "It's time. Time for you to live again. Feel again. Love again. Stop waiting to die and..." She squeezed my hand tight and I wondered how much of the remaining strength in her body she was using to try to strengthen me. "Live." She stretched the word out long and hard. "Live."

I knew she was speaking to my spirit – commanding life to come back to my soul. She said the word again and again and each time she spoke it, I felt like someone attached jumper cables to my heart and was revving a spiritual engine.

Tears poured down my face. I began sobbing loudly and lay my head on her chest.

She rubbed my back. "That's it, baby. Let the Lord heal you."

Charlene got up and left quietly. Momma Bey began praying like my life depended on it. Her voice and spirit got stronger the more she prayed. I knew the Holy Spirit had risen up in her to resurrect me from living death.

I wanted to tell her to stop. To save her strength for herself. And for the children. But I knew Momma Bey wouldn't have it any other way. She lived and breathed intercession.

Soon her breathing was heavy and I knew she was asleep. I gently lifted her arm and lay it at her side. I kissed her cheek and wondered if it was the last time –

"You ready? We should let her get some rest," Charlene whispered from the doorway.

I nodded and stood.

As I reentered the family room, the scent of Momma Bey's macaroni and cheese wafted toward me. How could she have cooked in her state of health? My question was answered when I saw an older teenage girl in the kitchen checking pots on the stove. Momma Bey had trained her well.

When I got out to the car, I noticed a child's booster seat and several presents on the backseat. Charlene followed me out with

24

Hope in her arms. Her large fluffy coat and scarf made it almost impossible to see her cute face.

After Charlene fastened her into her booster seat and slid next to me, I gave her a questioning look.

"I can't leave her here with Momma Bey being so sick. She's staying with me tonight. She'll open her presents at my house and then we're coming back to have dinner with Momma Bey and the other kids. You're welcome to join us."

I didn't answer. All I wanted was to get back to the safe, quiet aloneness of my home. No people, no conversation, no one making me feel anything.

Momma Bey's cry, "live", echoed in my spirit. I felt that electric jumper cable thing charging my soul.

"I'll think about it."

- - -

"What in the world?" Charlene stared out the window as we turned onto her street. Her house was pitch black. We had left it aglow with millions of Christmas lights.

"My power is out." She looked at me sheepishly. "Guess I had too many lights, huh?"

She dug into her purse for her keys. "Just give me a minute to pack up some stuff."

"You're going with me?"

Charlene frowned. "Unless you want me and the baby to sleep in the dark and cold." She looked back at Hope. "I'll be right back, okay sweetie?"

Hope nodded and gave a heartwarming smile. She seemed to sense my trepidation about her coming to my house. "I promise I'll be good, lady. I won't break anything and I won't be loud. I'm Momma Bey's good girl."

I turned around to Hope and willed all traces of anxiety to leave my face. "Of course you are. Don't worry – we'll be fine." I patted her little leg. "By the way. My name is Faith." I couldn't let her continue to reference me by my gender status.

Her eyes grew big. "Faith?"

I nodded.

Her smile lit up the entire car and probably had enough wattage to heat Charlene's house. "You have a fruit name like me."

I frowned. "A fruit name?"

"Yeah, a fruit name. Momma Bey teaches us about spirit fruit. My name is one. Hope. And your name is one too. Faith. The only one missing is love." She wrinkled her little nose. "Well there's a whole bunch more, but Momma Bey says the most important are faith, hope, and love."

I stared at her. "How old are you?"

She held up four fingers. "I'm about to turn five. My birthday is on Christmas."

"Your birthday is on Christmas? Mine…is too."

"Really, Miss Faith?" She giggled and clapped her hands like it was the best news she ever heard. "You must be special like me."

"Special?"

"Momma Bey says I'm God's special Christmas gift to the world."

"I bet you are." I had to ask. "How long have you been with Momma Bey?"

"Since I was two. My parents went to heaven when I was two. At Christmastime."

I looked into Hope's eyes. They lacked the haunted sadness I knew mine held. I guess she was too young when it happened.

"My parents went to heaven at Christmastime, too."

Hope held out a chubby hand. I closed mine around hers.

Charlene came flying out of the house and jumped into the car, slinging a large bag into the backseat. "It's got to be ten below in there."

She looked at Hope's hand in mine and gave me a curious smile. "Guess you guys were okay without me."

I shifted into first gear and headed home.

- - -

After Charlene tucked Hope into bed in the guest room they'd be sharing, she joined me for hot chocolate at the kitchen table.

"Should we have taken her to the hospital?" I asked.

Charlene shook her head. "There's nothing they can do. The doctors said she'd go months ago. The cancer has eaten up her whole body." She blew the steam off her hot cocoa. "She wants to go at home. She's prepared the older kids but doesn't want Hope to be there when it happens."

I sipped my chocolate.

26

Charlene smiled. "That little girl is something. Before we left, she ran back into the room to kiss Momma Bey goodbye. She told her she knew she was ready to go to heaven but made her promise she wouldn't go on Christmas Day."

"Yeah. She told me about her parents."

Charlene almost dropped her cup. "She did? Are you…okay?"

I shrugged. "Why wouldn't I be?"

Charlene frowned. "What exactly did she tell you?"

"That her parents went to heaven on Christmas." I stood to get an ice cube from the freezer to cool off my cocoa. "Why?"

Charlene let out a deep breath. "I don't know whether to tell you this or not."

"What?"

"Hope's father died in a car accident three days before Christmas. Her mother committed suicide on Christmas Day. Momma Bey heard it on the news and called Family Services to get her. She's had her ever since."

I shrugged, wondering why Charlene thought that would bother me. It was a sad story, but why should it affect me personally?

Then I remembered.

I had heard that story before. On the news. After my husband was killed. When I was in the ER after my miscarriage.

"Hope is…" I staggered back to the table and sat down.

Charlene put her hand over mine and nodded.

"She's…" I shook my head. I couldn't say the words. *The daughter of the man that killed my husband?*

Charlene nodded and waited for the information to sink in.

"I didn't know…I didn't realize he had a …daughter. That her mother had…"

"You okay?" Charlene studied my eyes.

I hung my head. "I guess I never thought about *his* family. I spent so much time wishing he were in hell for killing my husband that I never thought about the hell he left behind for his family. Her mother…killed herself?"

Charlene nodded.

"And Momma Bey has had her all this time?"

Charlene nodded again.

"Why didn't you tell me?"

Charlene shrugged. "Why would I have?"

27

She was right. It wasn't like I would have rushed over to offer comfort to Hope if I had known about her.

I looked up at Charlene. "It's been a long day. I think I'm gonna turn in."

I was drained. I had experienced more emotions in one day than I had allowed myself to in years. I couldn't handle the feelings developing in me for Hope. I was being overwhelmed with love for her. Something in me wanted to protect her little heart from any more hurt. I tried to push the feelings away. I knew protecting her would put my heart at risk.

As I settled into bed and snuggled under my comforter, I had to wonder. What if this was one of those situations where what Satan meant for evil, God meant for good? Did God bring me and Hope together for a reason? Were the two people who lost the most at Christmas three years ago to bring love to each other's lives?

I fell asleep wondering if I would be able to do what the Holy Spirit, through Momma Bey, had commanded. Could I choose life?

- - -

A whimpering sound woke me up from a deep sleep. I rolled over to see a small figure standing in the doorway.

"What's wrong, Hope?"

She ran over to my bed. "Miss Charlene sounds like a bear. She scared me." Her eyes were large as saucers.

I chuckled. "Yeah, Miss Charlene makes some pretty bad bear noises at night." I hesitated then scooted over and patted the bed next to me. "Come on."

I lifted the covers and she climbed into the bed. The child had a sixth sense for my apprehension. "I promise I won't wiggle too much. Momma Bey says I sleep bad, but I'll be still. I promise."

"You're fine, sweetie. Get some rest, okay?"

She lay her head on the pillow. Her squeaky voice cut across the darkness. "Momma Bey's going to heaven soon, isn't she?"

I couldn't answer. I hated lying to children, but I didn't want to scare her.

"It's okay. I know she is. She's going to live with Jesus. She says heaven is the most beautiful place and she's ready to go there."

I didn't know what to say.

"Is that why I came to your house? Is Momma Bey going to heaven tomorrow?"

28

I let out a deep breath. "I don't know when she's going, Hope. Only God knows, really."

She seemed satisfied with that answer and closed her eyes, fluttering her long eyelashes. She tossed and turned for a good ten minutes. She finally snuggled up close to me and laid her head on my chest.

Instinctively, I reached out to stroke her hair and rub her back. She sighed. Within minutes, her breathing had the heavy pattern of sleep.

- - -

When I awoke the next morning, Hope was sitting up in bed, staring at me, like she had been waiting for hours for me to wake up. She threw her little arms in the air. "Happy Christmas and Merry Birthday!" She covered her mouth with her hands and giggled. "I mean Merry Birthday and Happy..." She fell over on the bed, giggling – tickled that she couldn't seem to get it right.

I couldn't help but giggle with her. I tickled her tummy and set her off into another fit of girly giggles. Instead of pain, her laughter brought me joy.

She sat up and wrinkled her eyebrows like she was concentrating. "Happy Birthday and Merry Christmas." She threw her arms in the air, obviously pleased that she finally got it right.

"Happy Birthday and Merry Christmas to you too, Miss Hope." I reached out to her and she jumped into my arms, squeezing me tight around my neck. I kissed her cheek.

"Are we going to Momma Bey's for Christmas?"

I pinched her cheek. "Yep. As soon as Miss Charlene wakes up."

Her smile faded. "I want to go soon in case Momma Bey decides to go to heaven today."

"Are you worried about what's going to happen to you when she goes to heaven?"

Hope's curls bounced when she shook her head. "Momma Bey says if I just have enough faith, God will always take care of me. All I need is faith."

All I need is faith. The words rang in my ears. In my spirit. Like God was speaking to me.

It made sense. All she needed was Faith and what I needed more than anything was Hope.

I heard Charlene's cell phone ring from the guestroom. The hairs on my arms stood up. Something about that ring. I had gotten enough bad phone calls at Christmastime to know what news was coming.

I gathered Hope in my arms, pledging at that moment to always take care of her. To be the Faith she needed for God to take care of her. I knew she would be Hope to me. I smiled, remembering her telling me about the spirit fruit. We would have everything we needed.

Faith. Hope. And a whole lot of love.

Chapter Three

Angela January has a heart to encourage individuals in their Christian walk. She is a Bible study leader, inspirational speaker and founder of Career Renewal, a career development company dedicated to helping women realize their true potential, find the right career fit and manifest their life's calling through their work. Angela holds a Master of Education (M.Ed.) degree and is pursuing licensure as a professional counselor.

Angela is an avid reader, and particularly enjoys stories about women at transitional points in their lives. Recently, she took a leap of faith and moved beyond her love of reading inspirational stories, to writing them as well. She believes God has called her to this work, and is currently crafting her first full length novel. Her mission is to share a faith affirming message of hope relevant to women at all stages of life.

Angela is happily married to Roy, her biggest supporter, and is the proud mother of one teenaged son. She resides in Durham, North Carolina where she attends Duke Divinity School.

Her contribution to *The Midnight Clear* is entitled, *A Season of Love and Grace*. It is her first published work

A Season of Love and Grace

Jordan fought back a flood of tears, as she struggled to close her overstuffed suitcase. She was going home for Christmas break. It should have been a happy time, but instead, she felt nothing but dread. Her first semester at college was over, and she had finished it with a near 4.0 average. Even before the ink was dry on her grade report, Jordan's mother had called everyone in the family to tell them about her daughter's success. She'd already received a congratulatory e-mail from her Aunt Sheila. No doubt, others would be clamoring to celebrate with her when she got home.

Trying to regain her composure, Jordan dried her damp eyes with the palm of her hand and took one last look around the dorm room she had come to love. She and her roommate, Brenda, had spent hours there, studying together, gobbling down microwave pizza, and talking about their hopes and dreams.

"How could I have been so foolish?" she wondered aloud as she slowly gathered her belongings.

She didn't want to go, but the time had come for her to leave behind the bland white walls, gray floors and lumpy twin beds that filled her home away from home. With all the courage she could muster, Jordan opened the door, whispered a soft goodbye, and walked into an uncertain future.

"Don't let one night of pleasure give you a lifetime of pain."

If Jordan had heard it once, she had heard it a thousand times. Her mother's stern words of warning had been all she needed in high school to keep her on the straight and narrow. But secretly, she had decided that college would be different. Away from the watchful eyes of her mother, she planned to explore her passions.

What Momma didn't know wouldn't hurt her, Jordan had thought carelessly. But, now as she sat stuck in traffic on the crowded highway headed toward her hometown of Bentonville, she remembered the sermon Pastor Mayfield had preached in church the Sunday before she left for college.

"Your sins will find you out," he'd said, clutching the podium tightly with beads of sweat pouring down his large ebony face. Over and over, he recited, "What's done in secret will surely come to light."

Filled with guilt, Jordan wondered if she had the strength to face the weeks, months and years ahead. Everyone was going to be so disappointed in her. After all, she was the first in her family to go to college. She'd won a full academic scholarship and her mother couldn't stop talking about it. It would be a miracle if anyone in Bentonville had escaped hearing the news, because in her small town, any news, good or bad, got around fast.

After driving for hours, Jordan saw the Bentonville exit in the distance. She was not far from home. Drawing a deep breath, she pulled her cell phone from the large Coach bag that occupied the passenger seat of her car, and called her mother.

"Hi, Mom, it's Jordan."

"Where are you? I expected you home hours ago. I've been trying to reach you; didn't you hear your phone ring?"

"I'm sorry – I'll be home in less than an hour. I'm not far from my exit.

"Okay, pumpkin - see you soon."

– – –

Jordan flipped her phone closed and her thoughts raced. Maybe she shouldn't go home. She could just keep driving past her exit. She could go to New York, and change her name. People disappeared everyday in the United States. She'd be just another statistic. Being a "missing person" was starting to look like a better option than shattering her mother's dreams.

Pushing past her fears, Jordan knew in her heart that she had to go home. Trying to escape the consequences of her indiscretion was fruitless. The only thing left to do was pray. Maybe God would be merciful.

Fervently, Jordan asked the Lord to forgive her. "I've made so many mistakes," she cried out. "But this is the worst. Please help me to be strong, and if anything good can come out of this situation, please let it happen."

A sense of peace came over Jordan as her car veered onto the exit ramp. Certain that God had heard her prayer, she drove in silence the rest of the way, enjoying a level of calmness she hadn't experienced in months.

When Jordan finally pulled into the driveway of the small white cottage where she had grown up, she almost forgot her troubles. The house looked warm and festive. Her mother had always loved

33

Christmas. It was her tradition to string hundreds of lights around the two large evergreen trees in the yard and place a bright green wreath on the door. This year, there seemed to be more lights than usual, in addition to some ornamental reindeer twinkling brightly against the darkness of the night sky.

The porch light was on, which meant her mother was waiting patiently inside for the doorbell to ring. From the car, Jordan could hear Sebastian, her fourteen-year-old black and white collie, barking incessantly. Quickly, she looked into the rearview mirror, checked her makeup and reapplied her favorite lip gloss. She wanted her face to look bright and cheerful. Jordan steadied herself, opened the door, and slid out of the hunter green 2000 Honda Accord she had received as a high school graduation gift. Walking toward the door, she tightened the belt on her blue all-weather coat, hoping the dark color would conceal her recent weight gain.

Within seconds of pressing the doorbell, the front door flew open, and standing there was Robyn Brown, her mother - the woman she loved with her entire heart. Alongside her was Sebastian, Jordan's best friend since she was four years old, wagging his fluffy tail to welcome her home.

Once inside, Jordan embraced her curvy, 5'3" mother and then stooped to rub Sebastian's shaggy head. The aroma of chocolate chip cookies and fried chicken filled the air. Wearing the apron that Jordan had given her for Mother's Day the year before, Robyn looked like she belonged on the Food Network. She loved to cook and spent most of her free time in the kitchen. After stuffing a warm cookie, fresh from the oven into her mouth, she pointed to the plate of cookies on the table and offered one to her daughter. Jordan couldn't resist her mother's cookies, so she grabbed two from the plate and gobbled them down.

"Sweetie, leave room for dinner. I made all your favorites," Robyn announced with glee. "Your Aunt Sheila and Uncle Bo are on their way over with the new baby and they can hardly wait to see you."

"They are?"

"Yes, they'll be here any minute. Take your coat off and get comfortable while I run in the kitchen to finish everything."

Jordan was scared. The ten pounds she had gained was right in her mid-section. If she took off her coat, her secret would be out. "Mom, I'm going to my room to change my clothes."

"Don't be long – as soon as your aunt and uncle get here, we'll be ready to eat."

Jordan went into her room and shut the door. Rummaging through her closet, she found a loose-fitting navy blue sweat suit. "This will work," she mumbled.

Taking off her coat, she took a look at her reflection in the full length mirror attached to her closet door. The first thing she noticed was her small protruding round belly. There was no denying she was pregnant. About two and a half months. Fortunately, everything else looked normal. Her long chestnut colored hair beautifully complemented her round caramel colored face and hazel eyes, and her arms and legs were just as long and lean as usual. From now on she'd have to select her clothes carefully if she didn't want anyone one to suspect her predicament. Finally dressed, Jordan took one more look in the mirror. Her secret was safe; at least for now.

"Jordan," her mother yelled. "Get the door - I'm still busy in the kitchen."

Jordan went to the door and opened it without looking through the peep hole. In front of her was a bouquet of pink roses. Michael, the reason for all of her trouble was holding them out to her as if they were some kind of peace offering.

"Boy, I don't want to talk to you."

"Jordan," he whispered. "Have you told your mother yet?"

"No! I just got home."

"So it's safe for me to come inside?"

"No! I don't want you here."

"Jordan, please talk to me," Michael pleaded. "I love you."

"Love? You don't know the meaning of love, or you wouldn't have said those awful things to me."

"Jordan, I'm really sorry. I want to work things out. I'm not going to leave you to handle this all by yourself."

"Michael, go away. I can't deal with you right now."

"Jordan, if that's what you want, I will. But promise you'll call me tomorrow, after you've had time to rest.

"If you want, you can come over to talk after my mom goes to work."

"Okay. I'll be back about 10:00 a.m."

Michael handed Jordan the flowers and sprinted quickly down the front steps. Jordan closed the door and went into the kitchen. The fragrance of the large blooms she carried made her feel faint, so she placed them on the counter and briefly covered her nose.

"Wow," her mother exclaimed. "Where did you get those gorgeous flowers?"

"Michael just brought them over," she sighed.

"Why didn't you invite him in for dinner?"

"Mom, I'm tired. I just want to eat and go to bed. I'll see Michael tomorrow."

Sebastian's barking ended their conversation in mid-stream. The door bell was ringing again and this time when Jordan opened the door, she saw her favorite aunt and uncle. Aunt Sheila was short and curvaceous just like her sister, Robyn, while Uncle Bo was slender and well over six feet tall. They'd always made an attractive couple, but this time when Jordan looked at them, she saw more than two beautiful people. They had a light emanating from them that radiated pure joy.

As they moved into the foyer of the house, Uncle Bo proudly lifted up the baby carrier so Jordan could take a peek at her new cousin. For years, her aunt and uncle had tried to have a baby of their own, but couldn't. Then three months ago, one of Jordan's distant cousins had a baby she couldn't properly care for and asked Aunt Sheila if she and her husband would adopt the boy. They agreed and suddenly they were parents. It hadn't happened the way they had planned it, but that didn't seem to matter. It was clear they loved their new baby very much.

Hearing the baby whimper, Jordan asked if she could hold him. Her uncle nodded and Jordan pulled the baby from his soft warm cocoon. Gently, she rocked him in her arms. He was a miracle and holding him made her glad that she hadn't listened to Michael about having an abortion. Now she wanted her baby more than ever.

"Everybody come and sit down. Dinner is ready to be served," shouted Jordan's mother from the dining room.

As soon as Jordan complied, she saw the nauseating flowers from Michael sitting in the middle of the table.

36

"Jordan, I put your flowers in a vase – I thought they would make a great centerpiece for dinner."

"You got flowers from Michael?" Aunt Sheila asked. "I thought he was in boot camp."

"He was; he finished about two and a half months ago," Jordan responded. "Since then he's been in training and now he's about to go to Italy."

"Italy? That sounds fun, Jordan. I bet you wish you could go with him," Robyn teased.

If her mother knew the truth, she wouldn't be speaking about Michael in such a positive way, Jordan thought, feeling her stomach quiver.

"Please everybody, sit down," urged Robyn. "Dinner is getting cold."

Bo graced the food and they began eating. Jordan relaxed and enjoyed the light conversation and delicious food. Little Stephen constantly cooed and gurgled. Whenever, Jordan looked at him, she tried to imagine the face of her own child. Would the baby look like her or Michael? Michael was tall and muscular with captivating brown eyes and mocha colored skin. He was absolutely gorgeous, but it was his smile that made her heart beat faster whenever he flashed it at her. She hoped the baby would be a nice combination of both of them.

Seeing Michael again made Jordan long for his presence. He'd been her constant companion since the ninth grade, when he asked her to the Freshman Dance. They'd always been on the same page, that is, until she told him about the baby. His response to her news was shocking. He told her that he wasn't ready to be a father and that she should get an abortion. He offered to send her the money to take care of things, but said he couldn't leave his training school to be with her. He had been downright mean to her and made it abundantly clear that if she decided to have the baby, she would be on her own. So they broke up, just when she needed him the most. Their four year relationship was over, without warning.

Jordan had been devastated, but each morning she took the time to put on makeup, comb her hair and practice her fake smile. That forced smile got her through the semester. Nobody on campus knew what was going on except Brenda, her trusted roommate. Brenda prayed for Jordan, took notes for her in class, and helped

37

her study so her grades wouldn't drop. Brenda was like the sister she never had. Without her support, Jordan knew she wouldn't have made it.

Now Michael was back in her life, acting as if he hadn't stomped on her heart. Just thinking about him made her head swim with confusion, but she did want to talk to him. Jordan wondered what he'd meant when he said he wasn't going to leave her to handle everything alone. Had he changed his mind? Did he want the baby after all?

She had to admit it – he was still in love with Michael Leon Jones, despite his atrocious behavior. Maybe he wouldn't abandon their baby like her father had abandoned her. Feeling exhausted from the long drive home and Michael's unexpected visit, Jordan asked to leave the table so she could go to bed.

"I know you're tired – go get some sleep," There was a note of concern in her mother's voice.

Jordan kissed everyone goodnight and left the room. As she walked away, she could hear Aunt Sheila ask her mother if everything was alright. Then she heard her mother say softly that she wasn't sure.

"Maybe you should have a little talk with her," suggested Aunt Sheila.

"I will tomorrow. When I get home from work, Jordan and I are going to have a heart to heart," her mother responded.

Knowing that her mother wanted to talk made Jordan tense. She didn't feel ready to tell Robyn about the baby. She'd hoped to keep her secret for at least a couple of weeks while she decided on her next steps.

- - -

Worrying kept Jordan awake. She tossed and turned in her bed all night. Even though she wasn't asleep, hearing the blaring sound of the alarm clock on her bedside table was a jolt to her system. She'd set the alarm for 8:00 a.m. so she could get up and dressed before Michael stopped by. Lack of sleep made her body feel like a sack of potatoes – heavy and awkward. Dragging herself from her bed, she turned off the alarm and made her way to the bathroom, tripping over Sebastian's tail as he slept quietly next to her bed. When she saw her face in the bathroom mirror, she was appalled.

Dark circles ringed her eyes, her complexion was splotchy, and her hair was in disarray – she looked absolutely frightful.

She had to do something to make herself look presentable for Michael. But unfortunately, her luggage was still in her car – she'd forgotten to bring it inside when she arrived the night before. Thinking she could borrow a comb and brush from her mother, she padded down the hall and was startled to hear an angry voice coming from her mother's bedroom. Obviously, her mother hadn't gone to work yet and was talking on the phone to someone.

Listening intently, Jordan figured that it must be her father. George Brown was the only person on earth that ever made her mother this angry. She'd never heard her mother say one good word about the man.

"Why do you want to see her now?" she heard her mother snarl. "After all of these years, you think you can just waltz back into our lives? We've done fine without you! Don't call back later, George! I really would prefer you didn't speak to Jordan, you'll just upset her. Since we got divorced, you haven't even attempted to call and check on her. Much less, send any money to help out. It's been just the two of us.

"Jordan doesn't need you now. She's doing great! She got a scholarship to college and she's an A student. What can you do for her? It's too late to play Daddy."

Hearing the phone slammed back in its cradle, Jordan scurried back down the hall. She didn't want her mother to know she had been eavesdropping. Back in her room, Jordan got into bed. She needed to think. Her mother said she didn't need George, but that wasn't true. She did need her father; every girl needs her father.

Jordan had some good memories of him. But she knew from stories her mother told, that he was an alcoholic who made the mistake of getting violent one night after coming home drunk. The next day, Robyn put George out and changed the locks on the doors.

"No man is going to hit me and get away with it," Robyn would often say if someone mentioned her ex-husband. In her mother's book, an abusive man was the lowest kind of human. Jordan's father didn't get any mercy.

Jordan heard a quiet knock on her door, bringing her thoughts back to the present.

"Are you sleep?" her mother asked.

"No," said Jordan.

"May I come in?"

"Sure."

When her mother opened the door, Jordan sat up and carefully pulled the blankets up around her tummy.

"Honey, I want to have a talk with you when I get home from work this evening."

"Why, Mommy?"

"We didn't get a chance to really talk last night. I just want to catch up on what's happening in your life. I want you to know, I'm proud of you, Jordan. You've always been a good girl. You've never gotten into any trouble, and that has been a real blessing to me. Being a single parent isn't easy, but I've always been able to count on you to be responsible."

"Thanks Mom," Jordan said with tears threatening. "I've never wanted to disappoint you."

Jordan reached out and hugged her mother. Tonight was the night, she decided, as she rested her head on her mother's shoulder. The secret she was harboring had become too much to bear.

Robyn peeked at her watch as she bounced up from the bed and toward the door. "I've got to get out of here – I'm late for work."

"Okay, I'll see you later," Jordan responded, clutching her blankets.

After her mother left, Jordan relaxed her head against the big fluffy pillows on her bed and drifted off to sleep. Intending to sleep for just ten minutes, she awakened to the ringing of the doorbell.

"Oh no, it's Michael. He can't see me like this," she panicked.

When the doorbell rang again, Jordan rushed into the bathroom doused her face with water, rinsed out her mouth, brushed her hair down with her fingers and pulled a few balls of lint from the sweat suit she'd put on the night before. This wouldn't be the first time Michael had seen her look awful. She really needed to talk to him.

Jordan got to the door and opened it just as Michael was leaving. When she called his name, he turned around, ran up the front steps and embraced her with a warm loving hug. For a moment, it felt like old times.

Jordan pulled away from Michael's arms, closed the front door and motioned for him sit down on the couch in the living room.

"Excuse my appearance, Michael," she said, wishing she had on some makeup.

"Don't worry; you always look beautiful to me," he said with his eyes twinkling. "Please come and sit near me."

Jordan joined him on the couch, feeling nervous and unsure of what he might say.

"Look at me baby," he said. "I acted like a fool and for that, I am truly sorry. When you called to tell me that you were pregnant, I felt afraid. I didn't think I could handle being a father at eighteen. I didn't want the responsibility and some of the guys on base kept telling me that I all I needed to do was offer to pay for the abortion. So that's what I did."

"Michael, I don't think you know how you made me feel when you told me to get an abortion. I was so hurt. I thought you loved me and that we'd always be there for each other no matter what. We'd even talked about getting married some day and then you acted like I was just some kind of one night stand."

"I know baby – there is no excuse I can offer for my behavior, except to say I'll never do anything like that to you again."

"Both of us were foolish, Michael. I was the one that seduced you – I invited you up to my college campus. I made the reservation at the Holiday Inn and then I told you I was finally ready to make love to you. Up until then, you tried to respect my wishes to remain a virgin until we got married. It's my fault that we have a baby on the way."

"It's not your fault," Michael replied. "I could have said no. We both grew up in the church. We both knew what we were doing was wrong in the eyesight of God. I could have helped you stay strong, but I didn't. I always respected the fact that you wanted to stay a virgin until you got married. Jordan, I can't give you back your innocence, but I've been thinking we could get married. I love you, and I always will – there is no sense in us waiting to get married now that we have a baby to take care of."

"Michael, I don't know what to say – of course, I want to marry you. I just thought I would be finished with college first."

Rubbing her hands over her stomach, Jordan decided to accept Michael's proposal. She didn't want her baby to grow up without a father in the house. Besides, who could resist a proposal from a man who wanted to take responsibility for his family?

41

"So, when do you want to get married?" Jordan asked.

"What about Christmas Day?"

"That's only ten days from now."

"I know, but I have to leave for Italy the day after. I don't want to leave the country without you being my wife."

Jordan felt happiness overtaking her. Eighteen was terribly young to be getting married. But she had asked God to work things out, and if this was God's plan for her, then she would do her best to be a good wife and mother.

"Michael, I have to admit that I thought I was going to have to raise the baby all by myself. I'm so happy right now – I could burst with joy," said Jordan, throwing her arms around Michael's neck.

"Christmas can't get here soon enough," Michael chuckled. "Can I touch your stomach? I want to say hello to our baby."

Jordan took Michael's hand and placed it where her belly had begun to swell. Overcome with emotion, one big tear slid down Michael's face, then he kneeled before Jordan and pulled a small black velvet box from his jacket pocket.

"Will you marry me? I was going to wait until tonight to give this to you, but right now feels like the perfect moment." Opening the box, Michael revealed a small, but tasteful solitaire diamond mounted on a gold band.

"Yes!" rejoiced Jordan as Michael took the ring from its box and slipped it slowly onto her finger.

"It fits beautifully," she observed, holding out her hand for Michael to see. "I can't wait to show my mother."

"Jordan, I don't think she's going to be very happy about our baby, engagement, or upcoming marriage. She'll think we're too young."

I know, but I believe she'll be okay when she sees how happy we are."

"I hope so," Michael said. "I'm going to leave in a few minutes so you can get dressed. I'll be back tonight so we can share our news with your mother – together. But first, I have to tell you something really important."

"What is it?"

"I met your father yesterday."

Jordan sat up straight. "You did? How'd that happen?"

42

"I went to the barber shop where my Uncle Charles works. He asked about you and I told him that I thought I was going to ask you to marry me. He started teasing me saying, 'Jordan Brown is going be Jordan Jones.' Your father was waiting to get his haircut and he overheard us. The next thing I knew – he came over to me and pulled out his wallet, showing me a picture of you at about four years old, and asked if his Jordan and my Jordan were the same. That's when I realized he was your father. I could hardly believe it. We made plans to meet for lunch and ended up talking for two hours.

"He told me how he and your mother broke up, and that he had been sober for over a year. He moved back to Bentonville about three months ago hoping to reestablish a relationship with you. But he heard through the grapevine that you were off at college, and he knew better than to contact Robyn to get your number. So all this time, he's been praying that God would connect the two of you somehow. He's really sorry about running out on you, Jordan. He told me he wishes he could turn back the hands of time just so he could be a real father to you. I felt sorry for him. Talking to him made realize that marrying you and being a father to our baby was definitely the right thing to do. I don't want to end up like him, with nothing but regrets.

"I don't think this is a coincidence, Jordan. God is doing something special for you, me…our family. I do believe in miracles and it definitely looks like we are in the middle of one right now." Michael paused and then added, "Oh…by the way, I gave your father the phone number here – he'll probably call sometime today."

"He did call, but I didn't talk to him," Jordan revealed. "Mother answered the phone and it wasn't pretty." She shook her head at the remembrance of it. "Michael you'd better go; I have to get ready for tonight. Help me get my luggage out of my car before you leave."

After Michael left, Jordan took a shower and brushed her teeth. Feeling refreshed, she slipped on a warm terry cloth robe and looked at herself in the mirror. She noticed that her face held a new radiance – kind of like Aunt Sheila's. She was happy – pure and simple. The happenings of the day were almost too much to take in. She was engaged to be married on Christmas Day, her father

43

wanted to see her, and in less than seven months she would have a new baby to love and care for; not alone like she thought just yesterday, but with Michael.

"God you are wonderful." she said with her arms lifted up. "God I love you. You brought me out of a dark place and into your light. You forgave my sins, you showed me your love and extended your grace – thank you!"

Jordan had seen some of the older ladies in her church shout – leaping about and jumping for joy. She had even laughed at them once or twice, but now she had her own reasons to shout.

"Hallelujah – God, you are awesome!" she continued.

Before long, she was dancing around her room and singing *New Season*, the praise and worship song that Israel and New Breed made popular.

"What's going on in here?" Jordan's mother inquired.

Oh…I didn't hear you come in," responded Jordan.

I guess you didn't. It looks like you're having church all by yourself."

"Mom, let's go in the living room so we can talk," said Jordan with excitement. "Remember when you said you wanted to have a heart to heart talk to find out what's been going on in my life?"

"Yes."

"Well, you'll want to sit down." Jordan smiled as she escorted her mother to the couch. She knew this conversation would be the beginning of a new season in both their lives.

Chapter Four

Patricia Haley, national bestselling author of *Nobody's Perfect, Blind Faith, Baby Blues*, and *No Regrets* is a trailblazer in the mainstream faith-based genre. She self-published *Nobody's Perfect* in 1998 and her faith-based debut novel was the first of its kind to repeatedly make numerous bestselling lists, including #1 on the *Essence* list.

With her engineering degree from Stanford University and M.B.A. in marketing and finance from the University of Chicago, she works part-time as a project manager.

Patricia is a born-again believer, former chaplain and committee chairperson in her local chapter of Delta Sigma Theta Sorority. She is an active member of New Covenant Church in Pennsylvania where she sings in the gospel choir, serves on the building committee leadership team, heads a financial mentoring program with her husband, Jeffrey, as well as volunteers for the free-tax return assistance program.

Her latest novels, *Still Waters* and *Let Sleeping Dogs Lie*, released in Nov. 2005 and Sept. 2006, respectively. Visit Patricia online by visiting www.patriciahaley.com.

Her contribution to *The Midnight Clear* is entitled, *The Greatest Gift.*

The Greatest Gift

Lee stood by the door, periodically peering through the open blinds, letting his worries fall away like the fresh snow covering the streets. If only it was that simple, to wash away his troubles with a few flakes of snow. He was learning that life was mixed with doses of ups and downs; and downs he had aplenty, but times were changing. Grief had strangled the joy out of one holiday. He was determined to not let it claim two. His four little angels deserved some happiness and he was going to make sure they got a big dose of it tonight.

"All right Mr. Warner, I'm heading out," the store owner said, plunging her arm into the sleeve of her coat and flicking the scarf around her neck while juggling a stack of stamped letters. "We haven't had a customer in nearly an hour. Looks like we've done all the business we're going to do today. So, if you don't mind, I'm leaving a few minutes early this afternoon."

"I don't mind at all," he responded, mostly thinking ahead to his list of to-do items. Once he was off work, he'd have to hurry in order to get home and get the children ready for the holiday. The past year hadn't been easy, but his children had brought more fulfillment into his life than he'd ever dreamed possible. They were the single source fueling his motivation to keep going. Without them, the looming grief of losing his wife probably would have claimed more than a mere holiday.

"I want to make the bank deposit and drop these letters at the post office, although nothing is getting delivered tonight. Nothing that is, unless it's on the back of a reindeer sleigh," she said, chuckling at her own little joke.

"You're probably right," Lee agreed, still focused on tasks outside the doors of the business.

"Don't hang around here too late, Mr. Warner. It's Christmas Eve, get on home."

"Don't worry. Four o'clock sharp I'll be locking up," he said, unable to contain the swelling joy.

"Look at you. I haven't seen you smile like that in the entire six months that you've been here. You must have special plans for the holiday."

Jovial and unable to contain his glee, Lee said, "My kids are going to have one of the best Christmases they've ever had. My wife is gone," he said with voice dipping temporarily but unwilling to let the dab of grief overcome his plans tonight. "This will be the first Christmas without her, but I'm determined to give them the best holiday ever."

"Good for you," she said, patting him on his bony arm.

Lee hadn't eaten right for months; really for the whole year. The kids ate regularly, but not him. He could probably blame the loss of appetite on his jobs. Working from six in the morning until two and then hustling to The Packaging Store to work a two-thirty to five shift every day, didn't leave much room for luxuries such as proper eating. Food was his last priority. Sleeping, earning a living, taking care of the kids, and leaving a little time for God was the best he could do.

"Four o'clock, I'm out of here. That gives me enough time to cash my check, grab their toys off layaway and pick up a smoked turkey and trimmings before everything shuts down at six."

"Wow, I didn't know you could buy an entire pre-cooked Thanksgiving dinner. My goodness, how times have changed! Years ago, using a can of yams and a box of stuffing was the only shortcut on the market."

"You can buy everything down to the gravy and cranberry sauce, which works for me. Easter was my first attempt at cooking the holiday meal and it didn't go so well. We ended up eating hotdogs and canned beans," Lee said with laughter erupting from both of them. "It will be better for me to buy dinner than to try and cook it myself."

"You're a great dad, Mr. Warner."

"I'm trying, but it's not easy with my wife gone," he practically screamed, elevating over the speck of emotion lingering. Lee watched Ms. Gill pull her last boot up to her knee and scoop up her stack of letters and money bag which were blanketing the floor. "Get on out of here, and I'll see you after Christmas."

- - -

Lee pulled the black blinds down to the floor and double checked the lock. Four o'clock, right on time. Turning off lights along the way, he hustled down the back hallway, reconstructing the to-do list in his head. Final light off, he opened the back door.

47

"Oh my gosh man, what are you doing?" he said, glaring into the face of a man who was close enough to kiss him, causing Lee to take a step back. The black hood pulled over his head made it difficult to see his eyes or any other distinctive characteristic with detail.

"I need to pick up a package that was delivered here for me."

"We're closed."

"I have to get that package," he demanded, pushing past Lee.

"Hey wait a minute, I told you that we're closed. You'll have to get the package after Christmas," Lee said pushing the man back into the doorway. Feeling a hardness press into his abdomen, Lee repelled, pushing the door toward closure.

"I told you, I'm not leaving until I get that package," the intruder reiterated, overpowering Lee and pushing inside, this time drawing from inside his coat the pistol Lee felt when they bumped a moment earlier.

"Hey, hey, hey," Lee said with his hands extended and retreating into the store, "take it easy. I don't want any trouble."

The man pointed the gun at Lee and wouldn't take the barrel off the line of fire. He closed the door behind him and locked it, stepping toward Lee at the same snail's pace in which Lee was retreating. Ten degrees outside and this man was sweating like it was the middle of August. Lee wasn't sure which one it was, the cold or the holiday scent in the air that brought out the weirdoes. Get this crazy man out of the store, get the door locked, and get on his way; that's what he had to do. No time for confusion, an hour, maybe two to finish his errands and get home. Tonight was special and he wouldn't be deterred. Lee stepped fervently toward the assailant.

"Don't try to be a hero, just give me the money," the man commanded.

"What money? There isn't any money."

"Don't lie to me, there's always money at the end of the day. I know there is. I used to work here a long time ago, long before you took my job."

"*Your* job? What are you talking about? I started this job six months ago and I have no idea who you are, but you have to leave otherwise I'll have to call the police and that's not good for either of us. It's Christmas Eve and I want to get home. You should want to

48

do the same," he said, closing the gap between him and the intruder by taking a step.

"Don't tell me what to do," the man bellowed, clearly agitated. "Don't tell me what to do," he repeated in the same tone, carelessly flopping the gun around.

"Okay, calm down, let's not make this any more of a problem than it is. There's no money. You can turn around, walk out the door and I'll forget this ever happened. Consider this your lucky night," Lee told the man.

"I don't need luck, I need the money. Now give it to me," he demanded, this time taking aim with a dark coldness deposited deep in his pupils that caused Lee to shiver. This man was serious. He wanted some money and didn't seem to care how far he had to go to get it.

"Whoa, wait a minute, what are you doing?"

"Give me the money, man!" He screamed loud enough to be heard outside, and probably would have been if it had been a regular night with folks moving along the sidewalk. But tonight those who had a family were home with them or trying to get there.

"The owner left early and took the money with her. There's nothing here."

"You're lying. Give me the money man so that I can get out of here. You think I'm playing with you? Don't make me hurt you. I don't want to but I will if I have to," he spoke, fidgeting. I need that money."

"I swear to you, I'm not lying. She left about twenty minutes before you got here. Seriously, there's no money, it's gone."

"Please tell me that you're lying," he said charging toward Lee.

A struggle ensued and the hood fell off the man's head, exposing his neatly trimmed, short blondish colored hair. Although Lee had lost muscle mass over the past year, he was strong enough to overpower his smaller opponent and get to the gun. Seconds felt like hours. Finally, Lee had maneuvered his hand onto the barrel and was forcefully grabbing at the handle when a popping sound rang out.

Time paused. The room went silent. No one spoke, or moved, or seemed to take a breath. Thoughts darted around Lee's mind at the pace of a high speed train, zooming through a no name town. His wife, the kids, securing the store…Christmas gifts, his

49

kids...did he turn off all the lights, the kids...images of falling snow against his dark skin...dinner, his wedding day...thoughts swirled uncontrollably. His legs were like noodles and gave way, unable to sustain his weight. He collapsed onto the floor. His hand felt warm, soothing, wet.

Lee's assailant fell back against the door with the gun flopping from side to side, in unison with his head. "Oh my God, oh my God," he squealed. "Look what you made me do. Why did you do that? Let me think, give me a minute."

Lee pulled his hands from the pocket of wetness spreading across his stomach and stared at the bright red color saturating his hand. Visions were traveling haphazardly with increased intensity, but still slow. He didn't know what to expect. He'd never been shot before and didn't know anyone else who had. Wasn't it supposed to hurt? Oh no, what about the layaway? The toy store would close at six. What time was it? Was it still Thursday? Did he turn off the lights in the front of the store? Were the kids behaving with the babysitter? He had to hurry. The teenage sitter from down the block had to leave at six-fifteen, not a minute later since she had to go caroling with her church. So much to do, struggling to recall the to-do list he'd begun crafting earlier. He pushed into his abdomen, sucking in air, and pulled his hand close to his eyes this time. The reddish color seemed brighter, warmer. The ringing coming from his pocket drew him back into the moment. Instinctively, he reached for the phone.

"Don't move."

"I have to answer the phone, it's my kids," he was able to squeak out pain free. "I always talk to them the second I leave work. I have to answer the phone," he said commandeering his waning strength.

"Don't move. I'm sorry, but I need time to think," the crazy man said with both his hand and gun shaking.

"Man, I need to get to the hospital," Lee said, letting the back of his head rest on the floor.

"You can't go anywhere, not until I figure out a plan."

The weight of Lee's thoughts was too heavy. God would have to get a message to his children, otherwise they would worry and he couldn't let them worry. Daddy would be home soon and they would have the biggest Christmas ever. Excerpts of Lee's list bounced around in his mind. He would pull himself up, wipe away the little blood, turn out the lights, lock up and get to the bank and toy store before six. Picking up the food was questionable. Another hotdog holiday was highly likely and they'd make the best of it again. Nobody, not even a person pointing a gun at him would keep him from his children. He was all they had and he would never leave them. His wife had cancer, and she couldn't help leaving them. This man would have to kill him first. Maybe he already had.

"I can't believe this. I really am worthless," the man said, letting his back lean against the door as his legs slumped. "I can't do anything right," he whimpered before pointing the gun at his temple.

Lee raised up far enough to see what was happening. "What are you doing?"

"Shut up, you shut up; this is all your fault. If you'd given me the money like I asked, none of this would be happening. I can't go to jail. My kids would be ashamed of me and my wife would use it to turn them against me, and I can't have that."

Lee felt no pain, but lying in a flat position on the floor was uncomfortable. He squirmed for better positioning oblivious to his attacker's next step. Ringing came from Lee's pocket again.

"Don't answer that."

"Man, it's my kids. I have to answer it," Lee responded without lifting his head from the floor this time, feeling too tired to move.

"I don't want to kill you, but I will if I have to. I'm not going to jail. I'll die first," the man said matter-of-factly.

Lee hadn't begun to panic; not yet. He was bleeding, but not gushing out pints of blood. He had to get out of this mess. His children would not be orphans, not so long as he could collect his thoughts and come up with a plan. "Mister, I'm begging you to call the ambulance. I have to get to the hospital. I can't die like this. My children need me. I'm all they have in this world. You have to let me get out of here."

"I can't."

"I won't tell the police anything about you. Just let me go," Lee said, easing his head back on the floor.

"They're mother will take care of them. Mothers always do. They don't need us," the man responded.

51

"Not my kids," Lee said, recognizing the small crack in the man's defensive armor. He mustered as much strength as he could to pull himself up in a sitting position and scooted back against a stack of big boxes lining the back room. "My wife died last year. I'm all they have."

The man let his glance drop to the floor and allowed it to linger there for some time. "I'm sorry, really I'm sorry. Children deserve to be raised by both their parents. If only my wife believed that, I probably wouldn't be here right now in this mess. If she just wouldn't ride me so much. I'm doing the best I can."

"How many children do you have?" Lee asked, unsure where this conversation was headed. But if it was in the direction of freedom, he would gladly dance down the path.

The darkness which seemed to live in the intruder's eyes brightened and spilled out into his facial expression. "Two; a boy and a girl," the man conveyed, setting the gun down on the floor next to him. "Amy and Dillon. They love me. What about you, how many do you have?"

"Four. Three boys and one girl. Jason, LJ, Mark, and my little princess, Elaine." Talking about the children felt like medicine. There wasn't any pain, hadn't been from the beginning, but even the anxiety seemed to flush away when he concentrated on the children. They were Lee's hope, his reason for living.

Silence rested in the midst, with both thinking but not speaking. They had engaged into a conversation, but Lee couldn't forget the fact that this man was crazy, and that because of him, he had a bullet lodged in his abdomen. Not sure of what else to say to the man, Lee braced his head against the box, applied pressure to his stomach, closed his eyelids and spoke to the only one who could help him.

He said a silent prayer, careful not to move his lips, not wanting to agitate the disturbed man any more than he already had. God had allowed challenges to fill Lee's life in recent months, but he never lost sight of the peace and hope that He had also supplied in the midst of tough times. As Lee reflected on the situation, he had a lot to be thankful for. His children were healthy, safe, loving. He currently had two jobs when some people couldn't get one. His situation looked a lot better from his side of the room than that of the man with the gun.

The man broke the silence when he asked, "What's your name?"

Somewhat caught off guard, Lee took a few seconds to gather himself and respond. He followed with the same question.

"Most people call me Marty," the man answered. "It's short for Martin, but I like Marty better."

"Marty, it is," Lee affirmed, unwilling to strike up additional conversation. He was tired.

"My children love Christmas Eve. It used to be our favorite night together as a family. My wife would make cookies, while Amy and Dillon would help me toast marshmallows in the fireplace and string popcorn around the house. About seven o'clock, we'd each get a glass of hot apple cider and a handful of cookies and gather in the den to watch *It's a Wonderful Life*. Afterwards, we'd each open one gift. To see the faces of my children light up meant the world to me – still does." For the first time since he began speaking about his children, Marty was quiet. He drew in a big gust of air and Lee could see that Marty was unsuccessfully trying to camouflage his emotions. It was difficult for Lee to reconcile how Marty could be brazen enough to wield a gun in one instance and then struggle to fight back tears when talking about his children. Lee wanted to have compassion for Marty, the father, but it was hard staring at Marty, the robber.

"Enough about my children and Christmas Eve. This year won't be the same. My wife and kids are living with her sister and I'm out of work. Just seventy five dollars, that's all I need to get Amy's doll and Dillon's rollerblades. That's not much to ask for. This place owes me that much. If they'd let me keep my job, I could have kept my family and bought my own gifts. I wouldn't have to rob anybody," he said with voice elevating and becoming agitated.

"It's not the end of the world," blurted out before Lee could contemplate his words. "It's not the end of the world because you can't buy gifts. There are other things more important to a family than gifts, like having love for one another. That's what's important."

"Tell that to my wife and to her family. I'm a loser. They know it and maybe I know it too."

"Come on, how can you be a loser? I bet Amy and Dillon don't see you as a loser – you're a hero to them. You're Daddy. I know; I've been where you are."

"No you haven't. You didn't lose your job and 401K plan because some hot shot executive decided to steal the money. Worse yet, I get a part time job, one that pays no where near what I was making or even what I need to take care of my family, but a job is a job and I took it. I hired on right here at The Packaging Store. I was late three lousy days and the next thing you know, I'm fired. No questions, no mercy, no job."

Telling Marty the obvious about the consequences of his irresponsibility would produce no fruit and possibly lead to more erratic behavior. Appealing to him as a father was working better. "Being a father and husband can be tough, I know. But you have to hang in there. Amy and Dillon need you. Ellen, Mark, Jason, and LJ need me."

"My kids don't need me. They're mother is doing a fine job all by herself. Nobody needs me. Why would they? I can't get enough money to buy a few Christmas gifts. What kind of a father am I? They deserve a better father. I'm no good for them. I know it."

"You can't think that way or you'll end up doing something you'll regret."

"What…like robbing The Packaging Store and shooting a father of four? What could be worse?"

"Marty," Lee uttered with his gaze locked directly on the troubled man sitting across from him, "it's not too late for you, not as a father, not as a man, not even with this situation. It's not too late. Get me to the hospital and then we can sort out the rest of this. I'll help you in whatever way I can."

"Why would you help me? I shot you and you could still die."

Lee refused to embrace the concept of death. He would live and not die, that much he knew deep, deep down in his spirit – the place where God planted and nurtured his seeds of hope. "I've had my share of misery and I know how it feels to want to quit; but thank God, He didn't let me."

"Man, don't talk to me about that God stuff. He let your wife die. And what has He done for me?"

The mood was delicate. Marty was softening but he still had a gun and not much reason for living – a bad combination and one Lee didn't want to stir too briskly.

"Marty, He let you live."

"So what? I'm alive, big deal. I don't have a job or a family and I'm of no value to anybody."

"Your life has value to me."

"Yeah right. What do you take me for, a complete idiot?"

"Seriously, I value your life."

"Why?"

"Because I value mine." Lee sat up as straight as he could with his gaze still aimed directly at Marty. "Marty, yes, you've done a bad thing and some day you'll want to take responsibility for this and deal with the consequences."

"See, that's what I thought. You're trying to fool me into turning myself into the police. I told you that I'm not going to jail, period. I'll kill myself first," he yelled, raising the gun to his head for the first time in a long while.

Lee repositioned his body on the floor to help alleviate the tingling from his waist down, careful not to make any intimidating gestures. "If you kill yourself, how will Amy and Dillon feel? What will they say to the other kids at school when they're asked about their father? Do you really want them to deal with your death when it didn't have to be? My children lost their mother. It kills me every day to see how much they miss her and I can't do a thing about it. We couldn't stop her from dying but you have a choice. You can either do what you think is best for you or what you think is best for your children. You're the father, you make the decision."

Marty eased the gun back to the floor, held his head back and closed his eyes, not making a sound.

The ring of the cell phone buried in Lee's pocket broke the silence. Lee had lost track of time, but was sure that he'd missed both the bank and the toy store. No matter, so long as he could get home, alive to his children, no gift could compare to the joy he would experience. The phone kept ringing but he didn't bother to reach for it. He already knew the reaction coming from Marty.

"Go ahead, answer the phone."

"What?" Lee asked.

"Answer the phone. Your kids shouldn't be worried about you. Answer the phone and let them know that you're okay."

"Are you sure?"

"I'm sure."

The phone had stopped ringing, but Lee hit the button to redial the missed call. His heart was pounding. God had more than answered his prayer, the one where he'd asked to live.

While the phone was dialing, Marty interjected, "While you're at it, you might as well call the police."

After talking with his children, despair vanished and peace rushed in. The bleeding couldn't diminish Lee's intensifying strength. "I'll call the police; but not until you get out of here."

Marty leapt to his feet, grabbing the gun in the process and took two steps toward the door then stopped. "No, I'm not going anywhere. I can't leave you like this."

"Marty go, I'll be okay and like I promised, I won't say anything about you. I promise."

"I believe you, and I want to thank you, truly thank you. You're the only person that's shown me any kindness in months. I can't believe that I ended up robbing the kindest man in the city. Just my luck," Marty said.

"Marty, you don't need luck, you need hope, the kind that comes from a source, bigger than your problems, from somebody who cares about you, and you know who I'm talking about."

"I do."

"He cared about me when I was feeling awfully bad last year. I didn't know why and how I'd keep going, but God gave me the peace that I needed and now look where I am. I'm still dealing with grief, but the joy I have from being there for my kids far outweighs my sadness."

Marty didn't respond, but the intensity on his face confirmed that he was listening.

"He loves you, no matter what. He died so that you could live without having to rob anybody to make a few bucks. You have to hang in there for your children, man. Let God help you get through your tough time like He did for me." Lee paused for a second, giving Marty a chance to engage.

"Before I came in here tonight, nothing much mattered, not even God. He hadn't done me any favors. But sitting here with you, I actually feel like there's hope for me and for my children. I can honestly say that you saved my life, seriously."

"If you really believe that, then you've given your children the best Christmas gift they'll ever receive," Lee affirmed.

"What's that?"

"You."

Chapter Five

𝐵rittney 𝐻olmes was born in West Palm Beach, Florida on December 3, 1989. Currently a straight-A student in the gifted program at Redan High School in Stone Mountain, Georgia, Brittney's extracurricular interests include writing, reading and listening to music. Her club affiliations include: National Honor Society, Beta Club, PILOT (Preparing Innovative Leaders of Tomorrow), CIA (Christians in Action) and Peer Helpers. She is honored with being named in *Who's Who Among High School Students*.

In addition to writing novels, Brittney has also authored several poems addressing Christianity, peer pressure and social issues. Future plans after the completion of her high school experience include attending Spelman College in Atlanta, Georgia and majoring in English with a minor in Creative Writing. Among future undertakings, Brittney endeavors to become founder of a Christian magazine geared toward teens and young adults.

A budding author, *Living Consequences* (Urban Books/Urban Christian; Feb. 2007) is her first published full-length fictional work. For more information, visit www.brittneyholmes.com.

Brittney resides in Stone Mountain, Georgia with her parents, Jonathan Bellamy and Kendra Norman-Bellamy and her younger sister, Crystal.

Her contribution to *The Midnight Clear* is entitled, **Holiday Healing**. It is her first published work of fiction.

Holiday Healing

Against her will, Destiny Jackson walked through the mall with her friends. They were dragging her from store to store as if they thought she was really enjoying herself. She was not even pretending to take pleasure in being amongst the holiday shoppers. All that Destiny really wanted to do was go home and lie in her plush queen-sized bed; but she couldn't leave until the person who drove was ready to make her theatrical exit.

Destiny searched to find the drama queen that she called her best friend and spotted Kiana Boone looking through expensive lotions and perfumes along with their mutual friend, Marissa Holland.

"Kiki, are you ready to go, yet? I'm tried of walking around. We've been here for hours."

Kiana didn't even bother to look at Destiny. "Girl, we've only been here for about an hour and a half."

Destiny sighed at her friend's statement. Of all of the holidays on the calendar, Christmas was her least favorite and shopping during this dreadful time only made her more miserable. She didn't see the big deal anyway. People running all over the city, searching for the perfect gift for this person and that person, then they go home and waste time wrapping gifts and putting up decorations as if the celebration was going to last for more than just one day. In Destiny's opinion, it was a waste of time.

"Hey Dee," Marissa called to her. "I saw something in the jewelry department that your mother would love. Do you want to see it?"

Destiny stood with her arms folded across her chest. "No thanks."

Marissa and Kiana glanced at each other knowingly. They walked over to their pouting friend. Marissa placed one arm around Destiny's shoulders and Kiana looped her arm with Destiny's.

"Dee, I know how you feel about Christmas, but don't you think it's time you get over the past?" Kiana asked as sincerely as she could.

"Nope," Destiny said matter-of-factly.

"You don't feel bad about being upset with God?" Marissa asked.

"Nope," Destiny responded in the same tone. "He could've prevented what happened if He wanted to."

"But, Dee—"

"Look guys," Destiny said moving away from their grasps, "I don't want to talk about this right now."

Thankfully, her friends honored her wishes and continued their shopping. She was grateful that they didn't condemn her for being upset with God or for despising Christmas. For the past two years, the Christmas holiday had brought her nothing but heartache. Her grandmother had always said Christmas was a time to give thanks to God for what they had and for Him sending His Son to earth just for them. But for the past two years, Destiny was unable to thank God for anything. As far as she was concerned, He had taken so much from her that what He had given didn't seem to measure up anymore. First it was her father and then her boyfriend. This year, she refused to allow God to snatch another loved one out of her life. She wouldn't get that close to Him again. Never again.

- - -

Kiana dropped Destiny off at home, to go right back to the mall with Marissa. Destiny figured they were just tired of her holding them back, but she couldn't care less. All she'd wanted to do was stay home in the first place. Her mother was the one who'd suggested that she get out of the house. Destiny remembered a time when she would have to beg her mother to allow her to go out with her friends, but in the last two years, the outgoing Destiny that most people knew had dwindled into an introvert just waiting for the next tragedy to strike in her life. Ever since, the death of her father, Destiny felt she had nothing to look forward to.

She had been the light of Thomas Jackson's life and the joy down in his soul. She was a Daddy's girl for sure and very proud of it. Destiny nearly died herself when he was killed in a house fire two years ago, almost a week before Christmas Day. Food that he'd left cooking on the stove and eyelids that were too heavy for him to stay awake after a ten-hour shift at work the night before were the factors, the investigators concluded, that led to Thomas' death. But Destiny added God to that list. Her father was a God-fearing man who put the Lord above all earthly things. So why hadn't God spared him? Destiny knew, through many of her own experiences, that He could have rescued her father. God had spared her life from the same fate. He'd allowed her to safely be pulled from the inferno. He could have done the same for her dad, but He hadn't. She had never pardoned God for taking the person who protected and loved her like only a father could.

Distress had worn Destiny thin. She even looked older than her seventeen years. Though she still caught the eye of several male admires, no guy had been able to take Calvin Young's place.

Calvin had been Destiny's first love. Many people often commented that they made a very attractive couple. Calvin had been there for Destiny through her roughest times, especially after her father died. So Destiny couldn't understand how God could've allowed Calvin, too, to perish in such a horrible way; and on Christmas Eve at that.

He was a wonderful boyfriend, an even better friend, and a loyal servant of the King. Being in the wrong place at the wrong time happened a million times a day. Why couldn't God have allowed Calvin's car to dodge those misguided bullets. He was only going to visit his father for a few hours. It wasn't his fault that his father lived in a bad part of town where drive-bys were a part of everyday life. Why couldn't God have saved him? Destiny had yet to receive an answer and until she did, she and God would forever be on bad terms.

With a heavy sigh, Destiny moved around her bed toward her dresser and turned on the radio so that soft jazz filled the silent air that floated around in the room. As she listened to the saxophonist, she realized he was playing "The Christmas Song"—better known to most people as "Chestnuts Roasting on an Open Fire." Immediately, she turned off the radio to dodge the tears she felt building up inside. The last thing she needed to hear was a song the put fire in a positive light. Fire was evil. It killed her father. And it was a *fire*arm that killed Calvin. A song Destiny used to love now made her cringe. She absolutely hated this time of year, especially now when she had no one to comfort her. She wanted to ask God to send her hope or at least peace, but that would require she actually speak to Him, so she kept her prayers to herself.

"Destiny!"

Destiny moaned when she heard her mother's cheerful call. She really didn't feel like going downstairs. Seeing all of the white lights and gold ornaments made her sick on the stomach. Besides, she knew why her mother was calling her. Vivian Jackson was going to ask her the same question she'd asked her every year since her father died. With a pleading gaze, Vivian would ask if Destiny would like to place the star on top of the tree. Destiny's answer was constantly the same. *No.* That was her father's job.

Thomas would always wait until Christmas morning to place the star on the tree. He called it christening the day Jesus was born. Destiny used to love watching her father, without the help of a ladder, put the star in its place. When she was smaller, he would sometimes place her on his shoulders and allow her to do the honors, but now the tradition held too many emotional memories. Yet every year, Vivian would ask the same question, Destiny would say no, and Vivian would wait until Christmas morning to see of she'd changed her mind, which Destiny never did. It was a routine that was growing old.

"Destiny," her mother called again.

"Mom, I don't feel good. I'm trying to go to sleep," she responded exhaustedly.

She wasn't lying. Destiny truly didn't feel well. Just the thought of Christmas being celebrated in less than two weeks sickened her. It didn't help that all of her family would be coming to her home this year. Grandparents, aunts, uncles, and cousins would force her to join them, but they wouldn't make her be happy about it. Christmas was just not her thing anymore.

There were two more days of school left before the holiday break. Destiny was already preparing herself for the anniversaries of her father's and boyfriend's deaths.

Around this time last year, when Destiny began thinking about her father, Calvin had told her she would be fine. "Joy always comes in the morning" was his favorite saying and Destiny felt that he had worn that line thin. But then, she bought into it and just as she felt as if nothing worse could happen, Calvin was found dead in his car. So, Destiny was preparing to not be too surprised if another loved one happened to drop dead this year.

She remembered voicing those thoughts to Kiana a few weeks ago and was stunned by her friend's response.

"Girl, you need to find your way back to God 'cause you really talking foolish now. You act like this is a trend. That ain't nothing but the devil messing with you."

What was Destiny supposed to think? Two years in a row, two dead loved ones, a broken heart each time. She was left alone to draw her own conclusions. This had nothing to do with the devil.

"Hey Dee," Kiana greeted.

"Hey girl. Are you ready for finals tomorrow?"

Kiana laughed. "Am I ever? But I'm studying hard for Calculus because if I pass that final, it'll at least give me a passing grade."

As they walked down the hall, Destiny felt as if she were being followed. She turned around, but only saw other students who were trying to get to their classes too. She knew she was being paranoid when Kiana gave her a sidelong glance. Brushed it off, Destiny continued toward her classroom.

Just as she was about to enter the door, Destiny felt another's presence behind her again. This time when she turned around, she found herself staring into the most beautiful pair of eyes she'd ever seen. The brown eyes seemed to sparkle as they smiled at her and for a fleeting moment, they captured her soul.

"Hi." The possessor of the beautiful eyes spoke to her and his voice was a deep baritone that resounded melodiously against her ears. "Are you Destiny Jackson?"

Her name rolling off of this complete stranger's lips made Destiny smile, but when she realized that she had no clue who he was, she regained her composure. "Yes. Do I know you?" Her voice was steady, but her gaze curious.

"No, you don't." He stuck out his hand. "Dylan Murray."

Destiny could barely break her eyes away from his intense stare as she took his cocoa brown hand into hers. The sudden spark that shot through her as they touched made goose bumps arise on her skin. "I...umm. I have to get to class," she said, though for some strange reason she didn't want to leave at all.

His smile was hypnotic. "Me too." He gestured toward the door they were standing in front of and Destiny was surprised when he followed her into the classroom.

When the bell rang, signaling the beginning of the period, her teacher stood and introduced Dylan as a new student and sat him right next to Destiny.

"Hi." His eyes smiled at her again.

Destiny shocked herself when she blushed.

By the time lunch rolled around, Destiny had thought about Dylan countless amounts of times. It didn't necessarily help having him in each and every one of her classes. *How in the world did that happen?* It could be a coincidence, but if it was, it was *too much* of a coincidence.

She was eating lunch with Marissa and Kiana when she saw him again. She was beginning to feel as if he was following her, but when she saw him walking toward a table on the other side of the cafeteria, she let that paranoia go.

"Is there room for one more?"

Destiny suddenly heard his voice and her eyes shot up like fireworks.

Always the flirtatious one, Marissa smiled when she said, "Of course," and motioned for him to sit.

"I know I just saw you sit at another table," Destiny pointed out.

He smiled. "So you've been watching me?"

Destiny wondered if his eyes were always bright, even if he wasn't happy. "No" was all she could manage. There was something about Dylan's presence that was different. He seemed happy, elated even. It was as though he had constant *peace* from within. His countenance held *hope.* Those were the things Destiny had fought hard against praying for last night, but, yet, here they were, staring her in her face. Literally.

Destiny hadn't noticed she was staring at him until Kiana blatantly pointed it out. Destiny coughed to cover her sudden nervousness as she continued to eat. Her friends held general conversation with Dylan throughout lunch, but Destiny couldn't find one thing to say. She had never felt this way around a guy—not since Calvin—but Dylan had her heart fluttering and she couldn't figure out why. Physically, he was attractive, but she didn't even know him and she was acting like a lovesick puppy.

Get it together, girl.

By the end of lunch period, Dylan had told the girls everything about him, going as deep as he pleased. Destiny had never met someone so open and honest. It was a little overbearing, but she hadn't felt at all uncomfortable.

65

As she prepared to head to her next class, Dylan asked, "Would you like to hang out with me this afternoon?"

She verbally agreed before she could think, but as he accompanied her to *their* next class, Destiny felt as if that one impromptu decision would change her life forever.

- - -

Destiny didn't know what had come over her as she sat in a coffee shop with Dylan that afternoon. They had been talking nonstop for nearly two hours and she had had been so comfortable with him that she had practically told him her entire life's story. Dylan had listened attentively as she talked about her father and boyfriend. As she vented and shed several tears, Destiny wished he had never asked what her plans for the Christmas holiday were.

"I'm sorry," she told him as she wiped her tears with a napkin. "I don't know why I just dumped all of that on you. You probably think I'm crazy." She chuckled slightly.

Dylan's face was sincere and his tone was calming when he said, "Actually, no, I don't think you're crazy. But I do know you're hurt. Your pain is understandable, but your anger toward God isn't."

Destiny sighed. He was another person who was going to tell her she was wrong for blaming and banishing God for happenings of the past. "Dylan, if you're going to ridicule me, please save your breath because I promise you, I'm not going to stick around and listen."

"I don't know you well enough to judge you," he told her. "But I want to help you."

"And how do you plan to do that?"

"With God's help." He smiled as she rolled her eyes.

"That's going to take a miracle."

"You don't know how true your words are. Just wait and see." He nodded. "Christmas morning, you'll be placing that star on the tree."

Destiny looked up in surprise. "What did you just say?"

They both knew he didn't need to repeat his statement. As she stared into his eyes, Destiny wanted to run as far away from Dylan as possible, but once again, his gaze had captured her soul. But this time, she felt herself drawing closer to the Spirit living within him.

- - -

"God has His reasons for allowing certain things to happen. He doesn't do things to hurt His children. Maybe to test their faith, but never to hurt them. Your hurt is coming from within and you've dwelled on it so much that it has turned into anger. Anger has to be directed toward someone and of course, you're not going to blame yourself. So, you blame God when you should really be drawing closer to Him."

Dylan's words rang out in Destiny's ears, even though he'd said them nearly seventy-two hours ago. He made a lot of sense and had somewhat changed her outlook on things in just seven days. In her opinion, though, he still had major work to do to get her to soften her heart toward God and celebrate the day of His Son's birth. She doubted Dylan could accomplish that task in just four days. It was fun watching him try though.

He was supposed to come pick her up for lunch in just a few minutes and Destiny knew Dylan would have another convincing argument for her to think about for the next few days. She knew he could tell she was wearing down. He knew so much about her that it was frightening, but intriguing at the same time. It was as if every time he gazed into her eyes, he would learn something deep and engaging about her internal feelings. How Destiny had allowed this stranger to smoothly flow into her life and turn her opinions and beliefs inside out was a mystery, even to her.

Destiny heard the doorbell ringing and when she heard her mother run to answer the door, she laughed subtly. Ever since learning Destiny had a new "male friend," Vivian had been floating around the house with a smile on her face as if she knew there was hope after all. Destiny had silently told her mother not to get her hopes up.

She quickly walked down the stairs, hoping her mother had not bored Dylan to death with old photos and stories.

"Hi Dylan," Destiny greeted him once she reached the living room.

Dylan's eyes smiled at her as they had done the day they met. "Hello Destiny. Are you ready to go?"

"Yes."

"Oh, Destiny, before you leave," her mother interrupted, "Sister Deborah from the church called and asked if you'd do a solo for the

Christmas service next Sunday." She looked at her daughter with hopeful eyes.

Destiny hated that her mother had mentioned that in front of Dylan. Every year, before her father's death, she had sung the solo in the church choir during their annual Christmas production. But even though the choir director would ask her numerous times, Destiny hadn't performed for the past two years and she hadn't planned to do it this year either.

"I didn't know you could sing," Dylan commented.

"Oh, Destiny has a beautiful voice," Vivian gushed. "You should come hear her at the Christmas service."

"Well, that would be kinda hard for him to do since I'm not going to be singing at that service. Tell Sister Deborah that I can't do it."

Without another word, Destiny left with a confused Dylan following closely behind. The drive to Jason's Deli was uncomfortably quiet. Destiny prayed Dylan wouldn't bring up the issue, but she knew he would. When they arrived at the deli, they took a seat at a table that afforded as much privacy as possible and were immediately served.

"So, why don't you want to sing?" Dylan instantly jumped into interrogation mode.

Destiny bit into her sandwich and chewed slowly so she could prolong her answer. "I just don't want to," she said after swallowing. Destiny knew that response wouldn't satisfy him, and she was right.

Dylan shook his head. "I would love a better answer."

She smiled slightly as she prepared to explain. "Neither of my parents can sing. They say God blessed me with the gift of course, but I inherited the ability from my father's mother, who died when my dad was in his late twenties. So when I would sing, especially during the Christmas service, it would be because my father requested it. He would always say I reminded him of his mother when I sang. After a while, I began doing it because I liked praising God. But when my father died..." She shrugged and allowed Dylan to draw his own conclusion.

He took a few bites from his sandwich and allowed silence to settle between them before saying, "You shouldn't allow things like death to hinder your walk with Christ. God gives you gifts to use for Him. It was nice that you sang for you father's enjoyment, but when you started to sing for Christ, you were fulfilling the purpose of your gift." He reached across the table and took her hand in his. "Destiny, God loves you so much and I wish I could get you to see that. He wants to be a part of your life again, but you are so adamant about being against Him that you are hindering His will. Thomas and Calvin also want you to draw closer to God. The closer you are to God, the closer you are to them because they are with Him. You've been dwelling so much on the physical loss that you haven't noticed that they're with you spiritually. Right in your heart." He used one hand to point to her chest, and then continued as he reached up to wipe her pooling tears. "I know it's hard, but you have to learn to get over the past."

"But I don't want to forget it," Destiny said, sniffling.

"You don't need to forget because you want to remember what has gotten you to this point, but don't *dwell* on it so much that you lose sight of *Who* is guiding your footsteps. Christmas is a time where you should be able to do nothing but rejoice, in spite of the circumstances."

"What do I rejoice about when every year I'm going to be reminded about my losses?" Destiny's heart was drawing nearer to the Spirit, and though she felt it, she tried hard not to let it show.

Dylan's gaze deepened. "You should rejoice in the reason behind Christmas. If Jesus had not been born, He wouldn't have died on the cross, which would leave all of us doomed to exist in transgression, trapped in a life of sin and a future of nothing but eternal damnation. Jesus' being born and dying on the cross are the only reasons why your father and Calvin were able to accept Him in this life and then go home to live with Him eternally when their time on earth was up. That's another reason to rejoice. They're in heaven for eternity. I know they would love for you to join them one day. You just need to let go of this anger and allow God to renew the right spirit in you."

- - -

"Girl, this boy had done something to you," Kiana said to Destiny over the phone on Christmas Eve.

"I know," Marissa said, sharing in the three-way call. "You're all happy and jittery."

69

Destiny laughed. "Look, I don't have time for this. Just answer the question."

"Of course we'll come to the Christmas service at your church tomorrow. But why?"

"I'm trying to take baby steps, okay? I figure if I go to church tomorrow, it'll make my mother happy, especially since I didn't get her a Christmas gift. I just want to have you guys there for support."

"We're always there for you, Dee," Marissa assured.

"Thank you. I have to go, but I'll see you guys tomorrow night, okay?"

They said their goodbyes and Destiny hung up the phone. She sat on her bed with an unconscious smile on her face. Over the last week and a half, Dylan had made her see things she hadn't seen in over two years. A massive change had occurred in her life. Destiny could see it. Her mother could see it. Her friends could see it. Though she wasn't totally where she needed to be in her walk, she was pressing on and praying that she would get there.

Destiny's smile stayed in place as she reached over to her nightstand to answer her ringing phone.

"I need a huge favor from you," Dylan said as soon as she greeted him.

"What?" she asked nervously.

"I need you to sing tomorrow night."

"What?" she exclaimed. "No way. You already have me going to the service."

"I know and I'm happy about your decision, but I got in touch with a couple of people who haven't heard you sing in a long time. They were hoping you'd do this for them and I told them you wouldn't mind."

"Who are these people?" she asked, wanting to strangle him for doing such a thing.

"They're a couple of guys I know from back home. They know you pretty well. I promised I wouldn't tell who they were, but I know if you do this you won't regret it at all."

Dylan's assertive tone made her wonder who the surprise guests were. She knew all of her family were coming in tomorrow morning and would be at the service, but as far as she was aware, none of them knew Dylan. He must have been referencing friends from wherever he'd lived before moving to Atlanta. Destiny's smile returned. She couldn't help but feel good knowing that he wanted to show her off to his hometown friends.

"Okay," she conceded, hoping her grin couldn't be heard in her voice. "I guess all I can do is trust you."

When they ended the call, Destiny began to think about the solo. She hadn't practiced with the choir, so she had no idea what she was going to sing. But something down in her heart said that her trust in Dylan wasn't misplaced.

- - -

Destiny had excused herself to the bathroom and was nervously pacing about in the foyer of the church. Her solo with the choir would be coming soon and Dylan was no where to be found with his special visitors. She was close to telling Sister Deborah that she'd changed her mind, but as soon as the thought presented itself, Dylan came through the church doors…alone.

"Where are your friends?" Destiny asked. "If they don't show, I'm not performing."

Dylan took her hands with a smile. "Calm down. They'll be here." His smile suddenly disappeared. "But we can't stay long."

"We? Where are you going?"

"I'm going back home to spend Christmas with them, but I promise I'll be here when you sing."

Before she had a chance to argue, an usher came out to get her for her solo. Destiny bypassed her family and walked up to the pulpit. When Sister Deborah announced that the choir's next song would be led by Destiny, the congregation was surprised, but pleased as they stood and applauded.

As the music began to play, Destiny took the microphone. She smiled to her mother who had the most surprised look on her face. She closed her eyes and began to sing the words to "Oh Holy Night." Her soft alto voice filled the sanctuary and caused several people to stand on their feet in worship.

Destiny felt a strong presence in the room, just like she had the day she met Dylan, but this feeling was much stronger as if it were fueled by more than one person. She opened her eyes for a fleeting moment and nearly passed out when she looked out into the congregation and saw Dylan standing in the back of the church with Thomas and Calvin. Was this some kind of joke? She stopped singing, but the choir behind her continued.

71

She stared at the three men in the back and noticed they all were aglow as if they were standing in front of a bright light. Dylan smiled at her and mouthed the words "Keep singing." Destiny heard the words like a whisper in her spirit and instinctively resumed her melody. She cried as she watched her father and boyfriend bask in the presence of the Lord. As they whispered words into her heart, Destiny sang with more passion. It seemed as if their spirits had surrounded her as they whispered promises that they would always be in her heart. Slowly, she felt her heart mending, piece by piece, as they continued to speak to her.

Tears trickled down her face as the song came to an end. Destiny watched as the spirits of those she loved left the sanctuary. The only one left was Dylan. While the congregation continued to worship, he once again, whispered to her soul.

"Thank you for believing again."

Dylan blew her a kiss. When he turned to leave, Destiny was sure that she saw wings on his back. Things were finally making sense. The way he'd slipped into her life, knew so much about her, and led her back to where she needed to be. Dylan was her guardian angel, sent straight from the heavens above.

- - -

As soon as Destiny got home, she went into the living room and found the small box that held the only ornament not on the tree. She held the golden star in her hand. Slowly she climbed on top of the small stool that would allow her to do what hadn't been done in two years. She raised the star above her head and placed it at the top of the Christmas tree. Stepping down, she looked at the completely decorated tree as the lights twinkled, illuminating the dim room.

"Merry Christmas, my guardian angels."

Chapter Six

Dwan Abrams was born in St. Petersburg, Florida. She has lived throughout the United States and Europe. When she graduated from King's Academy High School with honors, she enlisted in the United States Air Force where she served honorably for four years.

While in the military, she was promoted six months early to the rank of Senior Airman. In recognition of her outstanding service, she was awarded Airman of the Month and Personnel Specialist of the Quarter. She graduated from the University of Alabama in Huntsville with a B.S. in Marketing. She also has an M.B.A. in Marketing.

Abrams is the author of *Only True Love Waits*. In addition to writing books, she is founder and president of Nevaeh Publishing, LLC, a full-service self-publishing company.

Currently, Dwan resides in Atlanta, Georgia with daughter, Nia. She's working on her next book. Readers may contact her through her website at www.dwanabrams.com.

Her contribution to *The Midnight Clear* is entitled **Favor**.

Favor

Every time I converse with my sister, Cheyenne, I end up getting upset or feeling like beating her down.

"Cheyenne," I yelled into the receiver, "tell me now!"

"Sister," she whined in a nasally tone, "I'll be there in a little while. I'll tell you when I see you. K. Bye."

We hung up. I closed my eyes and prayed that everything was all right. Knowing my sister, it could be anything. It's the week of Christmas and Cheyenne is driving from Valdosta to Alpharetta, Georgia to spend the holiday with me. This is the first holiday we're actually spending in the house since our parents died. In previous years, we'd go visit relatives.

Cheyenne's a freshman at Valdosta State University. I'm proud of her for going to college because it was no easy feat getting her there. In high school, she was notorious for skipping classes. It was favor from God that allowed her to graduate. I'd never seen someone miss as much school as my sister and still graduate with honors. That's favor – it's not fair.

Our parents died when Cheyenne was ten and I was twenty-two. Fortunately, I had just completed my senior year at Auburn State University when I became her legal guardian. With my portion of the money that I inherited from my parents' life insurance policies, I was able to set up, Eat Your Heart Out, my own catering company.

I tried to raise my sister the way I thought my parents would want. We went to church every Sunday and were active members. I prayed and taught Cheyenne how to pray, too. I went to PTA meetings, checked my sister's homework, helped her with science projects and made unexpected visits to her school. I did everything I could to let Cheyenne know that I loved her.

When she went through puberty I didn't think I was going to survive. She was moody. Got on my nerves. From one day to the next, I couldn't figure out whether she was thirteen or thirty. It was hard for me to maintain a romantic relationship because I was too busy raising a child. Most of the men my age weren't interested in taking on that added responsibility. Thinking back, that was probably for the best. At that time I didn't need the distraction of being in a committed relationship anyway. I was dealing with my

74

parents' death, raising Cheyenne and starting a company. When I was emotionally and spiritually ready for a relationship, Greg came into my life.

Greg and I met at the Corner Café in Buckhead during lunchtime. We struck up a casual conversation while waiting to be seated separately. He told me that he sold insurance and was meeting a client. I told him I was dining alone. He said something about a beautiful woman should never have to eat alone. I quickly let him know that it was by choice. I happened to be getting my Range Rover serviced across the street at Hennessey and was simply passing the time. We exchanged business cards before being seated at different tables. Before he left the restaurant, he stopped by my table and spoke again. Flashed me a news anchor smile. He seemed nice.

When it was time for me to leave, the waitress informed me that Greg had already paid my tab. That made me smile. Not only was he good-looking, but considerate too. He earned major cool points with me that day. And of course I had to call him to thank him.

When I phoned him he seemed genuinely glad to hear from me. I deliberately kept the conversation brief. Didn't want to seem desperate. I let him know that I appreciated the gesture. Before I could get off the phone he asked me if I was seeing anyone. When I told him I wasn't, he made a point to tell me he wasn't involved with anyone either and asked me to accompany him on a date. I accepted and we've been together ever since.

I went into the modern kitchen, stocked with stainless steel appliances, to put the finishing touches on Cheyenne's welcome home dinner. I must admit that I put my foot all up in it! Baked chicken so tender it would melt in your mouth. Pots of collards, sweet potato soufflé and garlic mashed potatoes covered the eyes of the stove. Freshly baked yeast rolls coated with warm butter and cornbread dressing occupied the oven. The food smelled so good I wanted to throw down right then, but I knew I had to wait. So, I went upstairs and took a shower. Slipped into a chocolate colored shirt and matching lace skirt. Let my shoulder length hair hang down.

I went back into the kitchen and put the dirty dishes in the dishwasher before starting a load. Then I wiped down the marble counter tops because I can't stand a dirty kitchen. My mother used to clean up the kitchen as she cooked. She taught me that. She also taught me *how* to cook. As a child, I would watch my mother as she prepared our meals. Pleasant smells always emanated from our kitchen. My family loved her cooking. Sometimes when I'm throwing down in the kitchen, I can feel my mother's presence. We were so close. We loved exchanging recipes and trying new things. Even though it's been eight years since my parents died in a car accident, I still miss them. Especially during the holidays.

- - -

I was away at college. I had just completed finals and was excited about my upcoming graduation ceremony when I received a phone call from my mom's sister, Sylvia. She was a rambling mess, crying and screaming. "Your family...your mom and dad...They, they, they've been killed in a car accident!" I had a sinking feeling in the pit of my stomach. I wanted to faint. Surely, Aunt Sylvia hadn't just told me that my mommy and daddy were...gone. I could hear the anguish in Aunt Sylvia's voice and it cut me to the bone. She cried harder; sounded like she was hyperventilating when she said, "Drunk driver hit them. Come home right away."

I couldn't breathe. Felt like the walls were closing in on me. I dropped the phone; cried. My heart thumped so loudly that I could hear it. I wanted to die. Wondered why this happened. I felt as if I was trapped in a photograph - still and lifeless. Didn't think I could handle the severity of the situation. My life seemed about as clear as muddy water. I'd never be the same. I didn't think I'd ever smile, laugh or experience happiness again. How was I supposed to live without my parents?

- - -

I felt a tinge of sadness trying to creep up on me like a teenager sneaking into the house after curfew. I quickly thwarted it by focusing on more positive things. I realize that I have a lot to be thankful for. I'm healthy, woke up in my right state of mind, own a successful business and I have a great guy. I'm blessed. Reminding myself of the positive helps me not to linger on the negative.

My doorbell rang. I looked through the peephole and saw that it was Greg. He looked good in his crisp white shirt and jeans. His baldhead was freshly shaved and his goatee neatly trimmed. He was carrying a bottle of sparkling apple cider in one hand and a poinsettia in the other.

"Nice to see you," I greeted, kissing him on the cheek. I took the bottle and he followed me into the kitchen.

"What are you in here burning?" he said, placing the plant on the island.

"Got jokes?" I laughed.

He rubbed his stomach and said, "I'm playing. It smells good. Almost as good as you look."

He pulled up a barstool and sat at the island.

"Thanks." I placed the sparkling drink in the refrigerator. "Cheyenne and Jonathan should be here soon." I said that like it was no big deal, but in reality, I couldn't believe that I was about to break bread with Jonathan. He's the bane of my existence. I pray that Cheyenne wises up before she lets him ruin her life.

"Jonathan?" Greg crinkled his nose. "I thought you couldn't stand him."

"I can't, but that doesn't stop Cheyenne from dating him."

"Did he ever get his GED?"

"No. He's been popping the same old tired game ever since Cheyenne's known him. And she keeps falling for it. When they were both juniors in high school and he dropped out, I told her he wasn't going back. She gave me some sob story about his mother abandoning him and his dropping out of school to support himself."

"Is he still selling drugs?"

"Yes. What can I say? She's got a thing for bad boys."

"She needs to be careful. I don't get a good feeling about this guy. You hear stories all the time about people getting killed because of the company they keep. A bullet doesn't have anybody's name on it. She's got a lot going for herself and could do whole lot better. I would hate to see her ruin her life because of him or anybody else for that matter."

"I know. But it's like my momma used to say, 'A hard head makes a soft behind.' All I can do is pray."

I started transferring food from copper pots to sterling silver serving dishes. My mom used to use the same expensive silver pieces for holidays and any other occasion she deemed special. Greg offered to help, so I let him set the table. By the time we

77

finished, the doorbell rang. *Perfect timing*, I thought. I opened the door. Cheyenne and Jonathan greeted me. I offered them a warm smile and gave my sister a hug. I was glad to see her, regardless of how much she tested my resolve. I invited them in, locked the door behind them and we went into the kitchen with Greg.

Greg acknowledged Cheyenne and Jonathan and gave Jonathan daps. In the year we had been dating, Greg had met Cheyenne twice before. During a going away party I threw for Cheyenne to celebrate her going off to college, Greg met Jonathan.

"Sister," Cheyenne said. She never calls me by my real name, Shania. "I have something to show you."

I sucked air through my teeth and rolled my eyes. *What now?* I wondered.

She turned her back toward me, exposing angel wings tattooed on her shoulder blade. I didn't say anything.

"Well, do you like it?" Cheyenne asked.

"It's all right," I said. I don't know why she bothered to ask me. She knew full well that I wouldn't approve of a tattoo. That's why she waited until after she had already gotten it to tell me about it. Then she showed it to Greg. He simply shook his head.

"And wait." Cheyenne slightly lifted up her halter style top to reveal a second tattoo – a cross and rosary on the small of her back.

This just keeps getting better and better, I thought. *The devil is a lie. I'm not about to give in to this nonsense.* I recited The 23rd Psalm in my mind. I silently said that prayer whenever I felt an anxiety attack coming on, like right now.

"Sister, do you like it?"

"It doesn't matter if I like it. I'm not the one who mutilated her body."

"Why you gotta be so melodramatic all the time?" She laughed.

I could tell by the tone of her voice that she was disappointed that I didn't approve of her body art.

I exhaled and said, "Let's eat before the food gets cold."

We went into the formal dining room, held hands and closed our eyes as Greg blessed the food. Then we took our seats and each fixed a plate.

"So. Shania. How you been?" Jonathan said.

I hoped that my eyes didn't betray me because secretly I was throwing darts at Jonathan. I couldn't stand the way he talked all slow. Perhaps that's the only way his brain could keep up.

"I've been doing good."

Until now I hadn't really paid much attention to Jonathan. He looked as sloppy as he usually did – baggy sweat pants and an oversized white tee. However, he had something on the side of his neck. My eyes narrowed, trying to decipher the scribbling. Cheyenne. He had Cheyenne's name engraved on his neck.

"When did you get that?" I nodded my head in Jonathan's direction.

He placed his hand on his neck, said, "Oh, this?" He laughed, looked at Cheyenne.

"Not that long ago. Maybe two, three weeks."

I looked at Cheyenne and said, "Why did you let him do that?"

"Sister, I told him not to, but he said he wanted to do it." She went on to explain that Jonathan said he loved her and would still want her name on him even if they broke up.

I felt disgusted. They were so young and so naïve. They were a perfect example of the blind leading the blind. Not wanting to say the wrong thing, I stuffed a forkful of collards in my mouth.

"Jonathan, what you been doing with yourself?" Greg said, biting into a piece of chicken.

"You know. Tryna stay outta trouble."

I wanted to reach across the table and shake him. For the life of me, I couldn't figure out what Cheyenne saw in him. He had pimply skin and a chipped tooth in the front of his mouth. He had enough butter on his teeth to spread on every roll at the table. I had to wonder whether she was rebelling against me.

"You plan on going back to school?" Greg said, sounding like a parent. He reminded me of my dad. The way he used to interrogate my boyfriends.

"Nah. I wanna get my GED."

"So why don't you?"

"I'm workin' on it. I gotta get a copy of my birth certificate from my mom. We ain't speaking right now, so it's hard."

This guy must think that everybody at this table has about as much common sense as God gave to a rock. Who was he trying to fool? I've met his mother, Candace, and spoken with her in-depth.

79

She admitted to leaving her children for a while, but she came back. Candace said that Jonathan was trouble and warned me to get my sister away from him. She was the one who told me Jonathan was a drug dealer. According to Candace, she found his supply at her house and kicked him out. Having him living with her and her other children posed too much of a threat to the safety of their family. She refused to take him back in until he straightened up his act.

When I confronted my sister with my findings concerning her boyfriend, she tried to down play the whole thing. Insisted Candace was crazy. Not credible because she abandoned her family. I told her I believed Candace's story. Then Cheyenne flipped the script. Acted like Jonathan's drug dealing was justifiable since he had to fend for himself. I looked at her like she had lost her mind because along with his other siblings, their grandmother cared for them in their mother's absence. I told her to stop making excuses for Jonathan's bad behavior. He made a choice to sell drugs. She stopped talking. I could tell by the thoughtful look in her eyes that my words were getting to her. At least I gave her something to think about.

For the rest of dinner, we talked about the weather and college life, mostly Greg's recollections. Afterwards, Cheyenne and I cleared the dishes from the table. Greg offered his assistance but I assured him Cheyenne and I could handle it ourselves. So he joined Jonathan in the family room, where the Christmas tree was located. This was the first tree I had ever purchased, and Greg helped me put it up. It touched the ceiling. The tree itself was white and the decorations were primarily gold with red and green accents.

"How do you think you did this semester?" I asked Cheyenne as I scraped leftovers into plastic containers.

"I don't know."

I could tell she was lying by the influx in her voice. "What do you mean, 'I don't know?' Haven't you been going to school?"

She exhaled and closed her eyes. Acted like I was getting on her nerves.

She opened her eyes and said, "Sister, I don't want to talk about this right now." She unloaded dishes from the dishwasher, making room for the new batch, and put them in the cabinet.

Silently, I fumed. I wanted to go off but I knew that wouldn't accomplish anything – at least, not anything positive. Besides, we had company and I didn't want to show out in front of them. So I continued to put up the food.

Having finished our domestic chores, Cheyenne went into the family room and I put on a pot of coffee. A few minutes later, I grabbed a deck of Uno cards from the island drawer and joined the rest of them while the coffee brewed. They were as excited as school children at recess when I suggested we play. Greg dealt the first hand and I won. We were having such a good time laughing and trash talking that I temporarily forgot about my issues with Cheyenne.

I asked, "Anyone want some coffee?"

Greg and Cheyenne said, "Yes."

We momentarily interrupted the game as Greg and I went into the kitchen. I grabbed three cups and saucers from the cabinet and filled them up. Since the three of us liked our coffee the same way, I spruced up the hot liquid with hazelnut creamer and a couple of cubes of sugar that were housed in a small crystal bowl.

Smiling, Greg said, "I'm really having a good time."

"Me too."

Greg lifted the corners of two saucers that were balancing cups on top of them and went back into the family room. He sat both drinks on the glass table. I followed, carrying my cup.

We played another round of Uno. This time Cheyenne won. We finished our coffee and Cheyenne announced, "I'm going to drop Jonathan off at his grandmother's house. Be right back."

I nodded and waved good-bye.

Greg stood up, shook Jonathan's hand and said, "Take it easy."

Jonathan replied, "You too."

As soon as I heard the door close, I exhaled.

"You did good," Greg said, patting my hand.

I smiled.

He slid closer to me on the couch and looked me in the eyes. "Shania, there's something I've been wanting to say." He took a deep breath and released it. He seemed serious. "I was trying to wait until Christmas but I can't."

My heart raced and I gave him an incredulous look. He stood up and reached inside his right pant pocket. He wriggled his fingers around before pulling out his hand. I couldn't see what he was holding.

81

With a balled fist he knelt down on one knee. I swallowed hard, feeling a rising well of tears. He looked into my watery eyes, grabbed my hand again, and said, "I love you. You mean the world to me."

I noticed that his eyes were misty and his lower lip quivered. It totally surprised me. I was usually the one crying to him about my sister. I had never seen him cry. Sweet. Made my tears flow.

"Shania," he continued, "would you make me the happiest man in the world and marry me?"

I wiped his tears with my thumb. He seemed so sincere. Vulnerable. I didn't think it was possible but I loved him even more. I looked down and noticed a sparkling two-carat, pear shaped diamond ring staring at me. Looking back at Greg, I swallowed hard and said, "Yes. I'll marry you."

He slipped the ring on my left ring finger and stood up. I stood up too, and we hugged. This was truly one of the happiest days of my life. I say one of the happiest simply because I expected to have many, many more wonderful days to come.

- - -

"Greg and I are getting married," I said to Cheyenne, holding out my left hand for her to view my engagement ring. I was so excited I felt like jumping up and down. I had waited up for her in the family room. The lights from the Christmas tree lit up the room.

Inspecting my ring, she said, "I leave you alone for a couple of hours and you're getting married?"

"Yes. He asked me right after you left."

"Congratulations, Sister. I'm happy for you." She hugged me.

"Thanks. That means a lot to me."

"Greg's a nice guy. I can tell he loves you. And the ring," she paused, giving me two thumbs up, and continued, "very nice." She smiled, nodded her head.

She was about to go upstairs when I said, "Cheyenne, wait a minute. We need to talk."

"Can we talk in the morning? I'm tired."

I was in such a good mood that I agreed to talk to her later. I unplugged the Christmas lights and we both went to bed. That night I tossed and turned, excited about my upcoming nuptials. Eventually, I dozed off and slept soundly.

The next morning, I woke up feeling as good as an NBA player scoring the winning basket during a championship game. I prepared strawberry crepes for breakfast and woke up Cheyenne. She joined me at the breakfast table in the kitchen. We said grace and ate.

"So, what's going on in your world?" I asked.

She seemed thoughtful, rested her right point-finger on her cheek, and said, "Nothing."

I took a sip of freshly squeezed orange juice. Swallowed and said, "Okay, how are things with you and Jonathan?"

"Fine." She cut into the crepe with her fork and stuffed a piece in her mouth.

Obviously I was asking the wrong type of questions because she wasn't giving up any information. I decided to take a different approach.

"Tell me what you like about Jonathan," I said.

She became child-like. Shy. "Well, he makes me laugh." She rolled her eyes upward. Apparently she was thinking. "He loves me for me."

I nodded my head. "What does he plan on doing with himself? His future?"

"He's not sure. He says he wants to be a rapper. Then he said he wants to design clothes."

"How do you feel about that?"

"I'm okay with it. I did tell him that he better do something to put his life together. Because if he doesn't he won't have me."

"You really told him that?" I raised a brow.

"Yes, and I told him he needs to get his GED. I did some research and found out what he needs to do to get it."

"That's good." I ate another forkful of food. Dabbed the corners of my mouth with a napkin and said, "Do you plan on marrying him?" I don't know why I asked that question. She had never mentioned marrying him before.

She seemed stumped by the question but answered, "Yes. That's part of what I wanted to talk to you about." Her tone sounded serious. "Sister, I'm not going back to school."

"What?"

"I don't like school. Never have. The only reason I went to college is because you expected me to. Ever since I was a little girl I've been told to go to college. I didn't think I had a choice."

I felt a lump forming in my throat, storing all of my words. A few seconds later that felt like hours, I managed to say, "Why would you drop out of college?"

"I already told you."

"Okay. I won't lie. I am disappointed."

My mouth felt like cotton, so I drank some orange juice. I wondered why she would quit school when there were so many people who would give up their first-born child to be in her position. She was young, talented and affluent. She was blessed to have all of her college expenses paid for. She didn't have to work and she drove a cute car, a Nissan Maxima. I couldn't understand why she didn't realize what an enviable position she was in.

"Sister, I'm sorry. I didn't mean to hurt you."

"It's your life. You're an adult now. Even though I don't agree with your decision, I have to respect it. I can't force you to go to school."

A broad smiled appeared across her face. She got up from the table, leaned over and hugged me. Pressed her cheek against mine and squeezed my shoulders.

I grinned and pushed her away. Regardless of my disappointment, I still saw Cheyenne as my little sister. I couldn't stay angry with her.

"Don't get excited," I said. "If you're not going to be in school, you need to get a job."

"Sister," she whined, taking her seat.

"Don't 'Sister' me. I'm serious."

I had been so caught off guard by her admission to quitting school that I hadn't said anything about her plans to marry Jonathan. So I asked her what was up with that.

"We're planning on getting married."

I sighed, and said, "Let me share something with you. I don't think you should get married anytime soon. You've heard about two people coming together and making each other whole."

She nodded her head.

"That's not right. Two whole and complete people should come together and complement each other. If you don't know who you are or know where you're going, you aren't going to make a good wife. When you get married, I want your marriage to have the best possible chance of succeeding. Right now, Jonathan needs to get

84

himself together. He's not ready to be a husband. He's a high school drop out and a drug dealer. If you marry him you'll be living a dangerous life. If he keeps going the way he's going, he'll be dead or in jail. I don't want that for you or him."

She smiled and seemed to understand my sentiment.

I wrapped up by saying, "Now, if a couple of years down the road, you and Jonathan have your acts together and you still want to get married, I'll gladly support it. I'll give you the wedding you've always dreamed of. Just sit tight and enjoy your youth. You're only young once. Don't blow it."

We hugged again before putting up our breakfast dishes. I prayed that she plants my words in the garden of her mind and allows them to grow.

- - -

Christmas Eve. Every room in the house was lit up with Christmas lights. I put on a gospel CD while I prepared smoked turkey and macaroni and cheese for Christmas dinner. Cheyenne was hanging out with Jonathan. Greg spent the day with his family in Macon so that he could spend Christmas with me.

I was relaxing in the family room, drinking non-alcoholic eggnog, while the turkey and macaroni baked in the oven. Then the phone rang. It was Cheyenne. I could tell by the sound of her voice she had been crying.

"What's wrong?" My body became tense. I placed my milky drink on the coffee table.

"Sister," she sobbed.

"Calm down. Tell me what's the matter."

"I'm at the hospital."

My heart raced. *Lord, not again*, I thought.

She told me the name of the hospital and continued, "Come on." She sniffled.

I turned off the stove, put on my shoes and grabbed my purse. I was nervous. I hurried to the hospital. When I arrived, I parked at the emergency entrance and ran inside. I looked around and saw Cheyenne slumped over, sitting on a chair in the waiting area. I thanked God that she was all right. I rushed over to her and grabbed her face in the palms of my hands. Noticed that her shirt was soaked with blood.

"What happened?"

Still crying, Cheyenne said, "Jonathan. He's been shot."

"Who shot him? Why did they shoot him?"

"Some guy he'd been arguing with. I didn't know the guy. We were leaving the movie theater and the guy pulled out a gun. Shot him right there in front of me."

"How did you get to the hospital?"

"Somebody in the crowd must've called an ambulance because I was in shock. I couldn't move. I just rested his head on my lap. I rode in the ambulance with Jonathan."

I held her and stroked her hair as she cried on my shoulder. I assured her everything would be all right. Seeing her crying moved me emotionally. Made it hard for me not to cry too. Even though I wasn't fond of Jonathan, I didn't want him to die. In fact, I prayed that he would make a full recovery. Tears began to stream down my face too. I used the back of my hand to wipe away my tears.

"What's Jonathan's condition?" I asked.

"I don't know. They rushed him into surgery. I haven't heard anything else."

I excused myself while I asked the nurse behind the counter about Jonathan's condition. She informed me that he was still in surgery. I told Cheyenne and she requested we pray together. My heart rejoiced at the fact that she turned to the Lord. That let me know she knew the power of prayer. We held hands, closed our eyes, and I led us in prayer. Asked God to forgive Jonathan for his sins, oversee the operation and cover Jonathan in the blood of Jesus.

A couple of hours later, the doctor came out and told us that Jonathan was in stable condition. He had been shot in the chest but the doctor was optimistic that he'd make a full recovery. Cheyenne and I hugged and praised the Lord.

Although visiting hours had passed, the doctor made an exception and allowed us to briefly visit with Jonathan. We entered his room and he was heavily sedated. We stayed long enough to lay hands on him and pray some more. Then we left.

While in the car Cheyenne said, "Sister, I'm thinking about going back to school."

I didn't say anything. There was no need to. I understood the power of prayer – and favor.

Chapter Seven

Tanya Finney (pronounced Tonya) grew up seeking the love of others for acceptance and fulfillment. Her journey led her to several bad relationships that further fueled the emptiness felt in her heart. Enlightenment began in a physical move where she discovered the love she had been searching for – the love of Christ.

A participant and former leader in a women's ministry group, she has been sought after for counsel, prayer, and discipleship among church members and friends. Her poem "Do You See What I See?" has been selected for publication in The International Library of Poetry's collection, *Eternal Portraits*, and Tonya has been nominated for 2005 "Poet of the Year" by the organization.

The owner/creator of Divine Expressions, the company name under which she writes poetry, Tanya lives in the metro Atlanta area where she teaches high school English She shares her joy of reading various genres and writing poetry with her students.

Tanya is currently working on her first novel and second book of poetry. You can view updates concerning Tanya's literary career including a guestbook and calendar at www.tanyawrites.com.

Her contribution to *The Midnight Clear* is entitled, ***A Blessing in Disguise***.

A Blessing in Disguise

The cliché, "You can't judge a book by its cover" is certainly a familiar one. In this case, the cover was so horrible that Lisa Bryant had no desire to read its contents. The week before Thanksgiving, her father died, and at his funeral, it was discovered that he had a son by another woman.

Lisa's father, Nathan, was a hateful man and she didn't know why her mother, never divorced him. Tina tried hard to keep the family of two kids together with their parents; even seeking counseling from their pastor. But Nathan Bryant never saw that there was a problem. Part of the reason he didn't want to talk to the pastor could have been Tina's position as Pastor Moore's secretary, a high-ranking office in the church. On occasion, Lisa's father was mentally and verbally abusive and once, even hit her mother, but Tina remained a loyal wife to the end. His death was an end to the turmoil that she had been going through for ten years and now, they were being forced to face the fact that, on top of everything else that Nathan did, he committed adultery too.

The Bryant family was well known in Jonesboro, a city just outside of Atlanta, Georgia. Their name covered several body shop businesses scattered throughout town. Nathan inherited the business when his father died and worked hard to continue the reputation of doing quality work. Tina was the ever supportive wife and took over the philanthropic arm of the business, making donations to several causes, including cancer research. They both were featured numerous times on the society page of the local newspaper. Nathan's mother took his death the hardest, especially since he died of a heart attack – the same trauma that had caused the death of her husband.

Christmas was only two weeks away now, and although the family seemed to be slowly putting the pieces of their lives back together, Lisa's mind kept returning to the day her father died. On that day, Nathan and Tina were discussing the annual family Christmas feast that everyone on both sides of the family always attended. As usual, they planned to have the traditional turkey and dressing, but Lisa suggested that they try a fried turkey this time around.

Dessert was her area of expertise and she sometimes let her tremendous sweet tooth take over.

"So, Lisa, what sugary delight are you whipping up this year?" Her mom said.

"I haven't quite made up my mind yet. I know that I want to bake two red velvet cakes, but I'm not sure if I want to complement them with a caramel or an Italian cream cake."

"Don't forget to call the bakery and place the order for the brownies you love. And this year, would you try to let other people have some?" Her dad added.

Lisa's father knew her well. Richard's Bakery had the best chocolate and caramel brownies that she had ever tasted. Everyone in the family knew that she had to have them and gave her a wide berth when it came time for dessert.

As Lisa's parents pondered over the meal and seating arrangements, Nathan got a call from one of the body shops concerning an irate customer. He always liked to handle those types of situations himself and sometimes, to keep a customer happy, he was a little too generous. It was a good thing that they were rare occurrences.

Lisa often wondered how he could be so nice to customers but so mean to her mom. Alcohol was the main culprit of his anger toward Tina, but even when he was drinking, he never treated his customers with disrespect as he often did his wife. The holiday season always seemed to make even the meanest person happier, so for Nathan, the day of the call was a good day. Lisa knew that his good nature would only last long enough for the rest of the family to get the impression that he was a good husband. It was the only time that she could actually stand him being her father. The day after Christmas, he would start his tirades again and she often thought of how much easier life would be if he weren't around. Tina apparently loved him and was hoping for the reemergence of the man he used to be.

Shortly after Nathan left to tend to matters at the family business, they got another call from the shop. And life, as the Bryant family had known it, would never again be the same.

"Mrs. Bryant, this is Jimmy," the voice on the other end of the receiver announced. "They've taken Mr. Bryant to the hospital. He collapsed while trying to satisfy a very demanding customer. Things got really heated and he just grabbed his chest and fell."

Jimmy was the manager at the shop and had taken over the day-to-day operations as Nathan began semi-retirement. Gene, who was in their downtown store, was being prepped to take over as president and Lisa was to become CEO. Lisa and her mother gave Gene a call to inform him of what had transpired and then they raced over to Jonesboro Regional Hospital. Unfortunately, Nathan was pronounced dead on arrival. At least their last day together was a good one. The doctor told them that Nathan had had several small, undetected heart attacks and this one finally killed him. He attributed it to all of to the rich foods Nathan ate despite numerous warnings by several doctors.

Nathan loved greasy foods and would fry up his delights in lard – the worst thing possible. The rest of the family was very health conscious, but Nathan didn't care. He never liked going to the doctor and taking advice was pretty much out of the question. Even with the knowledge that heart disease had killed his father, Nathan wouldn't take the medicines that were prescribed to him. The rest of the family knew the consequences of Nathan's behavior could result in an early death, but no one expected him to die at forty-five. All of the warnings that he had so stubbornly ignored had finally caught up with him.

Tina immediately became the strength of the family and began the task of consoling Gene, Lisa, and their grandmothers, all while planning Nathan's funeral. She shed a few tears at the hospital and then went into overdrive as she met the family's needs. Lisa was very concerned that her mother was suppressing her grief to her detriment. In the days that followed, Tina kept busy, calling family members, making sure the body shop business was in order, and staying in constant contact with the funeral home. The news of Nathan's death was on the front page of the local paper and made the evening news on all three of Atlanta's top television stations.

The Bryants were high school sweethearts and Nathan was Tina's first love. She never thought that he would hurt her in the way that he had in the later years of their marriage. The obvious signs were not there – he never raised his voice or his hand to her while they dated or during the first few years of their marriage. It was the stress of trying to maintain their family's reputation that started Nathan's drinking habit and the release of his demons. His father was a tough man and he made it no secret that he thought that some of Nathan's ideas for the family business were not feasible. Nathan took this to mean that his father did not believe in him and he gradually turned to the bottle to find comfort for his wounded heart. Nathan wanted very much to please his father.

As the day of the funeral drew closer, Tina really didn't have time to grieve. The house was full of family members, friends, and community activists who extended well wishes and offered support. The funeral was scheduled for Monday, three days before Thanksgiving. It seemed as if half of the town, including news reporters, showed up at Greater Works Baptist Church that day. But no one could have guessed who else would show up.

After Pastor Moore gave the benediction, mourners gathered into the Family Life Center for the repast. It was then that Lisa noticed a young man staring at them as he stood with an older woman in the corner. He finally got the nerve to walk over, and when he did, he introduced himself as Corey Bryant. Hearing the last name immediately raised Lisa's suspicions. She knew that so called "relatives" always seemed to pop up, looking for money when someone died. All that the young stranger was able to get out of his mouth was that he was sorry for their loss before the woman he'd been standing with earlier walked up.

"Tell them the real reason that you're here," she urged.

Corey shifted his feet and it was obvious that what he was about to say wasn't going to be easy to hear. Still, neither Lisa, nor the rest of her family were prepared for Corey's next words.

"Nathan was my father."

When no one seemed to be able to voice a reply to the shocking reveal, Corey went on to explain the story of being Nathan's Chattanooga-born son. Nathan didn't continue a physical relationship with Corey's mother but would often visit and religiously paid child support. As proof that he wasn't fabricating his story, Cory brought pictures of himself and Nathan; the most recent one was taken at a football game at the University of Tennessee, where he was the star quarterback. Seeing the photos was enough to push Lisa over the edge.

"How could you come in here and do this to us!" she screamed. "Don't you see that we are already upset? How could you drop this bomb on us at a time like this?"

Her mother immediately faced her. "Yes, his timing is not the best, but you cannot cause a scene," Tina whispered.

Every eye in the building seemed to be on them as Corey quietly handed Tina a slip of paper bearing his number and offered his availability whenever they were ready to talk. After he walked away, Tina snatched Lisa up from her chair by the arm and led to the ladies' room.

"I know that I taught you better than to fly off the handle when you don't know all the facts. Your father wasn't the greatest of men and whatever he did is not the fault of that boy. We're in the Lord's house and you need to recognize that," she scolded.

As Lisa stood sulking, she couldn't believe her mother was taking the side of a stranger over her own daughter's. Her mind was riddled with questions. *How do we know for certain that he is my half-brother? Why hadn't our father told us of this? What was the relationship between my father and Corey's mother?* She knew that she couldn't ask her mother these questions so she fixed her face and obediently followed Tina out of the bathroom.

By the time they returned to their earlier vacated spot, Corey was gone and Pastor Moore came over to make sure that everything was all right. Lisa couldn't wait for the day to end so that she would be back at home, alone with her family.

Thanksgiving was a somber event. With the recent death and burial of Nathan, the Bryant family really wasn't in a festive mood. Lisa's main concern was for her mother who hadn't shown many signs of grief. All of her life she'd known that Tina was a strong woman, but until now, she didn't realize just how great her mother's strength was.

In the week that followed, Tina often had small talks with Gene and Lisa about their father. She told them that she suspected that he was cheating on her around the time that Gene was born.

"One day, several years ago, I opened a bank statement that came in the mail and discovered that money was being transferred to an additional bank account under your father's name. An account that I could not access. Since Nathan paid all of the household bills, I rarely looked at the incoming mail. I just happened to open the

92

bank statement that day since I was home with Gene, who was a newborn at the time.

"When I asked about it, Nathan told me that it was an emergency fund in case business began to decline. I was suspicious, but I let it slide. The thought remained in the back of her mind, though."

Tina said that the verbal abuse started not long after that when Nathan accused her of what he had apparently been doing – committing adultery.

As Lisa listened, she became angrier. She still couldn't understand why her mother chose to stay with him. *She was still young at the time and could have started over*, Lisa reasoned within herself.

"Despite everything your father did, I still loved him," Tina said, almost as if she had read her daughter's thoughts. "Besides, my vows were not only to your father, but to God and I trusted Him to see me through."

– – –

The days passed and soon Christmas season was in high gear. At two weeks to go, shopping was becoming more and more hectic. The family decided to put the finishing touches on the Christmas plans that were started before Nathan died. The menu would consist of fried turkey, baked ham, stuffing, mashed potatoes and gravy, turnip greens, and green beans. Tina was working on the guest list so that she could begin the seating chart. She was apparently riding high in the Christmas spirit when she proposed a question to Gene and Lisa.

"I think that we should invite Corey over to share in the festivities," she said.

"What!!" they exclaimed in unison.

"I feel that it is important that you get to know your brother," their mother explained. "There is nothing more valuable in life than family and now, more than ever, we need to hold on to each other."

"How can I embrace someone I know nothing about? He is just a reminder of what Dad did," Lisa piped in.

As Tina continued talking, it soon became apparent to Gene and Lisa that their mother had met with Corey. Lisa guessed her curiosity got the best of her, prompting her to give him a call. Tina admitted that she and Cory had met at Ruby Tuesday the week following the funeral. Corey told her more details about living in Chattanooga with his mother, Sherri. Neither he nor his mother ever knew about Lisa or Gene, just that Nathan was a successful businessman in Atlanta whose importance called for him to spend most of his time working. Sherri met Nathan while he was on a business trip in Chattanooga and she was working as the desk clerk at the hotel in which he was staying. A brief romance ensued and she became pregnant with Corey, not knowing that the man she'd been involved with was married.

Corey told Tina that for Nathan, Sherri was a way of escape from the ins and outs of the business. He wasn't much of a talker when things got bad and at the time, Tina's pregnancy with Gene had kept her ill and she spent most of her time in bed. Nathan's dad had just died and he was working hard to keep the business going. Since Tina was already under the stress and strain of her pregnancy, he thought that Sherri was a viable option for him. He occasionally made trips to visit and Sherri was later told that he was married, but not that he had any other children.

"Mom, aren't you mad at what Dad did?" asked Gene when Tina finished sharing the details of her conversation with Corey.

"Yes, but there is no need to continue to be angry at someone who is no longer here," she responded. "I've made my peace with it and God has revealed to me that my anger is justified; but holding on to it and trying to retaliate by being nasty with Corey would be a sin of my own. Besides, the wonderful thing about this life in Christ is that your father, not I, will have to answer for what he did when he faces God. My role is not to become bitter, but better."

Those were wasted words on Lisa, who was still too consumed with anger to receive them. She felt that it was just too soon after her father's death to have to deal with the revelation of a half-brother. All of the thoughts of her father's abuse came flooding back to her mind, ending with a mental picture of Corey who looked similar to Nathan. That image was just too much for her.

"If he's going to be here, I'm not. I can't stomach looking into his, rather, *Dad's* face, as a reminder of how he destroyed this family's trust and betrayed our love," Lisa said as she stormed out of the house.

Tearfully, Tina started after her but Gene stopped his mother's pursuit and offered her a supportive embrace.

"Just let her go, Mom. When she's like this, there's nothing that you can say that will get her to listen to reason," Gene said.

Lisa got into her car and went for a long drive through downtown Atlanta. She loved the look of the nighttime Atlanta skyline, bright with lights. Parking, she walked to the fountains at Centennial Olympic Park. Water always calmed her and it was at this time of year that those in authority turned a section of the park into an ice skating rink for families to enjoy. Christmas music played in the background as Lisa sat in the park listening to the gurgle of the fountain and the giggles of children as they played on the skating rink.

In the distance, Lisa noticed what appeared to be a father teaching his daughter how to ice skate. It brought back memories of happier moments she had with her own dad – him pushing her on the swing at six, and accompanying her at the father/daughter dance at thirteen. She still couldn't believe that he had been lying to his family the entire time.

Lisa's phone rang, notifying her of a received text message. It was from her mom who wanted her to call home so that she could be sure that she was alright. When Lisa dialed the number to calm Tina's anxieties, her mother suggested that she write a letter to her father.

"It will help you to get her feelings out and dissolve her anger," Tina assured.

When their brief conversation ended, Lisa continued to reflect on her life as she sat in the park. Her icy heart began its slow defrost and she soon found herself back in the car and headed for home.

- - -

Christmas was a week away and the Bryant family's house was a flurry of activity. Tina, Lisa, and Gene decorated the family Christmas tree with ornaments that the kids had made during their childhood as well as the angel ornaments that Tina loved. Each year, Lisa and Gene gave her a new angel ornament to hang on the tree.

Despite the festive mood that could be seen, heard and felt throughout the house, Lisa still struggled with residue anger toward her father. She couldn't yell at Nathan so despite her mother's warnings, she turned her anger toward Corey. When he called that day, he asked to speak to Lisa, but she refused. Tina made an appeal to her once again to reconcile her feelings about her father so that she wouldn't develop what she called, "the angry black woman syndrome." Lisa still had not taken her mother's advice about writing the letter and gradually, because of her refusal to face her anger head on, she was beginning to distance herself from her mother.

The children's Christmas play was to be held the next day at Greater Works and Lisa was the director. Tina tried to remind her daughter that the play was reflective of God's love for His children, despite what they did, as He brought His Son to earth to be the Savior. Lisa's healing was still being hampered by her anger, but she finally wrote her father the letter that she'd been avoiding writing. Upon finishing it, she decided to go to Nathan's grave to read it to him aloud, in spite of the dark clouds that threatened unfavorable weather.

"Father, how I wished that I could call you my daddy but I was blocked by how you treated Mom. How could you love someone and at the same time hurt them so badly? To make matters worse, we have living, breathing proof that you were guilty of what you falsely accused her of doing. Why couldn't you love her as a real man should instead of finding ways to tear her spirit down? I know that the stress of work got to you sometimes but I occasionally saw glimpses of your true self. I prayed for an end not knowing that it would be your death. At least the rest of the family still have each other without the fear of you going off the handle at any given moment. You turned the knife in Mom's back one last time when Corey showed up at your funeral. For that, I will never forgive you!!!!"

As Lisa finished reading, she was screaming, crying, and stomping on her father's tombstone while drops of rain showered down on her. Having said all she had to say, she ran to the car and headed for home.

That night, as she tried to find sleep, Lisa tossed and turned, still disturbed by the day's events. A few hours later, she began to have a dream that would impact her feelings toward her father. In it, Lisa was at church with Tina, awaiting her to finish a meeting. When the meeting ended, Pastor Moore came out and greeted her.

"Lisa, how are you?"

"Just fine. How are you?" she said.

"I'm good." He replied looked at her like a concerned parent. "Sweetheart, you need to release this anger that you have. Even though your father wasn't the best, your heavenly Father only placed on you what you could bear. You need to remember that the trials that we go through are not for us only, but to be a blessing to someone who is going through the same thing. You don't know who is waiting on the other side of this that might not get their release if you continue to hold on to your anger. Remember that God's love is in the good *and* the bad. Your father is not here anymore but your brother is, and you need to embrace him. You never know what blessing Corey holds for the future of your family."

At that statement Lisa awoke to hear Christmas music playing downstairs. It wasn't often that she had dreams that she remembered. When she did, she always took note of them. They were God's way of sending her a message, especially when she knew what He wanted her to do but was being disobedient. This dream was especially significant since Pastor Moore, a man she thought highly of, played a major role.

"Okay, God. I hear you. Maybe it won't be so bad to just hear what Corey has to say."

Getting dressed and going downstairs, Lisa found her mother preparing pancakes from a recipe she had gotten years earlier from a television news reporter. They were the family's favorite. She told her mom about the dream and Tina suggested that inviting Corey to stay with the family during the holidays would be a good start. Lisa wasn't too sure about that, but with the Christmas play being held that evening, she didn't have time to have a full blown discussion with her mother. Instead, she finished breakfast and headed over to the church.

The first person that she saw was Pastor Moore. They greeted one another and then Lisa got busy making sure that everything was ready for that evening's production. Pastor Moore expressed his pride in her for taking on the assignment while the youth minister was on maternity leave and suggested that she seriously consider working with the ministry full time. The kids loved her and treated her as a big sister and God seemed to send confirmation of the pastor's request. The play was a success and the children were

97

grateful that Lisa had taught them well and allowed them to showcase their talents as they reenacted Christ's birth for the audience.

That evening, the Bryant family held a discussion concerning Corey's invitation for Christmas. Instead of spending the holidays, they decided to invite him and his mother to share in the family festivities on Christmas day. Lisa was making a good effort to not pass the anger she had for the sins of her father onto her half-brother. But she just wasn't quite ready for a weekend visit.

It was Christmas Eve, and Lisa was busy in the kitchen baking red velvet, caramel, and Italian crème cakes. Her little cousin, Angel, had come over and was busy baking chocolate chip and white chocolate macadamia nut cookies. The house was filled with the smell of the delicious desserts. While Lisa and Angel were busy baking and Gene taste testing, Corey called to finalize plans for the next day. Gene answered, pressing the button that placed the call on speaker phone.

"Hello, Gene. Are you ready to watch the big game tomorrow?" Corey asked.

"Sure am. Just make sure that you are ready to root for the Atlanta Falcons," Gene replied, knowing that Corey's favorite team was the New Orleans Saints – the team the Falcons were playing against.

Christmas day arrived and Lisa nervously hoped that she could be as receptive and pleasant to her new brother as Gene had been in their telephone conversation the day before. This would be the first meeting that they had since her father's funeral. Lisa knew that it wasn't going to be easy, especially since he looked so much like Nathan. She only hoped that she could keep it together and remain calm during Corey's and his mother's stay.

If Mom can stand being faced with what my father did, I guess I can too, she thought.

Throughout the morning, Tina's sisters and their families arrived to help her with the meal. Lisa's favorite uncle, Teddy, arrived next and began to be the life of the party with his fun-loving personality. The afternoon meal was set for two o'clock and at noon, the doorbell rang. Gene opened the door to reveal Corey and Sherri. Tina was the first to embrace them and invited them in. The

98

dinner went surprisingly well and Lisa decided to even let Corey share in the tasting of her brownies.

"I am so proud of you, Lisa," Tina said with a beaming smile. "I'm glad that you let God into your heart. Forgiveness is not easy to give but if God can forgive us of our sins and send Christ to bring us back to Him, the least we can do is forgive our fellow man. Whatever sins have been committed against us is nothing compared to what our Savior had to go through here on earth."

As mother and daughter embraced, Corey approached and asked to speak to Lisa alone. As Tina walked away, giving them their privacy, Cory spoke.

"Lisa, I know it has been hard for you to accept me and I understand that. But I grew up thinking I was an only child and even in this sordid situation I can't help but appreciate the fact that I have two siblings. I hope that we can all get to know one another better."

For the first time, Lisa was able to look past her half-brother's all-too-familiar face and her heart went out to Corey as she reflected on the times that she had with her father and wondered how differently each of their lives might have been had they known about each other. When Lisa and Corey rejoined the others who were still feasting, Corey announced that he had a surprise for the family, especially for Lisa.

"I just wanted to let you know that your beloved Richard's Bakery, that had been up for sale due to the owner's retirement has just been purchased – by me. So, from now on, there will be two family businesses in Jonesboro," he said, winking at Lisa.

Lisa responded with a quiet smile. Instead of not attempting to open the book because of its cover, she not only opened it but began a new chapter – one that they, the Bryant siblings, could write together.

99

Chapter Eight

Laverne Lewis Gaskins is the 2005 recipient of the Memphis Black Writers Conference's Author Award of Merit. Her critically acclaimed debut novel, *Child Support and Other Guarantees* is available online at Amazon.com and Barnes and Noble.com.

Gaskins resides with her family in South Georgia.She is currently working on her second novel and may be contacted through her website at www.lavernelewisgaskins.com.

Her contribution to *The Midnight Clear* is entitled, *A Sparrow's Journey*.

A Sparrow's Journey

I feel a little awkward talking to you this way, so let me explain how I arrived at this point in my life. It all began a few days ago with a call to my favorite aunt.

"Aunt Sarah. It's me. Can you hear me?"

"Who is 'me'? Say your name, girl, and act like you've been raised right. I know who you are, but you need to show some kinda manners."

"Hello, Aunt Sarah. This is Danielle Lee Jackson, your lovely great niece, also known as River. Is that formal enough?"

"That's much better. Baby, you know I love you; it's just exhausting dealing with you young folks' ways."

"I know you do. Mom said you're not coming to our Christmas party because you're sick. Are you alright?"

"Yes, baby I'm just fine. My arthritis is acting up something fierce and I can't imagine getting through both a long drive and the party. Did you get the gift I sent you?"

"No, I haven't received anything."

"Well maybe the mail is running a bit slow because of the holidays. Y'all doing all right? I know there must be a house full of people."

My mother's bellowing voice suddenly floated up the stairs. "River, darling, please come downstairs and greet our company."

"Aunt Sarah, I've gotta go. The house is packed with folks. I wish you were here."

"I know it. So, you've finished your first semester of college. Girl, you know I'm so proud of you!"

"Well, it's just one semester. I still have a long way to go."

"I don't care where you are as long as you keep moving. You'll get there in due time. Have you been sleeping well?"

"Why do you ask? I was going to talk to you about..."

"River, did you hear me? We're about to sing. We need you on the piano."

"Coming, Mom!!"

"Mind your manners, now. Your mama is just excited, that's all. There's nothing wrong with a heart full of joy, especially around this time of year."

"Okay. Bye, Aunt Sarah."

"Bye, baby."

I slapped on a little makeup in a vain attempt to conceal the imperfections haunting my face, before descending into the pit of people, demanding repeatedly that I share details of my college experience. I should have stayed in the dorm during the break until Christmas Eve. For years, one week before Christmas, we've hosted a party where I've had to run through a gauntlet of over-affectionate relatives.

At the top of the stairs, I took a deep breath before walking down into the giant family room filled with my colorful family. As an only child, I had both benefited and suffered from being the center of attention. I was at the bottom of the stairs for all of a minute before someone spotted me.

"Lord, Pumpkin, I thought that baby would've grown up by now. Eighteen years old and still no bigger than a gnat! River, come over here and give your old Auntie Laura a hug."

Pumpkin? I never got accustomed to my mother's folks still calling her by a childhood nickname that suited neither her age nor dignity, and was inconsistent with her station in life. Maybe "Princess" or "Queen." But a food?

With a smile, my mom always responded to the rhythmic, delivery of the word as if it were her given name. The name reached far into her infancy, when her relish consumption of pumpkin pie gave birth to a nickname that endured the test of time. I could recite in perfect detail the pumpkin story without forgetting the required descriptors, "dirt poor farm family where food was plentiful."

At least my nickname made logical sense. I was told that while my mother was eight months pregnant, she returned to her mother's home for a short visit in the country. I made my surprise presence next to the river that flows near Aunt Sarah's house.

"Pumpkin, tell that baby to come over here and give her old Aunt Sister a hug. Girl, you know I can't hardly move with this bad knee."

"Hi Aunt Sister," I said. "I'm glad you could make it to our party."

"Chile, I wouldn't miss it for the world. You're just as sweet as you can be. Pumpkin tells me that you got a scholarship to Hampton University. I'm proud of you, but couldn't you find some good

103

schools here in Georgia or nearby? What about FAMU, or uh…
Hey, Marvin, what's that school in Carolina that Sharon's boy went
to?"

"What?" my cousin's voice echoed from the distance.

"Sharon's boy. The engineer. What school did he go to?"

Oh, yeah. The one making all that money. North Carolina
A&T."

"River, what's the matter with those schools?"

"Virginia is really not that far," I explained. "And Hampton
gave me two scholarships. Awhile back, I promised Grandma that I
would, in her words, 'go to the only university you should
consider.'"

"Well, your grandma ain't never led anyone astray and she was
a good woman. God bless the dead. And if that college is paying
you to go there, you go fast. But visit us as often as you can."

"Amen," chimed Marvin. "River, what's with the dark circles
around your eyes? College that bad?"

"Huh? Oh, yeah, I haven't been sleeping well lately. I guess I'm
excited about Christmas," I said as I quickly walked away.

Just one semester of college and you would've thought I had
already graduated the way my folks were treating me. Auntie June
chuckled real loud as she gave me some "sugar" which included a
near fatal, squeeze-the-air-out-of-the-lungs hug. That hug set off
some kind of psychic chain reaction, because immediately, relatives
from everywhere converged on my five feet, zero inches, ninety-
three pounds, for congratulatory hugs and sloppy across-the-cheek
kisses.

My best friend, Samantha Joe, laughed softly at the sight from
the safe distance of the sunroom. Between the numerous violations
of my personal space, I gave Sam a fierce, *what's-so-funny?* look.
Sam and I shared so many similarities. We were both the only child
of parents driven to make certain that our paths to success were free
and clear of any conceivable obstacles. We had seen our way
through various hair cuts: wraps, colors, braids, weaves, up-dos,
afros and now, twists. In high school, we both took the same
advance placement courses and managed to both graduate at the top
of our class.

"Listen up, everyone; River's going to play," my mother
announced.

As expected, Aunt May, began the first verse in her off-key rendition of "Silent Night" and then everyone else chimed in. I looked up from the keys to catch a glimpse of my mom's beaming face. With the huge decorated tree in the background, people surrounding her, and my dad standing next to her with his protective arm resting on her shoulder, the scene reminded me a beautiful Christmas card. After enduring five songs, I was ready to escape and take refuge under the sofa along with Fat Freddy, our cat.

Sensing my mood, my dad whispered to me, "River, let's test ride your car again."

Nothing was wrong with my new car, but I went along with the ploy to escape the crowd. As we weaved through the neighborhood, we were reminded of my mother's presence. Pictures of her face were plastered on the few sale signs that littered the neatly groomed lawns. Next to her plastic smile was her trademark slogan in bold letters: *Your dream house is waiting.* If I had a nickel for every time one of my classmates teased me about Mom's commercials, I would be rich. As a CPA and partner in a major firm, Dad would likely never be on television and that fact suited both of us just fine.

"Turn left and circle back to the park."

Frustrated, I asked, "Dad, are you going to try to teach me how to parallel park the *easy way* again? I mean, what's the problem? I have my license and I've been driving for two years."

Laughing, he admitted, "This has nothing to do with your pitiful driving skills." He paused. "River, you look tired. Sometimes, I don't sleep well either. I have a bad habit of keeping my concerns to myself. You shouldn't keep things bottled up inside."

Not ready to talk about the nights when I would sleep all night and wake up exhausted from it all, I blamed my woes on a handy scapegoat. "College isn't always easy. I'll be fine."

His brow crinkled like it did when he was in deep thought. I'd seen that look before. A few times, I had caught him staring out of the kitchen bay window early in the morning before I would go to school. I would speak to Dad and he would answer me with a distant acknowledgment of my presence. He was staring at me with that same worried look. I came to a stop in the lot of the park and he handed me a small box wrapped in brown paper.

"Your gift came in the mail today."

"I told Aunt Sarah I hadn't received it. Why did you keep it?"

Before he could respond, I had already ripped opened the package and an airplane ticket sprung up and dropped to the floor of the car. Peeking from the brown paper was a smaller package wrapped in brightly colored Christmas paper. Anticipation got the best of me and I opened the gift with the same delicacy I extended to the brown wrapping. Inside was a black Bible with frayed pages and my misspelled named: *Daniel*, engraved on the cover in gold. I was confused because Aunt Sarah certainly would have never given me something used or with my name spelled incorrectly on it.

After what seemed to be an enduring silence, Dad said, "The plane ticket is from your Aunt Sarah. Your flight leaves the day after Christmas. Grandma May left instructions that Aunt Sarah was to make sure you received the other gift. I guess she knew she was…leaving soon. Remember how special Grandma May treated Christmas?"

I didn't want to offend my dad's mother who'd just died last year, so I forced a fake smile of gratitude for the worn Bible.

Guessing my thoughts, Dad spoke with the full force of authority. "My mother may have acted different, but she was very wise. Maybe during your trip to Florida you can learn about …"

"Dad, it's okay. Sometimes, I misspell names."

"…the things you need to know." He finished his sentence despite my interruption. "River, appearances can be deceiving. As you mature, you will better be able to process and understand information. She also left you this."

In a bright, yellow envelope with pink trim was a letter written December two years earlier, in bold, deliberate strokes.

River,
Congratulations. Today marks the beginning of your journey. Listen and read. Trust what you see and you will understand what you need to know. Others have come before you.

Love,
Grandma May

Not a single word misspelled. Aunt Sarah must have helped her.

"River, we'd better get back to the party before your mother starts to worry."

\- - -

Inside the house, everyone had comfortably settled in various rooms to eat. Sam walked toward me with a plate piled high. The closer she got to me, the more we both laughed at the pig-sized portions.

"When I finish, I'm eating some of that red velvet cake," she said between the giggles.

I grabbed a piece of turkey from her plate. Laughing, I said, "Sam, you ought to be ashamed."

Once we finished laughing, Sam turned serious. "River, I saw you and your dad leave. He looked worried. Is everything alright?

"Yes...Sam, come go with me to Florida next week. Aunt Sarah sent me a round trip plane ticket."

"Lasonville, Florida?" she asked with a grimace. "It should have been named Lazyville, 'cause there's nothing to do there. And there is no such thing as a plane ticket to Lasonville. It's so far in the woods that we'd have to drive two hours to get there *after* leaving the airport."

I made a second plea. "Sam, we would only be there for one week and it's not like you don't have the time; and don't say anything about the money because knowing you, you probably still have money left from all those high school graduation cards stuffed with cash."

"Don't hate because I know how to save my money." Sam's cell phone interrupted her quip and she proceeded to have a conversation with her mom, complete with exaggerated facial expressions. "Are you kidding? Why? Okay. Alright, I'll go."

Ending the call and looking at me, she sighed and said, "Your Aunt Sarah sent me a ticket as well, so it's off to the woods of Lasonville."

\- - -

I could sense, even through a sky full of pillow clouds, the equally blended feeling of joy, buried fear, and a desire for understanding that always surfaced whenever I neared Lasonville.

"Are we here yet? River. River!"

"Huh? What? Sorry, Sam, I didn't hear you. I guess I was just

107

in deep thought."

"Are you alright? You look scared or something."

"I told you, I was just thinking."

The plane landed and we quickly boarded the surprisingly full bus headed for Lasonville. Sam and I walked to the rear toward two vacant seats. As soon as the bus left the station, the person seated across the aisle struck up a conversation.

"Y'all girls headed to Lasonville?" said a slightly weathered, high pitched, squeal of a voice.

I turned to my right to see an elderly woman with big smile that showcased two gold teeth and several missing spaces where white teeth should have been. Soft blue-tipped braids hung from underneath a multi-colored scarf that covered half her head. Our responding "yes" to her question was misinterpreted as permission to talk to us nonstop until we arrived at our destination.

"My mama wanted me to stay in Lasonville, but I had to go," she told us. "The city is where I belong. I knew it then and I know it now. Less than a month out, I got me a good job. I have a little time off this month, so I plan to visit for a few days. I need to catch up on what's going on. You know there is always something. The thang I missed most about Lasonville is the big orange moon. I mean, in other parts, the moon just doesn't seem as big or as bright. Sometimes that orange moon would scare me. Know what I mean?"

Sam was mesmerized but after awhile, "*Blah, blah, blah*" was all I could hear. I was irritated with the nonsensical talk about Lasonville and some orange moon. I didn't want to hear about any moon. Particularly since dreams of an orange moon had recently tormented my sleep. Finally, the screeching wheels of the bus signaled that we had arrived and that the incessant squeal from the intruder would end. Relief never sounded so sweet.

"Lawd, girls, that didn't take no time; and twenty minutes ahead of schedule! I see my ride's already here. Who you gonna see?"

"I'm going to visit my Grandmother May...I mean, Aunt Sarah."

"You some kin to May that usta stay up the ways near 'bout to the river?"

"Yes, she was my grandmother."

The woman reacted like she had accidentally swallowed a half

108

pint of extra-strength rage. She glared at me and left without another word.

Sam whispered facetiously as we got off the bus, "She must have an aversion to rivers."

The nice evening breeze felt good after being cooped up on the bus with the smell of feet, loud perfume, soiled baby diapers and doused-on aftershave. Within a few minutes of our arrival, everyone left, leaving Sam and me alone to share the tiny makeshift bus station.

"It figures we would be the last ones," said Sam with predictable pessimism.

"Mr. Nat will be here soon. He's never late. We're just early," I said with expected reassuring optimism.

Just as I calculated, our wait was soon interrupted by the sound and the sight of an old faded blue truck with the single headlight. Mr. Nat was a farmer and handyman who lived near Aunt Sarah and Grandma May. For a fair price, the two women could always depend on him to fix anything that was broken. Mr. Nat and his wife also ran an informal taxi service for the small, close-knit community. His "taxi" for the past eight years had been the old truck with a single front seat.

Worried that he may have made a mistake about our arrival time, Mr. Nat said, "Y'all girls ain't been out here long, have you?"

"No, sir," we answered.

"The bus arrived early," Sam said.

"Well, climb on in while I grab your bags. We'll be at your Aunt Sarah's house directly. How was your Christmas? I declare you two have grown since I last seen you. Now, I want to know about college. I been hearing some real nice thangs 'bout you two. I love to hear 'bout young folks doing good and trying to do something with their lives."

We effortlessly shared our plans for the future. Mr. Nat had a way of making you feel that you were a success if you had goals and that somehow, your success was his too. Soon, we were in front of Aunt Sarah's pink wood frame house decorated with a string of lights and a huge sign on the front lawn that declared *Jesus is the Reason for the Season*.

Aunt Sarah came out to greet us with outstretched arms. "You two, come give me a hug. I'm so happy to see you. Come inside, your dinner is waiting. Mr. Nat, you're certainly welcomed to have some dinner."

In customary fashion, Aunt Sarah handed Mr. Nat the taxi fare in an envelope. Years ago, Aunt Sarah told me that Mr. Nat, to ensure the dignity of all his patrons, preferred the envelope because some people could only afford change or an IOU.

"The wife is waiting for me to watch that preacher's show on TV," he replied.

"Well at least let me fix you two plates."

"Yes, ma'am. That'll be just fine."

After Sam and I wolfed down my favorite meal of fried catfish, stewed okra and tomatoes, macaroni and cheese, collard greens, cornbread, and sweet tea, we started the obligatory chore of washing dishes, prior to eating dessert. In Aunt Sarah's house, it didn't matter if you were company. If she cooked a meal the least you could do was wash the dishes. The only people exempted from this rule were the infirmed, the elderly, and males over the age of sixteen.

One time, I balked when my able bodied male cousin was allowed to eat the equivalent of three days worth of food in one meal and was not asked to lift a finger to wash not even the smallest cup. In response to my passionate plea for democracy, and desire to reorganize the social order, Aunt Sarah vetoed my attempted coup and simply said, "We need to encourage our boys to be men first. They can wash dishes later."

We quickly washed the dishes in anticipation of blueberry cobbler smothered in vanilla ice-cream. Between delicious gulps, we chatted softly while we made vain attempts to outwit the fatigue.

Sensing we were fighting a losing battle, Aunt Sarah said, "All right, girls, you've had a long day. Your rooms are ready. Sleep as long as you need."

- - -

She didn't really mean it.

"Time to get up. I said you can sleep late, not all day."

Despite my exhaustion, I was able to muster enough strength to look at the clock with one eye. The other was in sync with the rest of my body. It was eleven o'clock.

"Ladies, we are going to Winona Camp."

Both my eyes opened and my body instantly felt like I had just

110

received an intravenous shot of caffeine. *Winona Camp?* It was too soon.

Ignoring Aunt Sarah's constant demands to hurry, we didn't arrive until around four o'clock. I never knew why Grandma May's house was called Winona Camp. The tiny white house with a massive screened porch and short fence surrounding a small section of the yard, now had boarded up windows.

"Let's visit in the back," said Aunt Sarah.

Adjacent to the house, several yards in the back, was a gate that led to a heavily wooded area. In the middle of the wooded area was a small graveyard open to the world. We passed the few gravesites that I had viewed many times during my childhood summers. The faintly etched tombstones, with a few letters erased by time and neglect, conveyed a story deeper than the limits of the words.

Sarah   Resting in the arms of Jesus. Born 1855   Died 1875
Amos Smith. Loving Father and Husband. Died 1870.
Cora Phillips. Gone but not forgotten. 1900 – 1905.

Red, lilac, yellow and pink roses shared the ground near Grandma May's tombstone.

May Littlefield Jackson. Mother and Wife. Born 1905 – Died 2005. Come to me and I shall give you rest.

Without being told, we began to help Aunt Sarah clean the area of small weeds. A small gray dove watched us from beneath a nearby shrub. Satisfied that the area was clean, Aunt Sarah pulled herself up with a loud grunt.

"Sam, River and I are going to go inside and get a few things. We won't be long."

I gave Sam a reassuring slight smile that seemed to alleviate her fears of being left alone at the gravesite.

Aunt Sarah jiggled several keys to find the right one to open the back door and confidently said, "May said you'd know that I would give you something and by the look on your face, she was right."

The musty smell of the boarded up house and the sight of two mice scurrying across the floor assaulted our senses.

"River, flip the switch on behind the door. I kept the electricity paid." Directing my attention away from the condition of the house, she added, "In here," pointing to an antique secretary.

111

Aunt Sarah took out a small key and opened a drawer filed with papers. Inside the drawer was a small stack of envelopes held together by a strange ribbon.

"Take these. Some people thought May was a little odd, but she knew who she was. I've done my part. You can sit in this rocking chair and read. Let me turn on some Christmas music because I know if May were here she would be listening to it."

I saw this day before it came. So many times, I dreamed of rocking in a chair with Christmas music playing, an orange moon, and a dove standing in the yard looking at me and Sam. When I told Dad about it, he said in due time the dream would maybe make sense. I gently unfolded the first envelope in the stack, and instantly recognized the author's handwriting.

December 26, 1921

River,
Mrs. Lilly she the lady I clean house for. She learned me how to read and write. One day I want to learn numbers. I will write very good so you can read what I say. Granny said to write down what I needs to say to you so your journey won't have pain. You have not come in the world yet but I can see you. Tiny like a sparrow. I see you at the river crying. Making a fuss you cry loud. When you get here I will name you River. Your daddy is not here yet either. But I see him. I will tell him about your gift. My granny said in our folks the gift goes to the women. Granny said we all have purpose by God's will. I love you. Be strong.

Grandma May

My thoughts raced as I opened the next letter.

December 26, 1941

Dear River,
Forgive me for not writing you for such a long time. I let the world interfere with what's right and just. My Warrior is gone and

112

sometimes I get confused. Your daddy is here with me as a constant reminder of what I am missing. Let me tell you about my love. I call him my Warrior. When I was younger, I wanted to run away from my gift. I heard that Hampton Institute was looking for some workers for a government program they had. I took the fastest bus out of Lasonville. My people knew I would be back. I met my love at Hampton. My Warrior was from the Lakota nation and he was a young boy when he was taken from his folks and sent away for an education and civilization. His folks soon died and after having been taken from his roots, it was easy for him to stay put instead of going back to the reservation and cry for what was no longer there. My love was assigned to washing dishes and I got a job doing the laundry. He always found a way to be in the same area as me. When he finally spoke to me I just about couldn't understand him. He talked with a mixture of English and his native language. He called me his little sparrow, because of my size. He was six feet four inches tall, brown skinned, with long raven black hair. It did not take us long to fall in love and we would meet outside Winona Lodge dormitory for kisses that I will always remember. Some professors taught us both in their spare time for no charge. My Warrior taught me more. Because of him, I am not afraid of the world. He showed me how God's spiritual presence can be found everywhere in the natural world. My Warrior told me of others like myself and he understood my gift. We married and built this house. It was a long time before we had a baby. I can feel the sadness in my heart rising. I must stop writing now. I know God calls His children home when it is time. My Warrior was called home after your father was born. He always called our home Winona Camp. When the time is right I will tell you more.

Be Blessed,
Grandma May

I felt someone else was in the room but turned around to see an empty house.

113

December 27, 1950

Dear River,
Today, I am so tried of others seeking to use me for their dirty
deeds. A purpose, a calling and a gift should not be treated as
trash. Christmas is a time for all of us to remember the joy of our
Savior's birth and a beginning of a time of change. We are all
children of God and we must always remember who is in charge.
River, be careful not to forget why we even have this holiday. God
gave you a special gift. He speaks to you in your dreams so that you
may serve as an instrument of His message. I know sometimes you
get scared. Don't be afraid. Read the Bible I've left you and you
will understand better your work. Job 33:14-18 teaches us that
God can speak to us in dreams and the Book of Joel and the Book of
Act says daughters shall prophesy. There have been other prophets
before you, Isaiah, Jeremiah, Joel, Deborah, Micah. Your gift is not
to be used as an instrument for worldly gain, but a calling, to be
used to show others the way. Be prepared to feel the cold anger of
others who want to turn you into something that you are not. There
is a woman in Lasonville who blames me for her family's financial
hardship. There were others. I was young and didn't understand. I
would tell people about my dreams, about what I saw. River,
remember you can't predict the future, but you are only able to see
what God wills for your eyes. It is He who is in charge. I know you
will not be on earth for several years to come, River, but I eagerly
await your birth. I will write you soon.

Be Blessed,
Grandmother May

All the dreams! All the times I would see things before they
happened! I thought I was crazy! Dad knew! I turned my head to
prevent my tears from dropping on the next letter and sending its
fragile words into oblivion.

114

December 27, 1988

Dear River,
Merry Christmas! You finally arrived! Just like the vision, near the river. You were wailing and screaming at the top of your lungs. You're so beautiful! Your dad said it was fine for me to call you River, but your birth certificate would have to have another name. So, I wrote your name in the Bible, and had it engraved: Daniel Lakota Jackson. I named you after the prophet Daniel and your middle name in honor of your grandfather's people. River, may your journey through life's unexpected twists and thrilling turns be filled with the glory of His purpose.

Love,
Grandmother May

I didn't even hear Dad as he entered the room. He sat down on a wooden box and said, "Mom and I flew up yesterday. We wanted you to have some time by yourself. I have more letters. Your grandmother went through them and decided the ones she wanted you to read first. They were written for you so I have not read them.

"Baby, my mother was not tormented and she accepted her gift with responsibility. I know you are probably confused, but my mom found everything she needed in the Bible she gave you."

I broke the brief silence that lingered between us. "Dad, where do I go from here?"

"River, the Christmas season is not about Santa or things, it's a time for celebration and reflection. Read, pay attention to what you see, stay close to the truth and you will find the way."

- - -

December 28, 2006,

After everyone left, I stayed a little longer to write you this letter. Hopefully, you now understand how I came to this point in my life. You have not been born yet, but I see you looking up at the big orange moon in the sky. I will call you Sparrow because you are so

115

small in the world. I promise that your size doesn't matter. He will always see you and hear you. I know. I just put on one of Granny's favorite songs and I wish you were here to listen to it. I'm not afraid. I'll write you again. For now, I'm just going to lean back and close my eyes to soak in every word of, "It Came Upon and Midnight Clear."

Be Blessed,
River

Chapter Nine

Wanda **C**ampbell resides in the San Francisco/Bay Area with her husband of seventeen years and their three teenaged children.

After working years in healthcare, she is now a successful real estate agent. She enjoys traveling, reading and writing. Currently, Wanda serves as a minister at her local church and attends pre-seminary classes.

She's currently working on her first full novel, scheduled for release in the winter. For more information, visit her website at www.wandabcampbell.com.

Her contribution to *The Midnight Clear* is entitled **Mommy's Present**. It is her first published work.

Mommy's Present

Pamela Roberts threw her purse into the passenger seat of her Altima and quickly started the engine. She didn't have time to wait for the car to warm up so she prayed that one more cold start, coupled with the Bay Area's record breaking cold winter weather, wouldn't harm her only means of transportation. Pamela had thirty minutes to pick up her six-year-old son, Matthew from after-school care and then make it to Wednesday night Bible Study before seven o'clock.

After a quick glance over her left shoulder and without signaling, she pulled away from the curb and unto Powell Street. When signings at the title company where she worked as an escrow officer ran longer than normal, she was reminded of how much she disliked being a twenty-nine-year-old widowed single mother. It was days like this that caused her to rush and drive like a crazy woman down I-880.

A husband would really be handy right now to pick up Matthew, she thought. Sometimes she entertained the idea of remarrying, but in five years, no eligible candidates had surfaced, which was fine with her. Pamela had her hands full with Matthew, work, and her church activities.

Pulling into the after-school care parking lot, Pamela glanced down at the watch on her wrist; she made the drive in less than ten minutes. *Lord, please forgive me for the speeding records I just broke,* she prayed inwardly. Once inside, Matthew wanted to show her the popsicle-stick project he had been working on. Not wanting to disappoint her son, Pamela took a moment and listened to him explain that he was making a spaceship.

"I see," she said. The contraption looked more like a helicopter to her. "I can't wait to see the finished product, but now we have to hurry so you won't be late for the Christmas pageant rehearsal and I don't want to be late for Bible Study."

"Okay Mommy." Matthew smiled then ran to get his coat. There was no way he would miss his rehearsal since he had been chosen to play the starring role of Joseph in the church's annual Christmas pageant. Secure in his booster seat as they drove toward their destination, Matthew asked his mother what she wanted for Christmas.

"I don't know. What do you think I need?" Pamela answered, pulling into the church's parking lot.

Matthew thought for a while as his mother opened his door and loosed him from his child restraints. "I'll think about it and tell you later," he answered right before running in the direction of the fellowship hall where the Christmas pageant rehearsal was being held.

"Matthew, make sure you come inside the sanctuary as soon as rehearsal is over and listen to Sister Davis," Pamela called after him.

"Okay, Mommy." He said the words over his shoulder and was soon out of sight.

- - -

Before he went to bed that night, Matthew decided what present he would get his mother for Christmas. He liked the story of Joseph, Mary and baby Jesus, and wanted his family to be just like them, but without the animals. There was only one thing missing and Matthew thought that missing piece would make a great Christmas present for his mother. Matthew figured since Joseph married Mary and she already had baby Jesus in her stomach, God could send someone to marry his mother. His six-year-old mind told him, since his father was in heaven like baby Jesus' father, it was okay for him to have an earthly father like baby Jesus had.

On his Sponge Bob wall calendar he counted how many days were left until Christmas. Matthew had twenty-four days to search for the perfect present for his mother. When he said his prayers that night, Matthew didn't pray for the world like he usually did, he simply asked God to help him find the right present. Matthew didn't know where or how to look for his mother's present and he didn't want to ask anyone for help, for fear they would figure it out and tell his mother, so he relied on his six-year-old wisdom.

The way Matthew figured it, the present would have to be tall. His father was tall so he knew his mother liked tall men. And someone tall would be able to reach the top shelf and his mother wouldn't have to climb on chairs like she did now. The present would have to be brown-skinned like Matthew and his mother, so that Matthew and his future brothers and sisters would all look alike. The present's first name would have to begin with the letter "M". Matthew guessed his mother liked names that started with the

119

letter "M" because his father's name started with the letter "M" and so did his. The present's last name would have to sound nice too; Matthew didn't want the kids at school making fun of his new last name.

The present must like baseball because Matthew liked baseball and his mother didn't have time to play ball with him. The present must have a job, because Pastor Jackson said, "If a man doesn't work, a man should not eat." Eating was very important to Matthew, so this present would have to make sure his mother had money for food. The present must go to church and love God like his mother did, because Pastor Jackson also said, "Light and dark couldn't be together," and Matthew didn't want him or his mother to live in the dark. Since Matthew got the idea of the present at church, he'd figured he would start looking there first. So on first Sunday, Matthew went shopping.

The moment service began, Matthew's little brown eyes browsed over every unmarried man in the church. Some quickly got the big X because of their height and color. Matthew then sifted out all of the men he considered to be mean or unfriendly. That left only three possibilities: Deacon Blake, Minister Combs, and Brother Stevenson. While Pastor Jackson preached something about letting your neighbor slap you 490 times and giving all of your coats to your enemy, little Matthew assessed the three candidates.

Matthew decided Deacon Blake wouldn't make a good present because he was too old and wouldn't be able to play baseball with him. Besides that, Deacon Blake always fell asleep while Pastor Jackson preached. Matthew remembered his mother telling him that Pastor Jackson preaches the Word of God and that the Word of God is very important. With his six-year-old mind, Matthew figured if Deacon Blake could fall asleep on something as important as the Word of God, he would fall asleep on his mother when she needed to talk to him too.

Minister Combs was younger and he stayed awake while Pastor Jackson preached, but Matthew didn't like the bright colored shiny suits he wore all the time. In Matthew's opinion, the yellow suit he had on now made him look like an extra-large banana. Matthew also didn't like his last name. The kids at school were sure to poke fun at him for having a last name like Combs. That left Brother Stevenson.

120

Matthew liked Brother Stevenson because he was always nice to him. Even when he caught him playing around the water fountain, Brother Stevenson would speak softly and tell him to stop playing with the water. Matthew also liked his last name. Through little Matthew's eyes, Brother Stevenson looked about the same age as his mother, he was tall and he looked strong, like Matthew's father did in the picture on his dresser. Matthew knew Brother Stevenson had a job because every Wednesday he wore his cable company uniform to Bible Study and he drove the cable company's van. On Sundays he drove his big black SUV and Matthew liked big black cars. Brother Stevenson coached the church's baseball team so he would be able to play with Matthew. On Sundays, Brother Stevenson dressed nice too.

Matthew guessed Brother Stevenson really loved God because he always stood during praise and worship. He would sing and clap his hands; sometimes Brother Stevenson would even dance. When Pastor Jackson preached, Brother Stevenson not only stayed awake, but Matthew noticed he also took notes like his mother did. The only thing that troubled little Matthew about Brother Stevenson was that he didn't know if his first name started with the letter "M." Matthew decided to continue his investigation after service. Right now, he needed to listen to Pastor Jackson because he wasn't sure how many times he should let the kids at school slap him around before he was supposed to give them his new coat.

After service, little Matthew headed straight for the water fountain to wait for his prospect. "Hello, Brother Stevenson," Matthew said and then added, "I didn't play in the water today."

"I'm happy to hear that," Brother Stevenson said while smiling and rubbing Matthew's head.

Matthew looked around to make sure his mother wasn't coming. "Brother Stevenson, can I ask you a question?"

"Matthew, you can ask me whatever you like," Brother Stevenson answered and squatted so he would be eye level with the little boy.

"Brother Stevenson, what's your first name?" Matthew closed his eyes, held his breath and crossed his fingers.

"Matthew, what are you doing out here? Haven't I told you not to leave the sanctuary, unless I do? Were you playing in the water

121

again?" The sound of Pamela's voice startled both Matthew and Brother Stevenson.

Simultaneously, little Matthew opened his eyes, uncrossed his fingers and exhaled. Brother Stevenson turned to see Pamela glaring at her son.

"No, we were just having a little friendly conversation," Brother Stevenson answered and offered Pamela a smile.

"For real, Mommy. See, my clothes are still dry." Matthew stepped in front of Brother Stevenson so his mother could examine his shirt.

"All right," Pamela said to her son; although, she didn't see his shirt because her eyes were still locked into the smile of the man who squatted beside him.

"Sister Roberts, I hope you don't mind me talking with Matthew from time to time," Brother Stevenson said, rising to his full height. "He's a good kid and he loves baseball just like I do," he added and then once again rubbed Matthew's head.

"That's fine, as long as he's not a problem," Pamela answered returning his smile and taking her son by the hand.

"Matthew's not a problem at all," he answered still rubbing the boy's head.

Seeing the big smile on her son's face and the happiness in his eyes as he looked up at Brother Stevenson, reminded Pamela of how much her son needed a steady positive male role model in his life.

"Thank you for taking out time with my son," Pamela said sincerely," but we had better get going; it's a long drive to my parents' house."

"I'll see you later, little buddy," Brother Stevenson said to Matthew. He offered Pamela another smile before he said, "Have a blessed week, Sister Roberts." Then he walked away. Brother Stevenson had taken only three steps when he realized he never answered Matthew's question. "Micah," he called out to Matthew just as mother and son were exiting the vestibule. "My first name is Micah."

Little Matthew's eyes bulged. "Thank you, Brother Stevenson!" he yelled and started giggling.

On the forty-minute ride to Vallejo to visit his grandparents, little Matthew couldn't stop smiling. So far, Brother Stevenson was

122

perfect. Matthew tried to think of one thing he didn't like about him, but couldn't. He was almost sure Brother Stevenson would make the right present, but first he had a few more questions, just to make sure his mother would like him. Wednesday night Bible Study couldn't come fast enough for Matthew.

"What are you so happy about?" Pamela asked, looking through the rearview mirror.

"You'll see," Matthew answered through a returning giggle.

- - -

Wednesday night, during Bible Study, Pamela found herself looking in the direction of Brother Stevenson on more than one occasion. Up until this past Sunday when she realized how fond Matthew was of him, she hadn't given him a second thought. She didn't know that much about him except that he was Pastor Jackson's nephew and had joined the church about a year ago. By the inscription on the uniform he wore, Pamela knew he worked for the local cable company and she knew he coached baseball, but that was it. Tonight she noticed how intently he listened to Pastor Jackson and vigorously took notes.

He's definitely a good influence on Matthew and he's cute, she thought, then quickly tried to refocus her attention on Pastor Jackson. Pamela was careful not to read too much into his relationship with Matthew. It was very possible for Micah Stevenson to be interested in her son and not interested in her. That was fine with her because she thought Matthew needed a male in his life more than she did.

Micah took so many notes, that he filled his entire yellow pad. Normally he didn't write that much, but he had to do something to stop himself from staring at Pamela Roberts. He found the mocha colored woman with the soft brown, almond shaped eyes and full lips, beautiful! And he thought her medium five-foot six-inch frame housed her shape well. Micah loved the way her brown, curly hair hung loosely around her shoulders.

Unbeknownst to Pamela, he'd been observing her since the first time he caught Matthew playing in the water fountain. He'd been studying Pamela in church and in her interactions with other members. One of his favorite church activities was watching Pamela dance in the spirit. Micah especially liked how well she

123

took care of her son and appreciated the fact that he never saw Pamela hanging around men and her name was never mentioned in church gossip.

Next week, I'll sit in the back so I can't see her, then I'll be able to concentrate, Micah thought to himself.

- - -

As soon as pageant rehearsal was over, Matthew headed straight for the sanctuary in search of Brother Stevenson. Since Bible Class and rehearsal ended simultaneously, little Matthew had to maneuver between the adults who were coming out the sanctuary at the same time he was trying to go in. Frustrated, Matthew gave up and decided to stand outside in the parking lot next to the cable van.

"Hey little buddy," Micah said when he saw his little friend playing with his door handle.

Matthew's face lit up. "Hello Brother Stevenson, I was waiting for you," he said excitedly.

"Matthew, are you supposed to be out here by yourself?"

"No, but I needed to talk to you."

"Is something wrong?" Micah asked, rubbing Matthew's head.

"No, I just wanted to ask you some more questions."

"Okay, but let's go back inside before your mother starts looking for you," Micah said, taking Matthew by the hand. "We can talk while we walk."

"Brother Stevenson, do you eat all of your vegetables?"

Micah thought that was an odd question, but he answered it anyway. "Yes I do, I love vegetables."

Good, Matthew thought, *Mommy likes it when I eat all of my vegetables.* "Brother Stevenson, do you make up your bed everyday and keep your room clean?"

Another strange question, Micah thought, looking down into Matthew's expectant eyes. "Most days, I make up my bed and on the weekends, I clean my room."

Good, because Mommy doesn't like a messy room, Matthew thought again. "One more question, Brother Stevenson. Do you have any kids?" Matthew reasoned if there were other children involved they should meet now, so they could see if they would be able to share each others' toys after Brother Stevenson married his mother.

At that question Micah Stevenson stopped walking and looked down at his buddy. "Why did you ask me that?"

"Because I want to know," Matthew answered honestly. "Are you mad at me for asking?" The boy looked worried.

Micah reassured him by rubbing his head. "No, I'm not mad at you and no I do not have any children, but I will like some one day."

Little Matthew was smiling again; Brother Stevenson had passed the test. He was going to make the perfect present for his mother. Now all Matthew had to do was figure out how to wrap him up and put him under the Christmas tree.

- - -

With two weeks left before Christmas, Pamela and Matthew spent Saturday morning shopping for her parents' Christmas presents. Pamela really hated shopping in malls. If it weren't for Matthew, she'd do all of her shopping online or through a catalog. Matthew enjoyed going from store to store trying to find the perfect gift for his grandparents but today, Matthew also wanted to take a picture with Santa Claus. For Pamela, that meant at least an hour waiting in line with a bunch of loud and impatient children bumping into her and stepping on her feet.

To her surprise, the holiday crowd at Stoneridge Mall wasn't as bad as she thought. The wait for Santa was only half an hour. Pamela's eyes were glued on Matthew as he told Santa what he wanted for Christmas. It was a blessing to her that Matthew was a kid who was simple to please. The only things her son wanted for Christmas were to play Tee Ball in the spring and some new animated movies.

"Hello, Sister Roberts." Micah's deep voice from behind, startled her and Pamela suddenly turned around.

"Brother Stevenson, what are you doing here? I thought men didn't shop until Christmas Eve," She said in light of the bags in his left hand.

"Not this man. I hate waiting until the last minute. I like to take my time and pick out the perfect gifts."

Pamela took a good look at the man in front of her. This was the first time she'd seen him outside of church and in casual clothing. The milk chocolate brother was well put together with his dark brown eyes and full lips that were surrounded by a neatly

125

trimmed goatee. Climbing poles for the cable company sure had done his six-foot-plus body some good.

"Hi, Brother Stevenson!" Her son's voice interrupted her inspection.

"Hey, little buddy." Micah set his bags down and kneeled so he could fully return Matthew's hug.

"I took a picture with Santa," Matthew announced happily.

"I know; I saw you while I was speaking with your mother."

Little Matthew looked at his mother and smiled when an idea popped into his head. Turning back to Micah he said, "Brother Stevenson, we're going ice skating after we finish shopping, do you want to come?"

Pamela couldn't believe her ears. "Matthew, I'm sure he has plans already; isn't that right, Brother Stevenson?" Pamela looked at him apologetically.

"Actually, I don't," Micah said, standing up. "I'd love to go ice-skating with you, little buddy." He then faced Pamela, "Sister Roberts, please call me Micah."

Pamela kept her cool. "Only if you call me Pamela." Micah smiled at her and Pamela nearly blushed.

Out of habit, she took Matthew by the hand before they started walking. With his free hand Micah took Matthew's other hand. As the three of them walked through the crowded mall, Matthew couldn't stop smiling; he knew for sure, his mother was going to like her present. To him, she already liked it.

Although Pamela had reservations about Micah joining them, she had to admit she enjoyed his company and watching him interact with Matthew on the ice.

Micah spent so much time picking up both Pamela and Matthew from off the ice, he barely skated. But that was okay; seeing Pamela smile and hearing her laugh was worth it. Pamela enjoyed being picked up by Micah's strong arms so much that a couple of times, she fell on purpose. Before the three parted, Micah was tempted to ask for her number but changed his mind. He didn't want her to think he was using her son to get to her.

Later on that night when his grandmother called and asked Matthew when he wanted to go shopping for his mother's Christmas present, little Matthew told his grandmother he didn't

126

need to go shopping and that he wanted his grandparents to come to the Christmas pageant on Christmas Eve. After the pageant, Matthew was going to give his mother her present.

- - -

The following Sunday, during service, Micah caught Pamela staring at him during praise and worship. Upon realizing she'd been busted, Pamela closed her eyes, jerked and waved her hand, like she suddenly felt the spirit. To make it look even more convincing, she shook her head from side to side and yelled, "Thank ya!" Micah laughed, not buying the cute act for one second.

With Christmas Eve only two days away, Matthew still had to figure out how to get his mother's present ready for her. First, he had to make sure his present would show up, so as soon the final rehearsal ended, Matthew went looking for Brother Stevenson and found him walking in the parking lot to the cable van. When Matthew grabbed his hand, Micah slowed his pace for his little buddy.

"Brother Stevenson, are you coming to the Christmas pageant on Christmas Eve?"

Micah rubbed his little friend's head. "You know I wouldn't miss seeing you perform."

"Good." Matthew smiled, "Can you wear a blue and gray suit?" Matthew heard his mother say she liked men in blue and gray suits.

"Uh, okay," Micah answered cautiously.

"And can you buy some flowers?"

Micah narrowed his eyes but continued walking. "Why do I need flowers?"

"Because, my mother likes flowers..." Matthew stopped walking. "Oops," he said, covering his mouth with his hands.

Micah squatted to Matthew's level, "Matthew, why do you want me to bring your mother flowers?" he asked in a gentle voice. Micah had an idea, but wanted to hear Matthew's plan.

"Because." Matthew looked scared; just like he did the first day Micah caught him playing in the water fountain.

"Because what?" Micah asked.

Matthew covered his face with his hands but didn't answer.

"Matthew, do you have something planned for your mother and me?"

127

Matthew nodded yes from behind his little hands. Micah gently removed the boy's hands and held them in his.

"Okay, little buddy, why don't you tell me all about it?"

- - -

Two days later, after the pageant, little Matthew ran to the reception in the fellowship hall in search of his mother and grandparents. He found them standing near the Christmas tree. *Perfect*, he thought. Brother Stevenson couldn't fit under the tree, but at least Matthew could give his mother her present near the tree. After receiving hugs and accolades from his family, Matthew instructed his mother to close her eyes.

"Wait right here, Mommy, I'll be right back with your present." Matthew smiled at his grandmother before he went off to find his mother's present. He returned shortly thereafter and said, "Okay Mommy, you can open your eyes now."

Pamela assumed her son would have the present in his hand. Upon opening her eyes, she automatically looked down at her son who was wearing the biggest grin. Then she looked over at Micah standing next to him with a matching grin on his face.

"Merry Christmas, Mommy!" Matthew shouted and started giggling.

"Merry Christmas, Matthew; Merry Christmas, Micah," Pamela replied, wondering what happened to her Christmas present.

"Do you like your present, Mommy?" Matthew asked with expectancy.

"I don't know," Pamela shrugged, "you haven't given it to me yet."

"Mommy, it's right here," little Matthew said, holding out Micah's hand to his mother.

Pamela searched Micah's eyes for an answer; he didn't give her one, just continued grinning. Pamela then turned to her parents for an explanation, they had the same goofy grins on their faces that Matthew and Micah had. It was obvious to her they knew more than she did.

Finally, Pamela kneeled down to Matthew. "Sweetheart, I don't understand."

Matthew blew into the air in frustration. "Mommy, Brother Stevenson is your present!"

Pamela looked up at Micah who was still grinning. It wasn't until then that she noticed the flowers in his hand and that he was wearing a blue and gray suit. Since neither her parents nor Micah were going to point out Matthew's error to him, she took a shot.

"Sweetheart, Brother Stevenson is a person and you can't give a person away as a gift."

"Yes you can, Mommy," Matthew said nodding his little head. "God gave us His Son and Jesus is a person."

Pamela laughed at her son's analogy. "Baby, that's different. God gave us His Son so that we could have a chance at eternal life."

"That's not so different. I'm giving you Brother Stevenson so that you can have a chance at life and not be by yourself anymore." Matthew's revelation left Pamela speechless. "Mommy, you asked me what I thought you needed. You need a husband like Mary had."

Pamela looked back at her parents again. Now she understood why they where still smiling, they agreed with her son. Inwardly, so did she, which was why tears now rolled down her cheeks. Matthew, in his innocence, had reached a part of her she thought was hidden.

"Don't cry, Mommy," Matthew said after he handed her the handkerchief Micah had given him. "I made sure he was right for you. He's tall so he can reach the top shelf and he likes vegetables and keeps his room clean. And Mommy, he never falls asleep when Pastor Jackson preaches. I know because I've been watching him."

Pamela couldn't help but to laugh along with the group, at the scale that Matthew had used to measure the man he'd chosen for his mother. When she finished laughing and crying she looked at her son and wondered when he had become so wise and insightful.

"Thank you baby for looking out for me," she said while hugging him tightly.

"Does this mean you like your present?" Matthew just had to know.

On her feet again, Pamela looked over at Micah, "Are those for me?" she asked, referring to the flowers.

"That depends on if you're going to keep me or return me."

"My son didn't pressure you into this did he?"

"Matthew just told me his plan two days ago but I've been watching you for months."

Micah was still smiling, but the sincere look in his eyes told Pamela this wasn't a game to him. Micah was seriously interested in her. Pamela was definitely interested in him too.

"Mommy, do you like it?" Matthew pestered.

"Baby, don't be stupid," Pamela's mother whispered in her ear when she hesitated.

"Yes sweetheart, I like it," she said, finally answering her son's question, but holding a steady gaze with Micah. "Can I have my flowers now?"

Watching his mother accept the flowers from Brother Stevenson, Matthew jumped up and down; then giggled uncontrollably when his mother said, "Micah, that suit looks good on you."

"Thank you, Pamela. Does this mean you're going to keep me?"

"Well, I'm certainly not going to send you back," Pamela blushed.

"Once you get to know me, you won't want to send me back." The strength and confidence in his voice gave Pamela goose bumps.

"Confident, aren't you?" Pamela asked.

"I have to be, I come with a Life Time Warranty, 100% satisfaction guaranteed!"

Pamela giggled along with her son; she couldn't wait to get acquainted with her real-life present.

Chapter Ten

Kendra Norman-Bellamy was born in West Palm Beach, Florida and is a national bestselling novelist. Her current titles include: *For Love & Grace, Because of Grace, More Than Grace, Thicker Than Water, A Love So Strong, Three Fifty-Seven A.M., One Prayer Away* and *Crossing Jhordan's River*, which peeked at #1 on *Essence* magazine's Best Sellers list. She has also reached bestseller status on lists compiled by Wal-Mart, Black Expressions, and *Booking Matters Magazine*.

In addition to novel writing, Kendra is also a columnist for national periodicals, *Global Woman Magazine* and *Hope for Women Magazine* and a reoccurring contributing writer for *Precious Times Magazine*.

As the founder and president of KNB Publications, LLC, Kendra has helped many aspiring writers achieve their goals of becoming published authors. She is a member of, as well as the Georgia Area Coordinator for the national American Christian Fiction Writers (ACFW) organization. Kendra is founder and moderator of The Writer's Hut, an online support system for writers. For more information, visit her online at www.knb-publications.com.

Kendra currently resides in metropolitan Atlanta, Georgia with her husband and two teenaged daughters.

Her contribution to *The Midnight Clear* is entitled, **Three Wyze Men**.

Three Wyze Men

The Crave Building, a structure whose primary function was to house the activities of the youth ministry of Total Grace Christian Center, had never before been so immaculately decorated. The building was conveniently located on a main access road in Decatur, Georgia, a suburb of Atlanta. And as the sun was beginning to set, the holiday lights that surrounded the building's exterior drew double-takes from Friday evening commuters.

Steven, the second in command in the business that his family owned and operated, stood back and gave the inside adornment one last inspection. The decorating team couldn't call it a day until Steven said so; and after seeing him give the nod, the group of eight men and four women took a collective sigh of relief before starting the chore of packing away their tools.

"Dang man…and we thought Mr. W. was a tough cookie."

Steven flashed a half-smile at the worker who'd spoken the words, and then watched him walk away. Seems like they would be used to it by now. Although seventy-year-old Jake Wyze had founded the business forty years ago and indeed governed it with an austere eye, it was his son, Steven, who never settled for less than excellence.

- - -

"Hey, Steve. You just getting home, man?"

That was the greeting that Steven received when he finally walked into his house at ten o'clock. He'd been the last one to leave the building, making sure everything had been cleaned up, turned off and put away before the doors were locked for the last time before the big day. Tomorrow was the twenty-third, still two days before Christmas, but the day that the Organization of Christian Women would hold their annual holiday gathering. For more than one reason, Steven needed for the group to walk away impressed.

"Yeah, I'm just getting in." Steven gave his housemate a look of disapproval as he removed his coat and hung it on the coat rack near the door. "What have you been up to all day, Daryl? Why didn't you come and help out?"

"Man, this is Christmas break for me. Pop said I didn't have to spend it working with y'all if I didn't want to."

Steven narrowed his eyes, but didn't have the energy to make an argument of it. Instead, he picked up the basketball that Daryl had left in the middle of the living room floor and tossed it at him. Quick with his hands, Daryl caught it and then flashed a smile fit for any toothpaste commercial. It was a good catch. Steven couldn't help but return the grin.

At seventeen, Daryl Wyze was the third man in the enterprise of Three Wyze Men Events Planning & Catering Services. It was ironic, since he spent very few hours working there, except during the summer. Though there were seventeen years between them, Daryl and Steven had developed a relationship that was closer than most brothers. Like Steven was at his age, Daryl was a free spirit. But unlike Steven was as a high school student, Daryl was well-mannered, focused and most importantly, saved. It was the latter that kept Steven from worrying that Daryl would make the same bad choices that he'd made.

Steven made a brief stop in his bedroom to collect his pajamas and then headed to the bathroom where, for several minutes, he stood under the hot running shower, trying to rinse away the tiredness. It had been a long month. For Three Wyze Men, the last quarter of each year was always a busy time.

Busy is always a blessing. That's what Jake Wyze stressed to the family and staff that helped to make Three Wyze Men one of the most successful events coordinating and food service corporations in the city of Atlanta. Because of it, Steven made a conscious effort to never complain. His father was getting older now and although Jake was still in good health, he was no longer able to run the business with the same fervor as he'd done for the last four decades. Jake still came to all of the roundtable executive meetings and he still had a hand in all of the company's decisions. But three months ago, on his seventieth birthday, he'd all but stepped aside as the functioning director.

"You've come a long way, son," he'd told Steven with an embrace. "Once while, I thought I'd made a mistake when I gave the company its name. First of all, it looked like your mama wasn't ever gonna have anything but girls." Jake stopped to add a hearty chuckle. "Then when God finally gave us a boy, I thought you wouldn't even live long enough for me to know what it was like to be proud of a son. But you did; and I do."

133

Jake's seventieth birthday was a day of reflection for both of them. Daily, Steven thanked God that his parents never gave up on him. He'd been a rebellious child and his misbehavior shadowed him until he was twenty-four. Seeing one of his best friends shot at pointblank range, and then watching that same friend take his final gasp of breath as he lay in Steven's arms while Steven tearfully begged him not to die, was the moment that made him realize what a dangerous life he'd been living.

Instantly, he was scared straight. The next Sunday, Steven found himself at the altar of Vision of Hope, the church where his family worshipped every Sunday, giving his life to God.

Although she was ill, and not feeling her best, Steven had never seen his mother happier than she was on that Sunday afternoon. Her body was permeated with cancer, but on that day, she danced around the church like a healthy twenty-year-old. A few months later, Steven was helping his father and sisters bury her. He found comfort in the fact that his mother had lived to see him make a life change. When Melba Wyze died, she was at peace, knowing that all of her children were now walking in what she often called, "the pathway of righteousness."

"Daryl!" A sudden surge of cold water snapped Steven back to the present. Daryl must have heard him because the water quickly returned to its heated state.

As an unwritten rule, each of them knew not to turn on faucets or flush toilets while the other was in the shower. Steven had been running the water for quite some time and had not once soaped his cloth. Doing so, he quickly gave himself a thorough cleaning, rinsed away the lather, and stepped from the shower into a bathroom fogged with steam.

Within minutes, Steven had dried himself, gotten dressed and was back in his bedroom. Just as he finished his prayers, he heard a knock at his door.

"Come in."

Daryl opened the door and flipped the light switch so that he had a better view. "You going to bed already?"

Steven looked at the numbers that illuminated from the clock/radio on his nightstand. It wasn't quite eleven o'clock yet, but his body told him that it needed to catch up on some of the rest that it had been neglecting.

"Yeah. Why?"

Daryl shrugged. "I ain't hardly seen you all week, Steve. I thought maybe we'd watch a movie. You're the only somebody in the world who ain't seen *Ray* yet. I bought the DVD months ago and we still haven't watched it together."

"Man, you've seen that movie a million times."

"I know," Daryl replied. "But *you* haven't. I bought it so that you could see it and then maybe you'll understand why I've seen it a million times."

Steven sighed and after a brief moment of thought, shook his head. "Maybe some other time, Daryl. You haven't been working day and night, trying to keep up with the demands of the business. I'm tired, man. Let's do it after I get past the Christmas thing this weekend; okay?"

"Man, you act like you older than Pop," Daryl said with a curled upper lip. "I could have hung out with the guys from the church tonight. I told them I needed to get home to spend some time with you. Man, I betcha they just getting started having fun at Lee's house with that…"

Daryl's voice muffled as he stepped back in the hallway and closed the room door behind him. Steven sat on the bed and buried his face in his hands. Daryl was right. The two of them hadn't spent much time together since they'd attended one of the high school football games back in October.

Steven allowed his back to slowly fall against the mattress. His aching muscles felt better just being in a horizontal position. If he closed his eyes for two…maybe, three minutes, Steven knew that he'd be sound asleep. But he couldn't do it. Daryl needed him; and ten years ago, when he became a responsible and righteous man, he promised God that he'd always be there for Daryl. The teenager never asked for much; and when he did, it was never anything unreasonable.

Forcing himself off of the comfort of his bed, Steven went back into the bathroom and splashed his face with cold water. It helped; but not much. When he opened his bedroom door and stepped into the hall, the smell of buttered popcorn filled his nostrils and Steven's stomach rumbled. He'd failed to eat dinner and now, getting up to join Daryl seemed like a good idea on more than one level.

135

When Daryl saw him round the corner into the living room, the smile he'd flashed earlier in the night returned. Steven smiled back as he took a seat on the couch beside the boy that he knew admired him more than any other. Some things were worth a little sleep deprivation.

--- ---

The Christmas party for the Organization of Christian Women wasn't set to begin until six o'clock in the evening, but at five-thirty, the building was already almost full. The importance of having good work ethics was something that Jake Wyze had successfully passed along to Steven. Two hours before starting time, not only was Steven already at the venue, but he'd demanded the same of the supporting staff of Three Wyze Men.

He enjoyed sitting up with Daryl until two o'clock this morning, watching Jamie Foxx render an excellent portrayal of the late, great Ray Charles, but doing so made it hard for him to get up four hours later to begin the task of making arrangements for tonight's meal. With a spread that included everything from lemon pepper chicken, tender roast beef and fried turkey, to four choices of side dishes, three homemade desserts and freshly squeezed lemonade, it was a meal that took some time to prepare.

Born to the union of a sharecropper and a preacher's daughter, Steven's father rose from poverty and made a better life for himself when he attended the Culinary Institute of America in New York, the world's oldest culinary college, and received his formal training. Seven years ago, Steven followed in Jake's footsteps, relocating to The Big Apple for thirty-eight months, just long enough to achieve a Bachelor's degree to ensure that he would be equipped to continue the legacy that his father built from the ground up.

"Well, son," Jake said as he delivered a pat to Steven's back, "I think you really outdid yourself this time. Daryl said you'd been putting in a lot of overtime and I sure can see the fruits of it. Good job."

"Thanks, Pop." Steven beamed. Even at this stage of his life, his father's approval meant a lot to him.

"The folks out there are raving about the decorations," Jake added.

"Well, I can't take too much credit for that. The decorating team did the actual work. I just handed out orders." Steven laughed as he wiped his hand on his chef's jacket and then removed it to unveil a navy blue suit. "I guess I'll have to wait until they start their meals before I can really know whether or not I've achieved success tonight."

As if he could see better without them, Jake removed his eyeglasses and peered closely at his son's attire. "You're mighty dressed up to be on duty, aren't you?"

Steven laughed at his father's facial expression and then said, "I'm just overseeing, Pop. I'm not actually serving tonight. So I didn't see a need to wear the white jacket."

"I see," Jake said with a knowing smirk. "A lot of pretty women out there, too. I suppose you'll look better dressed like that than dressed like the help, huh?"

"Pop..."

"Boy, I ain't no fool," Jake said as he placed his frames back on his face. "I'm seventy—not dead."

Steven burst into a hearty laugh as he watched his father remove his white jacket to uncover a suit of his own; black and sharp.

"Like father, like son, I guess," Jake said. "I mean, this isn't just a crowd of beautiful women. This is a crowd of women who love the Lord. You and Daryl been telling me for five years that I'm a good catch with a lot to offer and I should allow myself to love again. Who knows? Maybe tonight's the night for both of us."

"You *do* look good, Pop," Steven remarked.

And he did. Even at seventy, Jake still had the handsome features that he'd passed on to his offspring. All of the Wyze children looked more like their father than their mother, but Steven was almost his replica. They both stood at just a hair shy of six feet tall, both were broad shouldered and both men had brown skin the color of maple syrup. Jake's hair was fully grey and at just thirty-four, hints of silver could already be seen in Steven's low cut fade and in his mustache and goatee.

"Listen, son," Jake said, struggling to keep a straight face as he spoke. "Let me apologize in advance if I catch the eye of whatever ladies you find interesting. These good looks of mine are a curse and a blessing all in one."

That drew another burst of laughter from Steven. He loved it when Jake was in a playful mood. It reminded Steven of the days

137

when he was a little boy, riding his father's back. The days before he became mischievous and wayward. Jake turned to walk away, but Steven's next words stopped him.

"Actually, Pop, I'm only looking to catch the attention of one lady."

"Oh?"

Taking his father by the arm, Steven led him to a corner as if he thought one of the workers who were now coming in and out of the area where they stood, would hear them.

"There's this girl that I went to high school with – Selena Ford. She's a part of this organization. When the president sent me an email of the headcount, attached to it was a list containing the names of all the confirmed attendees. Her name was on there."

"You know how many Selena Fords there might be in this big old world, boy? How do you know she's the same one you went to school with?"

Steven shifted his feet. "I hinted around and found out. When I spoke to Mrs. Peak over the phone, I cited that she'd sent me her entire guest list and commented that I knew a few because they were wives of some of the pastors in the area. Then I casually mentioned that I knew a girl by the name of Selena Ford, but the one on the list lived in North Carolina and the girl I knew lived in Lithonia, Georgia. She said that the Selena on her list used to live in Lithonia, but moved to North Carolina to attend Winston-Salem State University. When she graduated, she remained there after accepting a job offer."

Jake removed his glasses again. This time, he tucked them in the inside pocket of his suit jacket and readjusted his tie. "I know it's been some years, but I can't say that I ever remember you mentioning her when you were in high school."

"I probably didn't. You know the types of girls that I was drawn to and who were drawn to me back then."

Jake nodded and then shook his head as he recalled the bitter memories.

"Well, Selena wasn't one of those girls," Steven said. "She was a church girl. She was rather thin and kind of nerdy, but secretly, I always admired her. She was really pretty and smart, too. But she wasn't one of the cool girls."

"You mean, she wasn't one of the *loose* girls," Jake challenged.

138

"Yeah. She didn't put out. As a matter of fact, I don't even think she was allowed to *go* out. She got picked at a lot. I…I picked at her a lot." Steven dropped his head. "I was really mean to her back then."

Both men quieted as two staff members passed them on their way to carry out trays of food to set on the burners. Mixing and mingling had been going on for quite some time and Christmas music, both classic and contemporary, blasted through the speaker system. It was nearing time for the guests to be served.

"Well, one thing for sure," Jake said, "before you try to get her to take an interest in you, you're first going to have to show her how much you've changed."

"Honestly, I don't expect her to be interested in me, Pop. Not saying that I wouldn't want that, but I'm not expecting it. If she'll indulge me long enough just to allow me to apologize, it'll be more than I deserve. I think I owe her that."

"I think you do too, son."

"Mr. W., the guests are ready to be served," one of the women said as she peeked her head through the door, interrupting the men. "The lady in charge is introducing our catering service right now. Do you want one of us to address the crowd?"

After a thoughtful moment, Jake said, "No. Steven will do it."

It was a job that Jake almost always did, but Steven didn't ask any questions. It was all a part of the transition and he knew it. The open door allowed them to hear the president verbally acknowledge Three Wyze Men Events Planning & Catering Services. Straightening his jacket, Steven took a deep breath and walked through the doors to see a group of one hundred seventy-five women and men, standing and applauding.

"Thank you," he said.

The clapping died down and the people returned to their seats at the beautifully decorated round tables. Steven was accustomed to speaking to crowds, but today, knowing that somewhere in this one was Selena Ford, his heart pounded. So much so that he took a step away from the microphone for fear that the sounds of it would be amplified.

"To Mrs. Geraldine Peak, president of this God-inspired organization; thank you for entrusting your annual event to the expertise of Three Wyze Men. It is our sincere hope and prayer that

139

you do *not* find our services acceptable, but astounding. Our company was founded forty years ago by my father, Mr. Jake Wyze."

On cue, Jake walked through the doors and received his own standing ovation. When he grinned, Steven thought, for the first time, that while Jake had given him almost all of his other features, it was Daryl that had gotten his million dollar smile.

"Seventy has never looked so good, has it, ladies?" Steven remarked with pride as the cheers for his father increased.

When the people returned to their seats once again, Steven continued, feeling more at ease than when he first took the stand. "On behalf of Jake, Daryl, myself and our capable staff, I just want to reiterate how appreciative we are that of all of the professional caterers in Atlanta, you chose us to plan and carry out this occasion. Being that Three Wyze Men is built on the strong foundation of Christian principles, we are particularly honored when we host an event that in some way celebrates Jesus Christ. And as the Organization of Christian Women, you do that every day through the lifestyles that you lead and in the unselfish services that you offer others in your communities, your schools, and your churches. Merry Christmas to all of you. Enjoy your celebration and if there is anything that you need, please see me or one of the men or women in white. God bless."

As Steven relinquished the stage, he smiled as he watched his father go from table to table, greeting the women. Steven's eyes scanned the faces of those who had been the first in the food service line. Some of them had male companions; others didn't. Many threw him looks of approval as they passed him on their way back to their seats. Most of them were attractive in one way or another. But none of them was Selena.

Maybe she's not here. Maybe something came up and she was unable to make the trip. Steven felt a mixture of disappointment and relief as the thoughts flooded his mind. Selena's not being there would mean that he could breathe easier, not having to acknowledge the demons of his past. But it also would mean that he couldn't tell her how sorry he was that he'd helped to make her high school experience a trying and lonesome one.

"Son?"

140

Steven turned at the sound of his father's voice and his knees instantly weakened. Standing next to Jake was Selena Ford and in the fuchsia dressed that she wore, she was more beautiful than ever. The school-girl ponytail that she once wore, even as a senior, had been replaced by a short, sassy, feathered haircut that accentuated her face perfectly. Seventeen years had added about twenty pounds to her body, but every ounce of it had settled nicely.

"I believe you remember Selena Ford," Jake said with a toothy grin.

"H...Hi." Steven managed to extend his tingling hand, but Selena chose not to accept, choosing instead to make her hand unavailable by using it to tuck nonexistent stray hairs behind her ear. He wasn't surprised. Even her mumbled return greeting was more than he expected or merited, for that matter.

Breaking the elongated silence that followed, Jake asked, "Do you remember my son from high school?"

"Quite well; yes," Selena said, smiling at Jake, but not offering the same warmth to Steven. While her words were kind, the tone in which she said them erased any doubt that she recalled every bad thing Steven had ever said or done to her.

"And you remember her too, right son?"

Seeing the look on his father's face, that said *get it together and get it together now*, Steven swirled his tongue around in his mouth to try and replace the moisture that evaporated at the sight of his former high school classmate.

"Yes...yes, Pop, I do remember her. Do you mind...?"

"Not at all," Jake immediately said, happy to leave Selena and Steven to themselves.

"Can I talk to you privately for a moment?" Steven asked.

Selena paused, and when she raised her glass, for a split second, Steven thought she was going to toss the contents in his face. It would have been highly embarrassing, but quite justifiable.

Instead, she brought the glass to her lips and took a sip before quietly nodding and allowing Steven to lead the way to the area where, until now, only the staff members had been allowed. Pulling out a seat, he beckoned for her to sit and then did the same in one that was nearby.

As she sat in the offered chair, Selena seemed a bit more relaxed. Steven, on the other hand, fought to control nerves in the pit of his stomach that flopped around like fish out of water.

"How've you been?"

"I've been wonderful, Stevie. And yourself?"

Stevie. The name alone took him back nearly twenty years. Rarely did anyone refer to him by the nickname he thought he'd outgrown when he received his high school diploma. Steven thought it sounded juvenile and had dismissed it years ago. Now, coming from Selena's lips, the name had a strangely renewed appeal.

"I've been good. Not always; but lately, life has been great, actually."

She didn't reply.

"Listen, Selena…"

"Your father is charming. When I told him my name he instantly knew who I was. How is that?"

She wasn't sympathetic to his anxieties, and while Steven would have paid good money for more time to get his racing thoughts together, he knew this was his only chance to try and make things right. Selena was offering no grace period that Steven could use to tiptoe around the real issue.

"I told him," he admitted. "I saw your name on the RSVP list and learned that you were the same Selena Ford that went to Miller Grove High School. I told Pop that I owed you an apology and was hoping for a chance to offer it."

Selena's eyes softened, but she remained quiet, opting instead to drink more lemonade. Steven took a deep breath and accepted her silence as permission to continue.

"Listen, Selena. When I walked the halls of Miller Grove, I was a terrible kid. Funny thing is, I thought I was cool. All those years when I thought I had it going on, I was really just stupid, ignorant, disrespectful, callous, idiotic, heartless…"

Steven was running out of words, but the look on Selena's face told him that he could continue his list for the next hour and she'd have no qualms with any of the awful terms he used to describe the person he was back then.

"I'm sorry," he said. "I'm sorry for every wisecrack, insult and mean prank that was directed toward you and I hope you can forgive me. That's all I know to say, Selena. I'm sorry. I really am."

She nodded, but if she accepted his apology, her forgiveness remained unspoken. Steven found hope in her quiet tolerance.

"If one good thing came out of all of my foolhardiness, it's that I did finally get my life together," he added. "I know now what you knew a long time ago. That serving God is worth being different and unpopular."

"You?" Selena was visibly astonished, but her silence was finally broken.

"Yeah," Steven smiled. "Ten years blood-washed. Ten years clean."

Selena's smiled at him for the first time and she placed a supportive hand on top of his and squeezed. "That's wonderful, Stevie. Wow. Stevie Wyze got saved. God is good, isn't He?"

Steven stared at her left hand covering his right. There was no ring that symbolized a commitment. "All the time," he whispered.

"Hey, Steve!"

The door of the room where they sat flung open, startling both of them.

"Oops, my bad. I'll come back."

"No, no," Steven said as he stood and beckoned for Daryl to enter. He welcomed a moment to breathe. "Come here. I want you to meet someone." Selena stood as he gestured in her direction. "Daryl, this is Ms. Selena Ford. She and I graduated high school together."

"Dang, for real, though?" Daryl said as he shook her hand. "I hope the girls I graduate with look this good when they get old...er," he quickly added. "Older."

Selena laughed and said, "Thank you, Daryl. I'll take that as a compliment."

"It is," he assured her.

"Glad you could join us during your Christmas break," Steven teased, tugging on the company's white jacket that Daryl wore.

"Yeah, I thought I'd stop in and help out a little. It was the least I could do after keeping you up all night."

"Thanks," Steven said, giving Daryl's arm an appreciative pat. "You needed me for something?"

"Nah; I'm cool. I just wanted you to know I was here. You seen Pop? He's a chick magnet with the over fifty group. I'm gonna go out here and keep an eye on him."

"Yeah, you do that," Steven laughed. "I'll be out in a minute."

"He looks just like you did in high school," Selena remarked when the door closed behind Daryl. "I knew you had older sisters, but I don't think I was aware that you had a younger brother."

"Daryl is not my brother...well, he is, but he's not."

"Excuse me?"

"Daryl is my son."

"Excuse me?" Selena repeated.

Steven couldn't help but laugh at her dumbfounded expression. "Yeah. My parents adopted him when he was a baby and cared for him during the time that his biological father was a big zero. I've had full custody of him since he was eight, but on paper, legally, my dad and his dad are one and the same. So, in a sense, Daryl and I are brothers as well as father and son."

"He's taller than you are," Selena observed. "How old is he?"

"Seventeen."

"That would mean that you were..."

"Seventeen," Steven said, finishing the sentence for her. "You remember Eva Edwards?"

Instinctively, Selena grimaced, but tried to erase it before Steven could notice. Her attempt failed.

"Yeah," he laughed. "That's the one. I found out that she was pregnant right before we marched for graduation. Her parents wanted her to have an abortion and my parents didn't. They promised her folks that they'd pay for any expenses that their insurance didn't cover and they'd take full responsibility for the child once he was born. And that's what they did."

"And Eva?"

"The last time I heard, she was living somewhere in California."

"Does he ever see her?"

"No," Steven said, feeling surprisingly comfortable discussing the matter with Selena. "He doesn't even know who she is. That was a part of the agreement that my parents made too. They promised not to expose her identity. I guess you could say that her family really wanted nothing to do with him...or me, for that

144

matter. Eva and I weren't in love or anything like that. It was just…well, you know."

Selena nodded. "But what if he should ask about her?"

"If he ever wants to know, I'll tell him. I didn't make the promise and I feel as though he has a right to know. Daryl is aware that Eva doesn't want any affiliation with him and he's always said he doesn't want anything to do with her either. That may change in the future, but honestly, I don't expect it to."

"I can't say that I blame him," Selena said, almost as if talking to herself.

"Nor can I."

"So you've raised him as a single father?"

Steven nodded and smiled, suddenly feeling as though it was quite an achievement. "For the last nine years; yes. He even lived with me in New York while I was in culinary school. He's a great kid. Not at all like I was at his age. Daryl's an honor student, great basketball player and active in the youth ministry at church. I'm *very* proud of my son."

"As well you should be."

\- - -

The rest of the night passed quickly. Once Steven and Selena returned to the area with the others, he didn't get the chance to talk to her for the duration of the gathering. Duty called for him to return to his obligations as charge person of the event. Steven observed from a distance as Selena mingled with other guests. He also kept a watch on the men whose eyes she captured throughout the evening, constantly reminding himself to remain professional, constantly asking himself why it mattered to him.

As the festivities ended and the crowd thinned, Steven caught up with Selena as she stood near the exit door, reaching for her coat.

"Thank you," she said as he took it from her hands and helped her to slip her arms into the sleeves.

"Am I forgiven?" Steven needed to hear her say the words.

Selena turned to face him. "You said and did some vile things back then and they were very hurtful at the time. *Very* hurtful."

In renewed shame, Steven's head lowered. The brush of Selena's hand against his cheek quickly brought his eyes back to meet hers.

"It's Christmastime, Stevie. And isn't Christ's birth the beginning of the reason any of us are forgiven? If I hold those things against you after you've been so gracious and humble to apologize, then that would make my actions today, worse than yours were all those years ago. You're a different man now and who you are now is what really counts. Of course I forgive you."

Steven exhaled in noted grateful relief. Until that moment, he didn't realize the magnitude of liberation her pardon would bring. Grabbing Selena's hand and cupping it between both of his, Steven said, "Thank you."

After a brief mutual silence that consisted of shared smiles and lingering eye-contact, Selena slipped from his grasp and turned to walk away.

"I'll walk you to your car," Steven offered.

"No," she said, holding up her hand to stop him. "You go on and get back to work. I know you have a lot to do before leaving. Thank you anyway."

Steven wanted to insist, but didn't. "Can I...call you some time?" He braced himself for her answer.

Selena responded by reaching into her purse and pulling out a business card. When she placed it in his hand, Steven looked at it. She was a rehabilitation counselor, something he never would have guessed, but something he imagined she did well.

"Thank you," he said. "I'll definitely be in touch."

"Goodnight, Stevie." Her skin flushed.

"Goodnight, Selena." His heart raced.

With a quiet, almost bashful smile, she disappeared through the doors and walked into the darkness outside, brightened only by the blinking holiday lights. For several moments, Steven watched her and then turned, only to find his father and son standing in the entranceway with identical smiles.

"You wanna come and give us a hand in here...*Stevie?*" Daryl quipped.

As Steven walked toward them, he tucked Selena's card securely in his suit pocket. He already knew that this was a night Daryl and Jake would tease him about for many Christmases to come. Steven didn't mind, though. As a matter of fact, he looked forward to it; and hoped that Selena would still be around to share the memories.

Chapter Eleven

 **Dama Riles** was born in Atlanta, Georgia. She was called to the ministry at the tender age of fifteen, and began serving in ministry at seventeen. She is the Executive Visionary Officer of God's Butterflies Ministries Inc., a ministry that influences spiritual excellence in women from every walk of life.

Dama obtained her Associate and Bachelor of Arts Degrees in Biblical Education from Beulah Heights Bible College and Masters of Arts Degree in Christian Education from the Interdenominational Theological Center in Atlanta, Georgia. She is also certified in television production.

Her passion and gift to minister via dramatic ministry is evident by the success of her plays, which were written, directed and produced in 1995, 1997 and 1999. They reflect her diversity as a writer and producer. Dama has served as an editorial assistant and contributing writer for an entertainment and fashion industry magazine.

As an extension of her writing, Dama is preparing to release her first book, *Sister Stories*, which is a compilation of original short stories and poems, sprinkled with discussion questions that will help to provoke a dialogue among women. Visit Dama online by visiting www.godsbutterflies.org.

Her contribution to *The Midnight Clear* is entitled, *Just Like Snow*. It is her first published work of fiction.

Just Like Snow

I can't remember how long I've had a love for snow. I think ever since I could remember. Maybe it was because I grew up in *Hotlanta* where snowfall was rare. We've seen some snow during the winter of course, but not much. As a wide–eyed child staring at the television, I would see snow in other parts of the United States and wished with all of my heart, that I was wherever it was. I think the most beautiful thing I've ever seen, is snow as a covering during the winter. Covering rooftops, cars, trees, shrubs and bushes – it is absolutely gorgeous!

I have very fond childhood memories of visiting Auntie Sylvia, my mama's older sister, every winter break in the "Windy City." It was a time that I looked forward to every year. There was lots of rich and creamy hot chocolate, sweet and flaky cinnamon rolls, a blanket in front of the fireplace, and warm hugs and kisses from my Auntie Sylvia and Mama. In the north suburb of Chicago, Auntie Sylvia and Mama allowed me to play in the snow as long as I wanted. I would go for hours and hours. We would make beautiful snowwomen, using Auntie Sylvia's old straight and long Tina Turner wigs, big 80's red plastic hoop earrings, a long flowered scarf tied like a halter top, an over-sized scarf wrapped around her waist as a mini-skirt and a sassy Shy-town brim. We would use branches for her arms, a carrot for her nose, coat buttons for her eyes, and a red shoestring for her lips. Of course, we had to hang a spicy handbag from her arm to top it all off.

"Doesn't she look *foxy roxy?*" Auntie Sylvia would ask.

"And you know it," Mama would reply with her hands on her hips.

"Yeah," I would say in agreement.

There were other times when all three of us would lie in the snow in the front yard of Auntie Sylvia's home, in our snowsuits, making snow angels. Boy did I love those times! Mama and Auntie Sylvia were the coolest adults I knew and the snow just made me uncommonly happy. I remember looking out of the window of the airplane as we were leaving Atlanta and the southern asphalt was as dry as the Sahara Desert. The moment we arrived in Chicago and stepped off of the plane, it looked like a wonderful Winter Wonderland. I could feel the sharp crisp breeze of Chicago's winter, hitting my face as we got into Auntie Sylvia's 1981 Cadillac Deville.

"I feel snow air on my face," I would say to Mama.

She would reply, calling me by my nickname. "Oh, *Onesy,* that's just Jack Frost nippin' at your nose."

My daddy gave me the nickname "Onesy" because I was the "only child" for seven years; and then came my younger sister, Shallun. Daddy left our family when I was thirteen and Shallun was six years old. That was about twenty-one years ago and I have only seen him once since that time. Shallun saw him about two years ago with a young lady that looked to be about her age and he completely ignored her, for whatever reason.

He and Mama could not get along. They would argue continuously from sun up to sun down. Always screaming, hollering, slamming doors, cursing and calling each other all kinds of nasty names. My mother even got so mad a few times that she broke a few of our dinner plates, throwing them at the door as Daddy was heading out. I think she missed his head by a few inches. In my heart, I kind of wished that he would leave because I was tired of all of the fussing and fighting. By the time Shallun was born, their arguing tapered off and in the summer of '85, Daddy was officially *MIA.* The weekends turned into days, the days turned into weeks, the weeks turned into months and the months eventually turned into twenty-one solid years. Mama filed for divorce and just as quickly as their marriage started, it ended. She was now a single parent with a load of bills, a crazy busy schedule as a beautician, and dreams of owning her own salon.

It took some time, but Mama was able to grow the business. Her list of clients grew longer and she even began servicing a few celebrities when they would come in town. Mama was known in the cosmetology circle as the beautician with "growing hands." This meant that if Mama did your hair, it was sure to grow. Eventually, Mama's clientele consisted of celebrities only. She was one of the first *celebrity beauticians* in Atlanta back in the day. Nowadays we call them *celebrity hairstylists.* She made enough money to open her very own exclusive salon, *Diamonds and Pearls.* It was a cute little shop on Auburn Avenue. Mama had made a name for herself and had no problem filling her shop with other beauticians. By this time, I was sixteen years old and Shallun was nine. Mama had

149

stopped working in the shop, and would take her personal list of celebrity clients in the basement of our home, which she had remodeled into a private mini-salon.

Our home was always filled with fashion, fun and laughter. Mama often traveled with a few of her celebrity clients to do their hair for award shows, magazine photo shoots, album covers, movies, etc. Shallun and I had to spend most of our time at Grandma Sesylee's house. I didn't mind though because Grandma Sesylee was an excellent seamstress and I loved to watch her create garments. I think it was in those moments that I discovered what I wanted to do after completing high school. I was going to go to the Art College of Atlanta and major in Fashion Design and Marketing. I wanted to be the one that created and selected the outfits that celebrities would wear on all occasions. And of course, those outfits would come from the line of clothes that I would design.

Grandma Sesylee taught me how to sew when I was about ten years old. She made our church's choir robes and usher uniforms. Soon, other churches and their pastors started to call on her to make all of their robes and uniforms too. The pastors requesting robes became more popular than the choirs requesting robes. Pastor Shaw, our pastor, started showing off his different style robes and gained Grandma Sesylee a lot of attention and new customers. I often helped her to choose fabric, colors, designs for sleeves and the whole nine yards. Designing and sewing was something I was really passionate about. I designed my eleventh and twelfth grade prom dresses. Everyone thought that I had bought them at an expensive boutique. That's when I knew I was on to something. I had acquired a talent that had extended me far beyond myself.

My entire summer was spent learning some of Grandma Sesylee's sewing secrets and hanging out with my girls: Avery, Kristal and Jordun. This was one of the best summers ever. We were at Six Flags at least three times a week and at Greenbriar Mall the other times.

In the fall of '88, I met this guy named Damien Hill. He was tall, deeply dark and deliciously handsome, with biceps and triceps to spare. Damien approached me like a real gentleman; he was really a smooth operator and the star quarterback of his high school football team. When he approached me in the mall, I didn't have a

150

clue who he was. But my girls did. I was never into who was who in high school.

Avery, who is my best girlfriend to this day, said to me, "Girl, do you know who that was that you just gave your number to?"

"No," I answered.

"That was Damien Hill, senior star quarterback for Fredrick Douglass High School. He's been in the newspaper only every week, breaking some serious records. I hear he may go straight from high school to the NFL."

"Really?" I asked in a very nonchalant tone.

"Yeah *really,*" Kristal, my other girlfriend answered.

"He probably won't even call," I said.

"Let's just wait and see," Avery told to me.

A few days later, my girls were spending the night at my house and we were looking at a horror movie, when my phone rang. In fear, we all jumped and screamed at the same time. We busted out laughing when we realized that it was only my telephone. I answered.

"May I speak to Sarai?"

"May I ask who's speaking?"

"Damien Hill," the voice on the other end said.

"Hi Damien; this is Sarai."

"Hey Sarai." Damien sounded somewhat hesitant. "How are you?"

"I'm good."

"I am just calling to tell you that I think you are so beautiful."

"Oh really?" I blushed in laughter.

"Yep and I want you to be my girl."

"I bet you tell every girl that."

"Maybe," he admitted. "But with you, I mean it."

"Yeah right; how do you know you mean it?"

"Because it's just something about you. I'm gon' marry you, girl."

"You don't even know me, so how are you going to marry me?"

"You'll see. How about you meet me on the dance floor at *Jellybeans* on Sunday?" he spoke up like a sly fox.

"Maybe," I said, not giving in to his insistent flirting. "Good-bye, Mr. Hill."

"Good-bye, *Mrs.* Hill."

151

Avery, Kristal and Jordun were practically about to fall off the edge my bed, waiting to hear what Damien had said to me. I said nothing.

"What?" I asked, finally, looking at the girls eyeball to eyeball and pretending to be clueless as to why they were staring at me in anticipation.

Avery jumped up off of my bed and said loudly, "Girl, you betta' not leave out a detail. What did he say?"

"Okay, alright," I said, easily giving in. "He wants me to meet him at the skating rink on Sunday."

"*And?*" Kristal asked with a look of annoyance on her face.

I looked away and then turned my eyes to the ceiling, trying to appear as nonchalant as possible. "And, I told him I might."

"Honey child please; you'll be there." Jordun spoke up like she was somebody's mama.

"Ah, correction...*we'll* be there," I snapped back, rolling my eyes and neck like all teenaged black girls were born to do.

I ended up meeting Damien at the skating rink and the rest, as they say, is history. We started dating very strong in the next year. We went to the prom together, shopping together, movies together, and did just everything together. We were inseparable. By October of '89, we had been dating for one solid year. Damien had graduated and was on scholarship at the University of South Carolina; and again, breaking major football records. He came home at least twice a month to see me when he did not have to train or play.

By the latter part of 1990, we were talking about marriage. It was becoming hard for us to see one another often, due to distance and his football schedule. With Damien's popularity growing steadily, I never took his talks of marriage seriously. I was about to graduate from high school and was preparing to attend the Art College of Atlanta. My girls and I were planning a big graduation party. My mom had just bought a brand new five bedroom home out in the Cascade area, and we were anticipating "christening" it. We made our list and it looked like we were going to have at least seventy-five guests.

"Your little friends better not tear up my house, or I am going to tear up somebody's behind," Mama would constantly joke with me.

152

Avery, Kristal, Jordun and I were ready to throw the party of the year. After school one day, Avery drove me to Grandma Sesylee's house. I had not been feeling well the whole of that week.

"Are you alright? You look pretty sick," Avery asked, taking one hand off the steering wheel to feel my forehead.

"I don't feel good at all. I threw up a little yesterday morning, but mostly my stomach's been nauseous."

"You are a little warm; I heard that there's a stomach virus going around. Do you want to stop by the store and get a ginger ale or something?"

"No, my grandma keeps ginger ale at her house," I answered Avery with my head leaning back on the car's headrest.

We arrived at Grandma Sesylee's house. I got out of the car, headed toward the steps to the entrance of the house, stepped inside of the door, and everything went black. I don't remember anything after that, other than waking up in the hospital. When I finally woke up, Mama and Grandma Sesylee were sitting by my bedside.

I opened my eyes and everything looked very blurry and I heard Mama say, "Sarah, can you hear me?"

"Yes," I said, somewhat groggily. "What happened to me?"

"You fainted, honey."

"Why? What's wrong with me?"

"You were dehydrated....and pregnant."

"Pregnant?" I asked with tears welling up in my eyes.

"Yes, pregnant," Mama replied while brushing my bangs back out of my face.

I turned my head toward the wall and squeezed the bed sheet. All I could think was that I had made a major mistake. My life had been turned upside down and I was at the wheel of it all. I just wanted to express my love for Damien. We only had sex once. *What is going to happen now? Am I going to be able to go to college?*

The news of my pregnancy stung me like a wasp landing on my arm at a summer cookout. *How am I going to be a mother and a college student? How am I going to be a mother at all?* I was only eighteen and had only turned that a few weeks back. I was going to graduate from high school in less than two months. My life, as I knew it, was ruined.

"I'm so sorry, Mama," I balled in tears.

153

"I know, baby," Mama said, hugging me tightly.

"What are we going to do, Mama?"

"We're going to get through this... together."

"I messed up everything, Mama....everything. You, Grandma Sesylee and Aunt Sylvia showed me how to be a Christian and I failed ya'll...big time. I let you and God down."

"No you didn't, sweetheart. You had a moment when your humanness consumed you. It can happen to any of us. Now, do we agree with your having sex at this young age and before you are married? No we don't and neither do we agree with abortion. Yes, this whole situation has taken us all by surprise, but Christ is the head of this family and He has never failed us yet. So we're going to have to hang in there and know that God has our backs."

"That's right, baby and we're here for you," Grandma Sysylee said, holding my hand and rubbing my cheek gently. "This is a huge responsibility and it is going to take some time to absorb, but you can still reach your goals with a child. It may take a little more work and a lot more patience, but you can and will succeed in this life. I am a little disappointed that you didn't wait on marriage to have sex, but that's water under the bridge now. We can't dwell on *how* it happened; we are going to have to deal with *what* has happened. Baby listen, God is with us and He's going to see us through this. Psalm 127:3 says; *children are a heritage from the Lord and the fruit of the womb is a reward.* God has a purpose for this baby and we're going to believe that He does."

"I don't want God to be mad at me. I tried not to yield to temptation but I wasn't strong enough. Now I've just made a big mess of everything. I asked God to forgive me. I told Him I was sorry. I feel so bad. God hates me, and I hate myself. I really hate myself." I sobbed uncontrollably, pounding my fist down on the bed.

Mama grabbed hold of my fist and then forced me to loosen it so that she could hold my hand. "Oh, no my sweet baby," she said, "don't you think that for one moment. God loves you with all of His heart, He could never hate you. The first time you said you were sorry, He forgave you. As a matter fact, *before* you said anything, you were forgiven by God. Listen sweetie, with man, forgiveness is a process; it could take days, weeks, months or even years. But with

154

God, it is immediate and instant. No matter what you do or say, God is always going to love you."

The doctor came in and told Mama, Grandma Sesylee and me, that I was being released. My vitals were back to normal and the intravenous liquids had restored my strength. The next several days were hard for me and I went only to school and home. I avoided everyone for a few days, even my girls, Avery, Kristal, and Jordun. I just wanted to be alone.

"Sarai, at some point I think Damien and his parents need to be made aware of your pregnancy," Mama said to me with a certified tone of seriousness.

"I know Mama; he's coming home this week. Can I tell him first?"

"Sure. But as soon as you do I will call Damien's parents. We all need to come together and figure out how we are going to work together as a family unit."

"He's coming in Thursday night, I'll tell him then."

"Good," she replied. "I'll take it from there."

"Take it from there? Mama what do you mean?"

"I mean I'll make sure that we all come together to do what's right for this baby," Mama spoke gently as she kissed my forehead.

I didn't think anyone understood the precarious situation I was in. I felt all alone, with so much guilt and pain. I couldn't even believe it myself. How could I face the fact that I was going to be a mother? I felt so jumbled inside; like a jigsaw puzzle that I couldn't even find a matching piece to if I tried. I had to tell Damien. This was his child too. I knew that I could not get an abortion. That would only add to my overload of anxiety plus the fact that it's a horrible way to cover your mistakes. But how would I be able to care for such a tiny little life? What did I have to offer a baby? Could we be good parents?

Damien came home on Thursday evening and he called as soon as his plane landed. He said that he was on his way to his parents' house and then he would stop by to see me. I told him that I was tired and asked if we could see each other on Friday. That would be better. He agreed and I was glad. I did not quite know how to tell him that he was going to be a father. I finally mustered up enough courage to call Avery and she chewed me out for avoiding her. I told her that I was pregnant and asked her not to tell Kristal and

155

Jordun but to let them know that I was fine. I didn't have the strength to talk to them. I had to use what little I had left to tell Damien. It seemed that Friday came faster than a combo meal at a drive-thru window. It was like somebody sped up time. Damien came to the house and as soon as he came through the door he grabbed me, picked me up and hugged me tightly.

"I missed you, girl."

I began to sob heavily.

"Hey, it's only been a few weeks since I came home. I know I'm irresistible, but come on baby," Damien teased wiping my tears with his fingers.

"Damien, that's not why I'm crying. I think we should sit down. I have something important to tell you."

"Cool, what's up?" he asked with the look of curiosity in his eyes.

"Damien, I am six and a half weeks pregnant with our child."

He was silent for a moment.

"Come again?" he said, breaking the silence and stretching his eyes as wide as an owl's.

I looked down at the floor and up at him with crocodile tears rolling and said again, "I'm pregnant with our child."

Damien grabbed my hand and looked me in my eyes and asked, "Are you sure?"

"Yes, the doctor told me the other day. I fainted at my grandmama's house she rushed me to the hospital and the doctor found that I was dehydrated and pregnant."

"You know what this means," Damien said.

"Yeah; that we have a huge responsibility ahead of us."

"I was thinking along the lines of you marrying me."

"Damien, what are you saying?"

"I am saying, will you marry me, Sarai?"

I couldn't believe my ears. "You want to marry me?"

"Yeah, I want to give my child a family. What better family than you and I?"

"Damien, I think it's great that you want to take responsibility, but are we really ready to get married?"

"Why not? I love you and you're having my baby. It sounds like a good reason to me."

I needed more convincing. "Damien, are you sure you want to this?"

"I've dreamed about it, girl."

Those words erased my uncertainty. "Yes... *Mr. Damien Hill,* I will marry you."

Damien bought me a beautiful half carat diamond ring that I still have to this day. I keep it because it reminds me of real love. We told our parents and thank God, they didn't freak out. My grandmother set up a few months worth of premarital counseling with Pastor Shaw, for Damien and me. She said that we needed it because we were "too young and knew nothin' 'bout being married and nothin' 'bout raising no babies." She was right and so we delved right into counseling, which proved to be very revealing and helpful.

I graduated in June and by August, Damien and I were married. We had a simple wedding at my mama's house. As had been my dream for years, I started school at the Art College of Atlanta. Damien and I had agreed that he would come down every other weekend, until it was nearing time for me to deliver. I didn't start to really show until my eighth month, and by then, it was almost over. I was thinking of names that began with an "S". My mother gave both Shallun and me biblical names. My name means "princess" and Shallun means "peaceful and carefree." Mama said she named me Sarai because it reminded her of promises being fulfilled. She and Daddy had been trying to have a child for three years before I came. Mama said that she had been waiting on a promise and she finally received it when I was born. Just as Sarah received Isaac, her "promised child," from the Lord.

During my ninth month, I began to slow down. The reality that I was carrying human life inside of me started to set in. My first semester in college was going well and Damien and I were anticipating the birth of our baby girl. Our parents had agreed that the baby would stay with Mama and me until Damien graduated and we were able to look for our own place. The NFL was courting Damien and several teams were interested. As long as he stayed healthy and uninjured, things were looking good.

My mother was slated to be in Chicago for two weeks during my ninth month. I really wanted to go so that I could hang out at Aunt Sylvia's house. Mama didn't think it was a good idea, but we

157

called my doctor and she allowed me to go. My due date was December 31st, and I would be back home before then. Dr. Lark had a colleague at the University of Illinois Medical Center at Chicago that I could connect with once in Chicago, to make sure things were stable. As soon as I landed in Chicago Aunt Sylvia started spoiling me rotten. I didn't protest. I enjoyed it all.

"Sarai, I want you to promise me that when this baby turns sixteen years old, you'll bring her back here with a few of her close friends and I am going to throw her a fabulous Sweet Sixteen party," Auntie Sylvia said with all sincerity.

I stayed in Chicago about three weeks. Shallun and Grandma Sesylee came up a few days before Christmas. On Christmas Eve morning, I started feeling a little funny, so I called the doctor. She said that she would meet me at the hospital so that she could examine me. By the time I got there, my water had broken and I was going into labor. On the morning of December 25th at 7:01, I gave birth to a beautiful baby girl who weighed in at six pounds, five ounces. I named her Snow Reign Hill. She was as decadent and sweet as dark Belgian Chocolate. A tiny little work of art, created by God. That day, I saw God's awesomeness with my own eyes. Within a week, Snow and I were back in Georgia so that she could meet her father for the first time. She was immediately a "daddy's girl."

\- - -

Damien graduated with honors from the University of South Carolina and was headed back to Georgia to play professional football for the Atlanta Falcons. I had a beautiful home, a beautiful child and a loving husband. But when Snow turned two, Damien and I began to drift apart. By the time she was four, I was a single parent. Damien was a star Falcon and the tabloids had pictures of him cheating on me with some exotic beauty. I eventually filed for divorce and Damien moved out. He begged me to allow him to come back for Snow's sake. But I couldn't take back a man that I didn't trust.

Even though we were not married anymore, Snow was always our priority over the years that passed. Damien matured and soon realized that money, prestige and power were not all that he needed. He discovered that the love of God and family were more important, prompting him to turned his life over to the Lord and

158

become a new man. That opened up a whole new friendship and relationship for us and we started to date again.

- - -

It's now twelve years later and today is December 25th again, Snow's sixteenth birthday and our wedding day! Snow is having her fabulous Sweet Sixteen luncheon given by my Aunt Sylvia and I am having my wedding tonight at the Ritz Carlton here in Chicago. That's right; Damien and I are tying the knot again and this time, we are going to stay together because God is at the head of our marriage. I wanted to get married in Chicago because it reminded me of all of the love I experienced here as a little child, a teenage mother, and now, the mother of a teenager.

My life has come full circle in this space and it is amazing. I feel so honored and blessed. My life seemed to be heading down a road of guilt, shame, and pain. And yes, it was set on that course for a while. But God, in His infinite wisdom and power, restored my life unto Himself. I have really been "born again" and it feels so good! My daughter is healthy and beautiful and my marriage has been given a second chance. Only God can restore things in this manner.

I was reading somewhere, that most natural materials absorb some sunlight which gives them their color. But snow reflects most of the sunlight. As I look out of my hotel window and see blankets of snow atop buildings and trees, I feel that today and always, God's love for me, my love for my family and my family's love for me, is covering me… just like snow.

159

Chapter Twelve

Lawanda Johnson is one of the newest writers on the Christian-fiction scene. She is a native of New Orleans, Louisiana, where she graduated from Grambling State University in 1993. Although she majored in Computer Science, she has always had an unyielding passion for words and reading.

In 2003, Lawanda's desire to write merged with the Lord's call to restoration and ministry. Writing, for her, was a means of healing and cleansing that has since been used to inspire, motivate, and restore those hurting in the Kingdom. Through poetry and what she terms "Heartnotes," Lawanda is able to share God's desire for holiness, restoration, and victory to those in need.

Among her completed works are *Project-Restoration*, a collection of poetic expressions, and the *The Last Call*.

Lawanda is currently working on the novel, *Summer of Influence* and the poetic collection, *My Sister, My Friend*.

Her contribution to *The Midnight Clear* is entitled, **Slipping Through the Cracks**. It is her first published work of fiction.

Slipping Through the Cracks

To slip: an unintentional departure from truth or accuracy.
(See ERROR)

Crystal finds herself staring at the clock on the wall. Five o'clock, it seems, was taking its own sweet time today.

"You know, some of us would like to get out of here, so could you *please* hurry it up?" she says out loud to the clock on the wall. Crystal laughs to herself as she thinks about the clock deliberately slowing down to savor the season of Christmas.

Everyone but her is feeling like Christmas, festive and generous. She wants to get as far away from joy as possible. As the thought to check her email again flits across her mind, the phone rings. Glad to have an unexpected distraction from the time, Crystal eagerly hits the answer button on her headset.

"Good afternoon, Phillip Moore's office. How may I help you?"

Crystal has been with Arbor Investments for almost four months now. It is the first real job she's had since getting out of rehab nearly eight months ago. One of the things she learned during her tenure there was that she needed to establish a sense of normalcy in order to stay in control of her life. And what could be more normal than having a steady job to report to and bills to absorb all the money that the job provided? Although Crystal misses teaching, she couldn't face the embarrassment of losing her license, so she thought it best to just move on, relocate to another city, and get a fresh start. But she misses Reginald and Gia, too.

"Hey, Crystal girl! You busy?" It is her baby sister, her only sibling, KiKi. Although they are five years apart, they've always been more like twins. KiKi has always had a wise spirit that matured beyond her human years. Crystal is grateful for KiKi's support because she knows she couldn't have made it back this far without it.

"Yeah, busy trying to make it through the rest of the day so I can get out of here." The sisters enjoy a light laugh with one another. "What's up with you?"

"Same here. I'm just trying to *kill* some time before time *kills* me."

"Well you know what Mama always says…"

Crystal joins in and the girls sing the familiar line in unison as they raise their voices to imitate their mother. "Waiting ain't never killed nobody, but you can sho' nuff die waiting."

"You still coming to the Christmas Eve party at my house, right?" KiKi asks for what seems like the millionth time.

Crystal hesitates because she doesn't want to lie to her sister. She's been planning this party for weeks; mostly, Crystal imagines, to help her get through the holidays since this will be her first holiday without Gia.

Then tell her the truth, says the voice in her head.

Shrugging it off, Crystal carefully skirts around her sister's question. "Girl, why do you keep asking me the same question? You act like I'm your only friend." Crystal knows that will be enough to distract her sister who loves to talk.

"Ha, ha ha; very funny, Ms No-Comic View. I have droves of friends. I have an A list and a B list of friends. I'm so popular, I even have a C list of friends. You know – C if you ever get invited to one of my parties."

Crystal can picture her baby sister's eyes bugging out in animation like they always do when she gets excited. If she listens really hard, she can even hear her laugh waiting just over the horizon on her smart-aleck response. *Listening hard, hmm…*

Crystal tunes back in just in time for KiKi's wind down. "But seriously, even with all of the people on my lists, none of them, and I do mean *none* of them, can top my big sis, Trystal." KiKi always calls Crystal by the nickname she gave her when she was a baby and couldn't properly pronounce Crystal. Being called Trystal always sparks a tender moment between the sisters, much like finding an old friend.

"Crystal, you've done an amazing job of turning your life around. I know it wasn't easy, but you did it and I'm proud of you."

"I don't know, KiKi. It doesn't feel amazing to me. Why do I keep seeing where I messed up my life, where I messed up my marriage, and where I messed up my child's life?" Crystal takes a deep breath, puts her head down and begins to massage her temples. She doesn't want to talk about this right now because she is at work and doesn't want anybody in her business. She quickly reaches

163

across her desk to pull out a tissue and makes an attempt to pull herself together before anyone passes by.

"KiKi, I can't talk about this right now. It's just too hard, okay?"

"I know," KiKi says in a somber voice. "Just know that I love you and I'm here for you."

"I love you too," Crystal replies. "And I know you're there. Thank you."

"Do you have time to pray before we go?" KiKi asks with trepidation. Although they grew up in church, Crystal came into real fellowship with Christ again only two months ago when she moved to Chicago. So while she's been in church all her life, she's at the beginning of learning to walk with God. KiKi knows how tender her sister is, so she tries not to push her too hard.

"I've got a minute."

KiKi mumbles a silent "Thank You" to heaven when she hears the reply she was hoping for. "Okay, close your eyes. See, I'm bossing you like you used to boss me when we were kids. Remember that? Momma used to put you in charge of making sure we said our prayers before we went to bed and you used to pray extra long when you knew I was tired, just to see if you could get me to fall asleep on my knees."

"KiKi, how do you remember all that stuff? Don't you have things to do during the day? Crystal can't resist teasing her.

"Girl please, I have plenty of things to do. I have an A list and B list of things to do. Shoot I even have C lists – C if I'm going to get around to this..."

"KiKi, please come back! Girl your mouth is like the energizer bunny...it keeps going and going. And for the record, I wasn't bossing you." Crystal takes a deep breath before continuing with, "Anyway that was a long, long time ago." So long ago, Crystal thinks to herself, that she doesn't even remember how to pray anymore.

Let's begin again, says the voice in her head.

KiKi speaks up before Crystal can be swept away too far by her inner voice. "Okay, okay. Bow you head and close your eyes," she directs again. "Dear Heavenly Father, we come before you, grateful to be your children. Lord we thank you that you are concerned about everything that concerns us. God, we ask that you would

164

please forgive us of our sins; purge us and show us your path that we may continue on it. Lord, we confess that we are more than conquerors. Lord, we stand firm on your promises of peace and everlasting love. Father, I ask that you would favor us in this hour and meet our needs like only you can. Thank you for seating us in heavenly places that give us the ability to rise above every situation we face to find victory. It's in Jesus' name that we ask, believe, and receive according to your will. Amen."

"Amen," Crystal echoes. "Thanks sis, I needed that."

"No prob. Hey, guess what? I've got some good news."

"Really, what's that?" Crystal asks half-heartedly, not knowing what her sister will say next.

"It's five o'clock!" KiKi announces in a sing-song voice in an attempt to breathe a little life back into their conversation. And from the sound of the sigh she hears from Crystal, it is just in the nick of time.

"Now that *is* good news. Well, I'm gonna get my stuff together so I can get out of here.

"What are you doing after work?"

"I've got a meeting. Then, I'm just gonna go home and chill. I'll try to give you a call later, okay?"

KiKi knows that "meeting" was Crystal's code word for her counseling session with Pastor Donovan or therapy with her Fresh Start Recovery group.

"Okay. But if you feel like company, give me a call and I can come spend the night with you. Derek and I don't have any plans tonight because he's going over to a friend's to watch the fight, so I'll be home alone until really late."

"And when did you become the big sister?" Crystal teases. "I'll be fine, KiKi. Now let me go so I can get out of here."

"I love you, Trystal!

"I love you too." Crystal finds herself still smiling when she finally removes her hand from the phone. KiKi has a heart of gold and she is truly blessed to still have her in her life.

Crystal quickly shuts down her computer, transfers the phone to the operator, and grabs her purse from the file cabinet. It's 5:10 and she wants to get to the meeting early so she can talk to Pastor Donovan before anybody else gets there. Her mind has been racing for days and she needs to find an outlet, one that won't judge her or get too paranoid about what she's been thinking.

Crystal hits the garage button on the elevator and stares ahead as the doors quickly close her in.

- - -

"Crystal, you're a bit early for the meeting, aren't you?" Ms. Jackson asks with her left eyebrow slightly raised.

Crystal laughs to herself. *Why does the pastor's secretary remind me of the Mexican border control, always waiting to see if you're trying to make a run for it?*

"Yes, ma'am. I am a bit early." Crystal hesitates and then continues. "I was hoping I could see Pastor Donovan before the group met. There are some things..." Her voice trails off. "That I want to speak with him about privately. He told me if I ever felt the need to, I should just call."

"But you didn't call. You came by early."

Crystal can feel the terseness in Ms. Jackson's voice. So she holds her breath and whispers a silent prayer. *Lord, you know I need this. Please don't let her block me.*

Sometimes man is busy, but I'm always there, even when you don't want me to be, the voice answers back.

"Let me see if he's busy." She quickly dials the pastor to announce that Crystal showed up early and wants to know if he "has time" to see her. Crystal feels the urge to slap the phone from her hand, but throws out the thought as quickly as it flies into her head.

"Mm-hmm. Mm-hmm. Yes, I'll send her in." Ms. Jackson looks up from the phone and announces too politely to be genuine, that Crystal can see the pastor for fifteen minutes, but then, she would have to excuse herself so he can prepare to meet with the *entire* – and her emphasis was on the word entire – group.

"Yes ma'am." That is all Crystal can trust herself to say. And with that, she walks into Pastor Donovan's study.

- - -

"Good afternoon, daughter. What brings you by today?" Pastor Donovan is sitting behind his desk, wearing a starched white dress shirt, brown suit pants, a silk tie, and his legendary suspenders. When standing, he has a towering 6'3" frame, but his presence is softened by shining brown eyes that can lure one into telling their

166

deepest secret in total confidence. That's why Crystal needs to see him. She needs the trust she knows lives within him. "Ms. Jackson said you needed to see me before the group met at 6:30."

Crystal doesn't know if God had already shared her secret with Pastor Donovan, but if his eyes were any indication, she could put money down on it. She senses that he somehow knows something is up.

"Thank you for seeing me, Pastor. I know I should have called, but I probably would have lost my nerves."

"No need to apologize, child. This sounds awfully serious, so how about we begin. What's on your heart?"

"Pastor Donovan, I'm not sure what's on my heart but I can definitely tell you what's on my mind." Crystal sits up in her chair to give him the cliff notes version of her life. "Pastor, I find myself struggling with my recovery, with my salvation, with myself, and the biggest struggle is with Christmas. I hate that everyone is so happy and wants to spread cheer. When I look around, all I see is an addict that lost her family." Crystal hesitates a bit before she continues with the last statement. "And it makes me want to start using again. Because when I was using, I didn't feel anything and nothing mattered. Being sober means I have to live every single day...and feel it." Crystal begins to cry. "It's too hard and it hurts too much to pretend that it doesn't. How is it, that I'm a wife with no husband? A mother with no child? And a Christian with no relationship with God? Every time I count it all up, I keep coming out with a zero balance."

"Are you done, sweetheart?" Pastor Donovan asks as if his heart feels the weight of hers.

"Done is probably the best word to sum up how I feel. So, yes sir, I'm done."

He reaches into his pocket for a handkerchief, because he always has one. He reminds Crystal of her granddad; the kind of gentleman that seems extinct these days.

"Crystal, this morning while I was praying, God allowed me to see your heart, and I've been weeping ever since. First, He showed me a vision of an ant and how it works with the others to carry food back to the colony. Did you know that an ant can carry up to fifty times its body weight without straining? The reason ants can do this is because they are small and do not have extra mass on their

167

bodies. The more mass you have, the more force you must use to carry a load. Spiritually speaking, flesh means more mass and more strain. The smaller the creature, the greater its capacity to lift. Do you understand what I mean?"

Crystal isn't sure where all of this is going so she just nods and silently uses her eyes to urge him to continue.

"You see, it's the same thing in the Kingdom. The smaller you are in God, the greater your capacity to carry larger loads. Crystal, so much of your time and energy is focused on your problems that you are increasing your mass and are creating an undue burden." He pauses before continuing. "When the Lord showed me you, you were carrying way more than your body is designed to carry."

Slowing down his words, Pastor Donovan says, "Crystal, you're carrying too much, darling." He gets up from his chair to sit on the edge of the desk, directly in front of her. He slowly reaches out to lift her tear-stained face to meet his eyes.

"You, the Lord says, are trying to carry yesterday, today, tomorrow, your mistakes, your shortcomings, your tragedies, and your fears all in the same basket. And the basket is tearing because of the load. You *have* to let what's past be the past. We were not designed to carry the past, but to live in the present, and *hope* for the future. Crystal, when you came back to God, He came back to you. You must begin to trust in that and make peace with the past.

"Christmas time is a wonderful reminder to the world that we not only needed a Savior, but that we have one. This is the season of new beginnings. Please allow the snow, as it falls, to cover the things your eyes have been focused on for too long, so that God can begin a new thing in your life. Deliverance is a choice, just like defeat.

"You probably won't understand this right now, but I'm glad you can feel everything. It's a great reminder that you're alive and no longer drunken by the lies of the devil's words." With that, he pulled her up for a hug.

Crystal feels God's presence surrounding her when Pastor Donovan wraps her in his arms. She feels an incredible peace come over her.

There's power in my touch, the voice in her head assures her.

"Thank you, Pastor Donovan. You have no idea how much I needed that hug," Crystal says as she wipes her face and begins to grab her things.

"Actually, I did." Pastor Donovan winks at Crystal while pointing upwards. "He told me that too."

"Really? What else did *He* say about me?" Crystal is kidding with the Pastor as she mentally puts imaginary quotations around the word, he.

But Pastor Donovan is anything but playful when he replies, "He said to ask Him because He would love to tell you for Himself."

Crystal feels the truth behind his words and it scares her so she doesn't respond. She just gives him another hug and whispers that she will see him in the sanctuary.

- - -

When Crystal finally returns home, her first thought is to get out of her shoes. She quickly bolts the apartment door behind her and drops her keys and purse on the table nearby. *I don't care how cute a shoe is supposed to be, no shoe is comfortable after twelve hours.* Her second thought found her peeling off her sweater and trousers while making a beeline to the bathroom. *I'll clean this up after a hot shower.*

Showered, changed, and feeling better, Crystal finds herself keeping the promise to pick up her clothing trail. She hates a messy house. Once her things are put away, she decides to make a chicken salad sandwich and watch some TV before retiring to bed. With sandwich in tow to the living room, Crystal notices the red light blinking on her answering machine. She's not sure how she could have missed it before. *Probably because no one ever calls me, so there's usually not a message to check.* She hits the play button to listen.

"You have three new messages," the automated voice on her machine alerted.

"Wow, I must be popular tonight," Crystal says sarcastically to no one as the first message begins to play.

"Hi sis; it's KiKi. Just wanted to make sure everything went well at your meeting." Pause. "If you change your mind about company, I'll be home. It doesn't matter how late it is... I'll be up, okay? Okay. Bye."

169

"Friday, 7:39 p.m. Next message."

"Crystal, it's me again. I forgot to tell you that I love you. Okay. Bye."

"Friday 7:43 p.m. Next message."

"Hi, Mommy; it's Gia."

Crystal's breath catches in her throat.

"I know you're not home, but I just wanted you to know that I miss you and that I love you. Christmas is only two days away and Daddy said I could call you then, but I couldn't wait that long. Can you call me back? Love you."

"Friday 8:02 p.m. That was your last new message."

Crystal can't move. She can't breathe. She's stuck trying to hold the memory of her daughter close to her. It's hard for her to believe her ten-year-old baby girl could sound so grown-up. How much has she missed while being coked out for the last three years? And how can this amazing child still love her so much after how she's failed her as a mother?

Because love never fails, Crystal, the voice answered.

With her appetite gone, Crystal sits down near the phone, willing herself to pick it up to call her daughter back. But she couldn't. What would she say to her? And what if Reginald answered the phone? Would he talk to her? Would he even let her talk to Gia?

What if this is some crazy dream I'm having and it fades when I reach for that phone? she fretted.

"I need a hit. I need something to get me out of this nightmare." Crystal jumps from the sofa like a crazed animal and heads for the bathroom in search of anything that would get her closer to the high she desperately needs. She knowingly goes to the bathroom cabinet where she grabs the nail polish remover and a can of hair spray. She closes the cabinet and robotically reaches for the can of air freshener on her way out the door before turning out the light. Although she has never sniffed inhalants before, she learned enough from Michael's story in therapy to get where she needed to go. Crystal can see this scene playing out with eerie familiarity, and yet she can't stop it.

Back in the living room, she places each of the items in a single line facing her on the coffee table. She closes her eyes and subconsciously wrings her hands in her lap. *I can't do this. I've*

170

worked too hard. I've already lost too much. Crystal desperately searches her mind for something to anchor to, but the clamoring and noise are just too loud to make out anything. The tears begin to escape violently from her eyes, like rivers that have been dammed up too long. The weight of the water is so heavy that she finds herself being pulled to the floor. She willingly submits, because she simply does not have the strength to resist. The journey from the sofa to the floor, took mere seconds, but the ultimate journey of finally finding herself on her knees, seems like it took a lifetime. She opens her eyes in amazement, when she realizes where she is – she's in the position of surrender. And surrender she does. Crystal cries until she cries herself into a deep sleep.

- - -

When she finally stirs many hours later, Crystal begins with what's on her heart. "God, I need you. I am so lost." Crystal starts to find her voice. "I thought I could handle this on my own, but I can't. I need you. Please help me."

Psalms 34:4.

The voice is so clear that Crystal, at first, thinks she said the words. For a split second she hesitates, but then she realizes that it is God speaking. Crystal leans across the coffee table, past the polish remover and aerosol cans to her Bible. Sitting on the floor, she opens it to Psalms 34:4.

"I sought the Lord, and He heard me, and delivered me from all of my fears." Crystal reads the scripture again, and again, and again. *Lord, how could you know?* she asks with a questioning heart, but no real words.

Jeremiah 1:4.

Crystal eagerly flips over to Jeremiah and begins to read aloud, "Then the word of the Lord came to me saying: Before I formed you in the womb I knew you; before you were born I sanctified you."

I named you Crystal as a reminder to you that I can see through you to your heart. I know that it's hurting and I know that it's broken. Psalms 51:17.

With a trembling hand and hungry heart, Crystal turns to Psalms 51:17 and begins to read again. "The sacrifices of God are a broken spirit, a broken and a contrite heart – These, O God, you will not despise."

171

A broken spirit does not mean the end. A broken spirit means the beginning. You have tried everything to appease the pain in your soul. You have availed yourself to every drug and emotional stimulant in hopes of sedating the pain, but nothing can ease what ails you except my touch.

And this went on for hours. God would speak and Crystal would obey, read, and be filled.

- - -

At three o'clock, the Lord speaks for the last time.
Psalms 65: 9.

In obedience, Crystal turns to the Word, but this time she drinks it into her soul. She reads the words with clear understanding, as if they were written expressly to her in a love letter.

"You visit my earth and water it,
You greatly enrich it;
The river of God is full of water;
You provide my grain
For so you have prepared it.
You water my ridges abundantly,
You settle my deep hurts;
You make it soft with showers,
You bless my growth.
You crown my year with your goodness,
And your paths drip with abundance.
Your abundance drop on the pastures of my wilderness,
And my little hills rejoice on every side.
My pastures are clothed with flocks;
My valleys are also covered with grain;
They shout for joy, they also sing."

Crystal can feel the weight of her world slipping from its axis. She kneels in confidence and begins to pray for herself, for the first time in years. "Lord, please forgive me for giving my past more credit that it deserves. I was so used to looking down, that I'd forgotten the beauty in looking up. For so long I've been stuck. Stuck in a place where I didn't want to die, but kept refusing to live." As her voice begins to tremble, she confesses, "I have felt you with me all of my life, even through the storms, and I am so grateful that you are still here."

172

Crystal announces, "Lord, I'm ready to live again. I know I can't change what's happened, but I know that I can change me. If deliverance is a choice like defeat, then I'm choosing deliverance. I don't want to live my life in defeat anymore. Teach me how to live for you.

"Father, I simply ask you, *please* take me to a higher place. Take me to a place where I can see none of me and all of you. Take me to a place where I'm forced to look up, because I'm too high to consider looking down."

Crystal's prayer pleases the Lord, and He honors her request. He grants her peace, and allows her to rest and sleep right into a new season of expectation.

- - -

When the dawn finally breaks, Crystal awakens with a new sense of purpose. She closes her eyes and prays silently to God. She thanks Him for not allowing her to slip through the cracks last night. Crystal is still overwhelmed by God's concern for her. When she finally slept, she felt warmer. Never before had she been so safe.

After lying in the bed, thinking on God's goodness for what seems like hours, Crystal finally sits up to reach for the phone. Although there are several people she wants to call, like KiKi, and Pastor Donovan, Crystal first has a past to settle for good. She dials the number and patiently waits for the phone to ring. The line is answered by a sleepy, but familiar voice.

"Hello."

"Good morning," she whispers. "How are you?"

Reginald, Crystal's ex-husband sits up in bed too. He can't believe he's talking to Crystal. He figures he must still be dreaming. How did she know he dreamt about her just last night and somehow knew that he would speak to her soon?

He clears his throat. "I'm good. How 'bout yourself?"

"I'm better. Thanks for asking." Silence falls between the two. There's so much to say and yet there aren't enough words.

"Reginald, I am truly sorry for everything that I've put you through and everything I put our family through. I tried to blame you for my problems. But the truth is you were more than I deserved to have. You were always there to make sure Gia got what she needed when I was too concerned with hiding my problem, or

173

looking for my next hit. I can't imagine how much I've hurt you and I am truly sorry. Will you accept my apology?" Crystal fights back the tears. She never would have found the courage to ask for forgiveness, let alone risk rejection if she hadn't encountered a loving God last night.

With his eyes closed, Reginald responds, "Consider yourself forgiven. Crystal, I knew for a long time you needed help, but I didn't know what to do. I was scared and angry, so I quit, and I'm not exactly proud of myself. So, will you forgive me too? I never should have left you like that."

Crystal could hardly trust herself with the words she'd just heard through the receiver.

I can do exceedingly and abundantly above all that you could ask or think, the Holy Spirit reminds her.

Crystal smiles to herself. "You're asking *me* to forgive *you* after all I've done?"

"Yes."

"Then the answer is yes."

That's one hurdle, Crystal says to herself before she launches into why she called. "Reginald, did you know that Gia called me last night?"

"I'm not surprised," he says. "She's been asking for you a lot lately. She really misses you…we both do."

Before she has a chance to respond, even if she knew how, he asks, "Do you want to talk to her? I can wake her up."

Clearly, he isn't sure what to say either, so Crystal allows the moment to pass as he directs.

"Yes, I would like to talk to her. Honestly, I *need* to talk to her."

"Okay, hold on; I'll go get her."

Crystal can hear him lay the phone down on its side.

Look out the window.

In obedience, Crystal walks over to the window to see a very light snow beginning to fall, and so do the tears of gratitude in her heart.

"Hi, Mommy."

Her heart leaps at the sleepy sound of her child's voice. "Hi baby, I got your message last night. It was very sweet of you."

"Mommy, are you okay? Why are crying?" Gia can hear the emotion in her mother's voice.

174

"I'm crying because it's snowing outside. And the snow is covering up everything I can see." Crystal not only welcomes the snow, but she accepts Christmas as her personal gift at a new beginning.

Chapter Thirteen

Tia McCollors, national bestselling author, entered the literary scene in January 2005 with her debut novel, *A Heart of Devotion*, which was named an *Essence* Bestseller and was also chosen as a Black Expressions selection. Her sophomore novel, *Zora's Cry*, has garnered praise from her devoted readers, book clubs and reviewers.

After being laid off from a job in 1999, Tia recalls questioning her purpose in life and going through a soul-searching experience. What she found was her destiny to creatively minister the Gospel through the power of the pen.

Tia is a member of the national American Christian Fiction Writers (ACFW) organization, and currently serves as the vice president for Visions In Print (V.I.P.), the Atlanta Southeast Chapter of the ACFW. She is also actively involved in on-line author networks and continues to participate in a writer's critique group she co-founded in 2003.

A native of Greensboro, North Carolina, Tia is a graduate of the University of North Carolina at Chapel Hill with a degree in Journalism and Mass Communications. She resides in Atlanta, Georgia with her husband and son.

Tia can be contacted by way of her website at www.TiaWrites.com.

Her contribution to *The Midnight Clear* is entitled **The Perfect Present**.

The Perfect Present

Simone Alexander saw the familiar brown uniform of the delivery man through the small opening of her office door. She wriggled her right foot back into her pointed-toe shoe and walked out to the receptionist area.

She'd expected that Reggie, their regular delivery guy, would be the one to hoist the hefty box from his hand truck to the floor. His presence had been replaced by a tall man with a deep cleft in his chin.

"You know, Reggie would've been here earlier this afternoon," Simone teased. She tapped her watch, then signed the electronic signature pad he held out to her. Something about the man's angular face struck her as familiar. When she glanced at him again, it seemed he was looking at her with the same curiosity.

"Unfortunately Reggie's mother passed away last night so I'll be covering his route for a while."

"I'm sorry to hear that." Simone made a mental note to remind Indrea, the office assistant, to buy him a sympathy card from the office. Like most people at Boyd & Braxton Consulting, Indrea had opted to leave after lunch at the gracious offer of the company's vice president. The Christmas season even had the regular workhorse closing down the office early in lieu of his usual late evening mandatory meetings. Simone, however, chose to wait for the delivery of her mother's Christmas gift – bath and body care sets in every fragrance from Carol's Daughter. Her mother had talked endlessly about the natural products since seeing the Harlem store featured on television.

Simone nudged the box with the tip of her pump. Online shopping had been her saving grace this year, keeping her out of the Christmas bustle.

The man readjusted two boxes that were threatening to topple off his hand truck. "Normally I would've been on top of this, but the holidays usually triple our regular deliveries," he said. "I've still got several floors to work in this building before I'm out of here."

Simone drew him into a few minutes of small talk about the blistery weather, trying her best at the same time to place his face. There was something familiar about the tiny gap between his two front teeth and the slanted smile surrounding them.

"I don't want to anger any other feisty tenants in the building so I better get out of here." He looked down at the electronic signature pad again. "Can you verify the last name, please?"

"Alexander. Simone Alexander. Sorry about that." It was evident that both her fingers and eyes were tired from sitting in front of the computer all day.

"Simone Alexander," he repeated. He chuckled and she wondered what had struck him as funny.

"I'm Lincoln. Lincoln Crawford. Regency High, class of nineteen-ninety, home of the Mighty Lions."

"Hear us roar like thunder," they sang, recalling the school's mantra at the same time.

Simone leaned her round, ample hips against the receptionist desk. She shook a well-manicured fingertip at him. "I knew it," she said. "I may forget a name, but I rarely forget a face. I can't believe you're the same shy guy who hauled his saxophone everywhere he went."

"Well now I'm bolder and about fifty pounds lighter – and that doesn't include the sax." Lincoln laughed then raised his eyebrows at Simone. "And I doubt you ever knew my name. I wasn't part of your popular clique."

Simone couldn't argue with his accusation. Bourgeoisie was her middle name in her late teens. Although she still held onto the fashion aspect, she'd let go of the attitude that accompanied it years ago as far as she was concerned. It was other people who wouldn't let her relinquish that title.

"You're not going to hold some juvenile high school stuff over my head, are you?" She crossed her arms and cocked her head. The pout of her lips said her defensive stance was all in good fun.

"Not if you let me take you out," Lincoln said, propping his foot on his hand truck.

Simone was taken aback. That was the last thing she'd expected from Lincoln. He was anything but daring in high school. If memory served her correctly, he was involved in little else than the band and some sort of Christian fellowship club. Neither had been her thing.

"I told you I was bolder," he said when she didn't respond. "There are a lot of things you wouldn't expect about me now.

That's the beauty in seeing a person for who they've grown to be and not who they used to be."

Can he read my mind or what?

"Tell me about it," Simone said.

Lincoln reached into his coat pocket for a pen. He picked up a cube of yellow sticky notes from the receptionist's desk. Scribbling his name and number on the paper, he stuck it to the sleeve of Simone's navy blue suit.

"Call me when you're ready for someone to see you for the real woman you are." He turned away and pulled his hand truck through the glass double doors. His gait was smooth -- almost as if he was floating.

Simone watched him until he disappeared around the corner, then bent down and attempted to pick up her delivery. "Yeah, right," she said to herself when it didn't budge. It was heavier than she expected and she wondered how she could make get to her car.

Maybe Larry down at the concierge desk. She laughed at her own thought. He was more petite than most women in the building. On top of that, Larry was a modern-day Scrooge. He complained daily about the Christmas carols floating from the intercom through the lobby, and the wreath the building manager tacked to the front of his desk. The only time he didn't raise a fuss was when the Christmas spirit led someone to bless him with a gift.

Simone was still squatting by the box when she spotted Lincoln rounding the corner again. She'd expected him to head toward the elevators, but instead he veered toward her office. She stood quickly, relieved that the extra leg squats she'd been doing helped her keep her balance.

That smile, she thought, as Lincoln pushed open the door. It was enough to warm anyone's spirit on a cold day. Even the weatherman's forecast last night hadn't prepared Simone for the sting of winter that had swept through Charlotte, North Carolina. Christmas was in the air. *Why don't I feel it?*

"I didn't know if you needed help getting your mother's gift to the car," Lincoln said. "Unless of course you keep a hand truck tucked somewhere in your purse."

How does he know it's Mama's gift? "I've probably got everything but a hand truck in there, she said, returning his smile. *Why is he looking at me like that?* Rarely a man caused her to avert

180

his glance, but Lincoln did. His eyes seemed to stare into her soul. Those same eyes must've been hidden behind his gaudy glasses when they were in high school, or else they would have caused many a teenage girl a major crush, even with his extra fifty pounds.

"Give me a few minutes to deliver the rest of these packages and I'll be back down," Lincoln said.

Simone scuttled back to her office, bidding goodbye to the only two women left in the office. She saved her files, shut down her computer, and stacked the dwindling pile of paperwork on the corner of her desk. She'd tackle them first thing Monday morning since she expected a slow work week. She couldn't wait for her three-week vacation.

Simone pulled on her camel brown wool coat and wrapped a plaid Burberry scarf around her neck. There was a time when she would've scoffed at her grandmother's suggestion for the extra wintertime layers. Now at thirty-four, she'd finally learned how to mesh fashion with common sense.

In less than ten minutes, Lincoln returned with an empty hand truck. She held the door open for him while he muscled the truck carrying her package out of the door and to the elevator. She pushed the button to take them to the lobby. They'd ridden five floors down on their seventeen-floor descent. Until then, the only sound in the elevator had been the computer-generated voice announcing each floor.

"So what exactly do you do at Boyd & Braxton Consulting?" Lincoln asked.

"I help my clients assess whether their operating procedures are effective."

"That sounds interesting."

"Some days. You know how that is. Some days you want to go to work, others you don't."

Lincoln shook his head. "I can't say I ever feel the way."

"Come on, Lincoln. Be real."

"I'm serious. To me, this job is more than delivering packages. I get to meet new people all the time, and my supervisor--," he shook his head in admiration. "There's not a problem he can't solve or a question he doesn't have an answer to."

"Who wouldn't want to come to work with a boss like that? You talk about him like he's God or something."

181

Lincoln laughed.

"I'm right over there under the street light," Simone said when they reached the parking lot. She clicked her car remote to pop the trunk and unlock the doors of her pearl white Lexus coupe.

She'd originally purchased it to turn heads. Simone used to pride herself on being the center of attention. If it was the latest release of – well, anything – she had to have it. She wanted to exude the epitome of being a strong, self-sufficient woman. And she'd done just that. So much so that she believed she'd run off every half-decent man, rationalizing that they were intimidated by her success. But she wasn't the same woman she used to be. Keeping up had been exhausting, and after a while, a bit boring. She was more than the designer labels she wore, but no one else seemed to notice. Simone was caught in a cycle of living in people's expectations. She could afford Dana Buchman suits, but she couldn't afford to dash people's expectations.

Simone watched as Lincoln lifted the box into the trunk.

"That'll do it," Lincoln said, closing the trunk. He wiped his hands off on the back of his pants as if her package were dustier than the grimy boxes he'd been delivering all day. "Your mother won't have to buy any more smell-goods for a while."

"Tell me about it," she said, pulling her scarf tighter around her neck. "Thank you so much, Lincoln. I would've had it delivered to my home but I didn't want to risk it being stolen from the front door. Thieves work overtime during the holidays." She rubbed her gloves together and opened the door.

She had to ask this time.

"How did you know what was in the box?"

Lincoln stuffed his hands in his pockets and shrugged. "Deductive reasoning. I looked at the return address label. I grew up with three females in the house and they've always kept me up to date on the latest female favorites."

"And how did you know it was for my mother?"

"You told me, didn't you?"

"Could have," Simone said. "I don't remember saying it though." She knew she had the tendency to ramble.

"Maybe it was a man's intuition."

182

"I thought only women had intuition. But anyway, we'll have to grab a cup of coffee one day," Simone promised. "For your trouble. In the cold and all."

"I told you to call me when you're ready," Lincoln said, closing Simone's door after she was buckled in. He took a brown toboggan from his coat pocket and pulled it down low over his head.

While Simone waited for her car to warm up, she watched Lincoln start the long trek to his truck across the parking lot. *Ready?* She lost herself in thoughts about how she'd treated Lincoln when they were in high school. *Could ignoring someone be considered as treating them badly?* During their brief chats, she hoped Lincoln could see she wasn't that same person. When she looked up again, his truck was nowhere to be seen.

"Maybe I will call you sometime, Mr. Lincoln Crawford," she said as she shifted the car into gear. She remembered the sticky note with his number. She hadn't bothered to take it off her sleeve. No doubt it had fallen off. She imagined it being scooped up into the janitor's trash bin. *I'll see him next week.*

Simone wheeled out onto the street. A few blocks down, she slowed to let a woman dressed in jeans, a short sleeved-t-shirt and a scarf, scurry across the street and inside a dimly lit coffee shop. *Short sleeves? Crazy.*

If it weren't so cold outside, Simone would've indulged in a simple pleasure to end her work week – reading the newspaper and sipping on her favorite cinnamon and spice, a special drink served during the holidays. It wasn't a single woman's typical Friday night rendezvous, but it suited her fine. She'd already turned down several opportunities to attend company and holiday mixers with her girls. She wasn't feeling it. Who was she becoming? Maybe the person she'd always been.

Besides, Simone was too tired. She had to wake up early in the morning to shop for gifts for her annual Christmas brunch with her girlfriends. She'd come up empty during her online escapades and had put off shopping for them until the last minute.

For years, the six friends had been caught up in exchanging lavish presents. This year Simone wanted to give everyone a gift they would cherish for a lifetime and not just until the trend passed. The same kind of gift she wanted for herself.

- - -

183

Even the banana-nut scented candles couldn't conjure up a cheerful Christmas spirit for Simone. She drank eggnog in her gold rimmed wine glasses that she used for entertaining. That didn't work either.

Simone sat Indian-style on the rug in front of her gas log fireplace with her mother's gift. Presentation was everything, she'd been taught. She tried to focus on making the perfect crease while wrapping it. Her neighbor, Carlos, had been the dutiful man who'd helped her haul it inside. When she added the finishing touch of a satin bow, she gently slid it under the Christmas tree.

If nothing else put a smile on Simone's face, her Christmas tree did. For years she'd adorned it only with white lights and her growing collection of angel ornaments. It was indeed heavenly. Her friends and family had made it a custom to purchase her an angel each year. It had become a Christmas tradition and a competition, of sorts, to see who could discover the most elegant or unique angel.

Simone's favorite so far was one carved in mahogany wood and carrying a harp. It dangled from the end of an artificial branch by a sliver of gold ribbon. She touched it with the tip of her finger and it swayed back and forth. Three times. It stopped at the same instance the phone rang.

"Hey, diva," Simone answered after she stole at glance at the caller ID.

"What's up, lady?" her girlfriend Renee asked in her usual jovial tone. "You still want help making favors tonight?"

Simone forgot she'd asked Renee to lend a hand with the personalized ornaments she was making for the Christmas brunch next Saturday. They were going to double as name placards for the table.

"Can we do it on Monday instead? I've got a packed day tomorrow and I've got to go to my parents' house on Sunday.

"That'll do. I'll come over there right after work. That should give you plenty of time to hide my gift. One shake of a box and I can have it figured out."

"More power to you," Simone laughed, knowing there was yet to be a box under the tree with Renee's name on it. She'd even been stumped on what to buy her friend of twenty-one years.

"You're going to love your gift from me this year. I can promise this year you'll get one of the best gifts ever."

184

Simone sighed into the phone. "I hope you didn't go overboard." She was already feeling pressured to go extravagant.

"Leave me alone," Renee insisted, then began to rattle off the gifts she'd purchased.

Simone looked at her family's gifts stacked under the seven-foot tall tree. She didn't feel the same joy and excitement as Renee. She could already feel the tight squeezes around her neck from her nieces and nephews after they opened their new video games. She waited for the joy in her heart to return after seeing that image. *Nothing*

- - -

Simone wouldn't be satisfied until the first sip of cinnamon and spice tea danced on her tongue. The craving was strong enough to draw her out of the house by seven o'clock. She'd dressed in a white and pink warm up suit and a matching pair of running shoes. Tucked snug in her white down coat, she shoved the latest copy of Money magazine into her oversized purse and went out the door.

The Java Junkie Coffee Shop was only ten minutes away from her house and another eight minutes from the mall. Most of the stores were observing holiday shopping hours and opening at eight instead of the usual ten o'clock. Even though Simone's early departure was initially to avoid the crowds, she decided to relax. The world was always in a rush.

Simone ordered a raisin bran muffin along with her tea and found a table near the back corner of the shop that two elderly women had just abandoned. *If only there was the crackle and warmth of a fire*, she thought, pulling off her overcoat. Simone wiped a smudge of sticky residue off the wooden table then opened her magazine. The tea warmed her throat. Simone let out a soft sigh. *Just what I needed.*

She was engrossed in the magazine feature, "Smart Money Moves for the New Year," for at least ten minutes when a familiar voice pulled her attention from the page.

"Excuse me, Miss. Could you sign for this package?"

Lincoln?

He handed her a red pen and placed the back of a receipt in front of her. Following his playfulness, she scribbled her name on the paper and slid it back to him.

"And what package am I signing for?" she asked.

"Me. Special delivery." Lincoln pulled out the chair across from her and paused as if waiting for her to signal that it was okay.

Simone nodded toward the seat. "I guess there's no return to sender, huh?"

"Not right now anyway," he said.

Cute. Suddenly, warmth passed through Simone's body. Not a feeling of passion, but one -- almost like peace. A feeling that even her desired fireplace couldn't have matched.

"I take it you're trying to beat the Christmas shoppers this morning, too," she said.

Lincoln opened two packs of sugar and dumped them in his coffee. "Not me. I'm not buying Christmas gifts this year," he said, picking up the wooden stirrer. "I stopped through on the way to see a sick friend. She likes the pumpkin muffins from here. I saw you over here in the corner and invited myself to that cup of coffee you promised yesterday."

His admittance about being on strike from Christmas gifts piqued Simone's curiosity. She blew the steam off the top of her tea. "Why aren't you buying gifts?"

"This year I decided to give of myself. That's a lot more valuable, don't you think? For a person to give of himself?"

"For you, yes. But it depends on who the person is." As soon as she said it, she wished she hadn't. There he was, digging in her soul with those eyes again. Simone looked away from his face and thumbed the page corners of her magazine. She watched him dump a fourth sugar packet into his cup. By now there seemed to be more sugar than coffee.

"I can imagine showing up to my family and friends with a red and green bow on my head." Simone threw her hands in the air. "Announcement everyone. Your gift has arrived. They would walk past me and straight to the trunk of my car."

The thought of it was amusing, but sad at the same time.

"It wouldn't be as bad as you think," Lincoln said.

"Worse, probably." She shook her head and looked away. Why had she opened the door to this conversation? This was her issue. Her private struggle.

The clank of the bronze bell on the coffee shop door announced the arrival of more patrons. A girl clung to her father's neck; her red-gloved fingers intertwined like her life depended on it. She let

186

her legs buckle when he tried to put her down, so the father picked her up again.

That's what I need. Someone to carry me. Pick me up when I don't feel like standing on my own.

Simone didn't know what made her start talking again. Revealing her heart.

"I don't know who I am, so how can I give 'me' away?" I already have nothing left of the fake Simone." She zipped up the jacket of her warm up suit.

"Everybody else knows me. Business consultant, volunteer psychiatrist, personal ATM, event planner extraordinaire."

Sometime during her conversation, Lincoln had reached across the table and put his hand on her wrist. She didn't notice it until then. It felt familiar there. Warm.

"I was locked up for years because I was so shy," Lincoln confided. "It wasn't until I had a true encounter with God that I discovered who I am. It was so liberating to know God and discover the person He created me to be, not what or who others said."

Lincoln leaned forward as if he had a secret to tell. "Do you know God, Simone?"

His question made Simone shift in her seat. No one had ever asked her that before. To her, God was an untouchable notion. The only experiences she could recount about God were a few stories she'd learned when attending church as a child with an elderly neighbor. The lessons on Noah's ark, The Ten Commandments, Moses, and baby Jesus in a manger were about as much as she could recall. For Simone's family, Sundays consisted of sleeping in late, stuffing themselves with a soul food dinner, and staying clear of the game on TV so her father wouldn't slap her bottom side with the remote.

Lincoln rapped his knuckles on the table.

"No. I know a little about God. I guess," she stammered. Simone swept a strand of hair behind her ear. "Nothing like you do."

"The awesome thing about God is that He gives everyone the opportunity to know Him personally. He wants to know you, love you."

187

He paused. Simone could've sworn he stopped to listen to someone by the way he cocked his head to the side. A smile lined his face. "Carry you."

A single tear slid down Simone's right cheek. One on the left cheek followed, until there was a steady trickle. She tried to brush them away with her pinkies, but it was useless. The door to both her tear ducts and heart were open.

Lincoln squeezed her hand, his calloused palm covering the softness of her skin. Right then, right there, Lincoln asked her if she wanted to know the Lord. Without a doubt, she said, yes, even though she didn't truly know what it meant. He led her through the sinner's prayer and Simone felt God touch her heart for the first time. He considered her special enough to save her soul early in the morning in the corner of a coffee shop.

"I know this seems sudden," Lincoln said after a few minutes of conversation, "but I've got to get going. My friend is waiting for me." He looked at his watch. "Oh yeah, definitely gotta get out of here."

Simone stood with Lincoln and accepted his hug before he walked out the door. She could still feel his arms around her; his embrace both kind and strong. She was sure it was how God's arms felt.

Suddenly shopping seemed so superficial. How could she ever find gifts to compare to the one she'd just received? She couldn't. Renee had been right. She'd received one of the best gifts ever this year. And at that point, she knew both Christmas and her life had found their meanings again.

She'd call Lincoln tonight and thank him for...*His phone number. I forgot again. Monday*, she reminded herself.

Simone pinched off a corner of her muffin. That's okay. She and God had more than enough to talk about tonight.

- - -

"Girl what are you talking about? Lincoln died about three years ago." Renee took a swig of eggnog and clanked the glass down on the kitchen bar. I think he was in a car accident or something."

"I never heard that."

"I remember somebody mentioning it at our fifteen-year class reunion."

188

Can't be, Simone thought.

She intended on telling Renee about Lincoln and seeing how comfortable she felt about sharing her salvation experience with Renee. Other than the occasional prayer they sent up when life was chaotic, God was never a topic of their conversations. She couldn't picture herself as a Bible-toting saint even though she'd been doing her best to decipher the scriptures she'd been reading whenever she got the chance. Simone had made a special trip to the Christian bookstore so a knowledgeable salesperson could assist her with finding a Bible and study guide she could easily understand.

She thought some of the scriptures could be confusing. But this? This was crazy.

"Renee. I saw the man with my own two eyes Friday and Saturday. I'm a lot of things, but crazy isn't one of them."

"You probably got him mixed up with somebody else."

"No. I'm sure his name was Lincoln."

"And I'm sure Lincoln died in a car accident," Renee said. "As a matter of fact, it was probably in the local community paper."

Vapors from the freezer chilled the side of Simone's face. She slid an ice tray from the rack and cracked two cubes over her glass of white cranberry juice. For a split second, she questioned her own sanity.

"Let's just clear up the confusion," Simone suggested, abandoning her glass on the countertop. She logged onto the Internet from her laptop on the dining room table. Within seconds, she'd pulled up the website for her hometown's small community newspaper. Simone searched the obituary archives in the Hillsboro Herald.

Renee hovered over her shoulder, both curiosity and mystery their silent partners. Simone could hear her own breathing as she typed Lincoln Crawford in the search box, then scrolled down the article that popped up on the screen.

"What did I tell you?" Renee said. She hit Simone on the shoulder.

"It can't be the same person," Simone said, scanning the page for a photograph. There wasn't one. The warm feeling – the same one from the coffee shop – permeated through her body again.

- - -

Simone stared out of her office door on Tuesday just as much as she had on Monday. Surely there had to be a delivery of some sort sometime soon, she thought. The office break room was still inundated with corporate gifts of assorted popcorn, chocolates and fruit cake that were delivered last week.

The moment Simone caught a glance of a brown uniform she jumped up from her seat, but only walked as far as her office door. It was almost as if she was scared of who she would – or wouldn't – see. With his back turned, she couldn't see the deliverer's face.

"Lincoln." She swallowed the lump in her throat. "Lincoln?" she said louder.

The man stood and turned around. A full beard covered the bottom half of his face. The skin that wasn't covered was rough and uneven. Nothing like Lincoln's.

Simone didn't realize she'd been holding her breath. "I'm sorry. I thought you were Lincoln. Did he take another route? I thought he was taking Reggie's place until he came back."

"I've been taking Reggie's place."

"What about this past Friday's deliveries for this building?"

"As far as I know I delivered everything I had. What's wrong? You missing a package?" His words were quick and harsh as if he'd been offended.

"No. I signed for a package on Friday. Lincoln helped me take it out to the car and everything."

"Must've been another delivery company."

"I'm sure it wasn't. He had on the exact same uniform."

"Anyway." It seemed he'd tired quickly of her. "This package is for Simone Alexander."

"That's me," she said. Her thoughts went back to Lincoln and their exchange just four days before in that exact spot. *If only Indrea had been here*, she thought, looking at the assistant's vacant chair. This time she'd slid out for lunch.

Simone handed the signature pad back to him. "And there's no one named Lincoln who worked your shift last week?"

If the scowl and irritation hadn't covered the man's face she would've continued to drill him further, even after he answered, "No." He shook his head and didn't bother looking back when he left.

190

Simone walked back to her office and closed the door. She almost felt like she needed to pinch herself to wake up from this dream.

That's strange, she thought, turning over the brown box addressed to her. *No return address*.

She stripped off the wrapping and stuffed it into the wastebasket under her desk. In its place was a bright white box with the top held on by a single pink ribbon embellished with gold silhouettes of angels. Simone turned the box over to see if there was a business card of one of her clients attached. Nothing

One tug at the bow dropped the ribbon to the sides. Lifting the hinged lid, she saw a plush stuffed lamb sitting on a bed of shredded tan paper. A scripture written on the inside of the top lid read:

"...but only those who are written in the Lamb's Book of Life." - *Revelations 21:27*

Simone picked up the stuffed animal and pressed it against her cheek. It wasn't until she sat the lamb back on the makeshift bed of hay that she noticed the white piece of paper tucked in the corner. Unfolding it, she realized it was the receipt she'd signed on Saturday. The last time she saw Lincoln.

Simone had never believed in real angels until then. She couldn't wait to get home and tie the lamb to her Christmas tree. Lincoln had been a true angel. He'd offered her an eternal gift. One that she wouldn't be ashamed of. One that she would share with others.

Simone unlocked her purse from the bottom drawer, then pulled on her ankle-length wool coat. She'd intended to run out during lunch to pick up a bowl of chicken chili soup. There was no reason why she couldn't squeeze in an extra errand.

- - -

"Okay, okay. Let us open the boxes already," Renee said. Her smile competed with the Christmas tree lights for its sparkle.

The gas logs sparked in the fireplace as the six women sank down into the coordinated red leather furniture. The torn remains of Christmas wrapping and bows from their other gift exchanges were strewn at their feet.

191

Simone passed a bottle of white grape juice around the circle so the women could refill their wine glasses.

"This toast," she said, holding her goblet in the air, "is for the hope of a new life."

They clinked their glasses in agreement, then Renee was the first to pull the top of her ribbon.

"Hold on a minute," Simone said. The women's hands stopped mid-air and their glances fell on her.

"It's my prayer." Simone paused and started again. "It's my prayer that what I have to offer you today will change your life forever. It's so awesome that it really can't be wrapped in a box and you can take it wherever you go." She took a sip of her juice then set her glass on a wicker coaster on the coffee table. "You can open them now," she said to the anxious faces.

"What's with the stuffed toy lamb?" Bonita asked. She pushed around the bed of shredded paper beneath it, obviously looking for what she thought would be the real gift.

Simone sat back and pulled her late grandmother's flannel throw over her legs. "Well since you asked."

192

Chapter Fourteen

Sonya Visor is a co-pastor, author and playwright. She currently lives in Racine, Wisconsin and shares her heart with her husband, Pastor Tony Visor, and two sons, Jason and Tony Jr.

Who I've Become Is Not Who I Am is her first authored book. For more information on that project as well as upcoming literary and ministerial works affiliated with Sonya Visor, please visit www.sonyavisor.com.

Her contribution to *The Midnight Clear* is entitled, ***Love Me For Who I am***.

Love Me For Who I Am

Coming home for the holidays was the last thing Rainey Thomas wanted to do. Rainey had been in town for three days with only one soul knowing she was home. Tears spilled from her hazel eyes, onto her lovely milk chocolate face as she stood in her hotel room. She had to get herself together because it wouldn't be long before the Thomas family would track her down and ask her why she paid to stay at the Hyatt Hotel, five miles from her mother's home. Rainey didn't want to be surrounded by her mother's perfection. Daily, Mother Thomas' words spoke loudly from the grave.

Rainey couldn't seem to shake her mother's last sadness with the church. The words kept playing over and over in her mind. Her mother repeatedly fussed about the women at the church and how they're actions were just shameful.

"Acting a plain fool," Mother Thomas would say. "I hate to even go ov'r to the church; seein' them womens over there makin' themselves look like fools, chasing the Reverend right up in the church. I'm show glad I didn't raise my girls like them hot church goers. Naw...not my girls, they keeping their honey to catch them some good ol' saved men."

Rainey didn't do any chasing but she sure did get caught. Her appointment tomorrow would free her from her sinful ways. It would be hypocritical for her to show up handling her church duties, knowing the secrets she had. Christmas was a time when the church would give back to the community. It would restore hope in the lives, but today Rainey needed some hope. Too many people came to her for help; today she had to seek her own refuge. Not even God could help her out of this one.

Lord, how did I get here?

Rainey was beginning to regret her decision to come back to her hometown church in Milwaukee, Wisconsin. She had just recently taken a job in Minnesota, but before leaving, she promised the pastor that she would once again lead the Christmas project, planning every detail. Rainey felt guilty about leaving her family, the church and the secret love of her life. Her guilt was the only reason she made the commitment to work on upcoming events.

This year would definitely not be the same for Rainey. If there was any way she could have gotten out of it, she would have.

"Rain, open up; it's me."

It had to be Zora, Rainey's oldest sister. She was the only one who knew about her time away from everything and everybody. Although, Zora was three years older, at twenty-eight, the two were very much alike. Even miles apart, they kept their special bond.

The two ladies were often mistaken for twins. This always made their little sister, Tory, realize that the spotlight couldn't always belong to her.

"I'm coming, give me a second." Rainey wiped her eyes and smoothed down her pink pajama top. Giving herself one more look in the mirror, she opened the door.

"What's up, sis?" Zora, always looking to be the ultimate rescuer, came in with ice cream and cookies.

"What's all this?"

"We are going to eat a little something."

"A *little* something? Looks like you cleaned out the store!" Rainey said, trying to muster up some kind of enthusiasm.

"What's really going on?"

"What?" whined Rainey.

"I see you about to lie...I know, what's going on," said Zora.

"If you know what's going on, don't be asking silly questions."

"Oh, now I'm silly? How about drug addicts calling Mama's asking for your number?"

"Drug addicts?" asked Rainey.

An unexpected sound caused both Rainey and Zora to stop talking and putting the goodies on the hotel table. They stared at each other in sudden silence, not moving an inch. Who could be knocking at the door? Zora was the only one who knew Rainey was in town. The knocking persisted.

"You let somebody follow you over here," whispered Rainey.

Zora shook her head and whispered back, "Didn't nobody follow me over here."

"I'm not leaving ...so open up!" the voice called from the other side of the door.

"Tory!" both sisters yelled.

"Yeah, it's me. Now open this door before I..."

Zora opened the door and quickly snatched Tory into the room. "How did you find me...us...girl, what are you doing here?"

"Uh-ah...y'all two answer the questions...I'm the one who has information," Tory demanded, pointing at her sisters, thinking she had the upper hand.

Of the three, Tory was the bold one. There was one time when Tory's audacity almost caused Mother Thomas shame at the church. One Sunday morning, Tory walked into church wearing the shortest skirt she could find. She waited right until Pastor Christopher Dockery was in the heat of his sermon and opened her legs. Of course, with the man being a man, he looked – but only for a brief moment. Tory wanted to see if he would take the bait that her shapeliness dangled in his face. She was happy when he didn't because it was then that she knew he was a man of God. The pastor had passed her test and she was then able to join the church. After the incident she'd asked Pastor Dockery to forgive her for the calculated temptation and she begged him not to tell her mother. He never did.

Tall, chocolaty dark and what people around town described as "knock-alive handsome," thirty-three-year-old Christopher Dockery had acquired the largest "black church" in Wisconsin. Possessing a powerful physique; finely sculpted like that of an NFL wide-receiver, nearly all of the single (and even some married) women in and around the state desired to catch him, and then bring in close to his fine-tuned body, their well-thrown passes. His dark brown bedroom eyes never failed to ignite a slow burn on the flesh by just a mere glance in one's direction.

Pastor had grown the church in numbers and now he was trying to cultivate it in love. That was the purpose of the Christmas outreach ministry, but the love first had to be on the inside of each member. However, in recent months, the people seemed restless. They were more about other people's business than God's business.

One would have thought that the women at Covenant House Temple would get a gold medal for the best first lady performance. As shameful as it was, a fight almost broke out just one week ago, between Lena Frank and Josephine Norris, the two biggest competitors and members of the pastor's aide committee. Lena, a petite woman who always looked like she'd just stepped out of the salon wasn't intimidated by Josephine's model-like attractiveness, which at first glance, reminisced that of Halle Berry. These two had been in competition ever since Pastor Dockery was placed in leadership of the church.

Lena wasn't about to let Josephine outdo her in getting the Christmas program together that Pastor Dockery requested. The committee was comprised of these two women and Rainey. The news flash that everybody other than the two of them had gotten was that the pastor didn't want either one of them. Frankly, he'd gotten tired of them making a spectacle of themselves at each gathering which was why he wanted Rainey to handle all church activities. There was no drama with Rainey.

The women of course, didn't like this but it was wisdom on the pastor's part. Jealousy was something they would have to work out between themselves. Rainey took care of business. She could have any available man in the church, but she intimidated most of them because of her portrayal of perfection. But behind the beautiful face, the many church functions, her designer wardrobe, organizational skills and ability to operate her consulting business successfully, Rainey *wasn't* the ideal Christian.

People thought that she was the mirror image of Mother Thomas, but she couldn't measure up to her mother. What Rainey really wanted to do was just be free. Free to make mistakes and free to live without living in the shadows of a legend. Rainey had grown tired of *pretending* to be together; she wanted her composure to be a reality. That would take the hand of God, and right now Rainey didn't think God wanted to have anything to do with her. In her eyes, her sins were more than those of Judas, the betrayer of Jesus.

After her meeting with Pastor Dockery, her life had changed. She wouldn't be able to stay at Covenant Temple if word got out. It's amazing how Tory could be such a great news reporter of the family.

- - -

"Tell us what's going on?" The sisters surrounded Tory, which didn't take much with her being so short and sassy. They weren't in the mood for games.

"How come Malik is calling the family like a fool looking for you?" asked Tory with her arms crossed. She was a little irritated that she couldn't play a little bit with her knowledge.

197

"He's calling?" Rainey couldn't believe what she was hearing.

"Yup. You didn't cover your tracks, girl...I thought you old school girls could do that." And Tory wondered why she couldn't hang with her sisters. Her nineteen-year-old jazzy attitude always caused irritation.

"Stop playing, Tory!" If anyone could make Tory talk, Zora was that person and right now, her no-nonsense attitude was needed more than ever. If Tory found her, it was only a matter a time before somebody else would come barging into the Hyatt Hotel. Zora was just a step away from going up side of Tory's head. Tory thought she had the upper hand, but Zora was on the verge of showing her otherwise. Zora could go from being professionally and politically correct to Ebonics in no time flat, while her makeup and outfit remained in tact. She was admired by both of her sisters. Zora had a flair about her that caught the attention of many. It was not only in her looks, but her total demeanor demanded respect. She was a near replica of Mother Thomas, but a much more modern version.

Mother Thomas had gone on to be with the Lord for nearly a year now. She was well known in the church community and had high hopes for her daughters. Mother Thomas always gave her nuggets of wisdom to anyone who would listen. She wasn't one to just tote a Bible; she lived by the Word. Her very presence, not the big hats, could change the atmosphere of any room. She wore truth and expected nothing less from her daughters. On her deathbed she left her three girls in the hands of Pastor Dockery. She esteemed him highly and knew that he too, walked in truth.

"Okay, okay...back up!" Tory was trying to get herself together knowing she was only a step away from being roughed up. "Everybody at the church talking about yo' business, Rainey."

"Who is everybody?" Rainey asked.

"Those people are supposed to be walking in love and they just as hateful," said Zora. "Then they wondered why people were leaving the church as fast as they were joining."

"They...well two in particular, were just saying that Rainey was up in the pastor's office for a long time."

"Who is 'they'...and what were you doing in the pastor's office?" Zora had minimal contact with Pastor Dockery, especially

198

when she knew about her mother's request to have him look after her daughters. Plus, it didn't help that she was attracted to the man.

"We had a meeting about the community Christmas play..." Rainey was lost for words. She knew the identity of the people Tory was referencing. Rainey knew that the two who had a whiff of her business would unmask her life. Lena and Josephine would be glad to get the dirt on her. They would love to take over her role as the outreach chairperson. The Christmas play didn't matter anymore. How could she talk and encourage the community when she had her own problems? She had forgotten that she didn't even tell Malik what was going on. How could she when all she did was run away or cover up everything? Rainey had to talk to him before the outreach tonight. There was no telling what Lena and Josephine were up to. She wondered if the two women had somehow overheard the secrets she shared with Pastor.

"I've got to get to the church," Rainey stated in a desperate plea.

"First, you tell us what's going on," Zora insisted.

Rainey knew that there was no getting out of this. Her sisters should know because it would effect the reputation that the Thomas family had in the church. Knowing how church folks could be, it was better for Rainey to tell them what they were walking into. It was better for her to start with Malik, the drug addict, as Tory called him. What Tory didn't know was that he was the man her sister loved with all of her heart. It was time for her sisters to know the real Rainey.

Lord, why didn't I listen to you?

- - -

Malik Donaldson was altogether fine, but his easiness on the eyes wasn't what attracted Rainey. She was drawn to his rawness, his ability to be real, unmasked. He knew who he was. Malik was the kind of man she thought she couldn't bring home to Mother Thomas. He had issues, but she did also.

Malik and Rainey had met at the summer outreach program hosted by the church. Rainey chaired the event and was in the wrong place at the right time. Before she could even look up from registering people who were interested in knowing more about the church and its ministries, Malik extended his hand, making it clear that his only interest was in Rainey. There was an instant connection that Rainey couldn't nor wanted to destroy. Malik would show up to all of the church functions until finally, Rainey made a deal with him. She agreed to go out with him on one date, if he would come to church one Sunday for all the right reasons. That was one year ago. Rainey had kept this man a secret from her family. How could she tell her family that she was dating one of the cities biggest drug dealers?

As Rainey brought the story of her dealings with Malik to an end, she shocked both her sisters with four little words.

"I'm almost three months."

"What?" Anybody on the third floor of the hotel would be able to hear Zora.

"See, that's why I didn't want to say anything. It's alright for others to mess up, but as soon as I do the world stops…"

"I can't believe you Rain, you gone sit up here and go through this alone and let us almost hear about this drama from a bunch of church hypocrites?" Zora sat on the hotel bed and put her hands over her eyes. She felt betrayed. Her sister, her best friend felt like she had to walk in shame alone. Why?

Zora's biggest fear was turning into her mother. She loved her mother and they all were very close, but Mother Thomas' bar of life was too high to hurdle. Zora wanted people to be free, not bound to an unrealistic lifestyle. There was only one Mother Thomas.

"Rain…I'm here for you…you could have told us," said Tory, who was quiet from the moment Rainey told them about her secret life. Tory was almost liberated that her sister had flaws. Not only her mother's life, but the lives of her two sisters seem to always overshadow hers. Tory did her best to make sure that she had her moments. People often mistook her ways for rebellion, but the truth was that she only wanted to be Tory.

"Thank you Tory…I appreciate hearing that…I'm sorry for…" Rainey began to weep. She too felt a little freedom from confessing the sins she'd been withholding.

Zora stared at her sisters and knew what she had to do. She walked over to her purse and pulled out two letters and handed one to each of them. It was time for them to step into their own. Mother Thomas had instructed Zora to distribute the letters at a turning point in life. This was the time.

Rainey and Tory read their individual letter. They could hardly see, blinded by tears that were glossing their eyes and washing their souls. All three allowed the spirit of Mother Thomas to hover in the room as they meditated on the words that served as an impartation of life unto them.

Mother Thomas had spoken from the grave once again. Each letter contained what each woman needed to hear. But both letters told Mother Thomas' daughters that Jesus loved them and He was their measuring stick. She told them of her mistakes, her failures – she told her daughters to be free. She left them with a scripture that was immediately committed to memory to be a road map for their lives: Jeremiah 31:3 ...*I have loved thee with an everlasting love*...

"How did Mama...I mean... this was...," started Rainey.

"Right on time," Tory added, humbled by the experience.

It was new life breathed into the dying lives of two broken women. It was wonderful. Words couldn't express. The power of the written words on the letters melted away years of trying to measure up. The letter was filled with confessions, love and integrity. These women were loved no matter what.

"Rainey, you need to cancel your appointment at the clinic," said Zora, realizing that her sister had originally planned to cover her sin to keep her perfect church image.

"You're right." Rainey started toward the telephone.

"Wait a minute. You mean...?" Again, Tory was lost for words.

"Yes, Tory; I was about to take my child's life all because of what the church folks would think of me." Rainey stood in disbelief of herself at the mere thought of what she had planned on doing. Her thoughts reminded her also that she needed to get to the church and find Malik. He had a right to hear the truth from her; not the church's two busy bodies. Rainey wasn't ignorant of what folks were capable of doing with just one bit of information. One of Mother Thomas' slogans was. "They only have a page, and think they got the whole story."

The women at Covenant Temple would make Rainey's life a disaster if they could. Jealousy, not her fall, would be the main reason for them embarrassing her. After all, Rainey held positions that they wanted. She wore the best in attire, perfume and jewelry. Her look was unflawed as well as her demeanor, but like many, her secrets held her captive. Today was a new day for Rainey. She would face all of her demons. She had to get to the church and the Thomas sisters made it clear that she wouldn't be going alone.

The church hall was decorated in festive Christmas colors. At each table there were balloons, displaying words of hope such as: faith, love, grace and mercy. Each visitor had been given a heart to be opened at the end of the program. Rainey had outdone herself again; every detail was a work of creativity. Love was this year's theme and Pastor had been preaching a series on the topic and was looking for a great manifestation.

"I know this ain't the preacher man coming on time!" said Trina, one of the attendees of the church outreach.

All kinds of folks came out to the event for free food and gifts. Trina didn't exactly fit in with the elite club, but she tried to dress the part. She probably could have passed if her purse were a real Louis Vuitton. Trina didn't make an attempt to join Covenant Temple because she didn't like the Thomas sisters, especially Rainey for one reason only: Malik.

"Thanks, for inviting me and my family, Pastor or is it Reverend?" Trina remarked.

"Pastor is fine, sister, I'm glad you could join us."

By this time, Trina had worked her way closer to the reverend as if she was the special one in his life. She was swinging her hips and hair in the same direction as she walked toward him.

"You want to sit at our table?"

When it took a moment for Pastor Dockery to respond to Trina's request, she snapped. "Oh, see…now I get it. We not good enough to be seated with the good ol' Reverend."

The scent of drama began to thicken in the air and it wouldn't be long before any previously unknown church gossip would be revealed. Trina never could take rejection well and she wasn't about to let the fine reverend dismiss her, even if they were on church property.

"No, sister it's not like that." Pastor Dockery eyed the fellowship hall to make sure that all eyes weren't on him, but it was too late. The people seated at the tables had already turned around with their sherbet punch drinks in their hands. Pastor Dockery didn't know what he had walked into but he wished he had delayed his entrance by five minutes.

"It's not like that? Save it, or better yet save yourself!" Trina barked like an untamed dog.

"Calm down sister...all I want to do is greet everybody."

Trina, knowing that she had the spotlight, dropped her napkin thinking that Pastor Dockery was going to pick it up. After realizing that the pastor wasn't going to fall for her daintiness, she knelt down to make sure all the other men were able to take a peep at her more-than-enough cleavage.

"Y'all preachers always got some meetings going on. I know all about your meeting. Especially the one with your girl, Rainey Thomas."

You could only hear the ice in the glasses as the people continued to drink and watch Trina's showdown.

"Oh, good you've met Ms. Thomas?" the pastor responded, not realizing where the conversation would take him.

"She calls my club all the time gettin' on my nerves looking for Malik." There was no stopping Trina now. Unbeknownst to Pastor Dockery, she had come to the outreach angry because Malik had just told her that he loved Rainey. Trina had lost another round to Ms. Thomas and she would make sure that her precious church family knew that Rainey was no saint.

"Your club..." Pastor was getting his thought process together. He remembered what Rainey had told him at the meeting. She told him how she loved a man that the world didn't deem loveable and how she was carrying his child. Rainey had told pastor that she wanted to step down from her duties so that she could spend some much-needed time with God.

"Yes, my club. She messing around with my man!"

From the fellowship hall, there were sounds of members gasping in unbelief. Folks repeating Rainey's name.

"Not the Thomas sister," others were saying.

"I know all about what you are about to share, Trina." Pastor Dockery tried his best to maintain civilized conversation with the woman.

"Oh, what happened to you calling me sister?" Trina's neck was rolling now.

Standing in the background taking it all in, Lena and Josephine were glad that Trina was allowing the members to hear the truth about Rainey. She was doing all the dirty work. The smirks on their faces sang, *"We've got the victory."*

- - -

Rainey entered the fellowship hall with Malik by her side, knowing the moment she walked in that her secret was no longer her own. Her sins were confessed as the result of somebody else's tongue. There was something different on Rainey. The people could see it. Her demeanor spoke loudly, *"There is but one judge."*

Ignoring the quiet, accusing faces, Tory passed out hearts from a basket to all attendees on cue from Rainey and Malik. Pastor Dockery smiled, knowing exactly what was going on.

"There's been a change in the program," Zora announced into the microphone, beaming with pride. "The message will be from Rainey Thomas, my sister." Zora then took *her place* next to Pastor Dockery. There was a strong chemistry between the two. It wouldn't be long before they would realize that God had made them for each other.

Immediately, Lena and Josephine marched over to pastor with demands of what was going on.

"Pastor I can't believe you will allow this woman, full of all kinds of sins, to preach to these people!" Josephine had a stance that clearly screamed, *I will leave the church if you allow this.*

Pastor Dockery had finally had enough. In his eyes, Josephine and Lena were acting far worst than Trina, who at least was a non-believer. He could no longer allow this kind of behavior. Their lack of love almost caused a greater sin – death to an unborn child. This was the season to celebrate the miracle of birth. To embrace and share love, drawing people with the love of Jesus Christ. Today was a new day for Covenant Temple.

"If you leave the church, God bless you and if you stay, you will learn to walk in love. Your hateful ways drive people away. The words you have spoken have crippled the church body and this can no longer be. Not at Covenant Temple. If you can't comply with the Word of God, then as you go, let others come," Pastor preached, looking at the three women who were apparently so unhappy that they needed to find pleasure in somebody else's fall.

Pastor's prayers were being answered right before his eyes. The women, including Trina, sat down with the little dignity they had left. Their obvious choice to stay was a shock to the Thomas family as well as the pastor. All eyes returned to the front when Rainey's voice echoed through the speakers.

"The theme of today's message is: He sent His Son for me. I was living a life that was pleasing to the church and not pleasing to God. I kept secrets, I lied. Yes, I've sinned but God sent His Son for me. He sent Him for you. Jesus is love, but church, we must love people too. It doesn't matter who they are or what they've done; love will bring them to the Son."

Responses of "Amen" and "Bless God" filled the air in the fellowship hall. Mailk took his place and shared his heart.

"The only reason I'm standing here right now is because of Rainey Thomas. She chose to love me despite my sinful ways, as y'all call it. No one from the church ever showed that kind of love. I didn't want to be 'round a bunch of hypocrites; at least I knew I was a sinner. I never thought I was better than anyone, but the church folks thought they were better than me. What's that scripture? We've all fallen short of the glory."

Laughter erupted from the congregation when somebody yelled from the back, "You better preach boy!"

"What I'm saying is…Rainey accepted me for who I was. And that love brought me a mighty long way. Our getting together started in sin, but it eventually brought me to the cross. Christmas never really meant much to me before, but today I know the true reason. I will leave you with this thought. The only one who matters is Christ, all else will fall into place. The hearts that were passed out remind us of the greatness of Christ's love."

The congregation read what was written on each heart: *Inside of me I have POWER; it's called LOVE.* God was in the midst. The people realized that they could be a true church only when they chose to love unconditionally.

Mother Thomas found me one day and told me this, "Even in your darkest midnight, Jesus can make everything clear."

Chapter Fifteen

Carolyn Forché was born in Chicago, Illinois and has been blessed of God to enjoy a career that spans many disciplines, all of which have been threaded with the prerequisite for writing skills.

She eventually saw her career segue to becoming a full fledged journalist/editor for a Chicago newspaper, and public relations specialist for a number of organizations and agencies.

During the administration of President Jimmy Carter, Carolyn was the first woman and first African American to be appointed to the six-state Midwest Region V, Director of Public Affairs, a sub-cabinet level presidential appointment for the U.S. Dept. of HHS. She served as Illinois Deputy Press Secretary for the Dukakis/Bentsen U.S. Presidential Campaign. During this time, she maintained her Christian leadership positions as teacher and PR Director for her church, eventually becoming an ordained minister. She is currently working toward obtaining a Masters in Divinity. Visit Carolyn online at www.CarolynsQuill.com.

Carolyn is author of the award-winning, bestselling children's book, *Colors come From God...Just Like Me!* She is also the author of *The Story of a Man Named Job* and the soon-to-be-released, *That's Not Nice What You Did To Me*, which is targeting for healing sexually abused children.

Her contribution to *The Midnight Clear* is titled, **The Best Christmas Promise Ever**.

The Best Christmas Promise Ever

Quickly dropping her luggage and winter coat inside her sister's isolated room in ICU, Carole rushed to RoseMarie's bedside. She had just flown in from Houston, Texas to be with her ill sister. The reports were not good. This was the third time in three years that Carole had stopped everything to fly home to be there for Rose. There were tubes of various sizes coming from and going into different ports in her now, frail body. She was semi-comatose, but upon seeing her big sister, Rose strained to lift her head and cried out in a surprised, labored, barely audible voice, just moments before the medications sedated her:

"Carole, what are *you* doing here?"

"I'm here on a mission from God!" Carole affirmed, startled at the words, which were involuntarily coming from her own lips. Then she gave her little sister's thin body a long embrace before being asked to let the medical staff administer yet another procedure. A breathing apparatus was rushed in. RoseMarie was in critical condition, but Carole had a *promise* from God!

The most difficult to bear was seeing doctors insert the large, accordion-ribbed breathing tube, which kept Rose's mouth uncomfortably and awkwardly propped open –while sending life-sustaining oxygen into her lungs. Amazingly, Rose was still very pretty despite her fragile state. Her chiseled features, large almond-shaped eyes, long black eyelashes, perfectly shaped nose and bow-shaped full lips, had not succumbed to the full-scale attack of leukemia on her otherwise weakened frame. Doctors and nurses would stand over her and say they'd never seen anyone go through what she was going through, who still looked as pretty. They made these observations even though radiation had significantly altered Rose's flawless, coppery bronze complexion, and chemo had left her completely bald.

Carole mused to herself. *Such a pretty picture would not have been, had I been the patient. Chiseled features? Hmmmm, I think not.* Plus Rose didn't have on a speck of makeup. Carole felt a tad guilty, realizing how vain she was to be wondering how bad she'd look without makeup had she been in her sister's place. Carole's motto concerning her makeup was, "I don't leave home without it."

Because of the white coats that were now surrounding RoseMarie's bed, Carole could no longer see her sister. Leaning her head back against the wall where she stood waiting near the ICU glass-walled unit, which looked directly out onto the nurses' station, she folded her arms to relax her posture. Carole reflected on the past half hour before arriving at the hospital. She had scurried through homebound Christmas travelers at Midway Airport and zeroed in on the wide-eyed astonishment of the Chicago cabbie, when she plunged herself in front of his moving taxi to insist that she not be passed up "one nuther time!" She *had* to get to the hospital at all cost. Carole pretended to ignore the "I've got a live one" cautious glare in his eyes as he looked at her through the rear view mirror after she rushed open his back door and threw in her bags, not trusting him to help.

"Get me to Methodist Hospital!" she ordered. "I've got to get there yesterday, and fast!" Remembering the golden rule, she added, "Please, sir!"

In the midst of holiday shoppers laden with brightly colored shopping bags crossing at the stoplights five minutes from her destination, it seemed each red light lasted an eternity. Carole gave the cabbie a thirty percent "hassle tip" when at last they arrived, and wished him a Merry Christmas. Taking note of her generosity, he quickly exited his door, rushed around to open the passenger door and helped her negotiate her luggage to the hospital entrance. He flashed a nervous, side-glanced grin, like he thought Carole was "certifiable" mentally, and might just lose it at any moment and swing at him with her purse. Silently amused at his cautious fear of her potential for violence, she remembered a lesson she learned a long time ago: Not only does money talk, but also it forgives insanity, rudeness and all forms of lawlessness.

She uttered a quick, "Forgive me, Jesus" for the hassle and a "Thank you" for sparing her life from the stupid prank she had just pulled with the moving cab that could have landed her in the nearest airport hospital emergency room.

Weighed down with luggage, Carole was ever grateful for doors that opened automatically upon approaching the hospital lobby. She was so focused on finding elevators, she hardly noticed the spectacularly large and tall Christmas tree. It stood gracing the center of the huge, round, three-story, window-walled lobby. Her eyes spotted the silver escalator on the other side of the tree and she ran for it, not wanting to waste another second looking for elevators. As impatient as she was to reach the main floor on the third level, Carole couldn't help but marvel at the gorgeous, glistening tree that rose with her as she glided up three flights of moving stairs.

For a moment, she was lost in the fantasy of childhood delights of Christmas. She was mesmerized with the variety of its colorful, shiny ornaments, which reflected all the joyous themes of the season. There were toys of every imaginable kind, from dolls to trains, and sugarplums to gingerbread men. There were sparkling icicles, snowflakes, snowmen, drummer boys, gift-wrapped boxes, angels, nativity scenes, and Santa with reindeer in tow, circling up toward the treetop star. Carole took special notice of the spectacular star at the top of the tree that had to span a diameter of at least five feet; and a height of eight feet. At its highest peak, it was studded with large, faux diamonds and pearls.

"OH MY GOD!" She blurted.

Suddenly and abruptly, the escalator plunged the always poised and sophisticated "Ms.Thang" (as her detractors would call her), into reality from her distracted day-dreaming. She stumbled and toppled backwards at the same time, as the disappearing top step teeter-tottered her to a landing halt, with her long, flailing arms, legs, skidding high heels and an overstuffed shoulder purse all fighting gravity at once. Gravity lost out when in the midst of all her flailing, she tripped the man just in front of her who came tumbling down, bringing her attempt to balance this comedy of errors to a fateful end.

What an awkward sight she became, and brought a stranger plummeting in tow. Carole was the brunt of uncontrollable laughter to several teens that had exited ahead of her and were trying unsuccessfully to hide their cackling amusement behind their hands. A few people rushed to assist, but were helpless to find which way to reach into the fray without falling onto the escalator themselves. Fortunately, Carole regained her balance, glancing back in a somewhat irritated manner at the moving steps, as though they somehow were responsible for her diverted attention and nearly treacherous fall. Embarrassed, Carole wondered within herself why people did that when they stumbled, as though it was the stairs' or the sidewalk's fault when they tripped? Meanwhile, she apologized to the man, who took the tumble with her.

His back was still toward her as he leaned over, brushed himself off and said, "Don't mention it; don't mention it."

She was glad not to have to face him and her obvious chagrin over the ungraceful display. Her eyes intentionally met no one's as she adjusted her skirt, smoothed her hair and straightened the luggage handle and shoulder strap of her purse. Fortunately, the escalator had delivered her directly to an elevator bank and she quickly slipped into an open car – alone.

Thank goodness, she thought, finally shielded from the amused eyes of pedestrian onlookers who saw the whole ungainly scene. "What-ever!" she exhaled under her breath, excusing herself for losing her cool.

But just before the elevator closed, a strong, dark brown hand belonging to a man, grasped the door, forcing it back open. He wore a clergy and was wielding another of Carole's bags with his free hand. It had apparently tumbled off her luggage hook just before entering the elevator car. He was a striking man with a quick smile and warm manner, but had the look in his eyes of a man with a mission. Something Carole had always dreamed of.

He introduced himself. "Hello, young lady. I'm the man you just tried to have admitted as a patient in this institution. But God!" He smiled reassuringly as he pointed to her smaller luggage he'd retrieved. "I thought you might be needing this."

Carole was speechless. First, because she was so embarrassed at having caused him to fall, and secondly, because she was clearly discombobulated at his manner, his persona, and his smile. And it didn't hurt at all that he was a minister without a wedding band. She couldn't believe that her own usual persona, which was always calm, poised and professional, had succumbed to having lost her cool twice in the space of five minutes.

Coincidentally, they exited at the same floor. He was there to visit hospitalized members of his church, he told her. They chatted briefly as she told him about her sister, and asked him to please remember her in his prayers. He assured her that he would, and gave her his card to contact him to let him know of Rose's progress. She (gladly) promised she would, but kept a serious look on her face, not wanting him to see she was instantly smitten. The card

211

read, Jonathan David, M.Div., Chaplain, and Licensed Christian Counselor. Carole's reflections of the last thirty minutes and the escalator incident were interrupted by the doctors who began moving away from Rose's bed, talking among themselves. They nodded politely toward Carole as they left the room. She stopped the last one and asked if Rose was going to be alright.

He responded in a well-trained professional tone, saying, "It's too early to tell. We'll know more in a few days."

What kind of a non-answer was that? she thought, and then walked slowly back to the bed where Rose's long black, silken eyelashes lay closed. She was motionless except for the heaving of her chest from the breathing apparatus. The rhythm of her breathing seemed to keep time with Christmas carols wafting into the room from a chorus of youngsters, who'd come caroling. She hung on to the words and began to sing along.

"All is calm, all is bright..." Then, *"Oh come, all ye faithful, joyful and triumphant..."* And their finale was the best of all. *"Oh...tidings of comfort and joy, comfort and joy. Oh...tidings of comfort and joy!"*

She smiled, and the staff and patients who could, applauded. By singing favorite Christmas carols and savoring the words of hope, these kids had ushered in the Christmas spirit for her, right there in the hospital, with a sister who was fighting for her life. The songs and their familiar, nostalgic melodies infused a greater faith, which rose up in her with anticipation and excitement to begin decorating Rose and Don's home for Christmas. She knew Rose would be home soon.

Nevertheless, as Rose's big sister, Carole could barely accept what was happening to her. But the promise kept her at peace, even in the midst of this tragedy. She found a sense of relief in knowing that Rose was not feeling the pain of her condition. The bombardment of foreign fluids and toxic cancer drugs being pumped into and coursing through her stricken blood stream seemed a vicious attack on the baby of the family. All the paraphernalia of prevention surrounding her – the machines, the beeping sounds on the heart monitor, the green, jagged lines on the life support system, fluctuating between flat-lining and peaked spurts – signaled a battle between the threat of death and Rose's indomitable will to live (even in an unconscious state).

Carole's eyes felt assaulted by what they saw. The scene was painted in marked contrast to the sassy, shapely, vibrant sister she knew, who would keep her, and anyone around, laughing till their stomachs hurt from her zinging wit and humor.

She leaned over and kissed her cheek. "How could this be?" Carole asked no one in particular. But immediately afterwards, she was checked by the promise, and rubbed Rose's face gently. She spoke quietly to her, wanting to believe she could hear in spite of the fact she had been sedated. Carole sang songs to her sister, and spoke words filled with confidence.

"We're going to beat this thing with our faith and the Hand of The Sovereign God," she said, assuring her in her unconscious state, she'd be home for Christmas.

At that affirmation, Rose's husband, Don walked in, smiling and agreeing with the words he'd just heard Carole utter. "That's right! Rosie is coming home; I don't care what anybody says!"

Carole loved his solid confidence. He never once appeared worried that Rose would not make it through this ordeal. Christmas was two weeks away, but he and his sister-in-law, Carole J. Fortier, were considered a little crazy and were bold in their defensive mode before others who attempted to gingerly prepare them for the worse.

"Thank God for crazy faith," Carole would often say.

After spending a short time with them, she left Don to be alone with his wife and meandered out into the hall.

"Rose will be home for Christmas," she affirmed again to herself. "It's a family tradition she just can't miss."

They looked forward to the holidays, beginning with Thanksgiving. For the Johnson clan, it was not so much about presents, but about reliving the childhood memories that always summoned warm and wonderful feelings of the season. Their presents were "*Little House On The Prairie*" kinds of simple gifts, which they cherished and delighted in as though Santa had brought bags full of fine toys and gifts from Swartz's Toys in New York City. For them, it was the excitement of trimming the tree, singing Christmas songs around the family piano, stringing popcorn for garland, the smells of a fresh pine tree, hot spicy wassail, homemade eggnog topped with whipped cream, the cooking of traditional dishes everyone loved, and the baking of special cookies, cakes and pies.

That was another reason why Carole wouldn't let herself think Rose wouldn't be sharing in this wonderful time of year. In the midst of the contrasting hospital scenes all around her, her thoughts began to segue into this one conviction, which she clung to like life itself ... hope for a Christmas miracle! That hope strengthened her for the difficult days, which lay ahead.

She thought of their precious parents, Larney and Hester Johnson, who had passed on to eternity. This ordeal would have been very difficult for them. They had already lost four children before Rose and Carole were born. Could they have taken the loss of Daddy's "Brown Sugar," which he called Rose as a baby? When Carole was only eleven, she had asked their mother how she and her daddy dealt with the loss of four children – three babies and one sixteen-year-old that died from a respiratory illness the very year Carole was born. Hester's answer was mind-boggling to a kid at such a young age.

She looked at her little daughter with those softly piercing gray eyes and quietly said, "I simply thanked God for loaning us one of His children for a while."

Wow! Carole exclaimed to herself.

Rose was always mistaken for a much younger woman, in her late twenties or early thirties at the most; but she was actually forty-two. She was a consummate Christian, and fervent prayer counselor. But as the executive assistant to the pastor of a mega ministry, she also loved life and was balanced, not stiff and pseudo-spiritual. Because she was such a vibrant, quick-witted personality, which she actually inherited from her mother (only her mother's brand of humor was once described by a family friend as "sugar, sprinkled with arsenic"), Rose's straight-faced barbs, often church culture related, rendered the most stoic, stuff-shirted people she encountered, weak-kneed, and doubled over with her sidesplitting wit.

Her banter once saved the day for a pastor, whose reputation for being in absentia at vitally important board meetings finally met the impatient, jaundiced eyes of fellow clergymen as they gathered to enter council chambers. As he came flying into the conference area, his chagrin at being late after months of missed meetings was neutralized in front of the Elders, when Rose mocked in a deep, resonant voice – *"Kill the fatted calf! Bring out the royal robe! Put*

214

a gold ring on his finger! Let us eat and be merry, for this our son who was lost is found!" Needless to say, Rose's quote from the Luke 15 story of *The Prodigal Son* broke everyone up and the delinquent pastor's embarrassment was spared.

Carole would often tell Rose that she could have had a brilliant career writing for sitcoms or comedians who would have competed heavily for her material. But with her, wit was something that came naturally and spontaneously. It was a gift she shared liberally with others. People were drawn to her as if to invite some clever, often self-deprecating, remark about themselves that would bring laughter and levity to whatever circumstance facing them – good or bad.

However, there was nothing humorous about this report of cancer. With the first clear prognosis now established, her age alone was a very certain death knell to the medical community. They assumed that even with radical treatment it was simply a matter of time. But God had other plans.

Chemotherapy, radiation, a Hickman port in her upper left chest to receive chemo injections and a host of other drugs to eradicate cancer cells made Carole's little sister *appear* to be at the end of her life. The persistent beeping of the heart monitor near the wall was a constant reminder that the rhythm of life is much like listening to the gentle beat of a song that stubbornly lingers in the mind. Only this – life's rhythm – was one song that few ever wanted to end. But there were times Carole wished the sound on the monitor would be turned off, because it sometimes drowned the faithful affirmation of "This thing shall not be" that she repeated often to herself.

Once, the erratic monitor suddenly sent one first-year resident, who had come to cherish Rose, racing furiously down the hall, pushing her on a gurney, rushing to wherever – and trying feverishly to pound life back into her fiercely resisting, yet gradually ebbing, life-line.

As the ninth child, or "next to the baby" as Carole was referred to growing up, she had to resist a nagging sense of guilt that tried to haunt her about why this should happen to the baby of the family.

"Why not you instead?" the demons of doubt taunted.

Carole quickly laid them to rest, because she had been given a promise about Rose. A promise from the only *true* Promise Keeper. She knew The Divine Physician would heal Rose. He had promised it. The family believed it. That settled it! Rose's life would be a

215

testimony for thousands around the world to hear about the "God of all flesh" who still worked miracles. She was surrounded by her devoted husband, and five siblings who refused to be moved in their faith that Rose would surely come out of this thing victoriously. But for Carole, the hope for victory was the gift of life at Christmas. This saga had begun three years ago, and this time, Carole was not returning home without knowing her sister was restored.

She first received the news about Rose's diagnosis after moving to Houston. She'd relocated there five years earlier from Chicago. She knew something was amiss when she received a call from Susan Smith, her pastor's wife in Chicago who, as graciously and calmly as possible, attempted to break the news about Rose's prognosis. Rose had asked her to call Carole because she couldn't do it herself. She knew it would devastate her sister. Rose was a close friend to Susan, and worked as executive assistant to her husband, Dr. Horace Smith. The fact that he was both a pastor and a physician, specializing in hematology oncology, with a wife who was also a medical professional, made this diagnosis seemingly impossible for them to receive with hope – because they fully understood the condition medically. They, too, were devastated by the news. They loved Rose passionately and she adored them as well, making her job working for one of the largest churches in the Chicago area, though high-pressured, an enjoyable position.

But the first miracle for Carole in this nearly three-year saga with her sister's health crisis was what happened upon initially hearing the horrifying report. The deep, gasping breath she took in upon hearing Susan's announcement that RoseMarie had been diagnosed with leukemia instantly shocked her senses; but her chest-heaving gasp was halted "mid-breath," by a voice that spoke gently, yet authoritatively, to her spirit.

"THIS THING SHALL NOT BE!"

By the time Carole exhaled, an indescribable peace had overshadowed her, calming every anxiety that was about to engulf and crush to pieces her very soul. In the three years that followed, Carole knew it was not mere coincidence that being self-employed afforded her the liberty to drop everything and fly to Chicago to be with her sister for eight weeks the first time, and six weeks another. She knew she had been chosen by God to be a guardian angel, of sorts, to her sister. He had orchestrated the arrangements for her

216

four sisters, Susan and herself to be there for Rose throughout this illness. As God would have it, Carole was available to stay by her side, sleeping next to her in a cot or chair in the hospital, and nursing her during her stays at home.

In Rose's totally weakened state, Carole was honored to do whatever it took to comfort, encourage and keep words of faith and songs of deliverance going into her ears. Even when she was unconscious, Carole whispered the words of God about healing throughout the days and during those dark, lonely nights in the hospital. However, the one who demonstrated the greatest faith was Rose.

From the moment she had returned from a vacation with her husband and opened the mail alerting her to report to her doctor immediately (although totally shaken at the prospect of beginning chemotherapy within a week), Rose's faith went into action.

She frequently whispered to Carole from weakened vocal chords as she lay so still, "I know the Lord is going to heal me."

She urged Carole not to deny that she had cancer. Not to be afraid of saying the "C" word. Now ministering to her caregiver, she urged, "Carole, we've got to be willing to admit what is happening in my body in order to pray effectively against it." She knew Carole had been refusing to speak the word cancer or leukemia in conversations and prayers – believing such a spoken admission of the disease would authorize its ownership of her. Her own faith in God was key to her restoration. Even when barely able to speak, Rose often uttered, "I believe God is going to heal me."

Preparing meals and keeping the house for Rose and Don, Carole refused to spend time with her Chicago friends who felt she needed to get out for a break. She didn't want to leave Rose. She fed her, brushed her teeth, and lifted her thin, fragile body into the tub to bathe her, praying for God to keep her from slipping or losing her balance as she tried to negotiate lifting and carrying Rose from the tub, back to her bed. Carol had never done anything like this before and knew God was with her.

It was now six months later, after Carole had returned to Houston from caring for Rose the second time for six weeks. The Christmas season was now in full swing. Carole's son-in-law, a pharmacist, received a call from Chicago to alert Carole about Rose's worsened condition. Reggie seemed very grave after she responded that Rose would be fine. However, because he was a medical professional, he told her with a somber and grave tone that he thought her prognosis this time was of such that she should prepare to go to Chicago immediately. Another crisis with her blood count had developed and things were not looking hopeful. Carole agreed. However, this time, she returned full of faith in the promise God had given her three years prior. She knew it was time for God's promise, "This thing shall not be!" to be manifest. She was returning this third time to stand in faith that this Christmas would be the best Christmas promise ever! She was resolute.

While Carole understood and respected medical professionals, she was glad not to be one of them. It might have stood in the way of her faith the way she had seen it obscure the faith of solid Christians, whose knowledge of medicine, compromised their total belief in and dependence on the workings of God through faith. Hopeless was not in her vocabulary where Rose was concerned.

"Hopeless," Carole would affirm, "is a word for those without faith."

She loved to quote a personal affirmation. *"For those who believe, HOPE is the desire of the heart backed up by confidence. But FAITH is the desire of the heart accomplished – without evidence."*

Flying at 33,000 feet, Carole didn't know what to expect when she would see Rose in a matter of hours. She had no clue that soon, Rose would be lying unconscious in ICU, only moments after she arrived. Spending time in a hospital gave much time for all these reflections of Rose's battle with leukemia. She decided to return to the room.

- - -

Don remained by his wife's side while Carole had gone to the hospital cafeteria to get a cup of coffee. Returning, Carole noticed that another team of physicians began filing into her sister's room. Don left to give them space to attend to Rose. Instead of joining Don in the hall, Carole walked into the room, joining the white-coated crew and remained standing there beside Rose until they asked her to leave the room while they examined her. She respectfully complied, but not before asking each of them to allow her to anoint their hands with oil and pray for them before they examined her.

218

Carole would later confess, "Bold faith will cause you to do some bold things!"

Surprisingly, each of the five doctors willingly held out their hands for her to anoint them with the blessed oil. Carole believed their open consent to allow her to anoint their hands without a question asked, to be an act of God Himself. It was much later that she realized under normal circumstances, physicians would question the germ factor of taking oil they knew nothing about, to be put on their hands before examining a patient.

Carole told friends later that, "Faith will cause you to do strange things when you're facing a red sea. But *obedience* parted the sea when Moses lifted up his rod at the strange command of God; and Noah kept on building that strange looking boat, before it had ever rained."

Those friends later laughed with her about that, but agreed that Rose was indeed facing a Red Sea experience, and the rod that was held up was the rod of obedience. Carole had learned from years of walking with God that one might be asked to do some strange things, but that God was a strong deliverer.

Most of the medical staff and Rose's wonderful attending physician observed their family with a curious tolerance. Others admired their faith, but with a sympathetic compassion for what they perceived to be obvious lack of medical knowledge – knowledge which would surely have caused them to be more "realistic" about any chance for their sister's recovery. Rose's personal oncologist, however, was a wonderful, kind and highly skilled woman in her thirties. Her manner was very professional, but she was also very warm and easy to talk with. When Rose was conscious, she spoke affectionately about Dr. Jacobs, and actually looked forward to the times she was to be taken to her office for examinations.

The evening Dr. Jacobs called for the family to come in for a conference about Rose's condition was five days after Carole's arrival. They sat silently, but unswerving in their faith that no matter what, they would believe God to restore Rose. She explained Rose's condition, saying that while she understood the family's faith – her condition could go either way during the night or before the weekend was over. She was very kind and as comforting as possible.

219

Finally, she said she would hope for the best and stood up to leave the hospital's family conference room, offering them the opportunity to call whenever they needed to talk with her. The family thanked her for her kindness and she quietly left the room, at which point, Carole turned to the family and asked the often-quoted scriptural question.

"Whose report will we believe?"

In a chorus of immediate response, the family quoted the rest of that verse. "We will believe the report of the Lord."

This was a reference to scriptures promising the report of the Lord saying, "You were healed" in I Peter 2:24.

Miraculously, the next day, a Saturday, that very weekend, Rose came out of the coma! Her vital signs incredibly returned normal. The news went through the hospital and the church community that Rose worked for -- locally and nationally -- like a lightning bolt. They had all been praying. Every doctor and medical professional familiar with Rose's case declared that this was truly A MIRACLE!!! Rose would be coming home for Christmas. She had been given the gift of life for Christmas. For Carole and her family, this was truly the greatest Christmas promise ever!

At the family Christmas gathering, Rose's husband was grinning ecstatically and hugging his wife endearingly throughout the day and evening. The Johnson family had held on to their faith, and Carole held on to her personal promise from God: "This Thing Shall Not Be!"

- - -

Today, Rose is *fully delivered* from cancer. She is again working full time, pretty as ever and squeezing her plumper figure into a size twelve! Six months after her Christmas miracle, a celebration was held in her honor. The medical staff of the hospital attended along with family and friends.

During the tributes, Carole was speaking reverently of the times she lifted RoseMarie's fragile body to bathe her, only to hear Rose quip behind her back within everyone's hearing, "Try that **now**, kid!" Rose is herself again – but with a part-time gig: Ministering hope!

Oh, and newlyweds, Carole and Jonathan David flew in from Morocco, having just ended their two-week honeymoon, to be with Rose, Don and the whole Johnson clan for Christmas.

As it turned out, Jonathan "fell for Carole"...in more ways than one.

Chapter Sixteen

 **Valerie Coleman** has been called to help writers get their books published. Walking in her purpose, she helped to establish Butterfly Press, a publishing company for Christian books and plays. She has since spread her wings and established her own company, **Pen Of** the **WritER or POWER** Press.

Her first compilation, *Blended Families - An Anthology,* released October 2006 consists of stories from novice and published authors from across the nation that minister to the unique demands of blended or stepfamilies.

With a heart to teach and serve, she founded the Pen To Paper Literary Symposium in 2004. This annual two-day conference draws participants from California to Florida. Presenters include national best-selling authors like Dan Poynter, Vickie Stringer, Parry "EbonySatin" Brown and Kendra Norman-Bellamy. In 2005, Valerie co-founded Write On! Workshops, which are seminars geared toward the novice writer. To read more, visit www.PenOfTheWriter.com.

Valerie has a bachelor's degree in Industrial Engineering from GMI Engineering & Management Institute and an MBA from The University of Dayton. She is a senior engineer in the automotive industry and a college mathematics instructor. A mother of five, she resides in Dayton, Ohio with her husband. They worship at Revival Center Ministries, International.

Her contribution to *The Midnight Clear* is entitled, *Safe In His Arms*.

Kaitlynn stood in the living room with her face pressed against the frosted window. Tears ran down her cheeks as she waved goodbye to her children. When the 1994 Ford Escort turned the corner, she crumpled to the floor.

"Babe, are you okay?" Jonathan, her loving husband, walked into the room and sat next to her.

"What am I going to do without my boys?" She shook her head and fell over into his lap. "After all these years, now he wants to be a father."

Jonathan stroked her hair and whispered, "They'll be alright."

"How can you be sure?"

"I asked God to protect them and I know that He will."

Thirteen years earlier, Kaitlynn graduated from high school at the top of her class. She had received her college acceptance letter and was scheduled to start her first job in three weeks — a co-op position with the largest auto manufacturer in the world. Excited about the news, she called her boyfriend, Donald.

"Hey Don," she said, with a grin as wide as the Atlantic Ocean. "I'm going to Flint!"

Without any enthusiasm or interest, he said, "That's great."

"What's wrong?"

"Look, I've got to go. I'll see you at church tonight."

After Friday night service, she caught up with Donald in the parking lot. As usual, the young sisters circled him like vultures.

"Hey Don." Kaitlynn shuffled through the groupies and kissed her man on the cheek. "Excuse me ladies, but I've got to talk to Don in private."

"Humph. She ain't all that," an unfamiliar female said.

Kaitlynn turned to the neophyte. "I'm sorry. Did my words offend you?"

"Well, we were trying to talk to him. You could have ---"

"Hey Janice. It's cool." Donald raised his hand. "We'll talk later."

"Okay, later." She smirked, rolled her eyes at Kaitlynn and then walked away with the rest of the entourage.

"Another one of your girlfriends?"

"Come on now, Kaitlynn." He threw his arm around her waist and pulled her in close. "You know you're my only girl."

"I know, but I'm not comfortable with those girls hanging around you all the time."

"That's what you get when you deal with an all-city athlete." He kissed her cheek. "Sorry I wasn't excited about your news earlier. I've got a lot on my mind. I'm really going to miss you though."

"I'm going to miss you too, but you can come up and visit. It's only four hours away."

- - -

In the second-floor office, Kaitlynn plowed through the piles of documents that needed to be filed numerically. After the hundredth seven-digit number, boredom rested on her shoulder and lulled her to sleep. In an effort to stay awake and maintain employment, she called Donald.

"I'm sorry, Kaitlynn, but this is not a good time," his sister said. "We just found out that Momma has taken a turn for the worse. We're on our way to the hospital."

"Oh my God. Which one? I'll meet you there."

"Saint Elizabeth. Gotta go, bye."

Kaitlynn paged her boss and left the factory in a sprint. By the time she reached the hospital, Donald was in a frenzy. When he saw Kaitlynn, he ran to her.

"She's gone. My momma's gone."

Kaitlynn hugged her man and caressed his back. In their four years of dating, she had never seen him shed a tear. His forceful crying made her heart heavy and his hurt soon overtook her. Together, they stood in the waiting room and cried.

- - -

A week before Kaitlynn left for school, she stopped by Donald's house. His sister, Paula was braiding her friend's hair.

"So Kaitlynn, what are you doing special for Donald before you leave for school?" the girl said as she sat Indian style on the floor. Paula tugged on a defiant lock. "Ouch! Take it easy."

"Be still," Paula said.

"Well, I hadn't really planned to do anything special. We talked about going out to dinner."

"Dinner?" She chuckled. "Is that the best you can do?"

"I think dinner is nice," Paula said. "I'll be back. I need some more beads." She left the room and Pocahontas turned to Kaitlynn.

"Girl, with a man that fine, I know you can think of something else to do for him."

"Not really," Kaitlynn shrugged.

"Well, let me say, do *to* him."

Grasping the girl's implication, Kaitlynn quickly said, "Oh, well, Donald and I don't do that. We love the Lord."

"I love the Lord too. But you're going to be gone for three months and you know how those girls are always on him. Do you really think he's going to wait for you?"

"I never really thought about it," Kaitlynn picked at her fingernails. "I've never had sex before. I-I don't know what to do."

"Girl, just follow him. *He* knows what to do."

- - -

Settled into her private dorm room, Kaitlynn studied for her first calculus exam. In the midst of solving the derivative of x, nausea consumed her. She darted to the restroom, flung the door open and made it to the trashcan just as her lunch escaped.

For the next several weeks Kaitlynn expelled her breakfast, lunch, dinner and sometimes, air. And with a cycle as punctual as the gushing Old Faithful geyser, she knew she was pregnant. When she returned home for Thanksgiving break, she shared the news with Donald.

"What do you mean, you're pregnant?" He pushed away his Big Mac. "How'd that happen?"

"What do you mean, how did that happen?" She rocked her head and propped an elbow on the table. "You were there. You know."

"How far along are you?"

"About ten weeks. And I've been so sick. Running to the restroom between classes and ---"

"It's not mine."

"Huh?"

"It's not mine! You have been at school sleeping around and now you want to put this off on me."

"You're kidding me, right?" Tears formed in Kaitlynn's eyes as her first love belittled her. "You're the only person I've ever been with."

226

"Tell me anything," he said, as he snatched her car keys. "Let's go."

- - -

As word of Kaitlynn's pregnancy spread through the church, shame settled on her shoulders. She understood why the pastor suspended her from the choir, but she did not understand why the father of her child, the pastor's son, was allowed to continue playing the drums and leading devotions. Seven months pregnant and unable to return to college, Kaitlynn endured the mockery of the so-called saints.

"Oooh," a parishioner moaned while she rubbed Kaitlynn's belly. "Are you sure you're going to have that baby when you think you are?" She whispered to the lady next to her and then laughed. With her head bowed, Kaitlynn walked away.

"Hey Kaitlynn," Donald waved. "Come over here for a minute."

Excited that he was speaking to her, Kaitlynn waddled over to him. "Hey Don. How've you…"

"I want you to meet my girlfriend. Sharon, this is Fatso. Fatso, this is Sharon." He put his arm around the new apprentice and planted a kiss on her lips.

"My name is Kaitlynn." She extended her hand dispite her breaking heart. "Nice to meet you." *Be careful of this one, he's a charmer.*

- - -

After dinner, Kaitlynn went to her bedroom and closed the door. She stared at the yellow and white walker, a baby shower gift from her co-workers. Picking up the yarn and needles from her dresser, Kaitlynn sat in the rocking chair.

"Okay now Mister, looks like it's going to be me and you." She rubbed her belly and then proceeded to crochet several more rows on the baby blanket she began weaving days earlier. "One, two, three, four, five. One, two…"

A knock at the door interrupted her.

"Come in."

Kaitlynn's mother, Mema, came into the room. "Hey baby. You counting to Mister again?"

"Yes ma'am. I'm teaching him early. He's going to be brilliant."

"Well, with you as his mother, he can't help but be brilliant."

"Thanks Momma." Kaitlynn dropped her head.

"How are you doing?"

Putting the unfinished blanket aside, she said, "I'm okay, but today was a tough one."

"What happened?" Her mother sat on the bed and patted the seat next to her. "Come talk to me about it."

"Well, I got the usual comments about being way too big for seven months." She looked at her mother with tears in her eyes. "They really believe him. They think I'm pregnant by someone from school." She shook her head then massaged her temples.

"You know how they can be — smile in your face one day and stab you in the back the next." Mema rubbed her daughter's back.

"But I heard the all-time winner today." Tears ran down Kaitlynn's cheeks and pooled at the top of her well-formed stomach. "One of the church mothers told me that Donald's been telling people that I raped him."

"What?"

"Yeah, I supposedly raped him. At first the baby wasn't his, now I raped him. He's got me by seventy pounds easy; so if I raped him, I'm a bad girl." She laid her head in her mother's lap. "He's stupid enough to tell it and they're stupid enough to believe it."

"Don't worry baby. The Lord will take care of him. You just stay focused on getting out of college and raising my grandson. The best revenge is a life well lived."

Kaitlynn lifted her head and looked at her mother. "Thanks."

"For what?"

"For loving me in spite of my mistakes and watching Mister when I go back to school. I don't know if I could do it without your and Daddy's support."

"You'll be surprised what you can do, when pushed." She rocked her daughter. "Need some aspirin?"

"I do have a headache, but I'm funny about taking medicine right now."

Her mother continued to rock her and caressed her temples. She hummed the tune of *My Soul Has Been Anchored In The Lord* until Kaitlynn fell asleep.

\- - -

The family cocker spaniel ran up to Kaitlynn and nudged her with his nose. "Jonathan, he wants to go potty. Can you let him out?"

228

Jonathan stood and opened the front door. "Come on Mogli." The white puppy ran to the door then disappeared in the snowy darkness. Jonathan flipped on the outside lights. "You need anything?"

"Can you get me a glass of water?"

"Sure babe."

Kaitlynn crawled around the living room floor and picked up stray tinsel. She tossed the strands onto the Christmas tree. Jonathan returned and handed her the water. "Thanks." She poured it in the tree stand, as Jonathan sat on the floor. "Got to keep this fresh until the boys get home."

- - -

Eugene, a.k.a. Mister, arrived on his scheduled due date. Almost nine pounds, he cooed at his mother as she tried to breast-feed him. Karen, the young mother in the adjoining bed, called out to Kaitlynn.

"Hey, how's your baby doing?"

"He's latching on pretty good. A little painful, but I know it's best for him. How's your son?"

"The doctors won't let me see him. He has jaundice." She sniffed to fight back the tears. "They've got him under a special light."

"I'm sorry to hear that, but he'll be fine. The Lord watches over children. They hold a special place in His heart."

"Don't know much about the Lord, but would you pray for my baby?"

"Sure," Kaitlynn agreed. "Dear Lord, we thank you for being our protector. You promised that if two or three are in agreement on something, you're in the midst. Father, we ask that you bless Karen and her son. Let your peace fill her heart as she takes on motherhood. Let your joy be her strength. And Lord, bless Little Man. You said that we were healed by your stripes, so it's already done. Help him to have full recovery from this condition without any negative side affects. We thank you for what you have already done and bless you for what you're going to do in *his life. In your blessed name, the mighty name of Jesus, amen.*"

"Thanks."

Later that day, Donald came to the hospital. Suited in jeans that fit his frame like a customized piece of art, he sat in the chair next

229

to her bed. "Let me see your stomach," he said, as he reached over the railing.

"See my stomach? For what?" She smacked at his wandering hands.

"Just let me see."

"No, it's nasty. It's all lumpy and discolored," Kaitlynn said, then noticed the expression of disgust on Donald's face. "The nurse said that it's normal." She adjusted her pillow and elevated the bed. "Did you sign the birth certificate?"

"Let me see," he climbed onto the bed and tried to pull open her gown.

"What are you doing?" she said, as she snatched the cover over her body.

"It's been a while. And besides, I heard that it's better after a woman has a baby."

She cocked her head to one side and stared at the assailant. "Oh, you have lost your mind. I have stitches from stem to stern."

"Yeah, I know."

"Have you even bothered to see your son?"

"No, I'll see him later." He continued to tug at her gown.

"Kaitlynn, do you need me to call the nurse?" Karen offered.

"Please do."

Donald jumped off the bed and ran out the room. "I ain't going to see that boy and I ain't signing the birth certificate."

- - -

With her newborn only three months old, Kaitlynn left her child and returned to school. She committed to providing a good life for her son and that meant finishing her education.

Although she dated on occasion, her first love still had her heart. To keep her mind off of Donald and focused on her studies, she visited a church near campus. At the end of service, Kaitlynn went to the altar for prayer. Before she could close her eyes and bow her head, the prophetess spoke to her.

"The Lord told me to tell you to leave him alone."

"Huh?" She dropped her hands.

"The Lord said that he is not the one. Leave him alone." She anointed Kaitlynn's head with blessed oil and prayed.

Despite the warning directly from heaven, Kaitlynn foolishly reconnected with Donald during the next school break. Desperate

230

for his attention, she conceded to his advances. Although he didn't cry rape, he retaliated with minimal interaction with their second son, Dorrell.

Without financial or emotional support from Donald, Kaitlynn struggled to make ends meet. Every time she left for college, she needed $1,000 to cover daycare, office visit co-pays and diapers. Her co-op earnings barely covered tuition, room and board. So for books and incidental expenses, Kaitlynn took out student loans and worked on campus. It took her six years to complete the five-year college, but she did it. And she did it with honors.

Settled back in Dayton and reinstated to the choir, she stood in the pulpit with microphone in hand. The organist played the introduction to *Safe In His Arms* as the congregation stood. Kaitlynn's father had Dorrell, whom they lovingly called Super, in his arms and Eugene stood in the seat next to him. She winked at her boys, now five and three years old.

As she waited for her cue, Dorrell jumped out of his grandfather's arms and ran down the aisle. In the elevated position, he had spotted his father three rows in front of him. Halfway to his destination, Donald threw up his hand and motioned for Dorrell to turn around. Devastated, the toddler ran to his grandfather with tears pouring. Donald looked at Kaitlynn and smirked, causing her to miss her cue and then start in the wrong key.

Lord, I need Your help. It's one thing for him to mistreat me, but not my boys. Lord, not my boys. She closed her eyes and let the Holy Spirit minister to her heart, as she sang in reverence to her King. The song that Reverend Milton Brunson made famous in the 80s had never sounded so soul stirring.

Kaitlynn's father, Bebe, walked to the aisle where Donald was seated. He poked Donald in the chest and motioned for him to go outside. With eyes as bright as 100-watt light bulbs, Donald tipped out the sanctuary. As soon as the director dismissed the choir from the stand, Kaitlynn and her mother scurried outside.

"That's the last time you'll mistreat my grandbaby!" Mema's hands flailed in the air as she blessed out Donald.

"Huh? I don't know what you're talking about." Donald threw up his hands as though he was clueless.

"Don't play dumb with me. I saw what you did to Super." Mema stepped to him with flames licking the whites of her eyes.

231

"Come on Momma, let's go," Kaitlynn said, as she took her mother by the arm. "Daddy's got this."

"If you ever," Mema warned through curled lips and a cracked voice, "*ever*, pull a stunt like that again, I will have your ---"

"Momma!"

"Tail! I was going to say tail." She jerked her arm from Kaitlynn and stomped back inside the church.

Kaitlynn looked back at Donald. He didn't seem quite as proud, under the scrutiny of her father. His shoulders bowed forward, with each occasional glance at the authoritative grandfather. *He's done it now. You don't fool with Bebe's boys.* Kaitlynn walked inside the church, then peeked outside to see the interaction. As she squinted through the little window in the door, Donald seemed to shrink to the size of Tiny Tim.

"What's going on, Sister Kaitlynn?" Evangelist Murdock, one of the church's ministers said as she tried to peek around Kaitlynn to see the goings on outside.

"Oh, not much," she sighed. "My father's finally had enough of Donald and his games. He's been mean and nasty to me ever since I got pregnant, but he took it too far today."

"I know that you've had some difficult times lately." She took Kaitlynn by the hand and escorted her to the ladies' lounge. "You need to be released from the soul ties that have you bound to Donald."

"I don't understand."

"Does your stomach still flutter when you see him?"

"Yes ma'am." She dropped her head.

"Then you are still emotionally tied to him." She took Kaitlynn's hand. "And since you have children together, you've been physically connected to him. But what most people fail to realize is that intimacy creates a soul tie that can only be broken through spiritual warfare."

"That explains why I kept putting up with his mess, even when I knew he was doing me wrong. I couldn't shake him loose."

Evangelist Murdock took Kaitlynn's hands and lifted them to the Lord. "Today's a new day. Father God, we come before you as humble and sincere as we know how. Lord we ask that you manifest Your presence in this situation. Release Kaitlynn from the spiritual ties that have her bound to Donald. Let her trust in you and you

232

alone. Help her to put nothing and no one ahead of you for you are her true love. Be her encouragement as she parents her boys. Help them all find peace in this situation. And Lord, whip Donald. Until he comes to do right by his children, whip him, whip him, whip him. Wreak havoc and chaos in his life. You said that a man that does not take care of his own is worse than an infidel. An unbeliever has no part in your blessings and we stand on your Word. Lord we thank you. In Jesus' name. Amen."

"Amen."

- - -

Jonathan helped Kaitlynn to her feet, as she wiped the tears away. She walked back to the picture window and stared at the driveway.

"They'll be okay. You taught them how to make a long distance phone call, if they need to reach us."

"I sure did; one plus the area code, I've just never had a Christmas without my boys." She scribbled their initials in the artificial snow sprayed on the window. "He's only doing this because I'm married now. It's his attempt to cleanse his guilt."

"Well, whatever his motives, it's good for him to spend time with our boys," Jonathan stood by his new bride.

"Yeah, I know, but I've played this game with him before. He pops in for a while, then disappears. I didn't even bother to tell the boys that he was coming until he pulled up in the driveway. He's disappointed them enough." Kaitlynn sighed. "Even though he's never tried to have a genuine relationship with them, they were excited about staying with him. I guess I'm more anxious about the whole thing than anybody." She flicked the white stuff from under her fingernails. "He'll never be able to say that I kept him away from the boys," she paused. "Well, he won't be able to say it and be telling the truth."

"I'm sure his wife will help take care of them."

"I'm sure she will, and that's part of my concern."

"What do you mean?"

"I don't know much about Terri. We've only met one time and that was a disaster."

- - -

233

Four years prior, following Sunday morning service, Kaitlynn waited in the sanctuary for her mother and father. As she collected the boys and their snack remnants from the floor, Terri approached.

"Hi. You're Kaitlynn, right?"

Stunned that Don's fiancé acknowledged her, Kaitlynn nodded.

"I really enjoyed the song you led today."

"Thank you." She crossed her arms. "You're Theresa? Terri?"

"Terri."

"Hi, Terri. How's college?"

"Uh, it's going okay," she said, as she looked up at the ceiling.

"You're at UC, right?"

"Uh-huh."

"Management?"

Terri nodded and Kaitlynn noticed her confusion. She had no idea how Kaitlynn knew so much about her.

She doesn't know who I am, Kaitlynn realized; then she said, "Well, since you're a sophomore, you've gotten over the hump. The rest is down hill." Her supportive words were immediately followed by the thought of: *And these are Donald's boys, Eugene and Dorrell.*

"Yeah, that's what they tell me," Terri said, responding to Kaitlynn's encouragement. "Well, I've got to leave now. Pastor is taking me home."

Before Donald went away to college, he made sure that Kaitlynn knew all about his fiancé. But up until the day before their wedding, Terri had no idea who Kaitlynn was or that she shared two kids with her soon-to-be-husband. When the pastor finally told Terri about Kaitlynn's boys, she called off the wedding. But, with a little convincing from the gold-tongued snake, she retracted her statement and married Donald as planned.

- - -

The gold and ivory decorations on the tree sparkled in the flashing lights. Wood crackled in the fireplace. Cinnamon pinecones and potpourri scented the house, as the CD player loaded another compilation of Christmas songs.

"So how'd you get through it?" Jonathan asked, as he prepped the turkey.

"Prayer. Prayer and support from my family." Kaitlynn chopped celery for the stuffing. "My sister missed out on high school events

234

because she watched the boys while I was at college. And my parents, they pushed me to finish school."

Jonathan shook his head. "I don't understand how a man can turn his back on his children. And the boys are such great kids. He really missed out."

"Yeah, he did. His loss. I just hope he's consistent with his visits."

"Let's live in the moment and be thankful for today."

"You're right," Kaitlynn agreed just as the phone rang. "I'll get it," she said as she put the knife in the sink, wiped her hands on the dishcloth and grabbed the phone. When she heard the voice on the other end, she flashed a smile at Jonathan and pointed to the phone. "Hi Mister! How are you doing? I miss you."

"Hi, Mommy. We're having so much fun. Wait a minute, Super. I'll let you talk to her when I'm done."

"Have you been good boys?"

"Oh Mommy, of course we have."

"Now you know I have to ask."

"I know. We got fresh haircuts." He muffled the receiver, then said, "Mommy, Super wants to talk to you."

"Okay, baby. I want to talk to you again, before we hang up."

Kaitlynn smiled in silence while her boys switched places on the other end of the line.

"Hi, Mommy."

"Hey Super. Are you having a good time? I miss you."

"I miss you too, Mommy. And yeah, we are having a great time. Miss Terri really cooks good." He paused. "But not better than you."

She chuckled. "I'm glad you like Miss Terri's cooking. I know how much you like to eat."

"How's Jonathan? Can you tell him that I said hi?"

"I sure will, baby."

"Okay, gotta go. We're on our way to church. Here's Mister."

"Hey Mister, you take care of yourself and your little brother, okay?"

"I will Mommy. I love you."

"I love you too, baby." A tear rolled down her cheek. "Just think, you'll have two Christmases this year." She wiped at her face.

"I know. We've got a lot of gifts under Don's tree." He whispered, "We tried to open one of them, but Miss Terri has it wrapped too tight."

"I thought you said that you were being a good boy," Kaitlynn giggled and her her son's laughter on the other end. Then she said, "Well I'm glad that you're having a great time. I know you have to go, so I'll see you in two days. Protection in the name of Jesus."

"Thanks, Mommy. Bye."

Kaitlynn hung up and lingered by the phone. Satisfied that her sons were being cared for, she walked to the counter and chopped more celery. When she finished, Kaitlynn looked at Jonathan and returned his loving smile. *Today is a good day.*

Chapter Seventeen

Angela *D.* **Lewis**, known to family and childhood friends as CheeChee, is an Account Manager with UPS as well as a budding writer.

In November 2005, she founded Speaking Concepts & Publications, LLC, which is a public speaking, training, and publications company, specializing in helping small business owners and sales professionals improve their customer relationships, sales and marketing skills. Through it, Angela speaks to thousands of people each year.

She is also the publisher of her first work, *SSSS - We Sizzle!!!*, a nonfiction relationship help tool geared toward single women.

In addition, Angela teaches a parenting class in her church and writes a column on "Tips for Successful Parenting" in her homeowners associations' monthly newsletter.

Angela currently resides in Atlanta, Georgia. She is the mother of one son, Brandon. For more information, visit her website at www.speakingconcepts.com.

Her contribution to *The Midnight Clear* is entitled, **Do You Hear What I Hear?** It is her first published work of fiction.

Do You Hear What I Hear?

Lisa Evans glowed as she walked across the stage to receive her B.S. Degree in Business Administration from the University of Central Florida. Despite instructions to hold all applause until after each graduate had received their degree, her proud family members gave a roaring cheer when the Dean announced, "Lisa Evans, cum laude."

Lisa was the oldest of three siblings. And since neither of her parents had had the opportunity to attend college, she felt a dual sense of family duty and honor. As she exited the stage with her degree in hand, she praised God for seeing her through. She found herself praying and asking God to allow her graduation day to be a momentous occasion whereby her parents could feel proud and honored and her sister and brother could feel motivated and empowered to do the same.

At twenty-two years old, Lisa was intelligent, outgoing, ambitious, and had her life all planned. She often boasted to her friends that she would get a corporate job upon graduating from college, get married at age twenty-five, have the "American Dream" (house, 2-car garage, and white picket fence) at twenty-six, have a little boy at twenty-seven and a little girl at twenty-nine. Little did Lisa know at the time that the problem with her plan was that she didn't take any time to pray and consult with God about His plans and purpose for her life; nor was she leaving room for the plans of her future husband.

Upon graduation, Lisa moved back to her home in Washington, D.C. Three months later, she landed a corporate job just as she had planned. However, she also landed something or *someone* that she had not planned on, at least not for another year. Lisa met and fell in love with Phillip Pernell, a twenty-four-year-old who had, two months earlier, gotten out of the Marine Corps. He was quiet, shy and very reserved. Being a former Marine, Phillip was also confident, well shaven, tall and very handsome.

Unlike Lisa, Phillip did not have an extensive timed plan for this life. After his tenure in the Marine Corps, he enrolled in and graduated from a local technical college where he majored in automotive technology. Soon afterwards, he landed a steady job, working for Pep Boys. After only two months, Phillip realized that

238

he really didn't like the grungy nature of the job and shared this with Lisa. Lisa welcomed this news because she had always liked the suit-and-tie type of guy verses the blue collar worker.

"What type of work did you do in the Marine Corps?" she asked, hoping to help him find his passion.

"Several," Phillips answered with a shrug. "The one I enjoyed most was the time I drove buses."

"Then why don't you check into getting a job driving for the county or maybe public transportation for the city?"

The next month, Phillip was hired to be a driver for an airport shuttle company. He and Lisa both worked hard at their jobs by day and spent most of their evenings together at Lisa's apartment, which she shared with her best friend from college. They introduced one another to their families and friends and six months later, got engaged.

Phillips family and friends adored Lisa and vice versa. However, Lisa's mom had one area of concern about Phillip. He still lived at home with his parents.

"By all accounts, he seems very nice and respectable, but I think you should prolong the engagement until he gets his own place. That way, you can get a good feel for how he handles his affairs."

Her motherly advice fell on deaf ears.

"No, Mama," Lisa refuted. "That money that he would spend on rent can be used to pay for our apartment together, not to mention our honeymoon."

Lisa loved every minute of planning the perfect wedding. She talked Kim Lee, one of Phillip's cousins into being her wedding coordinator. None of her own family members would agree to do the job because they knew how bossy Lisa was and that the poor individual that took the job would be coordinator in name only. But Kim did not seem to mind Lisa's domineering presence. Essentially, they made a good team.

On July 26th, the big day arrived. The wedding ceremony for Lisa and Phillip was brief, but elegant. The reception followed at Bolling Air force Base because of a connection that Phillip had made while he was serving in the military. They had all the formalities: cutting of the cake, sipping from the champagne glasses, the nervous groom removing the garter from the sexy bride's thigh, the toast, the first dance and the throwing of the bridal bouquet and groom's garter. The family and friends cheered as the happy couple ran down the aisle of rice throwers, toward the limousine waiting to whisk them off to the airport.

Phillip and Lisa were off to Orlando, Florida for a romantic honeymoon week. Due to mechanical problems, their flight was delayed; and being that it was Lisa's first time flying, she became very nervous. But in Phillip's arms, Lisa felt so comforted, loved and protected that her nervous jitters vanished. The two of them were so in love and so absorbed by one another that for a moment, it felt as if time had stopped and they were the only two people in the airport terminal.

"Passengers for Flight 254 to Orlando, Florida may now prepare for boarding."

The announcement interrupted the couple's romantic embrace. As Phillip released the love of his life, he gave her a gentle kiss on the forehead. The love birds grabbed their bags and Phillip held Lisa's hand as they walked down the ramp to board the plane. Lisa was glowing to have her man, correction... her *husband*, being so attentive to her.

To Lisa's surprise, it was an enjoyable flight and she could not believe the two hours and forty minutes flight from BWI to Orlando was about to end. Both the flight and its landing were smooth.

Their waiting honeymoon suite was like a beautiful picture from one of the many brides' magazines that Lisa had been scavenging through over the past six months. There were a dozen roses and a bottle of champagne, compliments of the hotel, along with a card that read, "Best wishes to Lisa and Phillip. Please let us know how we may be of service to you."

In Phillip's mind, he answered the hotels note by saying, *You can be of service to me by not disturbing us at all this week...cause I got this.* For a moment, he stood gazing at Lisa as she walked through the entire suite, admiring its entire splendor.

"Look how soft and lavish this feels," she exclaimed as she ran to him with one of the hotel's towels in her hand.

Phillip looked mischievously at Lisa and said, "I'm in the mood to feel something soft and lavish but it ain't no towel." Then he pulled her into his arms.

240

Lisa was very flattered to feel that her husband wanted her, but she remembered that they hadn't exchanged wedding gifts. So she gently wiggled herself out of the strong arms of her husband and made her request known.

"I'm sorry," Phillip replied, his face set and serious. "I didn't know that after purchasing that quarter carat ring and paying for this honeymoon that I was supposed to get you a wedding gift too."

Lisa, trying to hide her disappointment, ran to her bag to get the gifts that she had purchased for him. As Phillip opened his gift, he was studying the demeanor of his new bride so he would know just the right time to announce to her that he was just kidding. He was glad that he had talked to Lisa's sister before the wedding to make sure he met every obligation that a groom should.

Lisa had picked out two gifts for Phillip: a nice watch so he would look professional on his bus route, and a sexy pair of silk boxers for him to wear on their honeymoon.

"Thanks, baby," Phillip said, deciding not to torment his new bride any longer. He excused himself from the sofa and said out loud as he walked toward his bags, "Well, maybe I might have a little something-something for you."

Lisa immediately felt a huge lift in her spirit because Phillip had exceeded her expectations throughout the entire wedding process. He had two separately wrapped gifts for her as well. The wrapping was so beautiful that she just held the gifts in her hands and admired the packaging.

"After all the trouble I went through to get those gifts, you'd better open them to see what's inside," Phillip remarked.

She opened the smaller one first. It was an angel. The most beautiful angel figurine she had ever seen.

"I chose it because you're my personal angel," Phillip said, "and I admire you just like you're admiring it." He sealed his words with a kiss to her forehead.

Lisa, now filled with excitement and anticipation, quickly opened her second gift. "Wow," she exclaimed.

It was a red hot teddy with matching thongs and slippers. From Phillip's expression as she lifted the garments out of the box, she knew that he was imagining her in the sexy ensemble.

"When do you expect me to wear this?" Lisa asked with a grin.

As though he was waiting for that question, Phillip replied, "There's no time like the present."

The romance began and continued all week long. They only left the room to go to the dining area for breakfast a couple of mornings. On their last morning there, it dawned on Lisa that she had brought two rolls of film and they hadn't done any sightseeing. Although most people realized that a honeymoon is meant to be romantic and passionate, Lisa thought it would be quite embarrassing to return home with no immortalized memories of their time in Florida.

"Phillip, come with me to the beach so we can at least use one roll of film," she urged.

With the love she'd shown him all week, her husband couldn't deny her the simple request. The sunrise over the water was beautiful and they used every frame on the roll, taking photos of each other and the breathtaking sights of the flying seagulls and ocean waves that caressed the shorelines.

When they finally returned from their honeymoon and entered their new apartment that Phillip had moved into two weeks prior to the wedding, they noticed all their wedding gifts had been placed on the bed in their spare bedroom. Lisa was sure she had her sister and Kim to thank for having the apartment so clean for their return.

For the first few weeks, Lisa and Phillip enjoyed being married. But after only two months, Lisa became pregnant and while Phillip was excited about the news, Lisa wasn't. She kept reminding herself that having a baby now was three years ahead of her plans and they didn't even have a house to call their own. To try to accelerate things to get them on track with her self-imposed timeline, Lisa began to nag Phillip.

"You need to get a better paying position on your job," she insisted. Other times it was, "Phillip, you have to do something more so that we can purchase a house before the baby is born."

It wasn't long before the couple that was once filled with marital bliss found themselves arguing daily.

Finally fed up with Lisa's know-it-all attitude, Phillip announced, "I'm not going to spend the rest of my life doing everything you want me to do."

When he spoke those words, Lisa panicked. *If he isn't going to listen to me now, what are we going to do? I'm a planner and he's perfectly okay with taking life as it comes.*

When Phillip walked into the room and her heart did not melt as it did in the past, Lisa thought that she no longer loved him. Based on her feelings, she slowly began to lose respect for Phillip because he fell short of her expectations. When she thought about her future with her husband they were filled with doom and gloom. Lisa's active imagination saw them living in a trailer park, with three or four ragamuffins running around wearing nothing but pampers, while she had a stupid scarf tied around her head trying to cook on a half broken stove.

Instead of encouraging her husband, Lisa became resentful of him and talked very harsh to Phillip. She justified her bad behavior by saying that there was no way that God would have her sacrifice and go to college for four years just to end up dirt poor. Lisa concluded that she did not love Phillip any more. She did not sign up to live in poverty and therefore she wanted a divorce and shared her decision with her mother.

"Don't go doing anything that you're going to regret," her mother warned. "When women are pregnant their hormones go crazy, Lisa. At least wait until after the baby is born before you go making any life-changing decisions."

Lisa took her mother's advice and on June 3rd, Phillip and Lisa were blessed with a beautiful baby boy they named Jamar. For a while, things between Phillip and Lisa were decent, but Lisa had said some pretty cruel things to Phillip that had deeply wounded his ego. He was hurt to learn that no matter what he tried to do it was never good enough for Lisa.

Time passed, and when Jamar was two years old and they still did not have a house, Lisa decided that she'd had enough.

"Phillip," she announced, "I can't take this anymore. I want a divorce. Jamar and I are moving to Atlanta to get a fresh start. I have friends there that will help us get situated."

Although Phillip was heartbroken at the thought of losing his wife and son, he muscled up enough strength to take them to the airport and to wish Lisa well. In the years that followed, Phillip and Lisa remained cordial toward one another for Jamar's sake.

243

Over time, Lisa accepted Jesus as her Lord and Savior and became very active in her church. She had always had a zeal for learning so she took advantage of a lot of the classes that her church offered its members. It was not long before Lisa learned that she needed to release her plans over to God and to seek His will for her life. The Holy Spirit also convicted her that the way she spoke to her ex-husband was out of order.

As 2001 neared an end, Jamar and Lisa spent Christmas Day together, but afterwards, he traveled to North Carolina to spend the rest of his Christmas break with relatives. Jamar loved going to Charlotte because he had two sets of cousins there and they would all vie for his attention.

On New Year's Day morning, in preparation for the drive to pick up her son, Lisa got up at 6:30, did her morning grooming, and then threw on her favorite blue fleece sweat suit. She grabbed a few of her favorite snacks (chips, sunflower seeds and raisins) then grabbed a couple bottles of water and packed them in an insulated carrier bag.

Before Lisa pulled out of her garage, she said a prayer, asking God for traveling mercies. Instead of turning on the radio or listening to her motivational tapes or sermons from her church as she usually did, she decided that she would just commune with God for a while. She began to enter a place of total praise, thanking God for all His blessings, His love and His mercies.

She found herself saying, "Instead of making a New Year's resolution, God, I just want to know your perfect will for my life."

Then a small voice crept up in her spirit and said, *"Okay, since you want to be in my will; what does my Word say about divorce?"*

Lisa had read the scripture many times before. She knew it well. "According to your Word, Lord, if one party has committed adultery the other party is free to divorce."

"What were your grounds for divorce?"

Lisa answered, "Irreconcilable differences."

"Where in my Word is this 'irreconcilable differences?'" the Spirit challenged.

Panic went through Lisa. "Lord, are you trying to tell me that after all these years you want me to get back with Phillip?"

There was no more still small voice and no answer.

244

She spoke again. "Lord, I do not have that type of love for Phillip anymore, but if that is your will I will need your help."

At that moment, Lisa felt a huge sense of peace overwhelm her spirit. She had spent three hours communing and fellowshipping with God and was now only an hour away from Charlotte. It was one of the most relaxing and carefree trips she had ever had. Although she hadn't eaten, she experienced no hunger or thirst. Just total peace.

As she turned on the radio and flipped through the stations, a female's voice caught her attention. Lisa did not catch the story from the beginning but she heard the lady state that she was engaged to a minister and after dinner one evening, as he was driving her home, he told her that he could not marry her. After she asked for an explanation for his sudden decision, he stated that he had sought some counseling on the matter and based on the grounds of her divorce that ended her previous marriage, the Holy Spirit would not release him to marry her.

"I even started quoting scriptures," the radio hostess revealed. "I told him that God said once we are born again, old things are passed away. But after a couple of minutes of that, I came to realize that as regretful as he was for having to call off our engagement, he had made his decision."

She went on to say that instead of throwing herself through the window, which was what Satan tempted her to do, she threw herself on the bed and began to weep. She questioned God, asking why she'd had to go through such a trial.

"If I weren't ever supposed to marry again, then why had God brought such a wonderful man into my life?" she asked, her voice radiating through Lisa's car speakers. "After crying for well over an hour, I heard a still, small voice say, *'My grace is sufficient.'*"

After a while, she said, she dried her tears and began to repeat the words, "Yes Lord, your grace is sufficient." After a week of praying and meditating over the words, *My grace is sufficient*, her spirit began to calm and she was then able to offer praises unto the Lord, saying, "Not my will Lord, but thou will. Lord I just want to know your perfect will for my life."

It was the same prayer that Lisa had just prayed. Now she had Lisa's undivided attention.

As if giving her listening audience a moment to take it all in, the lady paused and then continued. "That still, small voice spoke and said, *'Okay, since you want to be in my will what does my Word say about divorce?'*"

Lisa gasped as she listened to the rest of the woman's story as she told it on air. Each time she spoke, it was as though she'd had the exact same experience as Lisa. When the woman went on to say that her reason for divorcing her husband was "irreconcilable differences" Lisa knew this was more than happenstance. The story she heard mirrored her own, almost to the letter. Lisa was flabbergasted at the epiphany she had just experienced. It was as if God told her something and took the time to confirm it since He knew how head strong she was.

When she got to Charlotte, Lisa shared what had happened to her with her favorite cousin, Melba, who was also a Christian. Agreeing that God was definitely trying to get her attention about something concerning Phillip, Melba suggested Lisa speak to her pastor about it. Not only was Lisa convinced that she needed to talk to her spiritual leader, but she also decided that she should talk to Phillip as well. If God was dealing with her, He had to be doing the same with her ex-husband. And He had.

"Lisa, this is amazing," Phillip said when she finally mustered up enough nerve to call him and tell him what she'd experienced. "You've been on my mind a lot lately too."

It was then that Lisa made her courageous request. "Can you come down so that we can talk about it face to face?"

She barely had time to get the question out of her mouth before Phillip agreed. The idea of a possible reconciliation seemed to excite him and in early March, he arrived at the church to meet Lisa, as they'd planned.

"The pastor will see you now," Pastor Knight's assistant announced.

Together, the divorced couple stood and walked into the office and Lisa nervously introduced her pastor to the man he'd never met before. She held her breath as the two men shook hands and exhaled when the strong comforting arms of Pastor Knight greeted her with an embrace.

"Please, have a seat," the preacher offered, pointing in the direction of two chairs that were placed in front of his crystal desk.

246

As he always did, Pastor Knight began the meeting by talking to God and praying that all hearts would be open and receptive to hear from the Holy Spirit. Upon ending the prayer, he looked at Lisa and Phillip for a brief moment, then cleared his throat and in his very reverent voice asked, "So, Sister Lisa, what can I do for the two of you today?"

Lisa began the conversation by thanking the pastor for agreeing to meet with them. Then she shared with him a little background about her and Phillip.

"We were only married for two years and have been divorced for thirteen." As she continued speaking, Lisa squirmed in her seat and Phillip did the same. Uneasiness rested heavily between both of them, making their nervousness obvious.

"Jamar resembles you quite a bit," Pastor Knight imputed, bringing a proud and relaxed smile to Phillips lips.

The simple observation served as an ice-breaker to ease Lisa's disquiet as well, and sharing the rest of their story with Pastor Knight was far more effortless. Pastor Knight listened intently as Lisa shared with him what happened to her while on her way to Charlotte.

After a few minutes, the conversation shifted to Phillip and it did not take Pastor Knight long to uncover that Phillip was a wounded and hurt man. The confidence that Phillip had as a young man exiting the Marine Corps was nowhere to be found. Instead, he kept repeating that he could not believe that a woman like Lisa would even consider getting back with a man like him.

Pastor Knight determined that a listening ear was what the couple most needed at this point. He allowed them to talk and the bulk of his time was spent quietly taking in what was said and sending silent prayers to heaven on their behalf. As the meeting ended, he gave both Phillip and Lisa some homework, first admonishing Phillip to find a good church to join in Virginia.

"God has given you some valuable spiritual gifts," Pastor Knight said, "but they are raw. To polish and harness them, you need to be under the submission of a pastor with a vision." Then turning to Lisa he said, "You have the spirit of a go-getter and while that is a good thing, you must learn to wait on the Lord's direction. Moving toward any path on your own drive and without His direction is a mistake."

247

Lisa nodded, knowing that he was telling her the right thing.

"In the Bible, God told Abraham that he would be given a son," the preacher continued. "Sara, in her haste, made the error of not waiting on God, therefore pushing her husband into sin to gain what God had already promised him. God does not need our help, Sister Lisa," he said with love in his eyes. "Wait on Him to give direction."

Over the course of the next months, Phillip and Lisa had many telephone conversations, finding reasons to share the laughter that they used to enjoy years earlier. As she'd wanted to do for quite some time, Lisa finally apologized to Phillip for the horrible way she had spoken to him when they were married.

"I need you to know that you weren't a bad husband, Phillip," she assured him. "I didn't have the right expectations of what a marriage was all about. I bought into the Hollywood images and expected the same from you. You were a good husband and you are a good father. If I've not said it before; thank you for being there for Jamar."

Phillip was so touched by Lisa's apology and kind words that he had to excuse himself from the phone while he gathered his emotions. As their conversation continued, Phillip seemed to gain back that old confidence that he once had.

"Have you found a church home yet?"

The dialogue had been going so well that Lisa thought it was a good time to ask. She couldn't have been more mistaken and was taken aback by the harsh tone of his reply.

"I'll find a church when I'm good and ready," he snapped.

It was then that God spoke to her and revealed that her purpose for reconnecting with Phillip was not to remarry him, but something totally different. As a believer, it would be against His will for her to be unequally yoked with someone who was walking in rebellion, as was Phillip's current status. But a tug on her heart for fellowship with him continued.

An accident on his bus route a short time later resulted in Phillip suffering a herniated disc. For the next six months the doctors tried to treat him with physical therapy and medication. However, instead of getting better, the pain in his back worsened; so much so that at the young age of forty-two, Phillip was walking with a

248

pronounced hunched back, like that of an old man. With almost no quality of life, he opted for the last recourse: surgery.

On March 12th, Phillip called to speak to Jamar and Lisa to let them know that he was going in for surgery the following day. "And you'll be happy to know that I gave my heart to God last night," he said as their conversation neared an end. "I wasn't at church. It was just me and God, right here in my house, but it was a worship service just the same."

Tears of joy streamed down Lisa's face and she could hardly believe her ears. She wasn't surprised that God had drawn Phillip in. In fact, she knew He would; but she just didn't expect to hear of her ex-husband's conversion so soon.

"Pray for me," Phillip said, referring to his pending surgery.

"We will," Lisa promised. "Give us a call after it's over."

That was the last time she spoke to him. On the morning of Wednesday March 13, 2003, Phillip passed away during the operation. His death was as much of a shock as had been the news of his new life in Christ. Lisa had no idea that the conversation would be their last. She didn't know that he would no longer be a part of her son's future birthdays, summers and Christmas vacations.

Seeing his daughter's devastation, Lisa's father drove her and Jamar to Phillip's funeral. Lisa arrived at the funeral home only to find out that everything was in total disarray. Phillip's family had been fussing and fighting and no one would sign to be responsible for paying the fees associated with his burial. Phillip's mom was so upset with the loss of her son and with the family's behavior that she had to be hospitalized to stabilize her soaring blood pressure. Lisa stepped up to handle matters so that her son's father, her ex-husband, her friend would have a decent homegoing.

On the night before the funeral, while Lisa was preparing Phillip's obituary, she finally understood what the epiphany was all about. Although Phillip's death came as a huge surprise to her, Jamar and other family members, it was not a surprise to God. Lisa began to give praises unto the Lord for loving her and Phillip enough to allow them the opportunity to totally clear the air before his death. Lisa realized the she was given a chance to make amends for her actions and her hurtful words. Not only had God forgiven her but she had the peace of knowing that Phillip had forgiven her as well. Her heart was so overjoyed with gratitude that God had allowed her and Phillip to have shared a moment in destiny and that she had their adorable son, Jamar, as a living manifestation.

At the funeral the next day, Lisa reached over and grabbed Jamar's hand as she praised God for all the joy that her son had brought into her heart. She knew that Phillip's spirit would live on through the seed he'd left behind.

"Well done, my good and faithful servant," were the words that Lisa believed she heard Jesus say to Phillip.

As she looked at Phillip's remains lying peacefully in the open casket only a few feet in front of where she sat, Lisa smiled and thought, *Phillip...do you hear what I hear?*

Chapter Eighteen

Michelle Larks was born in Chicago, Illinois and is the author of several books including, *A Myriad of Emotions, Crisis Mode, Mirrored Images* and *Who's Your Daddy.*

Michelle was Literary World's Author of the Month for March 2004 and *Crisis Mode* was book of the month in March 2005. *Crisis Mode* was named Best Novella by Black Refer website in 2005.

She's an avid reader, and enjoys discussing books at her monthly book club meeting. She has written poetry for friends, and relatives, commemorating weddings, funerals, birthdays, and other milestones in life. Michelle is currently at work on a manuscript titled, *Til Debt Do Us Part.*

Michelle is married and the mother of two adult daughters. She continues to reside in Chicago.

Her contribution to *The Midnight Clear* is entitled, *Jesus Will Work It Out.*

Chantelle Dixon placed a manila folder inside the tray of her out basket. She peered at her watch, hoping the workday was winding down. Her eyes flitted to a gold frame which housed a snapshot taken two years ago of, her husband, children, and herself. Chantelle tore her eyes from the Dixon clan's smiling faces. She glanced over her right shoulder and glimpsed her boss, Leo Ross, walking down the aisle, stopping at each of her co-workers' cubicles. The date was Friday, December 24th, the day before Christmas.

Leo was wearing a Santa cap. Chantelle shook her head and suppressed a snicker at his jaunty holiday appearance. The rumor mill had it, that there was a possibility the staff would be released early that day. Chantelle hoped so, since she had a million and one chores to complete before the holiday officially began.

A few minutes later, Leo invaded Chantelle's space. He thrust out his hand at her and said, "Merry Christmas, Chantelle. Happy holidays to you and your family." He presented her with an envelope, "This is the company's and my way of saying thank you for a productive year."

"Thank you, Leo." Chantelle placed the envelope on her desk. "Merry Christmas to you and yours." A pair of dimples sneaked along the sides of her cinnamon colored face as she shook Leo's outstretched hand. Chantelle was an attractive woman of medium height and build, and wore her dark colored hair in a short blunt cut.

"I know this has been a difficult year for you," Leo began. "Hopefully the upcoming one will be an easier time for you and your family."

"Thank you. God willing, I'm sure it will be," Chantelle nodded.

"Upper management has decided to close shop early today, and I'm staggering the dismissals. You can leave now, if you'd like."

"I sure would. The timing is perfect for me. I have a few more gifts to pick up for my children. I've been wracking my brain, trying to figure out how to finish my shopping without tipping my hand to those little rug rats." Her eyes darted to the picture.

"Then I'm glad I could help." Leo nodded his head up and down. "To be honest, I decided to start in alphabetical order, and your last name starts with D. So…"

I can thank Derek for that. Chantelle thought as her eyes filled with tears, and a lump rose in her throat. Her beloved husband died from pancreatic cancer in June. She and her two children, eight-year-old Derek III, and six-year-old Cydney, were still mourning their loss. Chantelle and Derek had been married for ten years. She still hadn't come to terms with her beloved's death. Only her children and faith in God gave Chantelle incentive to keep going day after day.

Her telephone sounded. She looked up at Leo and then down at the telephone.

"Go ahead and take the call," Leo gestured, "I'll see you next week." He walked to the cubicle opposite Chantelle's to continue passing out holiday cheer.

"Hello," Chantelle said when she put the phone to her ear.

"Are you off work yet?" Chantelle's best friend, Deidre whispered.

"Yes, I just officially got the word. Thanks to Derek's last name beginning with a D, I got lucky."

"Perfect. I'm off too. Why don't we meet on the first floor, say in ten minutes? Then we can go hit the mall and finish our shopping," Deidre suggested. She leaned down, and placed her laptop computer in her bottom desk drawer, then locked it. She pushed a thin micro braid off her pretty bronze colored face.

"Sure. That sounds like a plan. I'm almost finished with my shopping. I just want to get new outfits for the kids." Chantelle locked her desk drawer too, and dropped the key inside her purse.

"You're one up on me," Deidre wailed. "I haven't even gotten started yet. Every year this time, around the first of the month, I say I'm going start shopping early, and before I know it, the Christmas season is upon us. I promise I'm going to do better next year."

"Why don't you get through this holiday season first, before you start making vows that we both know you probably won't keep. If I had a dollar for every time you've made that statement, I'd have a nice chunk of change by now," Chantelle teased her friend. "I'll see you in a minute."

She hung up the phone, and sat inertly at her desk, lost in thought. *Let me get going. I need to find outfits, and try to get home early enough to attend the Christmas Eve service tonight.*

She removed her shoes, and slipped her black flat-heeled boots on her feet. Then Chantelle stood up and donned her Kelley green down coat. As the elevator descended to the first floor, Christmas carols serenaded the smiling employees. They were happy to get a jump-start on the holidays. When Chantelle emerged from the elevator, Deidre stood near the receptionist's desk, impatiently tapping her foot.

"I take it you're ready?" she asked her friend as she pulled black leather gloves over her hands.

"Yes, let's do it," Deidre answered. "I'm ready to rock and roll."

A strong wind was blowing off of Lake Michigan in downtown Chicago as the women exited the building. Deidre pulled up the collar of her fur coat around her neck.

"How far away did you park?" Chantelle asked, looking up and down the street, scanning the automobiles for Deidre's gold Jaguar.

"Six blocks away. So start walking fast."

"Do you have a problem stopping at my house before we go to the mall?" Chantelle asked. "It's only eleven o'clock, so we should be the plaza no later than noon if traffic is light."

"Hmm." Deidre's voice sounded muffled from her coat collar. "If we stop then we're going to lose time. Why can't we go to the mall, and I drop you off at home after we finish?" Deidre glanced at her friend as they keep trekking.

"'Cause the kids might see me getting out of your car with bags. I told you that Derek told me last week, that there isn't a Santa Claus. It took all my powers of persuasion to convince him otherwise. That, my friend, is why I want to take my own car."

"Okay, I guess that's reason enough," Deidre conceded, walking around a patch of ice. "We don't want Derek spoiling the fun for Cydney. Hurry up, it's cold out here."

They picked up their pace, and were relieved when they arrived at the parking lot where Deidre's luxury vehicle was parked. Ten minutes later, Deidre was driving south on the Dan Ran Expressway.

She glanced over at Chantelle and asked, "What are you going to do tonight besides wrap gifts and play Ms. Santa Claus?"

"I'm going to church for the Christmas Eve service. Then I'll help Mother finish cooking. If I stay home, I'll think of Derek not being here with us, and get depressed. Not that I'm not already depressed."

Deidre nodded as if she understood. "I hear you, girl. This year will be tough, because it's the first year without him. Just lean on the Lord, He'll get you through these times."

Chantelle brushed away a tear that had gathered in her eye. "How right you are."

Deidre reached into the glove compartment, and handed her friend a tissue. "You know I haven't gotten as many presents as I would have liked to for my godchildren, so while you're shopping, if you see something you think they'd like, get it for me, and I'll reimburse you."

Chantelle blew her nose, and crumpled the tissue in her hand. "Now you know they don't need anything else. I went a little overboard with shopping this year. I guess I was trying to make up for the fact that they'll be fatherless this Christmas; although their Uncle Justin has been spending more time with them. In the past, Derek would get on my case and grumble that I'd bought enough stuff for our children, nieces and nephews, and all the children on the block." Her attempt to smile, failed.

"Derek was a good man. He's missed by a lot of people," Deidre said as she steered her car on the blacktopped driveway of Chantelle's tan brick bungalow house.

"Give me a few minutes to warm up my Galant, and I'll be ready."

The women arrived at the mall thirty minutes later. Chantelle trailed behind Deidre, and they parked in the upper level of the indoor parking garage. After she exited her car, Chantelle waited for Deidre, who parked in the space behind her. The women walked inside the mall, and joined the throng of last minute shoppers.

"It's one o'clock," Deidre observed as they walked through the flagship store, Carson Pirie Scott & Co. and on to the escalator. "Let's meet back here in two and half hours, I'll call you on your cell if I think I'm going to be longer."

"Sheesh, I didn't think you would need *that* much time," Chantelle said dryly.

"It shouldn't take me that long. I promise I'll hurry." Deidre waved from the moving staircase.

Chantelle ducked in the ladies' room and pulled her cell phone out of her purse. She dialed her home telephone number. When her mother answered, Chantelle said, "Hi Mom, I'm at the mall with Deidre. Hopefully I won't be too long. Do you need me to get something for you? How are Derek and Cyd doing?"

Helen, Chantelle's mother, replied, "Justin came and got your children about an hour ago, and took them to his house. Cydney was a little teary-eyed. She told Derek that she wanted her daddy to come home for Christmas. Derek became upset too, so since you were still at work, I called Justin. He told me tell you not to worry. He'll talk to the kids and see us at church tonight."

"I was afraid something like this might happen. Do you think I should go to Justin's house?" Chantelle fretted. Her brow was furrowed with worry lines.

"No. Stay where you are. Justin is good with the kids. He'll talk to them. I've started Christmas dinner. Relax, and let Jesus work it out," Helen advised her daughter.

"Okay." Chantelle sighed heavily. "I should be home in three hours tops. The mall closes at four o'clock."

"Take your time," Helen replied, peeping through the glass oven door to check the chocolate cake she was baking.

"Okay, Mom. I'll see you later." Chantelle closed her flip phone, squared her shoulders and joined the other shoppers.

Two and a half hours later, she sat in the food court, sipping a latte. Deidre walked up to her, carrying six bags, filled to the rim. She fell into the seat across from Chantelle.

"I should have known you would already be finished," she grumbled. She reached down, slipped off her shoe, and massaged the instep of her left foot. "My feet are killing me. I'm making a solemn pledge that I'm going to do all my shopping online next year."

"Yeah, right." Chantelle laughed and eyeballed the bags. "What did you do; buy out the entire store?"

"Not quite, although my checkbook and credit card probably look like I did." Deidre reached inside a bag, and took out two

256

boxes from Footlocker. "I bought a pair of Carmelo Anthony sneakers for Derek, and regular pink Nike's for Miss Cydney. They are so cute," Deidre gushed. "Do we have time for me to get something to drink? I'm hungry and thirsty."

Chantelle glanced at her wristwatch. "No we don't. The mall closes in twenty minutes. The garage will be packed with people trying to get out of here. Let's go while the going is good."

"Party pooper," Deidre mumbled, and then stood before adding, "I'm ready."

The women grabbed their bags. As they walked to the cars, snow was falling lightly, guaranteeing Chicago a white Christmas. When the women arrived at the spot where they'd parked the cars, Chantelle's automobile was nowhere to be found. She dropped her bags on the ground and screamed. "Deidre where is my car? I know I parked right here." She pointed to the empty spot. "Lord, someone stole my car." Her face paled, devoid of color.

Deidre quickly scanned the surrounding cars, and walked down a couple of the other nearby rows. Chantelle was correct. The blue Galant sedan was gone.

"All of the children's toys were locked in the trunk, and the car is gone. Deidre, I don't have anything for Derek and Cyd for Christmas. What am I going to do?" Chantelle wailed. Her arms flailed in the air.

"Now don't freak out on me," Deidre advised Chantelle, trying to maintain her own composure. "Try to calm down. Your car has got to be here somewhere. Automobiles don't just disappear into thin air."

They circled the parking area three times, and still there was no sign of Chantelle's car. She became hysterical, and several shoppers stopped to assist them, to no avail.

"I think we should go inside and talk to mall security and tell them what happened. Then they can file a report," Deidre suggested to a frenzied Chantelle.

The paperwork was completed within an hour. Deidre contacted Chantelle's insurance carrier. The representative informed the ladies that due to the late hour, and holiday rush, that the company wouldn't be able to provide Chantelle with a rental car until Monday.

Dusk was falling when they returned to Deidre's car and stuffed the bags in the backseat and trunk. Chantelle began weeping anew when she entered the car. "This is going to be the worst Christmas of my life. I didn't want to risk the kids finding their gifts ahead of time so I left them inside my car. I feel so stupid; now I don't have anything at all for them."

Deidre opened her mouth to suggest they go to another store, but thought better of it. Most stores closed early on Christmas Eve to allow store personnel time to prepare for their holidays with their families. "I feel so bad about what's happened, Chantelle. Maybe we can go by Walgreen? It stays open twenty-four/seven."

"Never mind, just take me home," Chantelle replied somberly. "I don't know what I'm going to do."

Chicago looked ethereal, like a winter wonderland. Snow accumulated on the grassy areas, but not on the sidewalks. When Deidre pulled in front of Chantelle's house, they saw that Helen had turned on the red and white Christmas lights, adorning the windows. The seven-foot tall ornately decorated pine tree, stood framed in the middle of a large picture glass window.

Deidre shifted the car into park, and turned to her friend. "If you'd like, I can give you the sneakers I bought for Derek and Cydney. I picked up a few other items that I didn't show you. I feel so bad about what happened."

"Don't worry about it." Chantelle rubbed the bridge between her eyes. "I'll think of something." She opened the car door and got out.

"Call me later," Deidre yelled to her friend's bowed back.

After Chantelle opened the door, she hung her coat on the wooden coat rack. She looked at Derek's picture hanging over the mantle of the fireplace, and slid to the floor, weeping and moaning, as she clutched her mid-section.

From the kitchen, Helen called her daughter's name and rushed into the room. When she saw Chantelle rocking on the floor, she frowned, and ran over to her child. "I can tell by the expression on your face, that something is horribly wrong." Helen reached down and grabbed Chantelle's hand, pulled her up, and led her into the kitchen.

Sniffling and hiccupping, Chantelle collapsed on a kitchen chair, and managed to say, "Someone stole my car. And all of the gifts that I bought for the children were inside it."

"Lord have mercy," Helen murmured. Her hands flew to her cheeks and she shook her head in disbelief. "That's awful."

"The sad part is that with today being Christmas Eve, all the stores are closed. There's no way I can replace the items I bought." Chantelle rubbed her eyes.

Helen walked over to Chantelle and hugged her. "What are you going to do?"

"I'm going to stay home in my room, and bawl like a baby. Maybe by the time you return from church with the children, I'll have pulled myself together and thought of something. This is our first Christmas without Derek, and I messed up, Mama. I really messed up bad." Chantelle bit back a sob.

"You should go to church with us," Helen suggested. "Staying home alone won't serve any useful purpose. You need to be with your blood and spiritual family."

Chantelle lowered her eyes, and shook her head no.

"The problem with Christmas is that it's become too commercialized," Helen added. She stood and walked to the stove and turned off the burners under the pots. "December twenty-fifth has become a date for people to exchange extravagant gifts, and we tend to forget the true meaning of the holiday. It's Jesus' birthday; you need to focus on that."

"I know what you're saying is true, but this is not what I had planned for this holiday," Chantelle moaned. "I wanted the children to have a good time, so they wouldn't become sad because Derek isn't with us."

"Your children will be fine, as long as they have you." Helen scolded her daughter. "Nothing else matters. Try not to lose sight of that. I guess I can't talk you into going with us. I hate the idea of leaving you home alone, with your spirits so low. Your daddy and I never had much financially, and there were times when we didn't know how we going to buy presents for you and your sister and brothers. That's one reason why we tried to emphasize the birth, instead of the gifts and Santa Claus."

"I know," Chantelle sighed. "If my car had been stolen any night but tonight, I could have coped better. But this is too much. I feel like God is punishing me."

Helen reached out and grabbed Chantelle's hand. "You know the Lord doesn't work that way, child."

"Then why did He take Derek away from me? How come I don't have presents for my babies for tomorrow morning?" Chantelle whined sadly.

"There's more to life than material things, and I know you are aware of that. The Lord works in mysterious ways. It was Derek's time to go home. But you have to keep living, and trusting in the Lord. You have so much to be thankful for: the fact that you're alive, your health is good and so is the children's, you have a job and a beautiful home. There are a lot of people who can't make that same claim. They're blessings from our Father above. Why don't you rest, and when you get up, maybe you'll look at things differently."

Chantelle stood, "I know what you're saying is true, it just doesn't feel like I'm blessed at this minute. I'm going to lie down. I'll see you when you come back from church."

Helen looked at her daughter and sympathy shone in her eyes. "I hope you change your mind and join us," she added just before going into her room to prepare for church. Forty-five minutes later, she was gone, leaving Chantelle to herself.

The house was dark and quiet without the presence of her mother and children. Chantelle sobbed until she fell into a fitful sleep, tossing and turning the entire time. Derek plagued her dreams. He seemed to be telling Chantelle something important, but as hard as she tried, Chantelle couldn't make out what he was saying to her.

She awakened and sat upright in the bed. Her heart beat rapidly and she felt an overwhelming urge to be with her husband, knowing it was impossible. Chantelle jumped off the bed, walked to the closet, and flung the door open, searching for a possession of Derek's, anything to feel him near her.

Her head drooped. She remembered that her brother, Justin, had moved Derek's belongings to the basement months ago. Chantelle's footsteps clattered on the steps. When she arrived in the basement, her legs shook as she walked across the floor and pushed

260

open the utility room door. Chantelle flipped on the light switch. The light was dim, not very bright.

Her eyes traveled to Derek's clothing, which neatly hung on metal racks near the rear of the room. She glimpsed her late husband's favorite burgundy sweater and rushed over to touch it. It was the last gift she'd bought him.

In her haste, Chantelle reached up to pull the garment off the hanger, and stumbled over several boxes positioned beneath the racks. A frown marred her face as she wondered where the crates had come from. Chantelle hadn't noticed them before. She cradled the sweater in her arms, and put it underneath her nose, inhaling Derek's natural masculine scent mixed with Ice-Water, his favorite cologne.

Chantelle slid to the floor and held the knit material in her arms, hugging it like a child, as tears flowed from her eyes. "Derek I miss you so much. Why did you have to leave us? Why would a loving God do this to us?"

She sat on the cool tiled floor with her legs extended in front of her body, and cried. Then she sniffled, and her eyes flew to the boxes again as curiosity got the best of her.

Chantelle's stomach somersaulted when she recognized Derek's handwriting on the top of one of the crates. He'd written the word, *Christmas*, and the current year on every box. Her hands shook slightly as she opened the box nearest to where she was sitting. Nestled inside lay gaily wrapped gift boxes and letters, addressed to Cydney, Derek, and Chantelle. She dropped the letters on the floor, and proceeded to open the other boxes. Gifts were in each of them.

"Oh my God." Chantelle's legs suddenly felt as heavy as lead. She sat down on the floor and picked up her letter. The sight of Derek's handwriting caused her heart rate to accelerate. She picked up the envelope and placed it against her lips and kissed it.

Using the tip of her manicured fingernail, Chantelle quickly slit open the corner of the envelope.

Hey Telly,
I prayed you would find the boxes. I asked your brother to hide them for me back in April when Dr. Norris told me there wasn't anything else that could be done to halt this terrible disease that I knew would claim my life. My heart aches, knowing I won't be with

261

you and the children as always. I know my time is growing short. I couldn't let our favorite holiday go by without celebrating it in my own way with my family.

Now if I know you, and we both know that I do like the back of my hand, you've probably cleared the shelf of a couple of toy stores by now. Woman, take that stuff back to the store, because I got this one.

My last few months at the hospital have been difficult, but knowing that I was leaving my legacy on earth, with the woman I've loved with my entire being, has given me the strength to go home with our Father above. We all have to take that journey home one day; some of us sooner than others.

Telly, you've been an excellent wife. No man could have asked for a greater friend, lover, and helpmate. I don't want you to put your life on hold mourning me. Live your life to the fullest, and most of all, take care of Cydney, and Derek. They hold the keys to the other compartments of my heart.

I asked Justin to keep my actions a secret. So I'm hoping he kept that promise. He and Shelly wrapped the gifts for me. Don't cry, love; I can see a tear peeping out the corner of you eye now. Just enjoy life, raise my kids the way we said we would, when we learned the rabbit died. Don't be bitter or sad. Trust in God, and we'll see each other again in the sweet by and by.

I'll love you 'til the twelfth of never.

Your husband,
Derek

Chantelle couldn't finish reading the last line. Her eyes, awash in tears, didn't seem to function correctly. She rushed upstairs, and quickly put on her coat. Then Chantelle ran out the house as quickly as she could, and drove Derek's SUV to church to join her family.

When she walked inside the sanctuary, the choir was singing *O Holy Night*. Chantelle saw Helen, her sister, Noelle, and her sister-in-law, Shelly. At the end of the pew sat Justin. Chantelle slipped in the pew next to her brother, and on tiptoes, kissed her sibling's cheek.

"Thank you for your gifts to me and the children. I love you."

Justin looked down at his sister and smiled. "Oh, you must have found Derek's gifts. When Mother told me what happened, I planned on stopping by your house after church. Don't thank me, Chantelle. Thank Derek for his unselfishness, and love."

Helen stood between her grandchildren holding each child's hand. They looked down the row at Chantelle and smiled. Cydney and Derek inched by their aunts and uncle to join their mother. Chantelle reached down and hugged them. Then she stood erect.

"O holy night when Christ was born." Chantelle's body swayed to the music and she waved her arms in the air as her voice rang out, strong and melodically, along with the members of the choir.

Chapter Nineteen

Deborha Parham is a Georgia native born in Atlanta to Nathaniel Sr. and Alberta White. As a child she was involved in a car accident that left her handicapped. While incapacitated, she discovered that she enjoyed writing short stories, poems and journaling. Thus the writer in her was born.

The love of technology drove her to start her own desktop publishing company, Nite Shift Computer Services, while still working as a federal employee. The company has been in operation for 15 years. She is also co-owner of another company called Sekret Xscapes which creates and prepares nights of intimacy for married couples away from home.

The title of her first published novel, *Beyond the Ashes*, is very dear to Deborha's heart. Symbolic of her own healing process, the word, 'ashes', serves as an acronym for *Anger, Sorrow, Hatred, Empathy* and *Sickness*.

Deborha is a member of New Birth Missionary Baptist Church where Bishop Eddie L. Long is the senior pastor. She currently resides in Stone Mountain, Georgia with her husband, Wade and their three children, sons, Rashi and Ramoris and daughter, Ramaiseya. For additional information, please visit Deborha online at www.deborhaparhamwrites.com.

Her contribution to *The Midnight Clear* is entitled, **Mirracle's Promise.**

Mirracle's Promise

An exhausted Kyra looked at Kaleb, closed her eyes and shook her head. "Lord," she prayed, "please heal my husband and bring him home to his family again. We need him very badly." As she finished her prayer, Kaleb stirred. Kyra had been at the hospital every day since the accident, coming right after work.

If only he would open his eyes, she thought.

The nurse was making her rounds. Daily she came in and did the exact same thing; check Kaleb's temperature and IV and then change his bedding and fluff his pillow. After doing it this time, she mouthed to Kyra that nothing had changed and walked out. Kyra immediately got up, kissed Kaleb on the forehead, and left the room as well.

Once in the hall, she let out a deep sigh. Kaleb just had to pull through this. Kyra could not imagine life without him. It was exactly one week before Christmas and they had never been apart on a holiday. Christmas was always special to them because Kaleb had proposed to her on Thanksgiving Day in front of everyone and they had gotten married on Christmas Eve. That was nineteen years ago.

As Kyra walked down the long corridor her mind switched to her children, Mirracle and Maleek. Mirracle was sixteen and had secured the lead in a play at church. Kaleb had not seen her perform since she was thirteen and was really looking forward to seeing her this year. Seventeen-year-old Maleek was performing in the band where he played the saxophone. It would mean a great deal to both of them if their father could be in attendance.

In the car, Kyra turned on the radio and her favorite song, *Stand,* by Donnie McClurkin was playing. Singing along with the radio, she reminded herself that she needed to decorate the house. That alone would make it feel more like the holidays. Stopping at the red light, she noticed that the whole city was decorated with Christmas trees, candy canes and images of Santa Claus. Some stores and businesses, in their advertisements, chose not write out the word Christmas. Instead, they used an "X" for Christ.

Xmas. Mmm, Kyra thought. *If they only realized that they were eliminating the One who was the reason for the season, they would be more careful of the callous abbreviation.*

266

Turning in her subdivision, she was determined not to go in the house looking depressed. Her children needed her and she needed the Holy Spirit to empower her to do what she had to do. Pressing the garage door opener, she took a deep breath and prayed a little prayer before parking. Kyra's faith kicked into full gear and as she stepped out of the car, she felt the power of the Holy Spirit coming upon her. The children were getting an empowered mother.

- - -

Mirracle and Maleek were sitting in the den when Kyra entered the house. Mirracle had prepared spaghetti and salad for dinner and Maleek had set the table. Kyra was very proud of her children. They were handling the family's misfortune like champs. This was one of those moments wherein Kyra felt reassured that they had listened and grasped some of the things that she and Kaleb had taught them. Upon seeing his mother, Maleek stood and gave her a hug.

"Hi Mom; has Dad made any progress?" he asked while relieving her of her purse and briefcase.

Kyra gave him a look that answered his question and added, "I just feel in my heart that he's going to be alright."

There was an awkward silence before Mirracle chimed in and said, "The food is getting cold. We can talk at the table."

Mirracle went to the table and waited while Maleek and Kyra washed their hands. The truth was, she just didn't want to talk about her dad right now. Mirracle had always been "daddy's little girl" and the thought of him not being in her life scared her. Tomorrow she would go visit and read to him. He needed to know that she was there. She loved her father dearly. Mirracle regrouped so that her mother wouldn't be overly worried. But sensing that Mirracle's mind was on her dad, Kyra decided to try and lighten the mood.

"Hey guys, after we leave the hospital tomorrow, why don't we go and get our tree and decorations? The house needs to look nice for when your dad comes home from the hospital. You know Christmas will be celebrated at our house again this year and your dad and I will be celebrating our twentieth year anniversary. It will be fun. So what do you say?"

Both children mumbled their agreements under their breaths and then joined hands so that they could pray over the meal in front of them. Sounding a lot like Kaleb, Maleek led the prayer. As soon as the grace ended, Mirracle started passing the food. Just as Kyra was preparing her plate, the telephone rang and Maleek got up and answered it. It was his grandmother and she wanted to speak to Kyra. He handed the phone to his mother.

"Hello."

"Hi baby, how are you?" her mother inquired.

"Hi Momma, I'm fine. As a matter of fact, we were just eating dinner. Is everything okay?"

"Everything's fine. I was just checking on you guys. Has Kaleb's condition changed since yesterday?"

"No ma'am. If anything changes, I'll be sure to call you." Wanting to get off the telephone, Kyra created an untruth, telling her mom that another call was coming in and promised to call her back.

Kyra really loved and appreciated her mother. She was always there when she needed her and for that she was grateful. Since Kaleb had been involved in the accident, she needed all the support and encouragement that she could get. But for now, she was going to enjoy her children and pray that they could all get through the night in preparation for their visit with Kaleb tomorrow.

- - -

Kyra woke up with the sun glaring directly into her face. This, she determined, was a sign that it was going to be a great day. Kyra reached in the drawer and pulled out her daily devotional. As usual, the timing of the Word it provided for the day was perfect. After praying the prayer that accompanied the reading, she rose and went into her bathroom. Always praying that this would be the day that Kaleb would be awake when she arrived at the hospital, she felt a bit revitalized. Kyra could hear sounds that told her that the children were up as well. Hurriedly, she bathed, dressed, and went downstairs where her children had gathered.

Kyra and Kaleb had raised responsible children. Mirracle had cooked a light breakfast and set the table. Maleek was on the phone making sure that he did not have to report to work. Kyra sat down at the table and was immediately joined by the children.

"Mom, for clarification purposes, can you enlighten us with the details of Dad's prognosis?" Mirracle asked.

Kyra looked at her and then at Maleek who seemed to be waiting for the answer too. She knew she had to be honest. "Well, the doctors are saying that he's in a coma and that the prospect for a full recovery is not very promising. He was banged up very badly and has several bruises and cuts. There's a strong possibility that he may lose the mobility in his right arm or be totally paralyzed. His blood pressure is fluctuating and he keeps running a fever. They act as though they want me to give up on him but of course, that is not happening. Our prayers and faith in the Lord are going to bring your dad home. The young teenager who hit him has been released from the hospital, but he has been calling every day checking on Kaleb's progress. He feels so bad. You know, he told us that he only had one beer because he knew he had to drive. He had no idea that his friends would spike his drink, making it more potent."

Kyra's mind drifted to the day that she received the news from her mother-in-law. The accident had been the result of the teen driver going the wrong way on a one-way street. Kaleb was waiting on the traffic light to turn green and was less than two miles away from home when the accident happened. Kyra had just left home, headed to her sister, Ashley's house when her cell phone rang.

"Hey Momma Turk, what's up?" she answered cheerfully, recognizing her mother-in-law's number on the caller ID.

There was no sound on the other end.

"Momma Turk, are you there? Is anything wrong?"

Still, no answer; then suddenly the sound of crying could be heard in the background.

"Momma Turk, are you crying?"

"Kyra, I hate to tell you this but Kaleb has been in a bad accident."

That was all that Kyra heard. Her whole body went numb. "Is he, is he still alive?" she managed to get out.

"Yes baby, he's alive, but he's in critical condition at St. Luke Hospital. Don't worry about the children, I will call them. However, we won't tell them anything until they are over here. Call me when you get to the hospital."

Kyra made a u-turn in the road and headed toward the hospital all while using her free hand to dial her sister to let her know what had just transpired. Once there, she was escorted to the intensive care unit where she saw Kaleb's motionless body hooked up to many machines. Immediately, when Kyra entered the area that he was in, she started crying. The only ones there were his sisters, Sophia and Ezzia, and their husbands. Because it looked as though Kyra was going to faint, both her sisters-in-law grabbed her, led her to the waiting area that was just down the hall, and helped her to a chair.

A nurse stepped into the doorway and informed them that the doctor would be coming out to speak with them momentarily, and as the seconds ticked away on the clock, none of them could find words to speak. Even though all the news that the doctor delivered was not positive, it was not all negative either. He said that there was a chance that Kaleb's condition could go either way. It was too early to tell.

Following the doctor's brief report, Ezzia, her husband, and Sophia's husband left while Sophia and Kyra stayed. As the hour grew later, a nurse was kind enough to bring blankets and pillows as they settled down in the waiting room for the night.

When Kyra suddenly heard Mirracle telling her that the food was getting cold, her mind drifted back to the present. Quickly, they finished breakfast and left for the hospital; all of them praying that good news would greet them when they arrived.

- - -

Kyra had been at the hospital so often that the nurses recognized her and treated her with kindness. Going down the hall, all three of them were praying that they would see some sort of progress. A team of doctors was coming out of Kaleb's room when his wife and children arrived. As Kyra and the children approached the door, one of the doctors stopped and explained that Kaleb's vital signs were improving. There had been some eye movement, too; but even though they had seen some progression, the doctor reminded them not to get too excited. Then he left them alone to their thoughts while he rushed to catch up with the other physicians.

Mirracle looked at her mom and then at Maleek. "I don't care what that doctor said. I say that the Lord is showing us a sign that He has heard our prayers. I'm going in and talk to my dad."

Pushing open the door, Mirracle walked to the bed, pulled up a chair and started talking to Kaleb. Maleek and Kyra came in too, but they stood silently at the foot of the bed and listened.

270

"Dad, it's me, Mirracle, your little girl. I miss you so much. Mom, Maleek and I are going to get a tree and decorations today. Don't worry; I know what type of tree to get." She paused and then continued. "I've been practicing for the Christmas program. You are going to be so proud of me. I make you this promise; I promise I will sing your favorite song if you promise that you will get better. I need you, Dad. I'm not used to you not being here. Please open your eyes. Mom needs you and so does Maleek. I want my family back."

Holding his hands in hers, Mirracle began to pray. "Dear Lord, please let my dad open his eyes and be in his right mind. Breathe the breath of life into him once again, Lord, and allow him to finish his task on earth that you have destined for him. Please heal him so that I can keep my promise to him. Now Lord, strengthen us as a family so that we can support each other in a time such as this. Cover us and my dad. We love you, Lord and know that he is in your hands. Only you can make him whole again. It is in Jesus' name I pray. Amen."

Mirracle opened her eyes but didn't let go of Kaleb's hands. "And Dad, I always keep my promises just like you, so I know you won't let me down. Remember, you have to come home for Christmas so that you can tell the family for the umpteenth time why you told Mom to name me Mirracle." She then got up and joined Maleek and Kyra.

Maleek approached the bed and bent over his father's body. His lips moved, but no sound could be heard. After a while, he stood up and wiped his eyes. Kyra was the last one to go to the Kaleb's bedside.

"Okay sweetie, you've had enough rest. Now get up from there so we can go do our family Christmas shopping. The new mall is open and you know as always, I have many suggestions for my gifts." She pulled a list out of her purse. "See Kaleb, I made a list so that we won't overspend this year the way...*I* usually do." Kyra tried to laugh but instead she began to cry.

Seeing their mother breaking down, Maleek and Mirracle went and stood behind her. Kyra quickly dried her eyes and began speaking again. "We have your list as well. I'm not telling you which gifts we decided on; you'll just have to be surprised. So honey, we're going to go now so that you can complete your beauty

271

rest. Know that we all love you and will be back on tomorrow." She bent down and kissed him on his forehead and the children did the same before saying their goodnights.

Once outside, they regrouped and determined within themselves that they would make the best of the day ahead. As planned, they were going to purchase the tree and decorations before returning to the hospital the following day. In the car, everyone looked as though they were in another world. Kyra was thinking about seeing Kaleb's light brown eyes again; Maleek was thinking about playing chess with his dad and Mirracle was focused on the promise that she had just made. She knew her father had heard her.

He just had to, she thought. One thing she knew for sure. Kaleb Turk was big on keeping promises.

- - -

When Kyra and the children finally made it to the store, they discovered that everyone had apparently had the same idea as they did. The tree farm was packed with shoppers. Maleek guided his mom and sister to the area where they usually selected their tree. Inspecting the stock, they narrowed it down to two choices, and since she was the youngest, Kyra and Maleek allowed Mirracle to make the final decision. After the tree was selected, they moved inside to purchase the decorations. Before Kaleb's accident, he and Kyra had decided purple, silver, gold and gray would be the colors used this year. This way, their anniversary colors could be displayed as well.

Kyra picked out the decorations while Maleek chose the lights and Mirracle, the tree top ornament. Feeling very pleased with their decisions, they paid for their selections and left. The Turks decided to go home and put up the decorations before heading to the mall to shop for gifts. Barely inside the house, Kyra heard the phone ring. It was the doctor from the hospital.

"May I speak to Mrs. Kyra Turk? This is Dr. Stevens from St. Luke Hospital."

"This is Mrs. Turk. Is something wrong with my husband?" Kyra was beginning to panic.

"No. As a matter of fact, I have good news. Mr. Turk regained consciousness a little while ago. He has yet to speak, but he is alert. We are monitoring his progress and as anxious as I know you are to see him, I'm asking that you don't try to visit now. This sudden turn

272

of events has baffled us and we must run several extensive tests that will take quite some time to complete. I just wanted to call because I thought you would appreciate some good news."

"I certainly do. Thank you so much for calling. The children will be so happy to know that their dad has opened his eyes. When will we be allowed to see him?"

"How does late tomorrow morning sound?"

"Wonderful! We'll be there right after church. If anything else occurs, please don't hesitate to call. Thank you, Doctor Stevens."

Feeling a rejuvenation that she hadn't felt in days, Kyra dropped the phone and ran into the den where Mirracle and Maleek were placing the tree on its stand.

"Guess what?" Kyra was so excited that she didn't give them a chance to respond. "Your dad woke up! The doctor just called and said that so far he looks as though he's alert. He has not spoken yet, but Dr. Stevens thinks he is doing well." As soon as Kyra's ramble concluded, the room filled with joyous screams from her and the children.

Regaining her composure, Kyra added, "Now let's put on some music and *really* decorate this tree. We want Kaleb to be proud of it when he comes home."

Maleek put in the Temptations' latest Christmas CD and hands that once moved slowly under the uncertainty of Kaleb's prognosis quickly went to work, decorating the tree to showroom perfection. Once they were finished, Mirracle climbed the ladder and placed the harp-playing angel at the very top. Looking around, she saw that her mom had hung the wedding picture that she and Kaleb had taken twenty years ago on one of the tree's branches. With a twinkling light from the tree shining down on it, the photo glowed.

All three of them gathered around the tree, grabbed hands and Maleek began to pray. "Dear Lord, thank you so much for our family. Thank you for allowing my dad to open his eyes. Now Lord, please restore his speech and let him be fully coherent. Heal his body and take away the pain so that he can come home. We really need him here with us. Strengthen each of us to do what we need to do. Thank you Lord. Amen."

As Maleek's prayer came to a close, *The Christmas Song* was beginning to play from the stereo. Instinctively, Mirracle began to sing and the others joined in. By the time the song faded, they were

273

all doing something they'd not done in a long time; hugging and smiling. The only person missing from their union was Kaleb.

Kyra's heart leapt when she saw her children's happiness. Looking at her watch, she realized that Mirracle and Maleek had to get to practice for the Christmas program and she needed to visit her sister, Ashley, before they went to the mall later on. Each of them did their part in cleaning up the mess that decorating the tree had left behind and afterwards, Kyra dropped the children off at the church while she visited Ashley.

On the drive to her sister's house she phoned Mother Turk and told her about the call from Dr. Stevens. Kaleb's mother was elated, just as Kyra knew she would be.

"He's gonna be home for Christmas; just wait and see!" Mother Turk exclaimed.

Kyra didn't need to be convinced. All during her brief visit with Ashley, she spoke to herself in faith, believing without a doubt that God was indeed healing her husband. When she returned to the church to gather her teenagers, Kyra didn't even have to get out of the car. Rehearsals had ended and Mirracle and Maleek were waiting outside, still displaying the same excited smiles they had upon hearing the news of their father.

Since they all had their own lists and monies, the visit to the mall was going to be brief. Getting out the car, Kyra gave her son and daughter instructions on where and what time to meet when they were done. For Kyra, two hours was more than enough time to shop. She had finished and was headed to the meeting spot when she heard Handel's *Messiah* on the intercom system. It reminded her of Kaleb and she veered into the electronics store and bought him an iPod she had seen him looking at in a catalogue a few weeks earlier. She would get Maleek to add all of his father's favorite songs so she could take it to him when they visited the hospital.

When Kyra finally made it to the assigned meeting place, the children were already there, waiting with bags in tow.

"I know Dad is going to keep his promise," Mirracle suddenly blurted during the relatively quiet ride home. "And I have the perfect song to sing for him." She pulled a shirt from one of her shopping bags. "This is the shirt he's going to wear," she told Kyra. "And Maleek bought the pants to match."

274

Kyra was glad that her children had faith in the power of prayer and they grinned when she told them about the iPod she'd purchased. Anticipation was so high in the car that no one cared that the rain that had begun to fall would hamper any further outside activity. Looking up, Kyra knew that rain symbolized blessings and she knew that she would welcome one right about now.

- - -

Kyra didn't have to wake the children to prepare for church on Sunday morning. They were up and dressed when she emerged from her bedroom. The spirit of expectation was so great that even the pace of the church service seemed set on fast forward. Following the benediction, Maleek and Mirracle didn't even bother to stand around talking to friends. They raced to the car and were already buckled in their seatbelts when Kyra got there.

On the drive to the hospital, no one said a word. Once there, Mirracle was the first one out of the car, beating the other two into the hospital and to Kaleb's room door. Upon entering the room, she screamed, and Maleek and Kyra ran to catch up to see what the matter was. What they saw momentarily paralyzed them both. Kaleb's eyes were not only open but he was sitting up in the bed with the help of the attending nurse. His brown eyes smiled when he saw Mirracle. Kyra rushed to his bedside, stepped in front of the nurse and took over her duties. Maleek still stood in awe.

"Hi Dad, do you know who I am?" Mirracle asked while approaching his bedside with caution.

Kaleb nodded and smiled. The nurse explained that even though he was having trouble speaking and had been in a lot of pain, Kaleb had made miraculous progress. Mirracle heard what the nurse said, but all she really cared about was the fact that her father was awake and had recognized her.

"When do you think he will be able to go home?" Kyra asked the nurse.

"I don't want to give you false hope but I think he may be home for Christmas," the nurse replied just as Dr. Stevens was entering the room.

"Good morning Turk family. I don't know what happened between yesterday and today but Mr. Turk is determined to beat this thing. His body still needs a lot of internal healing to do but it looks like he might be home for Christmas." The doctor stepped closer to

275

the bed and began examining his patient. Satisfied with whatever findings he'd been searching for, Dr. Stevens completed his probing and gave Kyra the thumbs-up signal.

"I know you want to stay longer," he said with in an apologetic tone, "but Mr. Turk has been up a long time. He was too wound up to go to sleep because he wanted to see you all. Now that he has, we'll need him to get some rest soon. It's important for his recovery." He looked at his watch and then continued. "I'll give you an hour and then I'll have to insist that Mr. Turk takes his meds and get some sleep."

- - -

It was Christmas Eve and Mirracle and Maleek were preparing to go to church. The day of the Christmas program had finally arrived. Kyra was busy doing last minute chores around the house but her mind was on the fact that her whole family would be at her home in just a few hours; maybe even Kaleb. He had made remarkable progress over the past few days. Today was their twentieth wedding anniversary and she had never spent it alone. To lessen Kyra's burden, her mother offered to do all of the cooking. The free time gave Kyra a chance to relax a little before the children's performance.

Keep me, Holy Spirit, she thought as she completed her chores, determined not to let the thought of having to spend her anniversary without Kaleb take her into a state of depression. God had been too good and done too much for her to feel anything other than blessed.

It was already noon and the program was set to begin at three. After glancing around the house one last time, Kyra disappeared into her bedroom to get dressed. It was time to go and see her angles spread their wings.

- - -

With the exception of Mother Turk, Sophia and of course, Kaleb, the whole family was at the church to witness the fabulous Christmas program. Mirracle sang like a natural born songbird and Maleek played his heart out on the saxophone. Everyone was gathering for the finale when the mistress of ceremony came up to the mic.

"May I have your attention please? Mirracle, can you step forward?" Mirracle did as asked. The mistress of ceremony whispered in her ear and then turned to the musicians. The room was quiet. "Ladies and gentlemen, presenting Mirracle Turk accompanied by Maleek Turk and the St. Luke ensemble."

The music started playing, and Mirracle began singing *Because of Who You Are*, the hit song by Vicki Yohe. Hearing her daughter sing the lyrics was almost too much for Kyra to bear. It was Kaleb's favorite song and his little girl was singing it beautifully.

Suddenly, Mirracle stopped singing and stared straight ahead. Following the direction of her golf ball sized eyes, everyone looked around. There, being wheeled down the aisle by his sister, Sophia, was Kaleb. It only took a moment for Kyra to vacate her seat and arrive at her husband's side.

From his chair, Kaleb motioned for his daughter to continue. Tears nearly blinded her eyes, but Mirracle saw her father's urging and picked up where she'd left off. When she was finished, the congregation was on its feet; some clapping, some crying, but all rejoicing. While the ovation was still in progress, Mirracle ran to Kaleb and placed her head on his lap. Maleek was right behind her.

Another member of the ensemble walked up and handed Kaleb a microphone. A thick hush blanketed the room and every eye was on the man, who just days ago, was trapped in a world of an unshakable sleep.

Struggling, Kaleb brought the microphone to his mouth. Looking directly at Kyra he said, "Happy anniversary, baby; I love you."

Kyra was in tears, responding by placing several small kisses on Kaleb's face, being careful not to hurt him. When Kaleb made no effort to say anything more, the pastor stood behind the podium, led a prayer of thanksgiving and dismissed the congregation, wishing them all a happy holiday.

Well-wishers pressed together to greet the Turk family. When the crowd finally thinned, Mirracle looked at her father and smiled through lingering tears.

"See Dad, I knew you would keep your promise. You have never let me down. I love you so much."

"I heard your promise and I had to be here to hear my little girl." Kaleb spoke every word as if forming them took all of his energies.

Kyra chimed in. "I guess you could say that it was Mirracle's promise that got you out of that bed. The care from the doctors was okay, but for Kaleb Turk, it took a *Mirracle*, right?"

Those still standing around laughed at Kyra's light-hearted conclusion, but Mirracle and Kaleb exchanged glances, knowing that every word of it was true.

Chapter Twenty

Caterri Leaks, a native of Atlanta Georgia, has walked a vision that caters to teaching the Word of God. Her writing journey started in childhood and has come full circle. Her first poem was published in a citywide high school magazine and her first children's book was released January 2006.

Although most of her writing is geared toward young readers, she loves writing stories that inspire self-examination for women Caterri's writing passion allows the revelation of God's Word to come alive. She is the owner/founder of Willing Heart Creations, which produces Christian fiction books, games, products and curriculums for all ages. The company's visions is to mold the character of children, ages 3 to 7, build self-esteem in children, ages 8 to 12 and promote self-examination for teens and women. Visit www.willingheartcreations.com for future products and books.

Caterri currently resides outside of the Atlanta area. She is a full-time Plant Controller for a major corporation and has worked in accounting for the last fifteen years. She holds a Bachelor of Business Administration from West Georgia College and is currently enrolled in the Institute of Children's Literature.

Her contribution to *The Midnight Clear* is entitled, **What Child Is This** and serves as her first published work of fiction not geared toward children.

What Child Is This

Joy filled Sidney's heart as she listened to the hospital's piano player recite an instrumental version of "Joy to the World." There was a steady buzz in the air as families rushed through the hallways of the maternity ward, searching for their new additions. Looking through the nursery's window, Sidney smiled as she watched baby Joshua cry while receiving his very first sponge bath.

Oh, he's not going to like baths, she thought to herself. He was only half an hour old and already making his opinion known.

Sidney's moments of peace were shattered by the sound of, "Code blue to room 1208" that boomed over the intercom. The words, *room 1208* rushed through Sidney's head.

I know that room. "That's Carmen's room!" Her mental thoughts spilled out loud.

She rushed down the hall with a feeling of walking in place; she could not get there fast enough. The nurses and doctors arrived before Sydney and asked her to wait outside of the room. She waited as instructed, but on pins & needles. *What was going on? I thought once she got through the delivery, she would be fine.* Fear gripped Sidney as never before. She could hear the monitors beeping and the urgency of the doctor's commands on the other side of the door.

Every second felt like an hour. Sidney's heart was racing faster than the rapid chords of "Sleigh Ride", the song that was now being played on the piano in the distance. The musical sounds that just moments ago had filled her with the joy of the season were now an annoyance.

Do they not know something major was happening? Can't they all just be quiet until all was right in room 1208?

"All will be well; just trust God," said an elderly voice as a tissue was handed to Sidney by the stranger.

She had not even realized that tears were streaming down her face. "Thank you," she replied, as she took the tissue and gently wiped the moisture from her cheeks. Sidney was a woman of great faith and was glad that the stranger had helped her re-focus her energy. She started to pray for God to take control of the situation in Carmen's room. Within minutes of her prayer, the doctor came out of the room and shared with Sidney.

280

"She is stable now. Her blood pleasure dropped to 67 over 100, which is dangerously low. The delivery may have been too much for her body. The next twenty-four hours will be critical. Has she been taking her medica...?"

Before he could complete the question Sidney replied, "Everyday; I make sure she does not miss a dose."

"Good," he replied. "Now we will wait. I will check back in on her in a little while."

Sidney eased into the room where Carmen was resting peacefully. Her dark chocolate complexion was tinted with a hint of ash and her lips were gray. Her chest rose and lowered very slowly, as if her lungs were exhausted. Although she had just delivered a baby from an eight-month pregnancy, her body was frail. Carmen was only one hundred twenty pounds before the pregnancy, and she gained eighteen pounds, delivering a five-pound-six-ounce baby.

Sidney thanked God in advance for her friend's health being restored. She was relieved and hoped Carmen would grow stronger so she could get a chance to hold Joshua. The nurse had promised to bring him from the nursery as soon as he had his bath. Sidney had been by Carmen's side during the entire labor and delivery process and was a little tired herself, but she would not dare leave her friend's side now. As many children waited with great anticipation of Christmas morning, so would she. This would be a long Christmas Eve.

Standing at the bedside, Sydney brushed Carmen's shoulder length hair away from her face and then moisturized her friend's chapped lips with Vaseline. Then she walked over to the reclining chair to settle in for the rest of the evening. She pulled a hospital blanket over her legs and stared at the friend that she had grown to love as much as a sister. As Sidney sat in the recliner, she reflected on how they met and got to this point in their relationship.

- - -

It was a crisp May morning and Sidney had gotten up early to attend the 7:00 a.m. Sunday service. The praise team had just begun singing when an usher approached and asked Sidney if anyone was in the vacant seat beside her.

"No, the man that was here moved to the back to sit with a friend," was Sidney's reply.

281

The usher then instructed a young lady to sit in the seat. Sidney smiled and extended a cordial greeting as she looked down from her five-nine statue to the young lady standing at a height of about five-six. The woman returned a halfhearted smile and greeted her as well. As the service continued, Sidney could sense a spirit of heaviness on the woman who sat beside her and she said a silent prayer for God to lift the load and give her peace.

As Pastor Jordan began to teach that morning, he introduced his message by talking about seeking God's forgiveness, not only for others, but for self as well. Throughout the entire message, the young visitor cried silent tears. Sidney could feel her pain but did not want to intrude. Pastor Jordan closed his message by asking everyone to turn to Galatians 6:1-2.

The scripture read: *Brethren, if a man is overtaken in any trespass, you who are spiritual restore such a one in a spirit of gentleness, considering yourself lest you also be tempted. Bear one another's burdens, and so fulfill the law of Christ.*

Then he said, "Church it is time for you to minister. Turn to someone next to you. Everyone should have just one partner. Pray for your brother or sister right now."

Sidney turned to the young lady and began to pray for her. The sister continued to allow the tears to flow freely but the heaviness seemed to lift. After Sidney prayed, she heard the lady beside her say this simple prayer.

"God, thank you for sending a sister that could hear from you."

Sidney and the visitor embraced one another so long and tightly that they did not realize the pastor had given the benediction. When they released one another, each woman returned to her seat and sat in silence. Sidney was the first to speak.

"I'm Sidney."

"I'm Carmen," the girl replied.

"It's nice to meet you Carmen. Are you going to be okay?"

"I think I will, I have no choice but to try."

"They have breakfast in the fellowship hall. We could go there if you would like to talk." Sidney shocked herself. *What am I doing? I don't know this lady and I have too much to do to sit around talking.*

As a mortgage broker, Sidney usually caught up on her paperwork on Sundays after church. Just as quickly as the selfish thought came to mind, so did the last scripture that the pastor had read.

"I don't want to be a bother," replied Carmen.

"It is not a bother. Let's just go get some hot tea to help you settle your heart."

Both ladies picked up their Bibles and proceeded to the fellowship hall, making small talk as they walked.

"So, are you a member here?" Carmen asked.

"Yes, I have been a member here for eleven years. How about you?"

"I'm not a member but this is my favorite church to visit."

"Did you move to Atlanta recently?"

"Yes. My job relocated me here." Once again, tears rolled from Carmen's naturally hazel colored eyes.

This time, Sidney did not comment on the tears. "Let's grab this table over here."

Forgetting about the tea they'd originally come for, the ladies put down their Bibles and sat. The information they initially shared was general, but personal, allowing them to get to know one another better.

Sidney was a thirty-eight-year-old native Atlantan, and middle child with two brothers. She was single with no children and although she didn't yet divulge her position at the church, she also served as a spiritual advisor. Carmen, an only child, was a twenty-eight-year-old attorney from Macon, Georgia. Like Sidney, she too was single.

After about thirty minutes of small talk, Sidney said, "So Carmen, why so many tears today? Do you want to talk about it? I would be more than willing to listen. When Carmen seemed apprehensive, she added, "I won't be judgmental and you have my word that nothing you say will leave this table."

Carmen was hesitant, but desperately needed someone to talk to. "I just lost my job and boyfriend at the same time."

Sidney nodded in an empathetic manner. "Both of those can be heartbreaking, but both can be replaced."

"Yes, but there's more; *much* more."

This time, Sidney chose to remain quiet and just listen.

"My boyfriend was one of the senior partners at the firm. His wife…yes his *wife*, was the other senior partner." For the duration

283

of her explanation, Carmen hung her head low, as if she was too ashamed to look at Sidney. "We had been having an affair for the last year and a half. I never thought I would be involved with a married man, but it just happened. I joined the firm to be on their business law team. I enjoy helping small businesses set up their legal structure and legally protecting their inventions, products and services. Mack had the same passion. We starting working long hours and grew to really care about one another, or so I thought.

"His wife, Marcia, is an excellent attorney and focused on liability law. Last month, Marcia and Mack began to argue constantly; it seemed she despised his presence. Just before abruptly leaving the firm, Mack came to me and told me that he could no longer see me. I have not seen or talked to him since. Last Monday, Marcia called me into her office and told me that I was being laid off because the firm was only going to practice liability law going forward. The way she looked at me, I felt like there was more to my dismissal than what she said."

"Sounds like you fell in love with the wrong man," Sidney replied.

"Yes, I did; but you still haven't heard the whole story. Sidney, I grew up in the church. I sung in the choir from age five; I knew better. I had had only one other boyfriend in my whole life. I have become a person that I don't even like. Beyond all of this, I got a call from a fellow attorney on Friday. She is the only person that knew about Mack and me. She told me that it is rumored at the office that Mack has AIDS and had passed the infection on to Marcia."

Sidney read Carmen's thoughts clearly. "Now, you are afraid that you may have it also?"

"Yes. I called my doctor and I have an appointment to be tested tomorrow. I am so scared but I guess it serves me right for getting involved with a married man. God has really showed me this time."

"God would not punish you with AIDS. If you have AIDS, it is just a result of the circumstances. Know that God is a loving, forgiving and healing God. It is time for you to reconnect with Him and let go of the guilt that is gripping you so deeply. We do not always make the best decisions in life but let's look at those choices and grow from them." Sidney reached across the table and placed her hand on Carmen's chin, lifting her head. "Don't stay in condemnation. Seek God's forgiveness and trust Him to be in charge of your destiny. Would you like to pray now?"

Carmen nodded as tear continued to flow. Sidney prayed with her and then they exchanged telephone numbers and promised to keep in touch.

The next week was extremely long for Carmen. She received a call on Wednesday with the results of her test. In a state of shock, she called Sidney and was forced to settle for her voicemail. When she heard the beep, Carmen took a deep breath and spoke in as calm a voice as she could muster.

"Hi Sidney, this is Carmen, I met you Sunday at church. If you have a chance can you give me a call back?"

It didn't take long for the return call to be made. "Hi Carmen, this is Sidney. How are you?"

"Hi Sidney, I am as okay as I could be. Do you have time to talk? Could we meet for dinner or whenever you can fit me in your schedule?"

"I have a client coming into the office in about twenty minutes. I'm not going to Bible study tonight so, let's meet for dinner. Let's meet at 6:30 at the Beautiful Restaurant on Cascade."

Sidney thought and then replied, "Do you mind coming here instead? I think I need a little privacy to talk? I can cook us a light meal."

"No problem, give me directions." Sidney's spirit was quickened with concern as she wrote down the directions she was given and she said a prayer for Carmen before her client arrived.

It was six twenty-five when Sidney rang Carmen's doorbell. They greeted one another with a hug and sat together on the sofa.

"What a nice townhouse! I did not know these were here. It is such a central location in town." Sidney commented. Not wanting to waste any time on lengthy small talk she immediately asked, "How did the test go? When will you get the results?"

Carmen eyes swelled with tears. "They called with the results today, right before I called you." Not allowing a response she continued. "It's official, I have AIDS." She collapsed in uncontrollable sobs. This was the first time she had spoken the words. "How could he have done this to me? How could he say he loved me and give me AIDS?"

285

Sidney had no answers but tried to comfort her new friend. "He probably didn't know."

"That's not all," Carmen stated.

How could there be more? Sidney thought as she reached for the Kleenex from the coffee table and offered the box to Carmen.

"I'm pregnant. It's not just me in this mess. I don't care if I die but what about this innocent baby inside of me? What was I thinking? This is the worst thing I could have ever done to myself."

Sidney could only hold her. There were no words or scriptures that she felt would help or be heard at that time – only support was needed.

\- - -

The beeping of the IV monitor in the hospital room brought Sidney back from her reflections. She pressed the nurse's button.

"Can I help you?" was the nurse's response.

"The IV needs to be changed," Sidney answered.

"I will be right there."

Even while the nurse moved Carmen's arms to change the meds, she remained in a motionless, peaceful sleep.

Sidney looked at Carmen and recalled how hard she had pressed through the shame, conviction, and hurt to become a woman of faith. They found a good Internist to attend to Carmen's medical needs and an Ob/Gyn for prenatal care. Both doctors worked together to ensure Carmen's optimal health throughout the pregnancy.

Sidney and Carmen prayed together every morning and read and reviewed confirmation scriptures weekly. Carmen studied the lives of strong biblical women. Even though her pregnancy wasn't conceived in God's divine order, she was determined to turn it around to glorify Him. She joined a support group and began to keep a journal that she planned to publish one day to help educate other women. When the nurse left, Sydney's mind drifted again.

\- - -

At the beginning of September, Carmen told Sidney of an awkward situation she encountered as she rushed into her support group to escape an intense thunderstorm. Pulling her umbrella down with her back to the door, she bumped blindly into a woman who she hadn't seen standing there.

"Excuse me!" both ladies said. Then their eyes met.

286

Oh my God, thought Carmen. But she could not run from the situation any longer. Evidence of her pregnancy could be seen by this time. She had prayed for closure but had no idea an awkward opportunity such as this one would arise.

"Hello, Marcia," she said, looking into the eyes of her former employer.

"Hello, Carmen," replied Marcia, sharing Carmen's look of shock.

"Can we talk?" Carmen asked, wanting to get it over with before losing the nerve.

Marcia was hesitant, but agreed. The ladies went into an empty conference room across from the area where the support group met.

"I don't know where to start," Carmen said. "I guess the best place is to say I'm so sorry for interfering in your marriage. I've made some positive changes in my life since that time and hope you can forgive me."

Marcia was quiet for a minute and then tears began leaking from her eyes onto her cheeks. "You too, huh?"

"You did not know?" Carmen was surprised. She was certain that Marcia knew about her involvement with Mack.

"No; there were so many that it was nearly impossible for me to keep tabs. You were probably as much of a victim as the others. This means Mack was involved with all three of the new hires at the firm."

Carmen's eyes bulged with shock, as she was the only female among the new hires. "You mean,,,"

"Yes, Mack was on the DL. That's why I am here. He gave me AIDS. Did you get it also?"

With her head lowered, Carmen said, "Yes, I had no idea."

"Neither did I," Marcia replied.

For a moment, Carmen's shame turned to anger. *How could he do something like this?* "Where is he now?" she blurted with her eyes glaring, her shoulders back and her nostrils flared.

Marcia looked at her in amazement. "You didn't hear? He died last month. He'd been infected for years and he refused to accept it and would not take any of the prescribed medication. Carmen, you have to forgive him, let go of the anger and move forward to live the best life you can. He has gone on and even though he left us with great pain, the unforgiveness will only shorten our days." Her eyes dropped to Carmen's swollen belly. "Shall I assume this is Mack's baby?"

"I can't believe he's dead," Carmen said. Her embarrassment returned and she dropped her head once more. "Yes, this is Mack's child," she whispered.

Marcia looked dejected but said, "If you don't mind, I would like our son, Marcus to know his sister or brother."

"That would be nice," Carmen agreed.

"Are you working now?"

Carmen nodded. "I found a job but it's not the business law that I love."

"You have my office number and here is my home line," Marcia said as she scribbled the digits on a slip of paper she'd retrieved from her purse. "Call me and maybe we can discuss you starting that division back up for the firm. I was just so angry at that time. I had put Mack out of the firm and our home and I did not want any reminders of him. I took it out on the division by letting you all go, and for that I apologize."

"I understand. If I were you, I probably would still be angry."

"After many hours of counseling I have concluded that life is too short. I have to make the most of each day."

The ladies grabbed one another in an endearing embrace that lasted for several moments and then went their separate ways.

Carmen could hardly wait to share the encounter with Sidney that evening. She could not help but to shed a few tears for Mack's passing, but she was relieved to have forgiveness and closure with Marcia. Shortly thereafter, Carmen returned to the job she loved and worked with Marcia to reconstruct the business advisory division of the law firm and to get all of her personal matters in order.

- - -

Sidney's thoughts stopped as the nurse rolled Joshua into the room. "Here's your little prince."

"His mommy is resting, but bring him in anyway; maybe he will inspire her to wake up," Sidney responded.

She got up from the chair and leaned over Joshua's crib. His eyes were open and they were hazel like his mother's. He was a handsome boy with an almond complexion and a head full of hair.

288

Sidney had seen pictures of Mack and figured that baby Joshua had no choice but to be a handsome combination of both his parents.

A while later, the nurse returned to the room and said, "It's time for his bottle; should we wake his mother?"

"I'm not sure. Dr. Freemont just finished checking on her and said to allow her to awake on her own."

The nurse smiled and replied, "Well then, Auntie; do you want the honor of giving him a bottle?"

"I guess so," Sidney said as she cradled the child in her arms and placed the nipple of the bottle against his lips.

Initially, Joshua refused to take the milk, but once he began drinking, he did so until he fell asleep.

How precious! Sidney thought. She rocked him on her shoulder and began to sing softly, "What child is this that lay to rest on Mary's lap is sleeping. ..." Her words turned into a soft hum and Sidney's mind flooded with thoughts.

It must have been God's divine order for such a precious gift to be born on the eve of the day we celebrate God's most precious gift. Many obstacles had been overcome to bring this little fellow into the world. His father never knew about him. His mother could have chosen to abort him in conservation of her own health. Yet she forfeited certain medications and treatments to ensure he would not have any birth defects.

Sidney could not hold back the tears as she prayed, "God, thank you for the life of this precious gift. I know you have a mighty plan for his future and that's why it was such a battle to get him here. I prayer he will be all that you have created him to be on this earth. I ask that you cover him and shield him from the virus that causes AIDS. If he has any trace of it, may it be cleansed from his body as I pray this prayer. It is in your precious Son, Jesus' name I pray and celebrate this day and season. Amen."

"Amen," Sidney heard a faint voice say as she held the baby close. She opened her eyes in astonishment. Carmen was awake.

"Would you like to hold your gorgeous son?" she offered as she stood.

Carmen nodded. "He *is* gorgeous, isn't he?" she said while carefully checking his fingers and toes."

Sidney released a hearty laugh. "They are all there!"

289

Carmen was extremely weak but managed to ask the question that was most pressing on her mind. "Have they run the test?"

Sidney nodded. "Yes. They should have the results in the morning." Looking at her watch she saw that it was 12:12 a.m. "Well, Merry Christmas!"

Carmen's only response was a weak smile.

Sensing her friend's fatigue, Sidney asked, "Do you want me to put him back in his crib?"

"Please," Carmen replied. After a brief silence, she said, "Sidney, I saw an angel and it was so beautiful. There is nothing to fear anymore."

Sidney bubbled with joy. "I know girl. You made it through this and now we are just waiting for the manifestation of your total healing."

Carmen replied, "It is already here."

"Amen girl," Sidney said, taking note of Carmen's yawn. "Don't wear yourself out. I am going to slip home to shower and I will be back. Get some rest."

"I love you Sidney and appreciate all you have done and will do for me and Joshua," replied Carmen.

"I love you too; now rest. I will see you in a little while." Sidney kissed Carmen on the forehead and left the room.

While driving home, she had a great praise in her heart, singing songs and thanking God continuously. Sidney arrived home and took a relaxing bath, all while worshipping God for new beginnings. After lying down and getting several hours of rest, she woke up with the same sense of joy. Sidney got dressed and gathered some special gifts she had purchased for Carmen and the baby then headed back to the hospital, listening to her favorite Christmas CD during the drive. Pressing the repeat button, she sang the lyric to "Oh Come All Ye Faithful" all the way to the hospital and then walked to room 1208 with a joyous prance.

She was greeted by Dr. Freemont as he exited the room. "Ms. Sidney; let's talk," he said as he directed her to the empty waiting room.

"Good morning, Dr. Freemont and Merry Christmas. I didn't expect to see you this early in the day. Do you have the results from Joshua's test? A result of negative would be a wonderful gift for Carmen on this morning." Sidney chattered.

290

Dr. Freemont interrupted her questions and although the news was good, Sidney detected concern in his tone. "Joshua is totally virus free but we will want to test him every six months until we are sure that everything is well with him." His eyes dropped to the packages in Sidney's hand. "Sidney, Carmen won't be able to receive any gifts today. She was pronounced dead at 3:30 this morning."

Sidney's legs buckled and she collapsed into a nearby chair. "What? What happened? Why wasn't I called? Was she alone?" Sidney was beyond shocked. "Oh God, help me!"

Dr. Freemont sat beside her and continued, "She simply lost too much blood during the delivery and her body's system tried to recover but could not. She knew she wouldn't be going home. She left this note for you, instructing us not to bother you, but to give it to you when you arrived. I'm sorry for your loss."

The doctor left her alone and Sidney's hand shook as she opened the letter. She had to continuously take deep breaths and wipe away tears so that she could see the words.

Dear Sidney,

If you are reading this note, I have received my total healing in returning to our God in heaven. Sometimes healing means leaving the physical body – you taught me that (smile). I am sure this is very hard on you and I know after all you have done for me, I have quite a nerve asking for one last favor. However, here I go: Will you please be my child's mother? I know the love you have for me will overflow to him. I will rest in peace as I hand over this responsibility to the sister I love and admire more than anyone. Thank you for all you have shared with me and for reuniting me with my first love, Jesus Christ! I love you!

P.S. Please contact Marcia. A few weeks ago, at the firm, we drew up all of the legal paperwork for the adoption. You are my sole beneficiary on my life insurance plan, so all of your bills and home will be paid off. I knew I wanted you to be Joshua's mother when God was ready to call me home, so I had to make sure you would be totally free to raise him.

I'll see you on the other side- MUCH Love!

291

Sidney stared at her friend's neat, cursive signature at the bottom of the letter and then closed her eyes, with tears still flowing, and thanked God for the opportunity to know Carmen and for the gift she'd given her on Christmas Day.

Chapter Twenty-One

Cynthia Norman Slappy's love of writing literally began as soon as she could hold a pencil to paper. She began writing short stories and plays, and by age eight, she had won her first writing competition. She went on to win several poetry and short story contests in high school and college as an alumna of Valdosta State University and Macon State College.

Also a talented song writer and avid gospel music fan, she is the third daughter of Bishop and Mrs. H.H. Norman of Valdosta, Georgia, and the sister of national bestselling novelist, Kendra Norman-Bellamy.

After working several years as a licensed insurance agent, Cynthia is now a full-time aspiring writer. She currently resides in Macon, Georgia, with her husband, Minister Terry Slappy, a gifted singer and composer in his own right, and their two young daughters. Cynthia can be contacted by way of her web home at www.cynthianormanslappy.com.

Her contribution to *The Midnight Clear* is entitled, ***The Banjolin Player***. It is an abridged adaptation of her first full-length novel, which is set to become available soon.

The Banjolin Player

ban´ jo lin: *(noun) a rare, four-stringed instrument combining characteristics of the African-American banjo and the mandolin, used primarily in folk music.*

"You're going *where?*" Gerard laughed outright when Alicia broke the news to him over steak and shrimp plates at the annual Clover County Christmas Ball.

"I'm going to Africa," Alicia repeated, trying not to appear as disappointed with his reaction as she felt. "You know--*Africa*. The land of our mother."

"Who's mother? My mother is from Boston, and yours is from Savannah, in case you lost your memory along with your common sense," he teased. "What in the world do you plan to do in Africa? Catch malaria? Or a little jungle fever, perhaps?"

As the jazz band blared out Christmas carols and cheery couples danced all around them, slender, attractive, thirty-five-year-old Alicia Patterson looked intently at her fiancé. It was obvious that he was not taking the news seriously. She was tired of twelve years of teaching fifth grade in the coastal town of Cloverton, Georgia. Most of all, she was fed up with Gerard and his fickle ways. Their courtship was headed into its seventh year with a wedding date nowhere in sight.

"This is not a joke, G," she responded. "I'll be teaching at a school that Worldwide Christian Missions is supporting. My church will sponsor me, but I'll be more or less a volunteer for the year."

Gerard's fork slipped from his fingers back onto the plate. His gaze met hers attentively. "A year? In some wild, bush country where God-knows-what could happen? No way, 'Licia."

"Gerard, you don't seem to understand. I am not asking your permission. And if you are so concerned about what I do and where I go, then why in the world am I still just your fiancée?"

"Is that what this is all about?" The tense lines in his forehead relaxed. "Are you running away to Africa just to test my feelings for you? Come on, 'Licia. Please tell me you are a stronger, smarter, black woman than that."

Alicia just looked at him as he casually resumed eating his steak. From his nonchalant expression, it was as if they had just

294

been talking about the weather. That's when a bold revelation struck her in the face: *Gerard had become so comfortable with their engagement that he would forever be content for things to stay just as they were now.* Why hadn't she seen this before?

Her eyes fell upon the one-carat diamond ring he had surprised her with five Christmases ago. She had bubbled with excitement then. Now, with each passing season, it had become just another reminder of an unfulfilled commitment.

Father, you must have a better life for me than this, Alicia contemplated. Before she knew it, she had wrapped her napkin over the ring and pulled it off discretely. She then slid the ring and the napkin next to Gerard's plate.

"Okay. *Now* what's going on?" he asked, as he realized what she had just done. He looked up at her incredulously as she rose from her seat.

"I am," she answered with a soft smile, "I'm going to Africa."

"Whoa...Wait a minute," he protested, as she turned to walk away.

Alicia turned back for just a second to look at him. She then bent beside his chair and spoke softly in his ear. "I'm going to Africa, Gerard," she repeated. "I won't come back as your fiancée. Pray for me, but don't wait for me. I won't be waiting for you."

With that declaration, she stood gracefully. Carefully navigating between dozens of dancing couples, she exited the building, leaving her *ex*-fiancé in the smoke of her determination.

- - -

The bus, crowded with passengers, mostly Ghanaian, conveyed through the streets of Accra, Ghana's busy capital, carrying the volunteers for the African mission. Alicia hoped she would learn some of their native dialects, but was relieved that many of them spoke Ghanaian English.

She tried to calm her nerves by talking to Sarah-Sue McAdams, the 25-year-old art teacher from Atlanta, with whom she had shared a seat on the plane. In the air, the excited, pretty blonde had been almost too chatty, but she had now grown quiet. Alicia figured that it was because she was the only Caucasian female on the bus.

By the time the bus arrived at Juwani, the small village where the school was located, only the American group was still on board. There was Thomas Chi, an overzealous 27-year-old information technology teacher, Vincent Beckford a sixty-something-year-old retired English professor already experienced in overseas mission work, Tyrone Williams, a 33-year-old physical education instructor with overly-muscular arms, and finally, Ed Morgan, a high school algebra teacher and the least talkative member of their group.

Soon, the bus pulled up to what looked like a combination souvenir shop and miniature open-air market. The bus driver turned to them and in a thick African accent announced, "Last stop. Dis bus go no furder."

"Excuse me," Sarah-Sue said in her most pleasant Georgia twang, "We're the new teachers. We're supposed to be taken to the mission school here."

"I know who you are," the driver answered. "Mission paid me to bring you here. Mission school dat way." The dark-brown man pointed ahead to what appeared to be a small, rushing lake with a makeshift bridge leading to the other side. "Bus cannot drive over water. You walk two kilometers, follow de river, and school is on de right."

"What? Walk two kilometers? That's over a mile! We've got luggage." Thomas Chi was indignant.

"Aw, come on, guys. Walking is one of the best exercises you can do," Tyrone Williams piped in, the only one in the group to carry his bags with no trouble.

Within the hour, the weary Americans came upon a sprawling, wooden building about the size of a football field. An unsightly tin roof covered the structure. The place looked all but abandoned. Yet, an old, worn sign displayed, "Juwani Village School."

"Where are the children?" Alicia could not help but ask.

"Is this some kind of joke?" Thomas Chi asked, "Look at this run-down place!"

However, Sarah-Sue McAdams seemed to blossom into her cheery self again. Observing the lush, tropical greenery around them, and the rushing lake in the distance, she smiled and declared, "Well, I think it's the most beautiful place I've ever seen!"

"This *is* Mother Africa," Tyrone submitted, in a surprisingly accusatory tone. "She's the black man's land--abundant in natural resources. Why do you think your European ancestors invaded her land and enslaved her people?"

"My ancestors?" Sarah-Sue answered back, placing her hand on her hip and looking Tyrone straight in the eye. "You don't know anything about my ancestors, buddy. You probably don't know much about yours, either. Are you responsible for anything they did? Well, I'm not responsible for what mine did, either. So back off my grits, buster. I'm here to help like everybody else!"

Even the mortified Tyrone found himself laughing aloud with the others. Alicia immediately knew that she and Sarah-Sue would become good friends during their yearlong stay.

The front door flew open so suddenly, the teachers all stopped laughing at once. A little African girl, who looked about ten years old, stood staring at the Americans for a few seconds. Then a smile that revealed beautiful, white teeth and dimples as big as acorns lit up her face.

"Poppa, dey're here! De teachers are here!" she shouted. The excited child led them into the large entrance room. "Please sit down," she offered politely, then scurried away. The weary teachers were glad to get off their feet.

Thomas Chi soon got up and walked around the room. He paused at the desk, pressing keys on the computer.

"Windows 95? You have got to be kidding!" he said, laughing.

"Uh, young man, you ought to leave that alone," Professor Beckford suggested.

"Oh, please," Thomas said, continuing to press keys. "These people probably don't even know that Microsoft has put out newer operating systems since this one. The Neanderthal in charge of this place ought to be fired."

"Ahem!" The deep male voice echoed from the rear of the room.

The Americans turned to see a tall man, with skin as dark as a Georgia midnight. His austere expression could not conceal his striking features: chiseled cheekbones, small mouth, strong jaw, dimpled chin. He appeared to be in somewhere in his mid-thirties, and had a definite muscular build, but he was not muscle-bound like the showy P.E. teacher.

Alicia found everything about his presence fascinating, including the "V" shaped scar on the right side of his face, and the slight unevenness of his walk. She wondered if the scar was ceremonial or a battle wound. He stopped at the desk where the startled Thomas Chi stood.

"He's *beautiful*, isn't he?" Sarah-Sue whispered.

"Shhh!" Alicia whispered back softly, embarrassed that Sarah-Sue had articulated her own thoughts.

"Uh--who are you?" Thomas asked nervously.

"My name is Patrik." the African man stated. "Patrik Agyei Bolaru, apparently the *Neanderthal* in charge of this school. And you?"

"I, uh, I'm Thomas Chi. I teach computers at..."

"Thomas Chi, sit down, please." Patrik's statement was more of a command than a request.

Thomas masked his embarrassment with a simple, "Thanks," as he complied.

After proper introductions had been made, Patrik stated, "This building is in such bad shape, that classes have not been held here for over a year. I purchased it three months ago, determined to turn it into a proper school again. But it will take a lot of hard work. Nevertheless, my faith in God is strong."

"No offense," Thomas said, "But we're teachers, not carpenters, and certainly not miracle workers."

"Lessons can be taught by example, as well as in the classroom, Mr. Chi. Worldwide Christian Missions has arranged to supply the school with new books and computers once the repairs have been completed. The school will reopen in September, so you will get an opportunity to teach until your tenure ends next January."

As Patrik spoke, Alicia noticed that his accent was not nearly as pronounced as the Ghanaians on the bus. She wondered if he may have been educated in North America or Europe. She self-consciously averted her eyes, as she caught him looking at her with an intense expression.

"Some of you will no doubt drop out when you see just how much hard work and commitment is involved."

He's expecting me to quit because I'm a woman. He thinks that because my nails are manicured that I can't handle a hammer. The thought offended Alicia. She decided right then that she would work harder than the men just to prove a point.

The teachers were given dormitory rooms at the school, each with two beds. Alicia and Sarah-Sue became roommates and quick friends, as expected.

The first week's work proved to be too much for Thomas Chi, and he quit the project. Six weeks later, Professor Beckford slipped on a two-by-four, fracturing his arm in two places, and had to be flown back to the states. Volunteers from the village took turns filling in for the vacancies. Despite the differences in their personalities, the team of teachers worked well together.

Alicia was delighted to find that there was a little chapel on the campus. A traveling cleric would stop through every Sunday evening to bring the Word of God to the villagers who attended, as well as to the teachers and staff. The services were more reserved than the lively, hand-clapping services held at the Cloverton Church of God in Christ back home, but Alicia's thirsty soul was watered just the same.

Alicia almost cried the first time she heard Sarah-Sue sing "'Tis So Sweet to Trust in Jesus" in one of the services. The girl's strong voice was a little bit country and a lot of soul all wrapped up together. The old hymn seemed to minister to her in a new way, as she found her life anew in Africa. Alicia had never imagined that she could make so little money, not have a man, and still feel complete as a woman.

In the six months that had passed, great progress had been made. Alicia kept so busy, whole days passed without a thought to Gerard. Apparently, he wasn't thinking of her much, either, she realized, but not without some disappointment. She had not heard from him since her arrival in Ghana.

The most challenging part of Alicia's work was dealing with the temperamental Patrik Bolaru. She admired him for his dedication to the building and repair of the school, but grew frustrated with his criticism of her efforts.

"What in the world did I do to him to make him hate everything I do?" Alicia asked exasperatedly in the room she shared with Sarah-Sue one evening.

Sarah-Sue said matter-of-factly, "That man likes you."

"What?!" Alicia exclaimed. "He hates me. He can't stand anything that I do! And to tell the truth, I can't stand him, either!"

299

"He likes you, Alicia. That's why he gives you such a hard time. Can't you see through his smokescreen? He can certainly see through yours."

"What are you talking about?"

"You guys have had an eye for each other since the very first day we arrived here. Don't deny it. You know you like him, too."

"The heck I do!" Alicia snapped sarcastically. "That pompous snob? Limping around this campus like he owns the world!"

"Bet he doesn't limp where it counts," Sarah-Sue countered in a sultry, suggestive tone.

"That's it!" Alicia declared, changing quickly out of her work clothes and into a jogging suit. "I am going down to the gym, and when I come back, I don't want to hear a word about me and *Patrik Bolaru*," she said, imitating his accent. "And you? You need Jesus!"

- - -

Imani, the little girl who had opened the door to the school for the teachers on that first day, was Patrik's only child. The teachers were all soon aware that not only was Patrik Bolaru a rather demanding school proprietor, but was also a very overprotective parent.

Eight months into their stay, most of the repairs on the school were complete. In just a couple of weeks, the village children would once again fill the halls and classrooms. Alicia and Sarah-Sue were both in their dorm when the inquisitive Imani walked in. Sarah-Sue was lying in bed, trying to shake the lethargy that had plagued her for the past two days. Alicia was in front of the mirror brushing her hair, which had grown several inches since she arrived in Africa. The little girl watched, fascinated.

"Miss Alicia, please do my hair like yours. I want mine to be shiny and bouncy like yours and Miss Sarah-Sue's," Imani pleaded.

In her heart, Alicia had known from the first time she saw Imani, that the little girl could not have had a mother to tend to her hair. Patrik had no idea how to style his young daughter's coarse, thick tresses. On the day that Imani approached Alicia about her hair, he happened to be out of town on business. His much older cousin, Mandisa, was the school's cook. He had left Imani in her charge.

"Do whatever you like to her hair," Mandisa told Alicia when she brought the matter to her. "Her mother, rest her blessed soul, was a sweet, beautiful woman just like you. I know she would have wanted Imani to look nice."

Alicia wanted to ask Mandisa what had happened to Imani's mother, but decided not to. Even though Alicia knew nothing about the deceased woman, she was sure Mandisa was right about one thing. Every little girl's mama wanted her to look nice.

Making a special trip into town the next day, Alicia purchased the necessary hairdressing supplies. She gently washed, conditioned, and blow-dried Imani's thick tresses. She then carefully straightened her hair from root to tip with a heated pressing comb, using small amounts of pomade as a smoothening agent.

Once Alicia was finished styling the little girl's hair, it appeared to have lengthened at least six inches, draping past her shoulders. Now the hair matched the pretty face that it framed. Alicia smiled as she watched the little girl prance through the halls as her locks danced behind her.

She pranced right into her father, who had finished his business in the city earlier than expected.

"Poppa! Look at what Miss Alicia did to my hair! She says I'm a little Nubian princess!"

The school proprietor bent to get a better look at the little girl he barely recognized. He kissed his daughter on the forehead, and said, "Go play in your room, sweetheart." He then marched down the hall toward where Alicia stood in her doorway. "Miss Patterson, when I left yesterday, Imani was African. Who gave you permission to try to Americanize my daughter?"

"Imani asked me to do her hair herself. I wasn't trying to Americanize her. All little girls like to look pretty."

"She was pretty enough without all that--that grease and shine you've put on her," he said, his anger apparent.

"I only used a pressing comb to straighten it. When her hair is washed again, it will return to its natural state...."

"No, that's where you are again mistaken. Now you have ruined her. She'll always want to look like--like *that* even four months from now, after you have returned to America. And, Miss Patterson, the four months 'til your departure can't come quickly enough for me!"

301

He walked away leaving the stinging words to echo in Alicia's head. She blinked back the tears that threatened to betray her hurt.

Opening her top dresser drawer, Alicia pulled her large suitcase from under her bed, and began to fill it quickly.

"What are you doing?" Sarah-Sue asked in a voice weakened by increased fatigue.

"What I guess I should have done some months ago. I'm leaving."

"But you can't do that. Not now that the school's about to reopen. We've all worked so hard for this. Besides, you're not a quitter. I'm sick as a dog, and I'm not quitting."

"Bolaru didn't just get in your face and practically ask for your resignation, either!"

"He didn't mean it." Sarah-Sue could barely keep her eyes open.

"You don't look too good," Alicia observed.

"I'll be alright. Just don't leave, Alicia..." Sarah-Sue's voice trailed away, as she drifted back to sleep.

- - -

It was three in the morning when Alicia awoke to a strange sound. She turned on the lamp on the nightstand. Looking across the room at the bed where her roommate slept, she was immediately alarmed. Beads of perspiration glistened on Sarah-Sue's face. Her lips parted, but the only sounds emitting from them were moans. In a flash, Alicia was out of bed, shaking her friend frantically, in an effort to bring her to full consciousness.

"Sarah-Sue! Wake up!"

"Alicia," the young woman managed to speak. Her slurred voice drifted off again.

Panic seized Alicia and she ran down the hall and banged on the next door. A bleary-eyed Mandisa answered.

"Mandisa! I can't get Sarah-Sue to stay awake. She's drenched in sweat. I don't know what to do!"

"Sweet Jesus!" the plump, old woman exclaimed, wringing her hands. "You stay wid her. I'll get Patrik. He'll know what to do."

For a man with a limp, Patrik Bolaru could get around quickly. He arrived quickly and lifted the barely conscious woman as easily as if she weighed no more than his own young daughter.

302

"She's burning up with fever! Get some clean rags and a bowl of ice water," he instructed Alicia. "Mandisa, call emergency services so they will be waiting for us on the other side of the bridge. Once we make it to the river, we will have to carry her by foot over the bridge."

The only transportation the school had was an old, donated cargo van. After their sickly colleague was placed gingerly in a cot on the floor of the van, Tyrone Williams took the driver's seat. A silent and very solemn Ed Morgan sat opposite of him. Alicia and Patrik climbed in the back to sit on the floor beside Sarah-Sue.

Alicia drenched the rag in ice water and dabbed it all around Sarah-Sue's face. "Hang in there, girl," she said over and over.

"Miss McAdams, we are taking you to the emergency clinic in town," Patrik explained, hoping Sarah-Sue could understand him. "Don't be afraid."

As Patrik reached over to steady the bowl of ice water, which rocked with the jarring movements of the van, his hand brushed against Alicia's. Her worried eyes met his in the dim light.

"Don't be afraid," he repeated.

But by the next evening, Sarah-Sue had to be transported to the main medical facility in Accra. Patrik and Alicia made the two-hour trip into the city to wait for news. At the hospital, a concerned Alicia sat, praying silently. Patrik joined her, and offered her a hot cappuccino.

"I've contacted Miss McAdams' parents, and they are taking the next flight into Accra," he informed her.

Alicia nodded. "Thank you," she said, taking a sip of the beverage.

"I...I said some things to you yesterday that I should not have said. You are a good woman and a good teacher. I know because of the way you care for Imani. It would break her heart if you left. The school would be hurt by losing you," he said, briefly taking her hand in his, "and so would I."

Alicia was too weary to know what to make of his words. When she looked over at Patrik a minute later, his eyes were closed. His head leaned slightly on her shoulder, and she could feel the rhythmic pattern of his breathing. He had drifted to sleep. It had been a very long day for both of them.

303

As it turned out, even the more sophisticated hospital in Accra did not have the proper medicine to treat Sarah-Sue. Fortunately, her affluent parents arranged for a private medical jet to fly her back to Atlanta, where the staff at Emery Hospital was able to bring the infection under control. It took well over a month for her to fully recover, but her dream of returning to Juwani to teach at the school for the remaining three months was not to be.

- - -

The school reopened in September, as scheduled. It was renamed The Bolaru Memorial School, in memory of Patrik's late wife. Alicia saw a tender tear fall from his eye at the ribbon-cutting ceremony. She wanted to reach out to him, to give him some measure of comfort, but she held back. Although their working relationship had improved since the heart-pounding night of Sarah-Sue's departure, the display of affection that Patrik had demonstrated at the hospital was becoming a distant memory.

During the day, now that the school was in session, Alicia taught basic writing skills to the eager-to-learn children of the village. This brought her a great level of satisfaction. Their attitudes were such an about-face from the mumbling, complaining pre-teens she taught back at Clover County Middle. Still, she felt a nagging void.

The days passed slowly, but finally, December arrived. Alicia was surprised to find that even in impoverished Juwani, the anticipation of Christmas was still strong. On the last day of classes before the week-long Christmas break, she tried to recapture some degree of holiday cheer. She basked in the smiles on the faces of the children in her class when she handed out the inexpensive gifts she had managed to buy with her meager earnings. Still, her heart felt anything but merry. She spent time alone in prayer, hoping God would take away her melancholy spirit.

Quite simply, Alicia was lonely. She kept reminding herself that the six remaining weeks in the mission program would pass quickly. By mid-January, she would be in Clover County, Georgia among familiar scenes and people once more. However, each lonesome day seemed to pass more slowly than the previous.

To complicate matters, she finally received a letter from Gerard. Their year apart had made him appreciate what he'd foolishly let

304

slip through his fingers. He still wanted to marry her, and wrote that she could set the date for whenever she liked.

Instead of filling her with joy or anticipation, the letter left her more confused and discontented. Was this the answer to her prayers? Or was this a last-ditch attempt by Gerard to get them to pick up right where they left off? Could she even learn to love him again? Should she?

Alicia looked forward to the upcoming Sunday evening Christmas service at the campus chapel. The Ghanaian cleric seemed very approachable. She decided she would ask him for a few minutes of his time after the service for counsel.

But Alicia's heart was so heavy by that Thursday evening that her peace of mind could not wait until Sunday. As she approached the chapel, a song, wafting softly from the sanctuary made her stop and listen before she pushed open the door. It was "'Tis So Sweet," the same song that she loved so much when Sarah-Sue sang it.

This time, the words were unsung, but the simple calm of the stringed instrument that played the melody brought tears to Alicia's eyes. It reminded her of all the joy and heartache she had experienced in the past year. It was all too much.

As she was yet standing outside weeping, the door opened. There stood Patrik Bolaru, still holding the banjo-like instrument that had helped to foster the tears that she now shed.

"Alicia," he said, addressing her by her first name for the first time. "What's the matter?" He led the teacher to a wooden pew where they both sat in silence for a few moments.

Embarrassed at the thought of him seeing her in such an emotional state, Alicia attempted to stifle her tears.

Patrik simply handed her a handkerchief and in a gentle tone said, "Tears are purifiers of the heart, mind, and spirit. Never be ashamed of them."

This made her want to cry even more. Instead, she found herself talking to him, sharing with him all of the things that had burdened her heart so heavily: her seven-year relationship with Gerard, her reasons for coming to Africa, the delights and frustrations with her work at the school, the loss of the presence of her best friend, her love for Imani, and Gerard's letter. She could literally feel the heaviness drain from her as he listened attentively. By the time

Alicia had finished telling him her troubles, her fountain of tears had dried.

"You have had quite a year," he said. "I guess life never quite goes in the direction you expect. I...I..." He paused, seeming to ponder whether or not it was safe to go on. "Thirteen years ago," he began again. "I met a woman who would change my life. I was a champion marathon runner and received a four-year track scholarship to attend Oxford in England. I met her there. She was an Ethiopian beauty. Christian, graceful, smart, hardworking--not unlike you. We fell in love and were married while we were still students. That same year I got to try out for the Olympic team. But during practice, I badly injured my ankle. That was the end of my Oxford scholarship."

"So, your limp was caused by that?" Alicia had to ask.

"No," Patrik paused pensively. "No, that happened to me about two years later."

When he grew silent, Alicia figured he did not wish to share the event with her. Just when she was about to change the subject, he continued.

"Amari--that was my wife's name--Amari and I moved to Accra to complete our education. It was her dream to someday teach at the university there. However, she became pregnant with Imani in her junior year. She planned to return to school once Imani turned a year old.

"Meanwhile, I remained in school during the day. In the evenings, I played the banjolin for a folk band. That was how I supported my family for over a year. We mostly played for tourists, sometimes birthday parties, a few weddings, and such. Because I did not earn much, the neighborhood we lived in was not the best. Street gangs were a concern, but they generally roamed the streets stealing cars, not breaking into houses." Patrik's voice broke a little. He cleared his throat, and after a few seconds, he resumed speaking.

"A Christmas Eve Festival was taking place in Accra's town square that year. Another group was scheduled to play, but when they cancelled, the festival organizer called on my band at the last minute. Amari begged me not to go, because it was to be Imani's first Christmas. She knew the festival would last well into the wee hours of the morning. But I told her that we needed the money, so against her wishes, I went."

306

Patrik was blinking back tears of his own by this time. Compassion flooded Alicia's heart for him. She knew that whatever this story was, it would be a hard one for him to tell, a story he had not shared with anyone in a long time.

"Alicia," he said, looking at her directly, "there is an unbelievable amount of evil and ignorance in this world. Living in your comfortable existence in America, you are sheltered from much of it. Living in England for those years, even we were sheltered from it. You see, Ghana and much of Africa was at the height of the terrible AIDS crisis during that time. On the streets, men were being erroneously told that if they contracted the virus, the only way to cure it was to have intercourse with a virgin. Therefore, the three men who broke into my house that night were not after money, they were not after my wife. They were looking for my six month old daughter."

Alicia had to close her eyes and swallow hard to keep from getting sick on the stomach.

"I got home at about two in the morning, and I could hear my wife's muffled screams. Two of the men saw me and ran. The third--the one who was pressing the pillow over her face, *demanding to know where the baby was*--did not see me until I was on top of him. I tried my best to beat the life out of him. I am not a small man by any measure, but neither was he, so we struggled. He had a knife and a gun; I had nothing but my hands."

Alicia took a closer look at the facial scar that she remembered from the first day the teachers arrived. *It is a battle wound after all,* she suddenly realized.

Patrik went on. "He then managed to grab his gun as we struggled. I had one hand around his neck, trying to crush every bone I could get my fingers on. I was fighting for my life and for my wife and child. I couldn't think of anything else. As I felt the life leaving his body, I reached to take the gun away from him. But then it went off, shattering the bones in my lower left leg. At the time, I hardly felt the pain.

"That's when I heard the muted cries of my baby coming from somewhere in the room. I crawled over to where Amari lay, barely breathing. Her nearly lifeless hand pointed toward the foot of the bed. I opened the linen chest at the base of the bed, and there was Imani, safe and sound where she had hidden her from the men. By

307

some miracle, she had slept through everything, except the noise from the gun blast. Unfortunately, Amari could not be saved. A part of me went with her when she was buried two days after Christmas."

Alicia thought her heart would break into a million pieces. Suddenly, she felt very selfish to have burdened him with her woes--all of which now seemed minor when mirrored against his unthinkable tragedy. Before she could think of a proper-sounding apology, he began to speak again.

"I put down my banjolin that night, intending to never pick it up again. And I never did. Not until tonight. After all, had it not been for my love of it..." Patrik stopped short. After taking a deep breath, he spoke again, "That was over nine years ago. But for some reason, I had the strongest urge to play tonight. But I'm afraid it's been so long that I'm not very good anymore."

Almost involuntarily, Alicia reached out and touched his hand. "Oh, Patrik, don't believe that. God sent you and your banjolin to minister to *me* tonight. Everything you have experienced I could feel in your music. Everything I have experienced, too."

"I am learning," Patrik said with a little smile, "that even though our best made plans sometimes go terribly wrong, God is still faithful. He works an ultimate good out of our worst experiences. Otherwise, this school would not be here. Imani and I would not be here. And you, Alicia, would not be here.

"As you can imagine, this time of year is usually very difficult for me. Only for the sake of Imani have I always tried to make it as pleasant a time as possible. But just sitting here talking to you tonight has given me a reason to truly celebrate the season in my heart for the first time in a long time."

"No, Patrik. It is you who have helped me," she said, blinking back tears of her own.

He reached his arms out to her and they held each other close. Alicia thought Patrik would never let her go. *We've both needed this for a long time*, she thought. When they finally released each other from the embrace, his next words caught her totally by surprise.

"I am sorry, Alicia, for the way I treated you. The first time I set eyes on you, I was smitten with you. At the same time, you reminded me so much of my Amari that I did not know how to

308

react. You have eyes as beautiful as hers, a smile as bright as the sun, and you have her spirit. The proud way you carry yourself, the belief that you can accomplish anything you set your mind to. Then Imani became attached to you, which really magnified my dilemma. I…I was *in love with you* and couldn't stand to look at you all at once. I wanted to get rid of you so that I could deny my feelings. But now," he said, as he grasped her by both hands, "Now, with your departure so close, I can't imagine running this school without you here."

A thousand thoughts rushed through Alicia's mind. Sarah-Sue had been right. Alicia could no longer be in denial about the attraction she and Patrik felt for one another from the very first day they met. But attraction was one thing; love and commitment were quite another. Besides, she did not want to spend the rest of her life walking in the shadows of Patrik's late wife.

"You may never know how much just talking to you tonight has meant to me, Patrik," she began. "I must apologize to you, too, because I had misjudged you. It's so easy to make assumptions about people when you don't know their story. I appreciate the way you shared yours with me. I know how difficult it must have been for you.

"But before we complicate things, we really need to clear our heads. Without a doubt, the loss of your wife was very traumatic for you. As much as I sympathize with that, I don't want you to trying to recapture Amari through me. I couldn't live up to that. I would never *want* to live up that that.

"And to be perfectly honest, I, too, have some issues I need to work out." Alicia paused and concluded, "Patrik, I've decided to fly home for Christmas."

"Then, you are leaving," he said slowly, his disappointment obvious.

"Just for the holiday. I'll be back before the New Year to finish my six weeks."

"I see." Patrik picked up his instrument and began to strum a few notes of "Silent Night, Holy Night." After a few seconds of silence, he spoke again. "As genuine as the love that I have for you feels, I understand your apprehension. You fear that I am chasing a ghost. I fear that you will go home and resurrect your feelings for your former love.

309

"But go on home if you must, Alicia. If you don't return to me, I will have to accept your choice. But if you do come back, please allow me to me show you what true love really is."

- - -

Alicia's plane landed at Hartsfield-Jackson in Atlanta late that next evening. The excited group waiting to greet her included her mother and a few friends. She was so caught up in the greetings that she did not notice Gerard until he picked her up from behind in a surprise embrace.

"What are you doing here?" Alicia asked, startled by his forwardness.

"Baby, when your mother called and said you were flying in tonight, I knew I couldn't miss this for the world!" he declared.

"Mama, you called him?" she said, looking at her mother helplessly.

"Girl, what do you look like sneaking into town and not letting your fiancé know?" the woman, who looked like an older version of herself, said.

"Fiancé?" Alicia repeated, glaring suspiciously at Gerard.

"We'll discuss it later," he whispered in her ear.

A half hour later, they were riding south on I-75 in Gerard's two-year old, hunter green Ford Expedition.

"I don't know how you let this boy get away from you the first time," Mrs. Patterson went on. "You know, he is so sweet! With that big, new house of his, he said he wouldn't think of me having to drive all the way back to Savannah."

"Yeah," Gerard interjected. "When we get into Cloverton tonight, you and your mom are staying at my house. You're both spending Christmas Eve and Christmas Day with me. In fact, I've got a big dinner planned for you tomorrow, and I'm inviting all our friends. It's gonna be just like old times."

"Mama, I was looking forward to spending Christmas with you in Savannah. You know I rented out my house in Cloverton before I left for Africa."

"How was Africa? You and that principal still going at each other's throats?" Mrs. Patterson wanted to know.

Alicia knew she was referring to Patrik Bolaru.

Patrik. She had not stopped thinking about the man since she left Ghana.

310

"Everything's fine in Africa, Mama. Patrik and I are getting along great, now."

There must have been something about the way she said his name that caused Gerard to glance over at her curiously as he drove.

Within the hour, they could both hear light snoring from the rear of the vehicle, an indication that Mrs. Patterson had checked out for the night.

"'Licia," Gerard said, sliding a Tim Bowman inspirational jazz CD into the stereo, "you have no idea how much I missed you..."

"G, I cannot believe that you lied to my mother. You told her we were still getting married?" Alicia asked.

"Well, aren't we? You did get my letter, didn't you? I know that's what brought you home to me," Gerard said reaching over to hold her hand. "I still love you, 'Licia."

"G, I have spent a year in Africa finding myself. God has opened my eyes to see my life differently now. I'm sorry, but I just don't feel the same."

"You will," Gerard said confidently. He turned the volume on the stereo up a bit.   As the music filled her ears, Alicia couldn't help but marvel at Tim Bowman's masterful skills on the guitar. The particular song he now played, with its Latin flavor, sounded both familiar and sultry.

"Remember that?" Gerard said with a devilish grin. "That's our song, girl."

"Gerard!" Alicia exclaimed, pushing his wandering hand away. "Don't you have any Christmas music?" she asked, pressing the arrow on the CD changer. She hoped whatever played would break the sensuous mood that Gerard had fallen into.

The song that filled the stereo started out slowly and sweetly. She suddenly recognized it as a contemporary take on the hymn "'Tis So Sweet." by Commissioned. It was a version of the same song that had captured her heart anew in Africa, the very song Patrik had played so tenderly in the chapel!

By the time they arrived at Gerard's new home in Cloverton, Alicia couldn't remember anything else they had talked about during their ride. Looking around at the blinking Christmas lights in the neighborhood, she wondered how Patrik and Imani would spend their holiday.

- - -

311

A bright December sun met Alicia when she awakened the next morning. Gerard had respectfully extended her the courtesy of her own room to sleep in, next door to her mother's. The house *was* nice, she had to admit. Nothing back at the Bolaru school could compare in luxury. The designer drapes, the soft linens, the Jacuzzi tub in the adjoining bathroom. *A girl* could *get used to this*, she thought.

The Christmas Eve party was scheduled for five o'clock that afternoon. Everybody Gerard had invited showed up, plus a few extra. Alicia had managed to contact Sarah-Sue by phone early that morning, and was delighted when she arrived, having driven over four hours to get to Cloverton from Atlanta.

Despite the last minute planning of the dinner, Alicia did appreciate that fact that Gerard had put a lot of effort into it. Nevertheless, amongst the smiles, laughter, and the entire Christmas atmosphere, Alicia found her mind still wandering.

"You're ready to go back, aren't you?" Sarah-Sue whispered perceptively.

"Are you kidding?" Alicia teased back. "With all this good soul food?"

But in reality, Alicia did not eat much that evening. By six o'clock, while everyone else was still socializing, she slipped quietly out of the party and returned to the room she had slept in the night before. She lay down to rest and was soon sleeping.

A knock at her room door awakened her. Glancing at the clock, the time showed seven p.m. She couldn't believe she had been asleep for nearly an hour.

"It's just me," Sarah-Sue's twangy voice called from the other side of the door.

"Come in," her former roommate called back, still feeling jetlagged.

"Just wanted to make sure you were okay before I left," the blonde said, as she entered. "I really enjoyed the party. I guess Gerard ain't half-bad. Looks like he's got everything laid out for you for when you come home for good. I admit I was hoping things would go differently, but congratulations, anyway."

"Congratulations for what?"

"For your upcoming wedding, silly. Will it be held here in Cloverton?"

Alicia narrowed her eyes and looked at her friend. "Sarah-Sue, do I look like I'm in the mood for playing games?"

"Well, aren't we a grouchy bride-to-be!" Sarah-Sue exclaimed. "I'm just repeating what I heard Gerard telling someone at the front door before I came up to say good-bye to you."

"Who was he telling?"

"I don't know. Some guy, I think. I wasn't trying to see who it was. I just happened to be passing by the foyer when Gerard was talking to him. I don't think he let whoever it was into the house. Probably just somebody trying to crash the party."

"First of all," Alicia began, "what G is telling people is totally untrue. The fact that he is *assuming* that I want to marry him lets me know he really hasn't changed at all!

"Secondly," she pondered aloud, as she walked over to the window, which looked out over the front lawn, "half the people downstairs crashed this party. I wonder who it was that he didn't want to..." Alicia would never finish her sentence.

The sun had long ago set in the Georgia sky. Looking out of the window, the only lighting Alicia could see in the front of the house was a brilliant moon and a myriad of Christmas lights that twinkled like the stars. She could also see the silhouettes of two figures dressed in noble, white robes, which flowed gracefully in the cool December breeze. The twinkling lights behind them made them look like celestial beings. The taller figure helped the smaller one into a cab that waited by the curb in front of the house. The figure then paused, looking back toward the house.

Alicia gasped.

"What?" Sarah-Sue wanted to know. When she joined Alicia at the window, she gasped, too.

"Oh my God!" Alicia's voice was a whisper as she pushed past her startled friend. "Patrik!" Alicia tore down the stairs as quickly as her legs would carry her, through the hallway, dining room, and living room.

"'Licia...!" She heard Gerard's voice protest as she ran past him.

"What in the world...?" Mrs. Patterson wanted to know.

Conversations began buzzing immediately from the flabbergasted guests, as a few of them followed Gerard and Mrs. Patterson to the front porch to watch the woman run.

313

"'Licia!" Gerard called again.

"Patrik!" Alicia shouted at the top of her lungs.

The tall, dark, flowing figure was halfway into the cab when he heard her. Patrik reversed his steps and stood beside the car. No further words were necessary. A knowing smile, as bright as the Christmas Eve moon, parted Patrik's lips as he prepared to embrace his queen.